# THE SHINING HOST™

## Changeling: The Dreaming
### for Mind's Eye Theatre

# Credits

**Written by:** Peter Woodworth

**Development by:** Richard E. Dansky

**Editing by:** Cynthia Summers

**Previously published material has appeared in: Laws of the Night, Laws of the Wild, Oblivion, The Long Night** and **Changeling: The Dreaming, Immortal Eyes: The Toybox, Immortal Eyes: The Court of All Kings** and **Isle of the Mighty**

**Art Direction by:** Lawrence Snelly

**Art by:** Jonathan Rhea and Stefani McClure

**Front and back Cover:** Conan H. Venus

**Layout and typesetting by:** Conan H. Venus

**Character Sheet Design:** Sarah McIlvaine

## Special Thanks To:

**Justin** "Mouth Full of Silicon" **Achilli,** for giving the stuffed chicken a sucking chest wound — literally.

**Andrew** "Her Name Is Rio and She Dances on the Sand" **Bates,** for possibly the most novel use of a stuffed chicken known to man.

**Brian** "This is What I'm Giving Up?" **Petkash,** for bucking the trend and tying the knot. Congratulations!

**Rich** "I'm Blind!" **Thomas,** for knowing who'd be there for him.

**Fred** "Tattoo You" **Yelk,** for zeroing in on a certain navelly bulls-eye.

**Chris** "C!!!" **McDonough** for something that I cannot tell and must not recall.

**Greg** "Pop Up Video" **Fountain,** for telling us more than we wanted know about various cinematic masterpieces.

**Rob** "3 AM" **Hatch,** for letting us know how much debauchery was still on the clock.

**Mike** "No Coke. Pepsi." **Tinney,** for objecting to product placement.

**Playtesters:** Sarah McIlvaine, Jody Gerst, Jim Vasquez, Alyson Gaul, Larry Puccio, Steven McIlvaine, Cindy Silvestri, John Passanante, Steven Lovejoy, Tracy Miller, Suzanne Mlynarczyk, Heather McIlvaine, Michael Dappolone, Julie Miller, Richard Lovejoy, Kristie Mulieri, Trish Castallante, Justin Shilliday, Margaret Serota, Greg Heller, Travis Hughes, Larry Zoll, Jenny Stauder.

# TABLE OF CONTENTS

# One Enchanted Evening: A Cautionary Tale

I swear, I'm never going into a fistfight unannounced again.

Sounds pretty stupid, but when you're a beat cop, getting the snot beaten out of you kind of puts a crimp in your nightly routine. I thought for a while that I'd just quit and see if the auto body place would take me back. That fell through, though — Ernie would want to know why I quit the force, since getting the badge was all I used to talk about. Then I'd have to tell him what really happened, and he'd never believe me. *You* might, though. You look like you might be one of them.

Now, you might be a stranger, too, so let me tell you a bit about our fine city. There are times when I swear it looks like the Renaissance Fest has gotten loose in South Central around here. We've got street buskers and pimps, caffeine-freaked students and prostitutes, and above it all this air of genteel weirdness that means that most of the time all the various factions leave each other alone. I walk beat at night — Rank Hath Its Privileges, and I'm low man on the totem pole. Still, being around at night has its up side — you get to see some amazing things. Also, some really unpleasant ones.

That little kindness is also what let me hear the sounds of the fight when I came out of the Dunkin' Donuts on the corner off St. Charles; I can tell the noise of a beating over just a plain beat, even with the way the trio of busker drummers was feeling their groove. The ruckus was *loud* — at first listen, it sounded like a mosh pit lightly seasoned with pro wrestlers. Looking around, I realized that the noise was coming from one of those trendy new nightclubs off Esplanade Avenue. The sign read "Cat Turned Blue" in funky lines and neon squiggles — you could barely read the thing without seeing spots. Not the sort of place you'd expect to be home to a brawl, but then again, you'd be surprised how loose those preppies can get after a couple of those mocha-expresso-double-fudge-caffeine-shooter jobs they like. Loud, lewd and well-lawyered — the worst kind of perps. I radioed into central that I was going in to break up a bohemian brawl, got my nightstick ready, and waded in.

5

Man oh man, *nothing* I had seen prepared me for this. I walked in through the artsy smoked glass door and saw a company of hyperactive street mimes kicking the collective ass of the local high school freshman mixer — and all of them looked underage. These kids were jumping off tables, punching, kicking and screaming bloody murder. Even as I watched, one of the kids yelled some nonsense and did a little dance, at which point one of the mimes staggered like he'd been shot and fell over.

Then there was the sword-fighting — these kids were whaling away like extras from *Braveheart*, but if they had weapons, I sure as hell didn't see them. The fighting was real enough to them, though, and apparently mimes learn about things other than climbing out of invisible trash cans because they were cutting down kids left and right. And the kids played along! I've seen guys so whacked on LSD they'll believe you just killed them if you tell them that the cactus man has just stepped on their fifth foot, but never anything as precise and realistic as what these kids were doing — some of them were acting like they were really injured!

But they train you for the weird stuff at the academy. I looked around and figured, OK, I could deal with all this. I'd just slow the place down and wait for these guys to detox a bit before sorting out who did what to whom and what for. Perfect plan, right? I just didn't take into account the fact that the kid in the black hat hanging up in the rafters was going to turn into a coyote.

Actually, that was only one of the problems. The other was the young woman, maybe 20 or 21, who had been standing by the door. She saw me come in and did one of those mime overhead chops on my brainpan — and everything went to hell. All of a sudden, I started seeing things, things that I knew weren't real. For one thing, she had been swaddled up like some retro gypsy, silks and scarves all over the place, but now she was just in these gorgeous robes, with these weird pointed ears. Her hand had been empty a moment ago, but now she was holding a huge knife with a serrated edge. I looked around and things didn't get any better. At the back of the bar, a big dark-haired girl who'd been busting heads pretty good suddenly looked about nine foot nine, with blue skin and huge muscles and a set of horns poking out of the top of her forehead. All around me, the scene turned into something from an old storybook, with a collage of weird skin tones, renaissance faire outfits and wild body types suddenly replacing the kids who had been right in front of me. And the weapons! Jeez, these kids were armed like they were about to go on another Crusade, all swords and daggers and axes and knives! The only things that didn't look much different were the mimes, except they did — they were all sinister and dark, holding these wicked gray blades. And yes, there was still a coyote there, with some kind of black bird perched on his shoulder.

I must have screamed something then, 'cause everybody in the place stopped, just for a second, and got this weird look on their faces like someone let the dean into the frat party right when they were about to roll out the kegs. It actually would have been pretty funny if I hadn't been convinced at the time that I was insane, high or both. Suddenly one kid, now dressed in black and purple robes and the honest-to-God most handsome guy I've ever seen, called to me. "Help us! They're trying to take over the freehold!" he screamed, and then everybody started whacking at one another again. The kid shot me a look and went to go another round with a mime, but he was obviously on the short end of the duel. And even though my brain was taking some time off to consider what was happening, I knew he was right, that the kids were right, and that I had to help. So I stepped in and did the best I could for the forces of good.

It's amazing how much of a deterrent a big 9mm can be to a group of mimes, even evil ones. They put up their hands real fast and skedaddled, and I was too weirded out to even try to slap cuffs on any. They melted into the night like ice cubes on a skillet, and that left me with the Elfy Brigade, who of course had no idea what to do with me.

The guy in purple, who claimed to be some count of something or other, tried to explain things to me. He told me that the entire lot of them (except the coyote, whom I don't even want to go into) were quote-unquote "change-lings" — faerie souls in human bodies — and that the killer mimes were more of the same. He tried to explain kith and faerie magic, and why everyone was protecting this "freehold," and the rest of the kit and kaboodle.

Ten minutes later I still had no idea what he was talking about, and the backup I'd called for finally arrived. I went out to talk to the guys in the other black-and-white; that took a few minutes which the changelings apparently spent deciding what to do with me. So when I went back inside to see if whatever it had been was still in the air, the count came back with an offer.

The short version of the deal was this: They would knight me for my help, and keep me enchanted to see their world, if I would submit to an oath never to reveal them to the mortal world, and to help them to beat back the mimes and all the other creatures of darkness in the city. They even offered to supply me with proper weapons and armor for their enchanted world, but I couldn't take all that. The armor, yeah, but a sword? No thanks. I'd stick with my nine. I looked at the two knights in the corner, who were named Luke and Davis. They each gave me a big wink, and so I looked back at the count. I believe I said something like this:

"Why the hell not? Swear me in, and suit me up."

Not the best speech ever made, but it did just fine. So now I patrol the streets in the name of Count Brendan Beaumain, regent of the Principality of Jazz, defender of House Eiluned, as *Sir* Anthony Marks. I'm even allowed to fly the house colors right outside my window. Court sessions are every Friday, but until I learn a little more sidhe etiquette, I act as a door guard. It's OK, though; Davis and Luke come over every other night to give me a lesson in faerie lore, so I'm learning things pretty quickly. Davis is a card sharp, and Luke talks to his pet raven too much, but otherwise they're great guys. And believe it or not, this real fine faerie girl named Belladonna started making eyes at me. I think I'm in love, but who knows? Faeries are like that. Patrol is still the best part, and I'm already allowed to walk with the count's honor guard on their rounds. Apparently those mimes are called Oubliettes, and their leader, Vandermere, is some nasty Unseelie leader bent on the usual villain stuff: domination, absolute power, etc., etc. Still, we're making a difference, and we've kicked his elfin butt a few times already.

Besides, how can you fault a society in which they ask you to beat up mimes all day?

# Chapter One: Introduction and Background

## What This Book Is

The Shining Host is the live-action version of Changeling: The Dreaming for Mind's Eye Theatre. Like Laws of the Night or Oblivion, this book allows you to take one of the games of the World of Darkness and transform it into a live-action experience. With this book, you can leave the table and the dice behind and step onto the stage yourself.

## The Rules of Safety

Behave yourself so that everyone can enjoy this game. The Shining Host is to be played in the home, at conventions or at other safe locations. At all times, you should remember that it is a game, only a game, and nothing but a game. If you feel yourself getting too wrapped up in what's going on, take a timeout and step back from gameplay for a moment. It's for your own good.

## The Only Rules That Matter

Here are the rules of Mind's Eye Theatre (MET), the only rules that absolutely must always be obeyed. These are common sense rules to keep everyone safe and happy with your game: other players, yourself, strangers in the area and even the police.

These rules are designed to limit the opportunities anyone has to destroy the fun of your game. They're not intended to limit gameplay or cut down on your fun; they're just here to make sure that you play sensibly and safely.

# #1– It's Only a Game

This is by far the most important rule. If a character is killed, if a plot falls apart, if a rival wins the day — it's still only a game. Don't take things too seriously, as that will spoil not only your fun but also the fun of everyone around you.

Leave the game behind when it ends. Playing a changeling is a lot of fun; spending time talking about the game is great. There comes a time, however, when you need to leave the game behind. Don't call the local duke's player at four in the morning to try to badger some dross out of him unless he's told you that you can (and then maybe the duke needs to take a step back himself).

# #2 – No Touching

Never actually have physical contact with other players. No matter how careful you are, accidents happen, and someone will get hurt. Rely on the rules to cover physical logistics.

# #3 – No Stunts

Never climb, jump, run, leap or swing from anything during a game. Keep the "action" in your action low-key. If you can imagine you're an eight-foot-tall blue troll named Ølaf, you can certainly imagine that you're leaping from rooftop to rooftop. Avoid attracting the attention of people who aren't playing, and use your imagination to its fullest.

# #4 – No Weapons

Fake and real weapons of any sort are absolutely forbidden. Even obviously fake or silly toy weapons are not allowed. Such props give other people the wrong impression as to what you are doing, and in the dark could conceivably be mistaken for real weapons. Use item cards to represent weapons instead.

# #5 – No Drugs or Drinking

This one is a real no-brainer. Drugs and alcohol do not create peak performance. They reduce your ability to think and react, meaning that, among other things, your roleplaying ability will be impaired. Players impaired by drugs or alcohol use are a danger to other players, and to the game as a whole. There's nothing wrong with *playing* a character who's drunk or stoned, but actually bringing such stuff to a game is in bad taste at best, illegal at worst. Don't do it.

# #6 – Be Mindful of Others

Remember, not everyone you see, or who sees you, will be playing the game. A game can be unnerving or even frightening to passersby. Be considerate of non-players in your vicinity, and make sure that if you are in a public area, your gameplay actions are not going to alarm anyone. Just as in

10

**Changeling**, there are a lot of mundanes out there, and their disapproval can get a game shut down as quickly as Banality can smash a freehold flat.

## #7 – The Rules are Flexible

Feel free to ignore or adjust any of the rules in this book if it will make your game better. We at White Wolf call this "The Golden Rule." If some rule included in this book (beyond the ones listed here) doesn't work for your troupe, change it. But be consistent and fair. Nobody likes rules that change every week or "no-win" scenarios. If your troupe finds a new way to handle seemings that works better for you than the one in this book; go for it. The idea is to have fun.

## #8 – Have Fun

Not "Win." Not "Go out and kill everyone else." Not "Amass more treasure than anyone else." Just "Have fun." The object of **The Shining Host** is not to win. In fact, there are no rules for "winning." The goal is to tell great stories, not to achieve superiority over the other players. It's not about how the game ends, it's about the journey and what happens along the way.

## What is Storytelling?

We have been telling each other stories since the earliest days when cavemen acted out the tales of their hunts around their fires. We painted cave walls, pressed reeds into soft clay tablets, inked papyrus and vellum, acted plays, illuminated manuscripts, printed books, filmed movies, scripted radio and television shows, and programmed computers. Now, one of the newest methods of storytelling is actually a return to the oldest form. Live-action roleplaying (LARP), which grew out of the table-top roleplaying games of the '70s, is just the kind of "participatory" taletelling we can still view amongst cultures around the globe. It is the same emphasis on character and story which led to the creation of what we call "storyteller" games, that you can find in the myths of our most ancient cultures. The book you hold in your hands is an attempt to explore those universal tales of the Hero's Journey.

# What is Mind's Eye Theatre?

This game is probably different from any game you have played before now. In many ways, this is really not a game at all. **The Shining Host** is more concerned with stories than winning, rules, game boards or dice. You will find that this game has more in common with childhood games of adventure than with card games or *Monopoly*-type board games. This book contains all the information necessary to catapult you into the worlds of imagination. You create the action and you choose your own paths. We have a name for this style of game. We call it **Mind's Eye Theatre**.

Playing **Mind's Eye Theatre** is like being in a movie. You and your friends portray the main characters, but the script follows your decisions. The director of this improvisational movie is called the Storyteller; he, along with his assistants, called Narrators, creates the stage and the minor characters with whom you interact during your adventure. Most scenes are played out in real-time, and always in character. You should only break character when there is a rules dispute or a change of scene which requires adjudication from the Storyteller or Narrators.

## The Character

When you play **The Shining Host**, you take on the persona of a changeling, a fae soul born into a human body for protection from the cold winds of disbelief and Banality. Your character can be anyone from any walk of life. The only limit on your character concept (besides the rules) is your imagination. You create, then roleplay, your character over the course of a story and perhaps a chronicle (a series of connected stories). You decide what your character does and says. You decide what risks to accept or to decline.

During the game, you speak as your character. Unless you're talking to a Narrator or Storyteller, whatever you say is what your character says. Because most of what a **Mind's Eye Theatre** player perceives depends on the characters around him, players must be vivid and expressive. The characters direct the plot, but at the same time, the events of the game guide and develop the characters, helping them to achieve the story's goals.

To an extent, as a player in a storytelling game you have a responsibility beyond simply portraying your character. You need to consider the story as a whole and your role in making sure that other players enjoy the game.

Creating a character for **The Shining Host** is easy and only takes a few minutes. Only a few things are necessary to define a basic character, and once you've done that, you can play the game.

There's another phase to creating a character, though, and one that makes playing **Mind's Eye Theatre** all the more rewarding. Your character should be more than just a series of Traits and numbers. Rather, she should be a living, breathing personality with a past, motives, drives, likes, dislikes — everything you want to see from a character in a movie or a novel. So it's probably a good idea, before you start playing, to take time and figure out *who* your character is, as well as what she is. While certain details and personality traits will come out while you're playing her, you'll want to have the basics in place before you start playing. It's just like an actor asking his director for his character's motivation; if you know what your character wants, it's easier for him to get it.

Characters are the heart and soul of a story. Without them, all the patient efforts of the Storyteller would be for naught. Appreciate the Storyteller's efforts by following the rules and taking an active part in the game.

12

## Narrators

In **Mind's Eye Theatre**, Narrators are the people who help the Story-teller present the adventure. Narrators are the impartial judges who describe scenes and events that cannot be staged, adjudicate rules and occasionally play the roles of antagonists. Generally, enlisting the aid of one Narrator for every 10 players makes for a good ratio. The best number of Narrators for your game usually depends upon the gaming experience of the players; the more experienced your players, in all probability the fewer Narrators they'll need. Narrators usually play characters of their own as well as narrating certain situations. That way, they can be a part of the action instead of just trying to correct it from the outside.

## Storyteller

Every game must have a Storyteller, who serves as the ultimate authority and final judge in any game of **The Shining Host** you play. The Storyteller creates the basic elements of the plot, and makes sure that the story unfolds well — as well as doing everything the Narrators do. Storytelling is a demanding job, but it is also a very rewarding one, for it is the Storyteller who creates the framework upon which the players build their experiences.

The Storyteller makes certain the story has content, interesting hooks and a narrative flow. This does not mean that a Storyteller should just sit back and dictate the plot — characters who don't have free will are no fun to play. Instead, the Storyteller creates the "framework" elements of the plot, then turns the players loose in order see what happens.

During the game the Storyteller must be watchful and ready to create new elements to make sure that the story works out well. He is also responsible for safety, ensuring that all of the players have something to do and that everyone is abiding by the rules. Although performing all of these tasks simultaneously can be exhausting, the sense of accomplishment gained from created a successful story makes the whole process worthwhile.

In the end, the goal of the game is for everyone to have fun.

## Props

Props can be anything that the Storyteller approves that helps to define your character, including costumes, makeup and jewelry. Have fun and employ any props that you feel are necessary to enhance your character. However, if you have any doubts as to whether a prop, such as anything remotely resembling a weapon will be allowed in-game, consult your Story-teller and abide by her decision.

## Elegantly Simple

This game was designed to be easy to learn and easier to play. **The Shining Host** is a storytelling game. The rules are aimed at resolving conflicts quickly so that players can stay with the story without ever stepping outside their characters in order to figure out what happened. We have made every effort to create rules that maintain the integrity of the story and the background in which the story is set. And with that caveat, the world of **Changeling** is yours to explore. Welcome to **Mind's Eye Theater: The Shining Host**.

# A World of Darkness

*When we are young*
*Wandering the face of the earth*
*Wondering what our dreams might be worth*
*Learning that we're only immortal*
*For a limited time*
— Rush, "Dreamline"

The world of **The Shining Host** is, in many ways, just like our world. Children are born, grow up, go to school, follow careers, grow old and die. The sun rises and sets day after day. In the World of Darkness, however, everything is just a little grittier, a little more corrupt, a little more sinister. Gang warfare is rampant. Poor areas are even more impoverished. What little true art exists has been devoured by the maw of television, pandering to the lowest common denominator. True wilderness is even more imperiled, and even more savage. Even the "nice" places of this world are touched by a hint of something dark and dreadful.

This darkness is expressed in the ambiance of Gothic art, demonstrated by the motifs expressed in the architecture of high cathedral ceilings, gargoyles and towering structures that stab at the night sky like obscene arrows. The same shadows also express themselves in raw rage, random violence and rebellion — basic elements of the Punk movement. That is why we call the World of Darkness the "Gothic-Punk" setting, because it combines these two styles. **The Shining Host** represents it in a very different way than do the worlds of **Laws of the Night**, **Laws of the Wild** or **Oblivion**, though.

## Changeling: The Dreaming

The basic premise of **The Shining Host** is derived from the table-top roleplaying game, **Changeling: The Dreaming**. It is not necessary to own or know **Changeling** in order to play **The Shining Host**, but the world of **Changeling** has many useful source materials which can be easily adapted for live-action games.

# What Is a Changeling?

Contrary to popular legend, a changeling is not a fae child who has been exchanged by the Fair Folk for a mortal one, but rather a faerie spirit fused with a human one, born into a mortal body to take shelter from the ravages of the mundane world. It is no more a curse than it is a boon; it is simply the way of the fae, and has been the practice of the Kithain, as they call themselves, for well over five centuries.

## Myths Made Flesh

Faeries have walked the world since the first dream a mortal ever dreamt. Born from nightmare terror and romantic bliss, the first fae danced at the edge of mortal society, following the natures granted them by dreams and reveling in the power and mystique bestowed on them by mortals. Over the centuries, the fae inspired mortals to create great works of art, but always with their own eldritch agendas. The society of these dream-born creatures, the feudal ideal they originally inspired mortals to adopt, has survived the centuries and upheavals of mortal society, though it is much diminished by the passing of years. Even so, to this day, courtly romance and chivalric conflict light the pages of faerie history with transcendent passion, heartbreaking tragedy and immortal heroism.

However, the mythic times of the past are but a bittersweet memory now, and changelings have been forced to adapt their ways to an increasingly unimaginative modern world. Subsisting as they do on the power of creativity, changelings can be found wherever artists gather, inspiring them and urging them on to greatness. Some changelings strive to create art themselves, while others rip mortals' dreams away from them to fuel their own. Old customs long forbidden have begun to resurface as the young pay no heed to their elders, and the threat of commoner revolt underlies talk in far too many freeholds across the world. Banality, the force of mortal disbelief, slowly wipes away the faerie world, and true art becomes rarer and rarer all the time. Some changelings, weighed down by Banality, never awaken to their fae selves, and live out their lives entirely in the mundane world. Once truly immortal, changelings are now merely reborn into new bodies at the passing of their current ones, and even face the possible death of their faerie souls at the hands of Banality's agents.

Against these threats, the Kithain come armed only with their knowledge of the Dreaming, a realm which they themselves are forbidden by virtue of their mortal blood. Never anything less than heroic by birth and epic by temperament, the Kithain believe that they, as the legendary (if forgotten) heroes of humanity, are the only ones who can stop the world from destroying itself, and they face down the forces of Banality everywhere with magics as grand as a chariot of dragons and as simple as making a child's eyes grow wide with wonder.

15

# History

Although changelings have existed for as long as memory stretches, they divide their history into several distinct stages, beginning with the blissful world of the Dreaming and ending in the troubled modern era. Despite the air of finality that many mortals and Prodigals assign to the present, the Kithain refuse to give up, seeing everything as a cycle and this as only another down period in an endless cycle of progression. In many ways, they are the last true optimists of the World of Darkness, and all the rarer for it.

As the bards tell it, once all worlds were united, and Earth existed side-by-side with the Dreaming. Fae walked the paths of both Arcadia and Earth with ease. All life existed in a balanced cycle, Glamour saturated the air, and the fae could walk in their true forms without need for human bodies to hide in. Although the fae went largely unseen, pranking and beguiling their human cousins, both cultures embraced and learned from each other, and art and civilization flourished for a time that seemingly would never end. Then, for reasons unclear to this day, something changed, irrevocably separating both worlds. Known to the fae as the Sundering, this catastrophe impacted the fae like a tidal wave, making travel to and from Arcadia and Earth more perilous, and Glamour scarcer. Humanity began to embrace distrust and caution above imagination in an effort to pursue something that would be called "progress." The fae took comfort in the Glamour they had, which was still relatively easy to attain, and complacently hoped things would get better even as the first signs of the next disaster gathered.

Shortly before the Renaissance, humanity synthesized its faith, disillusionment and newfound hunger for scientific "reason" into a potent power of disbelief, and Banality first reared its cold head. This horrible event, called the Shattering by the fae, marked the final end of the Mythic Era. Taken aback at the power of this new foe, many fae were lost as the icy winds of rationality swept over the land, purging it of any trace of things that did not belong to the new "order" of the mundane world. During this time, nearly every sidhe abandoned Earth, returning to Arcadia through trods that closed after them, leaving the commoners stranded on a cold world. The remaining fae quickly developed the ability to create mortal seemings in which to hide, and went about surviving as best they could. They scavenged Glamour where it was found and held up a loose semblance of the noble order the sidhe had left behind, although the loyalty this new system got was shaky at best. Seelie and Unseelie fae even struck an unprecedented truce, which holds to this day. The commoners were simply too concerned with survival for the next several centuries to worry about matters of title and *politesse*, and it was during this time that they developed the strong "us against them" attitude that was to carry over into the modern age. It was also at this time that the fae discovered the deadly power of cold iron to destroy their faerie souls.

Over time, however, things improved, and commoners began to be truly born into mortal families instead of merely imitating their shapes. Though Banality caused many fae to forget what they were, times of art and learning came and went, giving the fae the opportunity to shape the world through their power to inspire mortal dreamers. Through war and inquisition, excess and famine, Kithain society survived. New changelings awakened all the time, and even the number of grumps was on the rise as imagination become a cherished trait once more.

It was with great surprise, then, that the commoners found the Resurgence upon them in 1969. As man first walked on the moon, the surge of Glamour triggered by a world transfixed with wonder opened trods long thought destroyed, and the sidhe returned to Earth. Exiled for reasons none of them could remember, the highborns nonetheless set about reclaiming their right to rule the Kithain, a right which the commoners — who argued they had done perfectly well without the sidhe for centuries — refused to recognize. The resulting conflict, known as the Accordance War, pitted commoners against nobility on a scale and with a viciousness not seen before or since. In particular, the Night of Iron Knives, during which much of the commoner leadership was slaughtered with cold iron after meeting under a noble flag of truce, and the murder of the sidhe commander Lord Dafyll still raise hackles on both sides. While the commoners, with their global home field advantage and better understanding of Banality, held the upper hand at first, the nobles brought with them many powerful Arts and treasures from Arcadia. After atrocities and heroics on both sides, a parley was eventually agreed upon. The coronation of the sidhe David Ardry, the long-prophesied High King, squelched the last of the tensions as he appealed to the values of both common and noble fae and built a kingdom sincerely dedicated to equality and the glory of the Dreaming.

The result is a society where open bigotry based on factors such as kith, Court or title is largely a thing of the past, but where many hatreds, new and old, still boil under a facade of politeness and daily affairs. Nunnehi raids plague parts of the nation, and the native fae have vowed to fight to the last to win back their glens from invaders both Kithain and mortal. After all, epic grudges are as much a part of the Dreaming as epic quests, and it seems some matters might never be settled. Still, the determination of High King David to overcome prejudices of kith and class has created an atmosphere of tolerance never before seen in the world of the Kithain, and motleys and households of many different kith and backgrounds are quite common. As True Thomas, Grand Bard of the High King's court, has said: "We haven't yet all learned how to get along, but we have found that our common enemies are too many to face apart."

# The Enchanted World

All changelings live a dual existence, interacting with both the mundane mortal world and the world of Glamour to which their faerie souls are heir. In this fantasy landscape, everything appears magical and different — castles rise out spaces where houses once were, forests glow with the life of nature, snow falls on the first of June just for fun, and fantastic beasts large and small roam the lands they once walked for real. What a character's mortal eyes see as a plain street might become a craggy cliff, a dark bayou or even the hall of an enormous fortress. The faerie selves of other changelings are immediately visible, as are any enchanted mortals and Prodigals, and even a changeling who has temporarily forgotten himself has his faerie marks peeking through the edges of his mortal frame. Anything that belongs solely to this enchanted world is known as chimerical, and any "imaginary" objects or creatures are called chimera. Formed of the very stuff of dreams (and nightmares), chimera can take any shape imaginable, and have degrees of free will and intelligence in accordance with the power ascribed to them by those who dreamed them up in the first place. Thus, anything from talking teddy bears and animated lollipops to fire-breathing dragons and fierce unicorns can be found in the chimerical world. More to the point, anything you can imagine often is.

Unless he has been overcome by Banality and forgets his fae nature, a changeling automatically perceives the chimerical world over the mundane one. This does not mean changelings are oblivious to the mundane world, but that they see the enchanted side as dominant. A changeling driving a car, even a car that chimerically spits flames and glows in the dark, is still able to navigate turns and traffic in the mundane world perfectly well. A Kithain can still detect a mugger approaching him, even if the thug isn't part of the enchanted world. Perhaps the best way to describe it is that a changeling's mind and spirit perceive other fae and the enchanted world, but her body (being mortal) instinctively recognizes and reacts to the mundane world. Consider the rule of thumb to be that any location the game takes place in is considered to be the mundane aspect of the setting, so that the characters' mortal forms are reflected in and react to the real world unless the game is specifically set at a freehold. In most cases, the Storyteller can simply describe what the changelings see for the chimerical landscape (including any staircases, structures and other notable — and notably different — features of the setting). Especially important chimera can be noted by props or prop cards, or perhaps even played by Narrators.

In the live-action world of **The Shining Host**, this means that many times characters will be forced to interact with chimera and a chimerical landscape that goes unperceived by the players themselves (and to characters who are unenchanted), a layer of make-believe on top of make-believe. Fortunately, as make-believe is the foundation of **Mind's Eye Theatre**, this shouldn't be too difficult. It can take some getting used to, however, even for experienced roleplayers. It bears noting that this also can be exceedingly unsettling to normal folk if the game is played in public places; routing a band of unseen Unseelie warriors in the comfort of your own home usually draws little notice, but chasing dragons on chimerical horses in the middle of the local mall invariably draws hostile attention, not to mention law enforcement. Even a friendly location, such as a gaming convention, can become confusing if the players are in the midst of unenchanted characters and wildly cheering a duel between two chimerical knights. The other players will feel left out, to say the least, and the game will quickly deteriorate into kill-the-changelings contests. Storytellers must take special care to describe to players what is mundane and what is chimerical about any locations in the game.

## Location, Location, Location

Any location which corresponds more or less directly to Earth is said to be the Near Dreaming, while those places without earthly counterparts are the Far Dreaming. Truly legendary realms of imagination are called the Deep Dreaming. The latter two can only be reached by faerie roads, or trods, which are rare on Earth these days. Note that many changelings take exception to having things of the Dreaming referred to as "imaginary" — everything there is very real to a changeling, perhaps even more so than the baggage of the so-called "real world."

# The Kith

Each changeling belongs to a "species" of faeries, called a kith. Born of legends and folk tales, each kith has its origins in a particular race or region, and once was restricted to living among the lands and peoples of its birth. However, the kith have since transcended such barriers, and now exist throughout the world. Indeed, though some families have carried faerie blood for generations, changelings are no longer restricted to being born to those families, and there is no rhyme or reason to the lineage of the kith. A pair of changeling twins might be born a pooka and a troll, for example. Contrary to modern notions of genetics, fae blood is also capricious, and may skip several generations, breed true in the next, and be absent once more. There is literally no telling whether a child will be born fae simply by her "pedigree."

Being born into a kith carries with it specific ties known as Bonds, certain inherent advantages and powers (called Birthrights) and some weaknesses or drawbacks (called Frailties). Birthrights can be everything from trollish physical might to sidhe beauty to an eshu's sense of direction, but to members of a kith they are as natural as breathing. In some cases, they are even strong enough to begin to surface before a changeling is aware of her true nature.

Frailties, on the other hand, can be anything from a sluagh's inability to speak above a whisper to the imperfections that haunt all nocker creations, but no kith can ever escape them. They are as much a part of that kith as the legends that forged them. While not all Birthrights or Frailties carry over into the mundane world, they are always on a changeling's mind, and often find ways to peek through into mortal habits.

For most fae, though, a kith is as much a community as it is a heritage. Many changelings only feel truly at home with others of their kith, who understand their shared idiosyncrasies. Most kith also actively seek out others of their kind who are yet unaware of their true lineage, or who have temporarily forgotten their fae natures, and the bonds formed thusly often hold local kith groups together. No matter how high a changeling rises in court politics or how many other kith form her motley, she remembers one of her own.

The process of awakening to one's heritage is known as the Chrysalis, a time when the Banality a changeling has endured in her life is sloughed off for the first time and her fae soul emerges. This event can occur at any time in a changeling's life, from childhood to old age, but is marked by powerful blasts of fae magic that often draw the attention of changelings (and occasionally other things) for miles around. A newly awakened changeling, called a fledge, is taken to the local noble to be recognized, and is assigned a mentor who guides her through the adjustment to her new life. When she has been determined to have learned enough and not constitute a threat to herself or the local Kithain population, the fledge is brought back to court, where she learns her True Name through a process called the Saining. At this point, she is fully recognized by the local nobility and free to pursue her own destiny. Any fledges who awakened with titles from a previous life take their places in the local court at this time.

## Seemings – The Mortal Shell

Long ago, faeries adopted mortal bodies and fused with mortal souls to avoid the fist of Banality. To this day, normal mortals still only see the mundane appearance of a changeling. Faeries and other enchanted beings, however, see a changeling for what she really is — a troll is a bluish tower of muscle, a sluagh is pale and thin, and a sidhe possesses breathtaking beauty. Indeed, in many cases the mortal shell often faintly resembles the fae spirit within — trolls' mortal seemings are usually tall and stocky, boggans' are short and plump, and eshu's are dark and handsome, although it is not uncommon to find a changeling whose mortal body hides a very different fae soul. Regardless of what the mortal shell resembles, however, the character's fae form is the character's "true" self, and he must act in accordance with both the chimerical and mundane world. For example, a troll must stoop when entering doorways that are too low for his faerie height, even if his mortal body fits through just fine. To do otherwise is to deny one's fae self, even if only for an instant, and is an invitation to Banality.

A changeling's mortal age and appearance is called his seeming. While some rare fae souls reflect a different age than their mortal bodies do, most fae selves echo the mortal frames that hide them. Kithain society divides the seemings into three groups: childlings, wilders and grumps. Childlings are any fae up to the beginning of adolescence, and they are viewed as innocents and protected by their fellow Kithain. Wilders, the teens and young adults of changeling society, earn their name with their passions and lust for adventure. They form the dynamic majority of changeling society. Grumps, those rare changelings who hold onto their fae selves after the age of 25 or so, are revered for their wisdom and experience, and often advise their brasher young counterparts. As a changeling's mortal body ages, so too does her faerie self, progressing from childling to wilder to grump until dying to be reborn again.

Keeping track of a character's mortal seeming is important to a character in **The Shining Host**, for while other fae will react with the character's faerie self, mortals and other unenchanted folk will react based on the appearance of the mortal seeming. A childling may be a duke of the surrounding principality, but is unlikely to intimidate a mortal police officer, much less a vampire, without the assistance of some fae magic.

## Courts

Though Seelie and Unseelie fae live without open hostility in the modern age, such was not always the case. In the old days, the two Courts warred, and switching from one to another was considered treason of the first water. Unseelie used to rule during the seasons of autumn and winter, while Seelie ruled the spring and summer; the exchange of power, which occurred every Samhain and Beltaine, was one of the fundamental rituals of faerie existence.

However, the Shattering changed all that. Out of the mutual need to survive the newly hostile mortal world, the Courts struck a truce which remains binding still. In modern times, Court is still important, however, as it determines a changeling's general personality and outlook as well as her likely allegiances, and fae who switch Courts frequently come to be mistrusted by both sides. Seelie fae tend to love tradition, courtly romance and chivalry, and prize true love and honoring one's oaths to be the highest achievements in life. Unseelie fae, on the other hand, embrace change and spend their Glamour and passions freely, trusting the countless mortals to provide more fuel for their adventures. Unseelie changelings hold the rights to speak and travel freely to be the highest freedoms a person can have, and bitterly oppose any attempts to restrict (read: restrain) these impulses on the part of their fellow fae and mortals alike.

However, despite the prejudices of both sides, Unseelie are no more inherently evil than the Seelie are good; the Courts are two sides of the same coin, and not necessarily constantly directly opposed. For every self-absorbed and anarchistic Unseelie, there is a stodgy and close-minded Seelie fae. What Court a character follows will affect the way other fae perceive him greatly, perhaps nearly as much as his kith or title, as many Seelie never quite trust an Unseelie, and an Unseelie often holds mild contempt for his Seelie cousins.

# The Shadow Court

Within the demesnes of the Unseelie Court dwells a second, secret power known as the Shadow Court. Although the Shadow Court makes a ceremonial appearance at several festivals during the year (most notably Samhain), it is more than a doddering relic. The actual nature of this order is far more sinister and mysterious than even the wildest drunken speculation would have it.

Rumor claims that the Shadow Court's ranks are composed entirely of devoted Unseelie determined to undermine the current Seelie rule. The truth is that the actual goals and leadership of this Court are unknown, but many foul deeds have already been traced back to this shadow player in Kithain politics. The more believable rumors flying around include stories that the Shadow Court's ranks include members of previously unknown Unseelie sidhe houses (the manipulative Ailil, the savage Balor and the disturbing Leanhaun), and that they have in their number the so-called Thallain, nightmare reflections of the more... acceptable kith. From goblins and ogres to foul beasties, bogies and boggarts, these wicked fae possess no Seelie aspect at all, existing only to serve the whims of their Unseelie masters. What's worse, it is said the origins of many Dauntain and the spread of Banality can be laid at the doorstep of the masters of the Shadow Court, who use these weapons to weaken their enemies before challenging them for dominance in the coming Long Winter.

And that's just the tip of the iceberg....

# The Power of Glamour

While artistic inspiration is perhaps the greatest, if subtlest, gift of the Kithain, it is by no means their only weapon with which to counter Banality. Changelings have always been suffused with a magical energy called Glamour, the power of raw creativity. Through this power, the fae can effect direct changes on both the mundane and chimerical worlds, using the stuff of dreams to shape magical effects to suit their whims. A changeling can achieve nearly anything imaginable — from levitation to prophecy to dream travel to unearthly manifestations of courtly grace — by invoking Glamour through one of the Arts of the Kithain. Each changeling begins play having learned the basics of one or two such Arts from her mentor. As she grows and understands better the nature of Glamour, she learns how to work more potent and far-reaching magics, and the workings of grump sorcerers can astound even the most jaded mortal or powerful Prodigal.

Chimera and the chimerical world, on the other hand, consist entirely of concentrated Glamour. This explains why mortals cannot perceive these fantastical creations and Banality causes them so much harm. Unlike changelings, chimera have no protection against Banality. Even the most magnificent chimerical manifestations, such as a cavalry charge on chimerical horses, will often disappear when faced with mundane observers. This forces Kithain to keep their most impressive chimera far away from relentlessly destructive humanity.

Not a thing to be tied to even such varied forms as chimera, Arts and kith, Glamour also comes in the forms of magical items, both chimerical and mundane, called treasures. Highly valued and much sought after, these items contain bits of the Dreaming which allow them to perform certain feats or endow their owners with mystical properties. Some lucky fae occasionally awakens from her Chrysalis to realize that Aunt Grizelda's tacky little seashell sculpture is really something quite magical, and winds up the proud owner of a potent treasure. There even exist temporary forms of treasures, called dross, which collect the creative and emotional energy of highly charged people and events into portable containers of Glamour. Changelings use dross both as currency and a means of fueling their magics.

If there is any one rule of Glamour, however, it is that Glamour can never be anticipated. Some things long thought lost to Banality can glow bright with the songs of a new generation, and some of the most unlikely people can attract Glamour with their ideas. Mortals may not perceive Glamour, but changelings always do. Glamour can be described in an infinite variety of ways, but it is always an dynamic and contagious energy. Creative mortals who are particularly in touch with the Dreaming can occasionally feel some residue of the "high" Glamour naturally gives off. Glamour is the essence and lifeblood of changelings, and the search for new sources of Glamour to cultivate can absorb much of a changeling's time.

# Banality's Grip

*You made your bed/That's where you lie.*

*No pearly gates/When you die.*

*We tried to teach/You didn't learn.*

*You're going down/You're gonna burn.*

— The Mighty Mighty Bosstones, "Holy Smoke"

Banality has existed ever since humanity first turned its back on the Dreaming to embrace cynicism, caution and doubt. A combination of cold reason, bitter self-delusion, apathy and pessimism, Banality acts as far more than just a kind of "anti-Glamour" — it replaces and prevents Glamour from reasserting its hold over something. Indeed, it sometimes seems to drive particularly banal mortals to seek out places and people full of Glamour just to destroy them.

Banality is as easy to sense as Glamour — excess mundanity produces a cold, heavy feeling in the stomach, followed by pins-and-needles feelings around the body and intense headaches. Changelings have trouble speaking and concentrating in areas of high Banality, and touching cold iron (the quintessence of Banality) produces violent stabbing pains, followed by a wash of lingering nausea. Unfortunately for mortals, Banality has turned on its creators in many ways, with the Mists that hide the effects of Glamour serving as the best example. Although the Mists cloud the minds of changelings who have forgotten their true selves, they also mask the power of Glamour, keeping those who would hunt the "insane" and "unholy" fae from being able to track their prey.

Those mortals who champion Banality often find themselves consumed by it, living dull, emotionless lives that they secretly long to escape from in any way they can. This painful truth is one of the strongest arguments the Kithain have against their enemy, and pointing out the self-destructive nature of Banality often leads its minions to reflect for a few painful moments on the joys and spontaneity that they have lost.

While the Kithain have no evidence of an actual animating intelligence behind Banality, this doesn't stop them from considering it the single greatest enemy the fae have ever encountered; those changelings who are temporarily lost to the Forgetting are immediately the subjects of rescue efforts by their fellows, and those who are Undone for a lifetime by the weight of Banality are deeply mourned. Those who are Undone by cold iron are mourned with soul-searing intensity, for with each cold iron death, another fae spirit has been lost forever, and a little more of the Dreaming has died with them.

Though childlings and wilders may think otherwise, grumps know that the greatest battles against Banality are not fought with guns and swords, but against mindsets of complacency and disillusionment, on battlefields where no sword has ever prevailed. Against such strong and subtle foes, only the willingness to dare to dream, and the urge to inspire mortals to live lives of greatness and imagination can ever hope to win out in the end.

# Changeling Society

Ever since the return of the sidhe, changelings have once again adopted the feudal system they maintained long ago, though the demands of the modern age has forced on it some democratic concessions of which the returning sidhe never dreamed. For all its romance and violence, pageantry and power, the feudal order seems to suit Seelie and Unseelie minds alike. Even the most radical commoner anarchists admit the appeal of crown and title; it's the lord and vassal part that most Kithain have trouble with. Since changeling society is based upon the progression of that simple unit — High King David counts the regional kings and queens as his vassals, who in turn get the allegiance of the dukes and duchesses of their domains, who have the fealty of their local counts and barons, who have the loyalty (at least in theory) of their commoner populations — not a few commoners have trouble with the whole setup from top to bottom.

Swearing loyalty to any one or more of the parties in the great chain of vassalage are the legion of knights and ladies of Concordia, who — squires and retinues in tow — act as errant defenders of the realm, soldiers against Banality and guardians against any other threat their lord or lady bids them challenge. Nobles hold sway over freeholds, and decide how those lands' resources are best used. In theory, every changeling has a lord or lady to whom he answers, who in turn watches out for his safety and provides shelter for him in times of conflict and need. Oaths backed by the power of the Dreaming keep both parties honest in their agreements.

In reality, the system works much as intended, with a few major differences. In deference to the democratic modern world and commoner appeals after the Accordance War, High King David created the Parliament of Dreams, a representative body which gives every noble freehold and commoner mew an equal voice in the politics of Concordia. However, there are still many pockets of commoners, children of the modern age of freedom and democracy, who refuse to accept the rule of the nobility, and carry out subversive tactics ranging from peaceful demonstrations to full guerrilla warfare in order to cause trouble for the "fascist" system. Similarly, many nobility, especially the elder sidhe, disagree with High King David's egalitarian tolerance of the commoner kith, and even refuse to recognize the legitimacy of commoners who have earned titles or held them during the Interregnum. These reactionaries constantly work behind the scenes to take freeholds away from commoners and restore the lands to their "rightful" owners, as well as to seize any opportunity to restrict the power and voice commoners have in changeling society.

The basic territory in changeling society is a freehold, a place of Glamour ruled by a lady or a lord. Identical sites run by commoners are called mews, but these have grown uncommon after the settlement of the Accordance War. A freehold can be anything from a New Orleans nightclub to an old Manhattan theater to an overgrown theme park — most often unobtrusive places away from easy mortal access, although it isn't unusual for Glamour to hide in plain sight. Wild places of beauty rarely disturbed by mortals, called glens, can also house freeholds and natural wellsprings of Glamour. All "official" Kithain business, such as settling disputes, Saining new changelings and conferring titles and honors, is carried out at a freehold, making the freeholds the center of Kithain society.

Each freehold has a court, but there are many positions for commoners in a noble's court, ranging from jester to steward to troubadour. The degree of involvement of the local commoners in a court is often a direct manifestation of the locals' feelings toward their lord, and a noble who finds herself surrounded solely by enchanted mortal servants is in deep trouble. Freeholds also possess some eldritch powers centered around the freehold's sacred hearth, or balefire. While in a freehold, changelings do not age in either their mortal seemings or their fae forms, and can freely adopt their kith shapes without using Glamour or worrying about the Mists. All magics used within a freehold do so without repercussions from Banality, even if mortals are present. Additionally, great healing powers manifest near a freehold's fire, making hearthfires ideal shelters for those ravaged by Banality. Given these advantages, it is no wonder the remaining freeholds are so fiercely contested and protected, and the discovery of a new freehold is a cause for great celebration.

Of course, beings of wild Glamour are by no means tied exclusively to dry bonds such as title, domain or noble succession; as much as they are creatures of tradition, the fae also have a long history of festivals and other merriment. Mortal communities used to go into hiding when the fae were out on the town, and for good reason — by enjoying and celebrating the cycles of life, fae can temporarily lower the local Banality and have a roaring good time, made all the better by the fact that the mundanes rarely remember it come morning. While many of the Kithain's festivals — such as Samhain, Beltaine, Yule and Imbolc — stem from Celtic tradition, the fae have borrowed holidays from just about every culture in the world, and invented some of their own when the mortals couldn't come up with enough. Some of them, such as Highsummer Night (known to the pooka as "Pranksgiving") and Carnival serve purely for merriment, while others remind the fae of ancient rites and transitions, and keep them hopeful and immersed in their heritage. Without such celebrations, much of the passion of the Dreaming would be lost; a changeling who consistently misses revelry with his kind begins to lose some of his fae aspect. Fortunately, eager childlings and wilders everywhere ensure that the old traditions will survive long past their current celebrants.

## The Escheat

One of the most ancient customs of the fae, this code of laws was revived with the return of the sidhe, and is now nearly universally upheld (or at least given lip service). Even the most staunch Unseelie admits it that the Escheat is mostly common sense, even if some of the semantics are disagreeable.

The Escheat is upheld through a practice called the fior, or trial by challenge. The local lord chooses the type of challenge, and the outcome — said to be dictated by Glamour, if the fior is performed properly — determines the guilt or innocence of the accused.

The Escheat consists of six tenets:

• The Right of Demesne — "A lord is the king over his domain. He is judge and jury over all crimes, large and small; his word is law. A noble is to be obeyed by his vassals, and respected by others. A noble is to respect his own lords in return."

• The Right to Dream — "Mortals have a right to dream unhindered by our needs. The Dreaming will die if we steal directly from the font. None is allowed to use Glamour to manipulate the creative process. Although you may inspire, you are forbidden to give direct instruction."

• The Right of Ignorance — "Do not betray the Dreaming to Banality; do not reveal yourself to humankind. Not only will humankind hunt us for our wisdom, but they will bring Banality on us and destroy our sacred places. The more humanity knows, the more it will seek to know, and the more Glamour it will destroy with its basilisk's gaze."

• The Right of Rescue — "All Kithain have the right to be expect rescue from the foul clutches of Banality. We are together in danger, and we must strive together to survive. Never leave anyone behind. Kithain are required to rescue other faeries trapped by Banality."

• The Right of Safe Haven — "All places of the Dreaming are sacred. Kithain cannot allow faerie places to be endangered. All those who seek refuge in such places must be admitted. Freeholds must not only be kept free of Banality, but of worldly violence."

• The Right of Life — "No Kithain shall spill the lifeblood of another Kithain. No Kithain shall bring salt tears unto the earth. No Kithain shall take from the Dreaming one of its own. Death is an anathema."

# Arcadia and The Dreaming

Lingering on the edge of every changeling's thoughts is the promise of Arcadia. Considered a paradise beyond imagination and the wellspring of all Glamour, Arcadia has been lost to the fae since the Shattering, and even the sidhe, who were exiled from Arcadia in 1969, can remember little about it. Supposedly, the taint of Banality and the limitations of a changeling's mortal body prevent Kithain from ever entering Arcadia, lest the returning exiles invite doom upon all the Dreaming. Even the mortal touch Kithain carry when dreaming forbids them from coming too close to Arcadia. It is only in rare visions and the occasional startlingly vivid dream that a changeling glimpses her long-lost homeland, but it is said that all Kithain instantly recognize the landscape of Arcadia.

The sheer beauty and appeal of even a dream of Arcadia has been known to revive and inspire even the most Banality-laden grump. Unfortunately, excessive homesickness for this ethereal realm also is a leading cause of wilders and grumps falling to the Forgetting, as they pine away for the unattainable paradise that lies just beyond the tips of their dreams. Disturbing rumors that some newly arrived sidhe recall a war in the declining Arcadian kingdom, and whispers of widespread turmoil and confusion in the heart of the Dreaming, contribute to the sense of loss and restlessness among the fae, as they worry about the fate of the land many of them consider their ultimate destination, and all of them realize is the source of Glamour.

Still, for all of the shadowy rumors extant, the fae still desire entrance to Arcadia once more. It is a common goal of the quests of many motleys and oathcircles to try to find a trod to take them home, and many Kithain bards draw inspiration from the notion of such a divine place.

## Seasons

Although changelings are creatures of a dynamic present and strive to recall a magical past, they know the future is gaining on them every minute. Unfortunately, the state of the world, with its growing pollution, violence and Banality, seems to bode ill for the fae. Many fae believe that the Earth is in the Autumn of its existence, about to slip into a Long Winter of cold Banality. In this coming age, the fae fear that Glamour will be completely smothered and the Dreaming weakened to the point of death as humanity embraces the carrion comfort of uninspired, unfeeling reason. It is a dark thought that haunts the fae even in the wildest moments of Glamour, and adds to the nihilistic fervor that many modern Unseelie fae feel — after all, if the world's about to end, who cares how a little Glamour's spent?

However, not all fae are without hope. Even if Winter is coming, many changelings point out, that must mean a new Spring lies beyond, when the Dreaming will rise anew from the ashes of the previous enchanted world. Such a cycle is only logical, these fae reason, and therefore they spend their time figuring out ways to store the Kithain's greatest treasures and deepest lore in safe locations. They also work to discover how freeholds will need to be bulwarked against the new ravages on the horizon, and make plans to preserve as many of the Kithain themselves as possible. These changelings are known as the Harbingers of Spring, and their arrival is sure to bring a flood of renewed hope and courage to dispirited fae and mortals alike. Indeed, it is this optimism, combined with a longing to return to Arcadia and an instinctive trust in Glamour, that keep the balefires lit across Concordia and the resources of every able changeling on the front lines against Banality. After all, even a hopeless battle has some appeal to the romantic in each fae — if the fight is for a good cause. And what cause could be better than the preservation of the Dreaming itself?

# The Prodigals

While they are certainly unique, changelings are definitely not alone in the supernatural community of the World of Darkness, as the wisest and well-traveled among them know (or quickly learn). Sluagh hold tea with vampires and the souls of the dead, trolls fight alongside werewolves to protect the dwindling wilderness, and human wizards seek to control the reality of the mortal world much the same as the fae seek to keep and shape their world of dreams. Believing all of the world's other supernatural denizens to be faeries who lost their way from the Dreaming and bound themselves to limited existences away from Glamour, changelings refer to these other beings as Prodigals. Some fae even long for a time when these other folk follow the parable of the prodigal son and return to the Dreaming, but as these supernatural "cousins" tend to be ignorant of the ways of the Dreaming they can accidentally bring Banality to a changeling's door. Most fae tend to work from behind the veil of the Mists when it comes to the Prodigals, using their mortal seemings and fae magic to keep the others ignorant of their true natures if at all possible.

### Vampires

Changelings and vampires often have little to talk about — faeries live and glory in the passions and fancies of life, while the Kindred, as vampires call themselves, are shut into a dreary half-life which depends on the suffering of others to continue. Indeed, the Banality brought about by a vampire's unnatural state and inhuman feeding habits is often enough to send changelings packing, although a few vampires, mostly those of the Malkavian and Ravnos "clans," seem to be onto the spirit of Glamour in their own way.

If a Kithain has to deal with the Kindred, it is best done through a member of one of these two clans at the highest possible speed and with the most possible precautions. The Kindred are known to be as paranoid as they are insatiable, and can have memories that span several of a faerie's lifetimes. Fortunately, they maintain a Masquerade that in many ways mimics the Mists, and share the faerie desire to remain unseen by mortals, which limits them to subtlety in most of their actions.

For more information on vampires, see **Laws of the Night**.

### Werewolves

Werewolves, on the other hand, have long had relations with the fae, as both groups move freely between worlds and fight to maintain a dwindling resource they hold dear; only, for the werewolves, it is the spirit of Gaia, the natural world, that needs defending. They are great shamans, able to control the spirits of the natural world, but they are also creatures of great rage and violence, born to kill and die for the Earth Mother.

Nonetheless, there are many ancient pacts between the Garou, especially members of the Celtic-born Fianna tribe, and the fae. Some Kithain also know of other breeds of shapeshifters, from bears to ravens, but of those, only the werecoyotes (or Nuwisha) share the true changeling spirit. Though the Nuwisha are extremely rare on Earth these days, when one of the prankster werecoyotes comes to town, laughter and good times are soon to follow for those fae wise enough to know when to laugh at themselves.

For more information on werewolves, see **Laws of the Wild**

## Mages

Mages, the modern descendants of the original Dreamers, are now locked in a war for the nature of reality itself, and are split into four factions — the mystical and eclectic Traditions, Bedlam-ridden knights of chaos called Marauders, the foul and demonic Nephandi, and the Banality-serving Technocracy. Of these, Kithain typically deal with the Traditions and Marauders the most; however, every mage of every faction is markedly different, and their thirst for Glamour — which they call Quintessence — makes changelings extremely cautious about inviting them to a freehold.

## Wraiths

Apart from the sluagh, who are inextricably bound to them, Kithain have very little to do with the spirits of the dead, or the Restless, as they dub themselves. Many fae troubadours speak of undying passion and love that reaches beyond death, but Kithain reincarnate, and thus think little about an actual afterlife; what they do know is that it is quite unpleasant, divided into quarreling factions and crowded with souls who try to cling to lives they've already lost. Denied direct access to Earth by ancient law and a barrier known as the Shroud, many wraiths serve dark and selfish dreams as well as noble love and guardianship.

For more information on wraiths, see **Oblivion**.

## Mortals

Often, Kithain fail to consider mortals in their world view; there are some mortals who live in fear and denial of anything that doesn't fit their notion of what's "right" and "real," and some of these hunt changelings. Those humans who serve Banality merely by their dedication to a boring existence are known as Autumn People, and while they do not actively hunt the fae (indeed, most do not know changelings exist), their excessive Banality makes Glamour scarce and every changeling's life that much more difficult. From overzealous librarians to overprotective mothers to overly rigid police officers, these folk are Banality-ridden obstacles in every Kithain's life.

The second group of those who hunt Glamour are known as Dauntain, and they are even more feared than the Autumn People. Many Dauntain were once changelings, but have rejected their fae heritage and are now driven to hunt down other fae and destroy them. Dauntain may believe all changelings to be deluded and in need of "help," or that they are demons sent to tempt "righteous folk", or (worst of all) they may know exactly what changelings are and hate them (and themselves) for it. Whatever their reason, the Dauntain track faeries with fanatical zeal and even employ weapons made from cold iron in their attempt to purge Glamour from the world. Such hunters, if once fae, may be very difficult to tell from normal changelings, at least until the fighting starts. Mortal Dauntain, on the other hand, often go unnoticed by the dream-struck Kithain, flying under their radar until it's too late. Such foes are the worst enemies a changeling can make, as they often know much about Glamour and Banality and the various kith, and use their knowledge to full advantage.

# Lexicon

A different existence calls for a new vocabulary. Below are some of the more commonly used terms from **The Shining Host**.

• **Ability**: The skills and knowledges and talents a character possesses.

• **Arcadia**: The land of the fae; the home of all faeries within the Dreaming.

• **Arts**: The ways of shaping Glamour.

• **Attributes**: The measure of a character's basic Physical, Social and Mental statistics. Measured in Traits.

• **Autumn, the**: The modern age.

• **Banality**: Mortal disbelief, as it affects changelings and their Glamour.

• **Bedlam**: A kind of madness that falls upon changelings who stray too far from the mortal world.

• **Bidding**: Part of the mechanism of challenges. The risking of Traits in order to win a challenge.

• **Bunk**: The price Glamour exacts for its power.

• **Cantrip**: A spell created through Glamour by using a combination of Arts and Realms.

• **Challenge**: The system by which conflict between two or more characters is resolved through bidding of Traits and the playing of "Rock-Paper-Scissors."

• **Champion**: A warrior chosen by one of higher rank to fight in his stead. A champion always wears the token of his patron, which he keeps if he wins the duel.

• **Changeling**: A fae who has taken on mortal form in order to survive on Earth.

• **Childling**: A child come full into his changeling nature; this lasts until he becomes a wilder, around 13 years of age. Childlings are known for their innocence and affinity with Glamour and are well protected by other changelings.

• **Chimera**: A bit of dream made real; unseen by mortals, chimera are part of the enchanted world. Chimera may be objects or entities.

• **Commoner**: Any of the changeling kith who are not sidhe.

• **Dauntain**: Human faerie-hunters, deeply twisted by Banality. They are usually changelings who have turned against their fae natures.

• **Dreaming, the**: The collective dreams of humanity. Changelings often travel in these realms both to seek adventure and to gather the raw dreamstuff that can be used in crafting chimera.

• **Dreamrealms**: The lands comprising Arcadia and the other realms of the Dreaming.

• **Enchant**: To imbue a mortal with the power to see chimerical objects.

• **Escheat**: The highest faerie laws.

• **Experience**: Points given to characters as they progress through multiple games. Used for increasing the character's statistics and powers.

• **Fae, Faerie**: A being indigenous to the Dreaming (though not always a current resident thereof).

• **Fathom**: A deep-seeking, protracted use of the Art of *Soothsay*. Also called "the Taghairm."

• **Fior**: A contest, the point of which is to determine justice.

• **Fledge**: A newly awakened changeling of any age.

• **Freehold**: A place that is infused with Glamour. Important to all changelings, freeholds are proof against Banality — for a time.

• **Gallain**: 1) "The Outsiders," those who may be Kithain but whose origins, customs and magical ways are not understood; 2) Any inscrutable creature of the Dreaming.

• **Glamour**: The living force of the Dreaming; changeling magic.

• **Grump**: A changeling of elder years, usually beginning at about the age of 25. Very few changelings reach this age — most succumb to Banality long before.

• **Health**: The measure of how much physical damage a changeling has taken.

• **Hue and Cry**: 1) A hunt called out against a criminal; 2) The call of all changelings to come and defend a freehold.

• **Influences**: The measure of how much control a changeling has on assorted institutions. Measured in Traits.

• **Kin**: Human relatives of a changeling who do not possess faerie blood.

• **Kinain**: Human kinfolk of a changeling who possess faerie blood and frequently have strange magical "gifts" because of it.

• **Kith**: All the changelings of a kind. One's kith determines the nature of one's faerie guise and soul.

• **Kithain**: Changelings' self-referential term.

• **Liege**: One's sworn noble sovereign, whether baron, count, duke or king.

• **Long Winter, the**: The prophesied eradication of all Glamour.

• **Mists, the**: 1) The tendency for mortals to forget the effects of Glamour and the presence of changelings after a very short time. The Mists protect changelings from being discovered. 2) The tendency for Banality-tainted changelings to forget their faerie lives.

• **Motley**: A family or gang of commoners.

• **Noble**: Any changeling raised to noble title; although nobles are traditionally sidhe, lately commoners have begun receiving noble positions.

• **Oathbond**: The mystical bond created by the swearing of an oath.

• **Realms**: The five aspects of the world with which changelings have affinity.

• **Retainers**: Any servants of a liege.

• **Saining**: "The Naming"; a ritual performed on a newly awakened changeling to determine his kith, True Name and title.

• **Status**: How well-respected a Kithain is. Measured in Traits.

• **Tara-Nar**: The great freehold castle of High King David. Beneath it is the Well of Fire, from which all balefire comes.

• **Trait**: The adjectives used to define your character.

• **Trods**: Magical gateways, faerie roads; some lead to other freeholds, some to the Dreaming itself. They are opened only at prescribed times.

• **Vassal**: The sworn servant of a liege.

• **Vellum**: A specially preserved chimerical hide on which changeling scribes write.

• **Wilder**: A changeling of adolescent years, usually from age 13 to age 25. Known for their wild undertakings and loose tempers, wilders are the most common changelings.

• **Willpower**: The measure of how strong a changeling's will is. Measured in Traits.

• **Yearning**: Also called "the Gloomies," the Yearning is the utter longing for Arcadia that overcomes grumps as Banality encroaches upon them.

# ChapterTwo:
# Character Creation

The cornerstone of any roleplaying game is the character. This is especially true in live roleplaying, where dice, character sheets and other typical trappings of gaming vanish. Below are the basic rules for generating a character for **The Shining Host**.

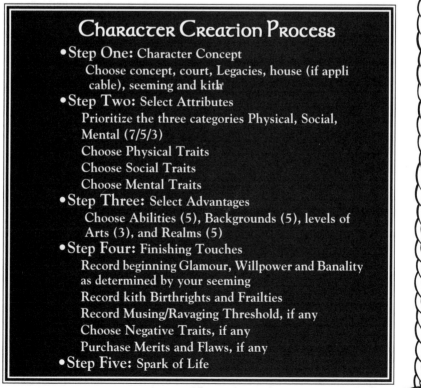

## Character Creation Process

- **Step One:** Character Concept

  Choose concept, court, Legacies, house (if applicable), seeming and kith

- **Step Two:** Select Attributes

  Prioritize the three categories Physical, Social, Mental (7/5/3)

  Choose Physical Traits

  Choose Social Traits

  Choose Mental Traits

- **Step Three:** Select Advantages

  Choose Abilities (5), Backgrounds (5), levels of Arts (3), and Realms (5)

- **Step Four:** Finishing Touches

  Record beginning Glamour, Willpower and Banality as determined by your seeming

  Record kith Birthrights and Frailties

  Record Musing/Ravaging Threshold, if any

  Choose Negative Traits, if any

  Purchase Merits and Flaws, if any

- **Step Five:** Spark of Life

# Step One: Inspiration

Before you write down a single thing about your character, you need to find inspiration for the type of character you want to play. Once you're inspired, you need to develop a rough idea of who your character is. This development involves choosing a concept, a kith, a seeming and a personality (defined by your choice of a Legacy). The better you interrelate these four aspects of your character, the more intricate and complete the end result will be.

A character's inner self is often completely different from his concept, and the stereotypical image of a kith can be contradicted by choosing a contrasting Legacy. There are many different types of people who exist in the enchanted world of **The Shining Host**, and a changeling can emerge from any class and nation imaginable. With imagination and a little thought, you'll find a character forming in no time.

## Court

In ancient days, the Seelie and Unseelie Courts warred openly, but this is no longer the case. Now the Courts nominally work together with Banality as their common foe, but ancient distrust still sets them apart. The Seelie embody tradition, honor and romance, while the Unseelie see their counterparts as stodgy, reactionary and hopelessly antiquated. By the same token, while the Unseelie see themselves as a force for change, new ideas and free expression, many Seelie see them as anarchistic, disrespectful and self-destructive. Current politics lean heavily to the side of the Seelie Court.

All prejudices aside, the Court a character chooses to follow says much, both about how he views himself and how he will be viewed by others. Switching Courts is always possible, but moving away from long-held beliefs is bound to raise suspicion and distrust from one's former comrades.

## Legacies

Over their many lifetimes, Kithain reincarnate, and no matter what kith or life a soul wears for a few years, the same underlying personality burns behind the mortal shell's eyes. Even the newly arrived sidhe possess legendary ancestors and powerful personalities, all the more necessary for them to survive the rough transition to Earth. As the drives of these old souls are what lead to the doing of heroic (or less than heroic) deeds, and are the essence of what is carried from lifetime to lifetime, they are known as a faerie's Legacies. Legacies are the marks and moods that determine the general personality of any given changeling.

Legacies still reflect the ancient division between the Seelie and Unseelie Courts, as Kithain have two parts to themselves. One tends to follow the honor-bound path of the Seelie, while the other adheres to the wildness and rebelliousness of the Unseelie. Unlike their ancestors, who were bound by

36

seasonal cycles that determined their Court, modern fae can switch allegiances freely. Most fae do tend to stick with one Court or the other, switching only on holidays like Samhain or Beltaine, or in face of great emotional or situational stress.

With the change in Court comes a change in Legacy, as the Seelie or Unseelie side of a Kithain's personality comes to prominence. Only one Legacy can be active at a time, but even so, the other finds ways to make itself known; fae Legacies are not catastrophic transitions, but rather complementing pairs. Trying to completely deny or repress one inevitably fails, with disastrous mental consequences for the Kithain in question.

Carried by each Legacy is a Quest, as well as a Ban. These are two requirements which the changeling's faerie soul has carried for several lives, and which have since carried into the character's current incarnation. The Quest is a goal or code that a Kithain with that Legacy strives to uphold and pursue, and is the destiny that refreshes and renews him. Any changeling who ignores his Quest often feels increasingly bereft and listless, having pushed away his true calling. On the other hand, a Kithain who embraces his Quest finds himself constantly invigorated, ready to challenge the world. Similarly, the Ban is a restriction or admonishment which the Kithain must attempt to abide by, or else risk being plagued with feelings of guilt, self-doubt and regret. Even the most callous redcap or arrogant sidhe finds that performing actions that go against his personal Ban leaves him drained and uneasy, and he often finds that his Ban is the one law he can't tolerate watching others break. (**Note:** The Ban does not prevent a Kithain from doing what it is the Ban describes; it only make him feel deep shame and regret if he does it.)

Fortunately, a Kithain must only honor the Quest and Ban of whatever Legacy is currently active. A character may also choose an entirely new Legacy for one or both Courts, rather than simply switching between them. However, this is a fundamental personality change, and should be done under a Storyteller's supervision and with a lot of soul-searching and roleplaying; the character is altering an essential part of herself, a painful and lengthy process. Such changes come about best when they are the result of events in the story (a Fiend develops empathy for one of her victims, a Stoic decides to embrace passionate public displays), not merely when the player feels like trying something new. As such, they should be worked into the chronicle accordingly.

For game purposes, Legacies serve several functions. Most importantly, they determine a character's personality. While not a straitjacket, a Legacy is still an excellent measure of a character's general attitudes and goals. Not all Paladins play fair, and not all Peacocks are completely irredeemable, but generally speaking it's safe to assume such cases are the exception and not the rule. Second, Legacies are one way to regain spent Willpower Traits; a Storyteller may allow a player who is roleplaying her Legacy (Quest, Ban and all) exceptionally well to recover a Willpower Trait as a function of her

37

increased self-confidence and self-respect. Conversely, a character who ignores her Quest and/or constantly violates her Ban may also find herself unable to regain Willpower Traits until she is more true to herself. Finally, Legacies serve to tell what Court a character is following at a given time; players should circle or underline on their character sheet which Court their characters are currently following before play begins, and update the sheet if the characters decide at any time to switch.

# Seelie

**Arcadian** — Human self? What human self? You much prefer your fae side to your human one, and long to learn more about the Dreaming. Your Quest is to learn new things about your faerie self, but your Ban is to never stay in your human seeming too long.

**Aspirant** — You see life as one long continuous quest for knowledge, and are constantly trying to expand your horizons with quests and questions of all kinds. Your Quest brings you Willpower whenever you overcome an obstacle, but your Ban requires that you never pass up a learning opportunity.

**Bumpkin** — You are a solid, practical sort, full of common-sense solutions for problems of every kind. Your Quest restores your Willpower whenever you find a practical solution to a problem, but your Ban requires that you never pass up a chance to solve a problem through common sense.

**Comrade** — You are the epitome of friendship, and value it above all other things in life; if you aren't a good friend, you're nothing. Your Quest affirms this bond with Willpower for risking your own interests for a friend, but your Ban requires that you never terminate a friendship, even if the friend violates your trust.

**Courtier** — You are a student of social interaction in all its forms, and love all the details that accompany such. Your Quest is to deflate volatile situations and bring peace and harmony to your motley, and your Ban that you never purposely make someone angry or upset.

**Crafter** — Your love is building, shaping and creating — bringing order to the universe, yes, but order in a beautifully crafted way. Your Quest rewards you when, through hard work and effort, you leave something better than you found it, but your Ban requires that you never leave a group or situation without improving it in some way.

**Dandy** — A social climber and career opportunist, you never miss a chance to advance yourself at court, and all manner of tricks are fair play to you so long as you get ahead. You have a Quest to succeed at being promoted or strengthening your current post, and a strict Ban never to pass up an opportunity to ingratiate yourself with your betters.

**Gadfly** — No one's 100 percent right, and you love to remind people of this. You are the social critic, the investigative reporter, the one who keeps the powers-that-be honest, be they mortal or fae. Your Quest goes one step further every time you win an argument with someone in power, but your Ban forbids you from letting anyone else get in the last word.

**Hermit** — You are introspective by nature, preferring your own company to that of others. When you do speak, it has weight, but most can count on one hand the times you've spoken on something without real consequence. Your Quest rewards you when inner reflection solves a problem, but your Ban requires that you rarely speak unless the situation is dire and you feel your view has not already been expressed.

**Humanist** — Fae side? Don't remind you! The opposite of the Arcadian and a reluctant changeling to the core, you may be frightened, disgusted or simply tired of your fae side. You prefer your human life and seeming to the chaotic world of the fae. You Quest to put human concerns above even the most pressing fae matters, and your Ban keeps you in human seeming and out of the Dreaming as much as possible.

**Knight** — Honor and glory aren't dead, and you're living proof. Your Quest rewards you whenever following your chivalric code puts you in danger, but your Ban prohibits you from behaving in an "unknightly" fashion.

**Orchid** — You have lived a sheltered life, but now you're out in the big, scary real world, and you desperately hope a hero will come along soon to rescue you. Your Quest supports you every time you escape a dangerous situation with your innocence and well-being intact, but your Ban requires that you never trust a stranger and never reveal yourself to anyone.

**Paladin** — You live for competition, and your story is that of the brave, stalwart athlete or hero. You advance your Quest whenever you overcome a truly challenging situation, but your Ban prohibits you from turning down a challenge you see as fair.

**Panderer** — You love seeing people happy, and will go to great lengths to make sure others are having a good time whatever way you can. You Quest whenever you bring others happiness without them realizing your part in it, but you have a Ban against ever knowingly doing anything to undermine another's happiness.

**Philanthropist** — You have a highly developed sense of morality, and live to help others and do good deeds. You may base these beliefs on anything from religion to your own moral code, but they are consistent (at least to you) and require you to give of yourself often. You fulfill your Quest every time you make a positive difference in someone's life, but your Ban forbids ever accepting payment for your generosity or deliberately harming innocents.

**Pishogue** — You live in a constant state of childlike wonder, and the conventional reality of your world is quite different even from other change-lings'. Your Quest rewards you every time you avoid an unpleasant truth, and your Ban requires that you never take anything too seriously.

**Prankster** — The fae have a long tradition as jokesters and masters of pranking, and you are proud to uphold this. Your Quest applauds you every time you pull off a particularly artful prank, but your Ban requires that you never verbally apologize for a prank and that you never take anything too seriously.

**Regent** — You are the leader, the living embodiment of the realm, the one who speaks for many. Though you may not actually rule a fief or freehold, you certainly feel that for better or for worse, the weight of the realm is on your shoulders. Your Quest is fulfilled whenever you resolve a tough situation through your own leadership, and your Ban holds you to abide by your own laws.

**Sage** — You are the advisor, the teacher, the wise one. You have seen much, traveled much and know much (including the fact that you know very little). You Quest to see others follow your advice and succeed at their chosen task, but you have a Ban to never stand in another's chosen way.

**Saint** — You feel the pain of others and constantly seek to ease the suffering of those in need. You are deeply concerned with healing, comforting, supporting and fortifying those around you. You achieve a step on your Quest whenever you ease suffering or protect another, but your Ban is never to cause distress, willingly or not.

**Squire** — You much prefer the role of sidekick to the glare of the limelight. You are Piglet to Pooh, Watson to Holmes, Patsy to Arthur, but wherever you are, you take the supporting role. You follow your Quest whenever you play a supporting role in some accomplishment but take no credit for it; you have a Ban against ever contradicting or undermining your current heroic companion.

**Stoic** — You take the joys and sorrows of life in stride, and rarely wear your heart on your sleeve. This isn't to be confused with having no feelings at all, but simply a calm, patient attitude toward life. Your Quest is to come through highly emotional situations with your composure intact, while your Ban is never to let emotions rule you.

**Troubadour** — You are an artist to whom the world is a beautiful, majestic place, and in which everything and everyone is an object of unique beauty. Your Quest supports you whenever you complete a task in the name of a higher ideal, but your Ban is to never hide feelings of love or affection for another.

**Virtuoso** — There are few who can claim to have mastered a given field, and you are one of them. You Quest whenever you learn or achieve something that brings you closer to mastering your field, but your Ban goes against focusing on matters not related to your field for too long.

**Wayfarer** — You are the endless wanderer, the rootless child with nowhere to call home and no one to call when you get there. You Quest whenever you survive a life-threatening situation through your own cleverness, but your Ban requires that you never plan for the future.

## Unseelie

**Beast** — You are the roaring monster, the Leviathan. You conquer all who oppose you, destroying them if possible. Your Quest rewards you whenever you remove a significant opposition to your goals, but you have a Ban against retreating or compromising your territory.

**Bogle** — You are a prankster, but unlike the Prankster, you don't care if your tricks harm and maim, emotionally or directly, as long as you get a good laugh out of it. You Quest every time you pull off an artful and mean-spirited prank, but you have a Ban against apologizing for a prank or letting a human intentionally slight you without pranking him in return.

**Cerenaic** — Pleasure is your quest, your motto and your area of expertise. You may favor a particular vice such as sex, food, drink, parties or all of the above, and your appetite is always increasing. Your Quest is to spend a day pursuing your vice, or to experience a new sensation, and your Ban is never to turn down an opportunity to fulfill your desires.

**Churl** — Manners are for wussies and momma's boys. Rude and ill-bred, you scoff (and fart, whiz and belch) at convention. Quest to get away with outraging polite society; you have a Ban against being polite.

**Craven** — Better a live coward than a dead hero; you have no guts whatsoever in any area of your life, and are always looking for a quick escape route. You advance your Quest every time you save yourself by running away, but you have a Ban against ever volunteering for dangerous assignments.

**Fatalist** — Everything in the world is flawed, and everything is doomed. You take a dark and sullen pleasure in seeing things go wrong, and love to prove that things are fundamentally flawed to others. Quest every time you prove your omens of doom to be true, and respect a Ban never to laugh except in bitterness and sarcasm.

**Fiend** — You inflict pain for no other reason than that you enjoy watching others suffer. You may try to rationalize this need for pain and control, or you may have just accepted it. **In no instance should you take this Legacy outside the bounds of the game, or violate the rules of Mind's Eye Theatre to implement it.** Your Quest advances every time you truly hurt someone, and you have a Ban against passing up an opportunity to inflict pain.

**Fop** — You are called "superficial" by many, those uncouth swine. Czar of fashion, sultan of style, you are one of the beautiful people. Peasants, prepare to be dazzled! You Quest each time you outshine others in a social situation, and have a strict Ban to avoid being out of style.

**Fool** — There is no meaning in the world, no deep purpose, no reason for anything. In this world of chaos you ride the waves like a master surfer — you are the divine trickster, the clown, the one who laughs last. Quest when you deflate the seriousness of a situation, but your Ban is to never search for the "whys" of your life — there are none.

41

**Grotesque** — You love disgusting others; it's an art, a hobby and a talent all wrapped up in one. The sicker, grosser and more horrible others find you, the more you like it. You Quest when your antics cause someone to falter or lose composure, but you have a Ban against ever revealing an overtly pleasing or appealing side of yourself.

**Humbug** — Grumpy, sour and just plain cranky, you never let anything satisfy you. Some think that under your exterior is a lovable softie; you live to prove them wrong. You Quest every time one of your dire predictions comes true, and have a Ban against ever looking on the bright side of life.

**Knave** — With a serpent's tongue and a wicked gleam in your eye, you lead others on to exploring their darkest desires with trickery, flattery and manipulation. You Quest when you get someone to enjoy something he'd normally be opposed to, but your Ban requires that you never protect anyone from the harsh realities of life.

**Outlaw** — You owe society nothing and it owes you everything, but you usually have to remind society of that fact. You Quest whenever you commit a completely selfish act that hurts someone else, and you have a Ban against doing anything that helps others more than it hurts them or helps you in the long term.

**Pandora** — It seems like such a simple thing, keeping your mouth shut, but you just can't do it. Your mouth flies open, and trouble comes crashing right out. You love getting people in trouble by exposing their secrets. Quest when you survive something dangerous you were strictly forbidden to do or warned against; even your Ban, never to keep a secret or obey an order, is fun in its own way.

**Peacock** — You are the loveliest, smartest, best person in the world, and you want to make sure that everyone knows it. If you're not the center of attention, you aren't happy. Sometimes you help other, lesser people, but only to make yourself look generous. You Quest when you prove that you're the best at something, but you have a Ban against admitting failure or fault.

**Ragamuffin** — The opposite of a *Fop*, you believe in substance over style, and you play the militant slob to prove just how deep you are. Al Bundy looks like Mr. GQ with your rejection of such unnecessary things as grooming, bathing, etc. You Quest to expose others as frauds, and have a Ban against ever dressing appropriately for a situation.

**Rake** — The world is one big bowl of pleasure, and you want the ladle. Material goods, sensual experiences, Glamour — you hoard anything that makes you feel good, even if it goes against your own self-interests. You Quest each time you succeed in your pursuit of personal pleasure, and have a Ban against giving anything away without hope of reward or a hard fight.

**Riddler** — You are an enigma wrapped in secrets, and never give a straight answer to any question. Maybe you feel ignored and thus seek attention through riddles, or you just like to lie; the results are the same regardless. You Quest when you confuse or mislead someone, but have a grave Ban against ever allowing others to discover the truth about you and your origins.

**Ringleader** — You have your gang, and you rule with an iron fist. You work hard to build and strengthen your organization, and any who won't submit to your cause and authority you crush mercilessly. You Quest whenever you achieve something through the devotion of your followers, and have a Ban against allowing anyone to endanger the whole organization and its goals.

**Rogue** — You don't want to work for a living; why should you when you can simply fleece others? You pick their pockets while they preach their sermons, and prefer to let the world work for you instead of the other way around. You Quest when you achieve something that you don't really deserve, and have a simple Ban — never work.

**Savage** — To you there is nothing but the law of the jungle; survival, reproduction and predation. Language, art, technology — all wastes of time. Fighting for dominance, mating when the urge strikes, eating what you can catch, those things are worthwhile. You Quest to conquer "civilized" foes through your own cunning and might, but carry a Ban against ever indulging in civilized follies.

**Schismatic** — Things fall apart. The center cannot hold. Why doesn't anyone accept this? You live to cause change and chaos. You Quest every time you cause dissension in a tightly knit social group, and have a Ban against joining any formal organizations except to subvert them or to use them to subvert others.

**Shade** — Like the *Pishogue* Legacy, you see the world in a very different way than even your fellow changelings, but yours is a vision crafted from nightmares. You Quest every time you encounter a horrific thing without losing composure, but have a Ban to never take anything too seriously — to do so would let the nightmare in.

**Sophist** — Most people hunger for knowledge, and you're happy to give it to them — for a price. You teach solely for self-gain, but unfortunately you tend to believe that people want what you are selling even when they do not, and you become... *agitated* if they do not meet your price. You Quest each time you win an argument or debate, but have a strict Ban never to admit you are wrong.

**Wretch** — You're wretched, and boy, do you know it. The only one who hates you more than everyone else you know is yourself, and you are so awful you can't even think of a witty insult for your reflection, sorry thing that it is. Your Quest (if it's even worthy of such a grand name) is advanced whenever others vilify you as worthless, or throw up their hands in frustration after failing to get through to you. You obey a strict Ban against ever admitting to your own success.

43

# Houses

When the sidhe returned from Arcadia, they came bearing the banners of several noble houses that had been gone from Earth for centuries. Only one house of sidhe, House Scathach, remained behind when their brethren fled to Arcadia; they are now considered impure and inferior by most of the new arrivals.

These are the descriptions of the six primary noble houses of the sidhe; all sidhe characters must belong to one of these houses, and any commoner character who is a servant or other recognized member of a house may write its name and add "(affiliation)" on the line for House. However, commoners do not receive the Boon or Flaw for the house.

### House Dougal

Members of this house are known for their strength, wisdom and technical acumen. The house's founder, Lord Dougal, pioneered the process by which fae smiths merge Glamour into steel to make it safe for fae to use. Members of this house tend to be gruff, practical and good with their hands. Order and precision are their allies, although they battle the Banality of mindless organization with all their souls. Dougal fae love artistic architecture and engineering of all kinds, and are often found as stewards, clerks and barristers in freeholds; those lands that are run by a Dougal tend to be orderly, practical domains.

**Boon**: Once per session, members of House Dougal may convert Glamour Traits to Willpower Traits, up their normal maximum. This must be done while working hard, exercising or in combat.

**Flaw**: All members of this house suffer from some handicap that they must compensate for, usually with cunningly concealed craftsmanship: a club foot, bad eyesight, poor hearing, etc. The handicap extends to their mortal bodies as well. Each must choose a permanent *Lame*, *Oblivious*, *Decrepit* or *Delicate* Negative Trait to reflect this Flaw. However, for practical purposes, the Flaw is considered to have been corrected or compensated for somehow by the time play begins. This Negative Trait can only be called if the character knows a particular Dougal's Flaw, and that usually requires a bit of digging.

### House Eiluned

House Eiluned is known for its potent sorcery and mysterious ways, and supposedly has many contacts among the Prodigals. They consider themselves to be in direct conflict with House Gwydion over the right to rule Concordia, and are constantly working to advance their house's power as well as their own individual holdings. Although such ambitions can lead to infighting and backstabbing, Eiluned quickly band together when the time comes to defend against a common foe or advance the greater cause of the house.

Many sidhe with high *Remembrance* seem to recall a great scandal in Arcadia that supposedly was the basis of this house's exile, a charge Eiluned fae vehemently deny. Many lords employ those of this house as councilors or advisors, as they have as much of a knack for unraveling problems as they do creating them. Lands ruled by this house tend to be as mysterious and dark as the house itself, and are often centers of great natural magical power.

**Boon**: All cantrips cast by members of this house are especially potent, and the magics worked notably durable; as a result Eiluned fae may spend a Mental Trait to receive a retest on all cantrips they cast. A Glamour Trait may be required to retest Advanced Arts (at Narrator discretion).

**Flaw**: Members of this house love intrigue, and cannot help being drawn into plotting and rumormongering. They receive a permanent *Untrustworthy* Negative Trait, and must spend a Willpower Trait to avoid listening in on or joining any mysteries or plotting they come across.

### House Fiona

This house embraces heroic passion and the spirit of adventure. Fiona fae are known for their love of drink and song as well as battle, and romance is their favorite pastime. Members of the house often hold radical views (compared to other nobles, anyway) and see their house as a catalyst for necessary change. Although members of House Fiona can sometimes be called from duty by appeals to base appetites, they are fierce soldiers when the trumpet calls, full of spit and vinegar and absolutely fearless. Despite their recent arrival and their role as one of the main military houses of the returning sidhe, Fiona are beloved by the common folk for their *laissez-faire* attitude toward rank, and they have quickly adopted the cause of the commoners in fae politics. Lands ruled by members of this house are typically happy and free-spirited, albeit a bit wild and disrespectful in the eyes of more formal houses and freeholds.

**Boon**: Sidhe of House Fiona are renowned for their courage; any attempt to induce fear in them, whether normal or magical, automatically fails. Though they understand it, fear cannot hold them, even in the face of death. The exception is if their true love is in danger, at which point they become deathly afraid for him or her.

**Flaw**: Fiona fae, due to their accepting natures, are given to tragic romances with "unacceptable" types like outlaws, mortals or even Prodigals. Such love often becomes such a complete and true passion that it cannot be denied; *Romeo and Juliet* looks like light farce compared to some of the tragic complications that frequently develop as a result. Members of the house can overcome the Flaw, but only by becoming utterly misanthropic toward the very notion of love — an attitude which will win the solitary sidhe no friends inside the house.

## House Gwydion

This house is perhaps the most "noble" of all the houses on Earth, and is generally held to have the best rulers among the fae. Indeed, this house spearheaded the Accordance War effort for the nobles, and still holds most of the power in Concordia. High King David and several of the other kings are of Gwydion. However, some say arrogance runs in the blood as well, and all Gwydion seem to display unusually hot tempers when roused to anger. Pain in particular seems to drive such sidhe wild with rage; however, it generally takes quite a lot to set them off in the first place. Lands ruled by this house tend to be fair and just, with a strong sense of protocol and tradition, but the local ambiance can also be described as somewhat cool and aloof.

**Boon**: Gwydion fae can, with a Mental Challenge using the *Kenning* Ability, determine whether someone is telling the truth (as the subject knows it). For some mysterious reason, members of House Eiluned are completely immune to this ability.

**Flaw**: When a member of this house reaches his *Wounded* Health Level, suffers intense pain, or has his honor directly insulted, he is in danger of flying into one of the legendary rages ascribed to the Gwydion. He must make a Static Willpower Challenge to avoid suffering the effects of the Derangement: *Crimson Rage* for the next 10 minutes. He may be talked out of this rage by allies as one would talk a vampire or werewolf out of frenzy (i.e., very carefully), with a successful Social Challenge, but if the target of his fury returns before the time of rage has passed, he will go wild once more.

## House Liam

The quietest (some also say wisest) of the houses, House Liam is known for its dedication to the mortal world and the protection of humans, a cause pursued with passion that even the Fiona notice. These fae do not see humans as perfect — far from it — but do feel humanity has a right to exist undisturbed. Members of House Liam are angered by Ravaging and hate Banality, and their normally peaceful demeanors are quick to change when presented with such.

The house is looked down on among the fae for its outspoken allegiances. Although law forbids Liam fae from being openly mistreated, the truth is that they are virtually pariahs among the sidhe; most are widely traveled and dispersed. Liam sidhe are often among the few nobles who truly understand humans, and are master sages, record-keepers and archivists. A wise king keeps a member of House Liam on staff as such. House Liam owns few freeholds, and the ones they do rule are often broken-down urban wastelands no one else would take.

**Boon**: Members of House Liam find it easy to enchant mortals; they need spend one less point of Glamour to do so than other changelings. Even this, however, has a downside — Liam fae begin with one more point of Banality than normal.

**Flaw**: Those of House Liam are considered oathbroken; no other changeling feels obligated to honor oathbonds, hospitality or justice so far as these fae are concerned. In addition, Liam fae begin with one less Status Trait than their *Title* would normally indicate.

### House Scathach

This mysterious house is named for its founder, one of Ireland's most famous warrior women. Members of the house actually remained on Earth when the other sidhe fled back to Arcadia, but were forced into hiding by the enmity the commoners held toward the vanishing sidhe. Like the commoners, they adopted the "Changeling Way" and have passed down through mortal families through the years. Scathach fae are master warriors, scouts, spies and assassins, and move with a grace and speed that is unnerving to their foes. Such fae are rarely seen, however, and are rumored to have contacts among the more nomadic Prodigals. The commoners have dubbed Scathach fae "Gray Walkers," and even the other sidhe admit that they have the best *Soothsay* abilities among the nobility. House Scathach neither possesses nor desires political power, and if any of its members own any lands, they are characteristically silent about it.

**Boon**: All members of this house are unnervingly quiet, even in combat, and are masters of blade and fist. Scathach fae receive a free level of *Brawl* and *Melee*, and are at a one-Trait advantage in challenges related to any kind of hiding or sneaking around. Because of their lineage, Scathach fae do not have the regular sidhe Frailty of *Banality's Curse*.

**Flaw**: The members of this house exhibit a strange madness in combat; once they enter battle, Scathach fae must either spend a Willpower Trait or be unable to leave the field until all foes have been defeated. However, friends and allies are safe from this madness. These fae also are forbidden by an ancient pact, enforced by the full weight of the Dreaming, from using the Art of *Sovereign*, and are down two Traits on Social Challenges with other sidhe (except those of Houses Liam and Fiona).

# Seeming

Trapped on Earth, exiled from Arcadia, changelings have managed to adapt to the mortal world in many different ways. One of the most important is the changeling's mortal seeming, the human body in which each fae soul clothes itself. These borrowed bodies act as shields against Banality and serve to hide a Kithain's true nature from the mortals around her. Without the protection the mortal seeming offers, Banality would quickly erode the obvious magical nature of a changeling into nothingness.

However, the age and appearance of one's mortal seeming has a great deal to do with how one is treated by mortals and fellow fae alike; a childling often has a problem being taken seriously, while a grump is considered over the hill by the youthful masses of the fae. While faeries were once capable of living for centuries, the nature of the modern world discourages such magics, lest mortals grow suspicious. Therefore, it is important to keep track of how a character ages; in the enchanted world, youth is critical to a character's belief in magic, wonder and trust. All Kithain are considered to belong to one of these three categories, collectively called seemings.

## Childlings

Childlings, the youngest of the Kithain, aren't always as innocent or naive as they seem. Though physically between the age of three and 13, most are wise beyond their years, having had several lifetimes of experience behind them (they just don't remember most of it). Outsiders in the adult-oriented mortal world, they can often see things their elders cannot or will not, and thus are prized for their perspectives by the sensitive Kithain.

No matter how many lifetimes childlings have lived, however, they are still children now — the world is their playground, and they delight in the pageantry and spectacle of faerie existence. Displays of Glamour fascinate them, as do clever jokes and pranks, and any treasures lying around a freehold are considered fair game. Despite what their elders may think, childlings are not necessarily peaceful and happy all the time; with so much Glamour in their bodies, and without the same emotional and mental safeguards as their elder cousins, they can be destructive and hellacious influences on the world around them. Some of the worst are feral and bloodthirsty; the best do what they do with grace and style.

One of the most serious threats to a childling is that posed by mortal authority figures, who often try to do "what's best" for the precocious little one. The number of Autumn People waiting to enforce normalcy and conformity in a child's life is also far higher than what most wilders and grumps think, and if a childling is forced into a corner by particularly banal parents and teachers, she may feel she has no choice but to run off to a freehold to escape. Unfortunately, few parents allow their child to run away without attempting some sort of rescue, and the childling risks having the freehold discovered by the authorities.

**Starting Temper Traits**: Glamour 5, Willpower 1, Banality 1

## Playing Nunnehi

There are no rules for creating Native American changelings, a.k.a. Nunnehi, in this book. If you're interested in playing a Nunnehi, more information on the kith indigenous to Concordia is available in the Changeling Players Guide, and you should feel free to improvise rules systems to recreate the unique abilities and Arts available to them. Note: As Nunnehi have the ability to step into the Umbra, Laws of the Wild might come in handy.

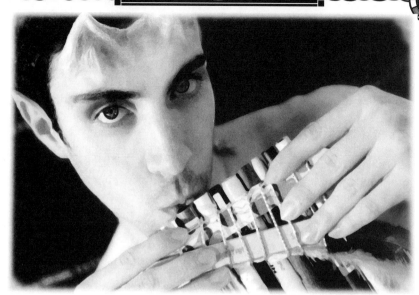

## Wilders

Anyone between 13 and 25 is considered a wilder, and most deserve the name. Typically rebellious, deviant and hedonistic, wilders are by far the most numerous of the Kithain, followed distantly by childlings and even more distantly by grumps. Because of this, wilders often try to assume the leadership of both Courts. After all, the childlings are too young, and the grumps just don't have the energy anymore, right? And anyway, it wouldn't be fair if a minority group represented the majority of society.

While these dynamic young Kithain have lost the naiveté of childlings, they haven't yet succumbed to the cynicism of grumps. Many can be quite caustic by temperament, and a certain degree of arrogance and self-importance can be counted on when dealing with these fae. After all, if you told the average 16-year-old that he's immortal, possesses supernatural powers and can stay out way past curfew, he's likely to be rather cock-sure of himself. Still, most of the time the passion and courage of these young fae make up for some of their shortcomings in wisdom, and a surprising number of them show as much skill at politics and word-play as the rest do at romance and fencing.

As they take risks and try experiences no other fae will touch, wilders often have brief, glorious existences as faeries; the thing these young hellions dread most is the notion of growing old, gaining Banality and simply waiting for the Undoing. A brief burst of light is better than a long, slow fade by candlelight to the mind of a wilder, and for this reason even the most cautious wilders make up some of the greatest heroes of changeling society.

**Starting Temper Traits**: Glamour 4, Willpower 2, Banality 3

## Grumps

Grumps are the "grown-ups" of the faerie world. Although some wilders can get to the advanced age of 24 or 25, there is something that happens to changelings when they pass on into their grump seemings, a change from the wild passion of youth to the cultivated tastes and lore of age. The fire of life doesn't die out, but rather dims. Many grumps miss the pleasures of youth, and some become irascible and bitter as Banality destroys some of the fiery idealism of their wilder days. A grump is far less banal than the average mortal, but by Kithain standards, he is stubborn and settled — a double standard which is a constant source of both amusement and frustration for grumps the world over. Many grumps play the part of the churlish mentor with a heart of gold, not out of inclination, but rather because it's what seems to tickle the young people, and if it means they'll listen to the "stern but kind old graybeard" when he speaks.

Only one changeling in 20 can keep his fae self alive past his late 20s, the official beginning of "grumpdom." The mortal world simply becomes too pressing to ignore, with careers to make and families to care for, and all too often the grump must choose which world he wants to inhabit.

The role grumps treasure most is that of advisor, for a grump can pass on his knowledge to the younger fae and try to prevent some of the mistakes he made as a youth from recurring. Despite what the wilders think, the grumps make up most of the true movers and shakers of Kithain society, having the experiences and patience necessary to play the games of shifting alliances and political maneuvering that are underlie all of the real decisions. Perhaps more so than childlings, grumps love the chance to show off their abilities and "teach the wilders a thing or two."

**Starting Temper Traits**: Glamour 3, Willpower 3, Banality 5

# Kith

The following are Western kith known to exist throughout Concordia. Though these sketches do little justice to the deep beliefs, abilities and ties of each kith, they shall suffice for now.

> Unless otherwise noted, the powers listed with each kith are free of charge, and do not require Backgrounds or Negative Traits to purchase; they are inherent to every one of the kith in question. If a Birthright or Frailty is marked as "Wyrd," it means that this advantage or drawback is considered in effect only when dealing with the enchanted world, unless the changeling calls upon the Wyrd to make his fae self temporarily "real."

## Boggans (BOG-guns)

Industrious, earthy and true, boggans are the glue that keeps Kithain society together. Ever ready to lend a helping hand and a sympathetic ear, boggans are wise enough to realize that even the mightiest heroes need a place to sleep, a bite to eat and the occasional parcel of goods to set them on their way. They are more than happy to oblige them.

Boggans claim they were the result of mortals wishing they had extra hands to help around the house, or just a helper who worked quickly and didn't complain too much. Tireless workers who hold by a store of common sense and household wisdom, boggans see themselves as the force that makes the larger achievements of the Kithain possible, taking as much pride in a simple well-kept cottage as a sidhe lord might have over an entire chimerical manor. It's all a question of scale, and boggans have suited their own more to their stature. As the hearth-keepers and tavern owners of the Kithain, their reputation for gossip almost rivals that of their craftswork.

Preferring comfort over fashion, boggan choose clothes that are often subdued when compared to those of other kith (although a boggan with a hand for sewing can rival the finest sidhe designers). In their fae forms, boggans tend to be short, with large, callused hands, twinkling eyes and large noses. They tend toward plumpness, with bushy hair and eyebrows. Most also have a second pair of eyebrows on their foreheads.

**Affinity**: Actor

**Birthrights:**

**Craftwork**: Boggans can perform any kind of task that requires hands-on craftswork in one-third the normal time, as long as there are no witnesses and they are undisturbed. Other boggans may assist without imperiling the time bonus, however. In addition, to reflect their expertise at their chosen trades, boggans receive a free level of *Crafts* that can never be permanently lost.

**Social Dynamic**: Social interactions of any kind are meat and drink to boggans, and they delight in figuring out the relationships between people. Each boggan receives a free *Empathetic* Trait which can never be permanently lost in a challenge.

**Frailties:**

**Call of the Needy**: Even Unseelie boggans are easily taken in by the sight of mortals in need. Boggans are also gossips without equal, and will buy almost any sob story or lurid tale, no matter how unbelievable. All boggans receive a *Gullible* Negative Trait that can never be bought off.

## Clurichaun (Cloor-uh-cohn)

Although many Concordian fae come from distant cultures and lands, perhaps none save the eshu have adapted to their new home quite as well as the clurichaun. Still strongest in their native Ireland, these endearing and resourceful fae have made the transition to America with grace and humor.

51

Clurichaun currently suffer only from one problem in their new home, which causes them endless frustration — the American perception of leprechauns (another term for the kith). In particular, Concordian natives seem disappointed to discover that a clurichaun doesn't wear green outfits with buckled shoes and carry a little hooked pipe, and more than one redcap band has fruitlessly tried to wrest the location of a clurichaun's pot of gold from him. Seelie clurichaun chide others for this misconception, while the Unseelie are always ready to pick a fight with any fae foolish enough to compare them to a certain cereal box character.

Clurichaun are strongly Irish in their mannerisms, even those who have been in Concordia for several generations. They often look the part as well, with bright red or tawny hair and deep blue or green eyes in both their mortal and faerie seemings; those born into families of African descent often have a red tint to their hair and striking hazel or light brown eyes. Clurichaun seldom grow very tall, and their faces typically get laugh lines very early in life. Although they wear what they like, most clurichaun decidedly prefer green, gray and brown, and in no case will they be caught without wearing green somewhere on their persons, whether it's a stone in a ring or a ribbon in their hair.

**Affinity**: Actor

**Birthrights:**

**Twinkling of an Eye**: Clurichaun have a knack for disappearing from potentially troublesome situations. Should someone take his eyes off a clurichaun, even for a moment, the clurichaun may automatically receive a Fair Escape as he disappears into cover and vanishes. No supernatural speed or sensory powers can counter this ability — only in-character watchfulness will. A clurichaun may not use this power if blindfolded or otherwise unable to see, or if bound with cold iron. This is a Wyrd Birthright.

**Insight**: When in a social situation, a clurichaun may spend a Social Trait and engage another person in a Social Challenge; if successful, he may then ask the player, "What would be the best response to this situation?" regarding the other character's emotional state. The other player must answer truthfully, although she can be as vague as she likes; in no case should this substitute for good roleplaying on the part of the clurichaun.

All clurichaun receive a permanent *Friendly* Trait as well.

**Frailties:**

**Tippling**: Clurichaun have a terrible time resisting alcohol in any form, and when in its presence must make a Static Mental Challenge to avoid drinking. When drinking, Seelie clurichaun must spend a Willpower Trait to do anything other than sing sad songs and tell pointless, depressing stories for the rest of the scene — and even with the expenditure, they still get maudlin drunk. Unseelie clurichaun must spend a Willpower Trait each time they wish to avoid picking a fight when the opportunity arises.

## Eshu (EE-shoo)

Explorers and entrepreneurs, dashing heroes and dastardly villains — eshu are never the supporting cast. These restless African fae embody the spirit of adventure, and as such can be found nearly anywhere in the world, pursuing quests and telling tales of their previous travels. Fae royalty in their homelands, eshu have since adapted to their involvement in Kithain society and the return of the sidhe with both humor and outrage. Few of their European or American brethren recognize their titles, and so the eshu take a loose view of title and nobility. Besides, it's hard to be a ruler on the open road anyway, and an eshu will take that freedom over some stuffy post anytime. Natural advocates of freedom and fierce individualists, eshu would no sooner lay claim over another than they would be held themselves. Eshu also have a deep love of tradition and custom, and abide by a wayfarer's code of sorts, which demands they respect the customs of their host and refuse no other traveler aid any more than they would wish for themselves. When slighted past the point of their considerable politeness, eshu make formidable enemies, and one will go to great and creative lengths to take revenge on the one who insulted her.

Although not hams in the way of pooka and satyrs, eshu are still consummate entertainers. They view life as a heroic movie or wonderful tale in which they are central characters, which makes them very intimately aware of their "audience." Eshu can become very cross if often interrupted or denied a dramatic entrance. Dignity and poise is almost as important to them as their freedom, and an eshu always takes pains to appear on top of things.

Eshu tend to find jobs as entertainers, gamblers, dilettantes, reporters — any trade that lets them indulge their thirst for travel. Although once primarily of African, Arabic and even Gypsy origin, eshu of all races now walk the roads of the earth; an eshu's fae form is tall and graceful, with deep skin tones and fathomless eyes. Eshu chimerical clothing tends to favor colorful Arabian-style flowing garb with sashes and adornments, or African tribal finery.

**Affinity**: Scene

**Birthrights:**

**Spirit Pathways**: Eshu have an uncanny knack for being in the right place at the right time, and although they may have to take the damnedest route to get there, the stories are always worth it. An eshu receives a "Spirit Pathways" card at the beginning of each session, which she may use to reach any given destination or find just the right place to be at any given moment. This translates into game terms in the following manner: When the card is used, the eshu may gain the advantage of a Surprise or a Fair Escape in combat; or, the eshu may state aloud a given purpose and/or destination with a Storyteller or Narrator present, and expect to reach it provided she actively travels toward it. Storytellers should take care that the intended spirit of this Birthright is not abused.

53

**Talecraft**: Eshu are all natural storytellers, whether they choose to practice it or not, and as such each receives a free *Expressive* Trait which can never be permanently lost as the result of a challenge.

**Frailties:**

**Recklessness**: Eshu can't resist any challenge that they have some chance of walking away from with any hope of success. To reflect this, they receive a permanent *Impatient* Negative Trait, and anyone savvy enough to try to lure an eshu with a challenge or proposition of some kind can also invoke a *Gullible* Negative Trait in any challenge that involves this flaw (although this Frailty never applies to obvious suicide missions).

## Ghille Dhu (YEEL-du)

Mortal legends abound with stories of nymphs and green men, Fair Folk who protected the glens and wild places. While all changelings savor the magic of the wilderness and seek to preserve it, there are few who can match the ghille dhu for their ferocity in maintaining the ways of the wild. Although the circumstances of the modern world have made these fae more scarce as time goes by, that has strengthened the resolve of those who stay bound to the earth still. Even the dedication of the trolls is put to the test when compared to the passion with which these strange and beautiful fae devote themselves to their chosen lands. Though once they held accords with the trolls, sidhe, pooka and even some Prodigal werecreatures to maintain the wild, nearly all of those old pacts now stand forgotten, and many of the Western kith aren't even aware of this kith's existence. This has forged a powerful "us-against-them" attitude in the ghille dhu remaining, and makes many of them suspicious and bitter toward their fae cousins. Only the pooka and the selkies, due to their natural affinity and shared disdain for Kithain politics, are granted exemption from this distrust.

Ghille dhu avoid any profession that takes them to cities for long periods of time, and have a deathly fear of Banality; the rapid aging of their faerie selves makes them fear chimerical death more than almost anything else. Even in the wild, members of the kith tend to avoid professions dealing with large numbers of people, and as such are commonly found as park rangers, naturalists and environmental activists. In their fae forms, ghille dhu have green skin, which goes from bright to medium to greenish brown as they advance in seemings. Ghille dhu are often adorned with plants: flowers as childlings, vines and grasses as wilders, and leaves and mosses as grumps. In their human forms, these Kithain make cute children, stunning teenagers and wizened elders, but they always wear something indicating their bond to nature.

**Affinity**: Nature

**Birthrights:**

**Note**: Ghille dhu have different Birthrights for each Season of their life, until their death in Winter, except for *Nature's Bounty*, which they have in all seemings. Thus, childling (or Spring) ghille dhu receive *Spin the Wheel*, wilders (Summer) get *Rose and Oak*, and grumps (Autumn) get *Wisdom of the Ages*. These Birthrights are not cumulative, as each Season's Birthright replaces the one before it.

**Nature's Bounty**: Ghille dhu may harvest Glamour from beautiful natural scenes. Consider this process a form of Reverie, only it allows the ghille dhu to take the *Dreamers* Background as a favorite park or vista instead of a person. The time taken to gain Glamour is the same as usual, the ghille dhu must be relatively undisturbed and the scene pristine. A natural site may be Ravaged, by accident or design, rendering it useless for the purposes of a ghille dhu.

**Spin the Wheel**: Childling ghille dhu can retest any challenge, no matter what it may be and without cost, once per story.

**Rose and Oak**: Wilder ghille dhu receive free *Gorgeous* and *Wiry* Physical Traits, reflecting the splendor of their Summer forms.

**Wisdom of the Ages**: A grump ghille dhu can use her deep connection with the Dreaming and its cycles to get the answer to a single question. She must meditate in a natural setting (not with a potted plant at the mall!) for one hour, out of game, during which time she cannot communicate with anyone, and spend a Willpower and Glamour Trait. She may then ask a single question of the Storyteller, and make a Simple Test. If she wins, the answer the Storyteller provides will be mostly straightforward; if she ties, a more cryptic answer may be provided. If she loses, the question may not be asked again for at least a month. She may retest, but only at cost of another Glamour and Willpower Trait per retest. This Birthright, meant to be used once per lunar cycle, can fail or even backfire with false information on the ghille dhu if used for trivial purposes. Those who use it too often may find themselves gone into the wilds for good one night....

**Frailties:**

**The Kiss of Winter**: Before the Sundering, this kith lived one-year lifespans before being reborn the next year, and ghille dhu still tend to live short lives even now. This Frailty is one reason. Any ghille dhu who is chimerically slain (reduced below Incapacitated chimerically) automatically ages to her next seeming. Additionally, if a ghille dhu acquires a permanent Trait of Banality, she must make a Static Challenge of her permanent Glamour against a difficulty of her permanent Banality or suffer a similar fate. If a ghille dhu grump is forced to age another seeming, her faerie self dies, leaving only the mortal shell. She may be reborn, however, although there is no hope for a return in this mortal life. Note that this "aging" applies only to the faerie mien, not the mortal seeming.

## Nockers (NOCK-ers)

The embodiment of creative inspiration brought to frenzied life, nockers are the builders and crafters of the faerie world, the artisans who shape palaces out of dreams and forge weapons out of hopes. Unlike the boggans, however, whom they jeer at for choosing quantity over quality, nockers focus on tasks large in both ambition and material. They are known for building some of the most spectacular landmarks and heirlooms of the Dreaming — as well as some of the most spectacular failures in engineering history. For, like it or not, even the greatest nocker invention carries some kind of defect, large or small, that mars any chance of its ever being perfect (at least in the eyes of its creator). This curse, the other kith say, is the reason nockers are often the most abrasive companions this side of a redcap, and the source of the streams of profanity and colorful insults that greet even the most intimate visitor to a nocker's workshop. The nockers, for their part, claim that language is just one more invention yet to be perfected, and until then they can do whatever they $%*@!@# like with it, thank you very much!

Whether or not the other kith appreciate it, nockers are the builders and makers of the enchanted world. While boggans may cook and fashion smaller items, nockers are responsible for nearly all the larger work when it comes to chimerical construction, and even for more complex crafts such as weaponsmithing and electronics. Although they often disparage the work they're currently producing (and machines work for them more out of fear than respect), nockers love being praised and constantly strive to build better and grander things in order to win additional praise. Praise a nocker's work well and often enough, and you have a friend for life; provided, of course, you can put up with their manners and their incessant cursing. Even well-respected nockers are on the low end of court invitation lists, but for their part nockers don't put much measure into politics — it's their craft that really matters, and little else.

Nockers have pale skin with red cheeks and noses that make them look drunk, and long pointed ears and noses. Their hair is a translucent white, and their skin tends to be tough and gnarled, making even wilders look fairly old before their time. Nockers are some of the most casual of the Kithain, and have been known to wear their workbelts and street clothes to all manner of court functions. When nockers do dress up, the angular and functional fashions can kill at a hundred yards — often literally! Many nockers become quite distracted without something in their hands, and are constantly fiddling with some device or another. In their mortal seemings, nockers flock to professions where they can spend most of their time tinkering and building and away from people; engineering, architecture, computer sciences and all manner of service/repair professions appeal to them.

**Affinity**: Prop

**Birthrights:**

**Forge Chimera**: Nockers are the craftsmen and artisans of the fae, and with proper time and tools they can create chimerical objects of all kinds, weaving them out of pure Glamour and hard work. These objects cannot require radiation, electricity or active chemical reactions to function, however. Nockers receive either a free level of Crafts or Repair to demonstrate this affinity. Created items require a Static Mental Challenge with a Storyteller-assigned difficulty, and also an expenditure of Glamour based on the complexity of the item:

**One Glamour** — Hammer, door, business card

**Two Glamour** — Locks, candelabra, knife

**Three Glamour** — Sword, siege engine

**Fix-It**: Nockers are master craftsmen, and everyone knows it, too! Most machines can be intimidated into working correctly by a nocker's baleful glare. Nockers may make a Simple Test to force a machine to work, and succeed on a win or a tie. If the machine is sentient, this becomes a Social Challenge, though no Traits are at risk for the nocker.

**Frailties:**

**Flaws**: Nockers are the greatest crafters of the fae, but something is always wrong with whatever they create — true perfection is beyond these Kithain. All items crafted by nockers have at least one Negative Trait (*Heavy*, *Loud*, *Fragile*), and should the artisan somehow correct this flaw, another one will appear to take its place. Nocker items may also have more than one flaw, depending on how rushed the nocker responsible was in the crafting. Nockers also receive a permanent *Obnoxious* or *Tactless* Negative Trait due to their abrasive attitudes.

## Pooka (POO-kuh)

One of the most quintessentially fae kith in outlook, the pooka are a diverse lot, and consider themselves one happy, funny, furry extended family. Notorious liars and pranksters, these shapechangers are the jesters and comic relief of Kithain society, and they play their part with great pride and enthusiasm. Pooka embody the daydreams of mortals who enviously watched animals and children playing freely, and maintain deep relations with both aspects of their protectorate. Imaginary friend, offbeat artist, class clown, favorite teacher and wacky neighbor are favorite pooka occupations, and any field where they can spend time with animals or innocents is a treasure to them. They take their protectorate quite seriously, and even the Seelie can become quite vicious with their "pranks" if they catch someone abusing animals or children; if the offender doesn't learn his lesson (quickly), he endures the same abuse his victims suffered several times over. Ever artful, pooka justice is often quite public and geared to humiliate as well as to punish.

Every pooka can change into one animal, and while the shape adopted is usually nonthreatening and mammal (cats, dogs, mice, sheep, etc.), tales of avian, amphibian, aquatic and even reptilian pooka are not unheard of. Some pooka even claim to have been born as animals, not people, but such are rare in the extreme; unless guided through their Chrysalises by a very gentle hand, these pooka often fall into Undoing from the experience. In addition, pooka tales of their kind who could change into insects, large predators or even legendary creatures are generally regarded as just that — stories. Often, a perceptive fae can guess at a pooka's animal affinity without even peeking at her fae mien, as pooka tend to look and dress in styles reminiscent of their animals — long shaggy hair for a sheepdog, bright clothes and a large nose for a parrot, sleek fashions and grace for a cat, and so on. As mortals, pooka tend to choose very "impractical" professions, which they somehow make work: stand-up comedian, actor, avant-garde poet and street mime are just a few. Other kith (usually those who just suffered at a pooka's cleverness) call their lying a malicious streak, but the pooka defend it by saying they can't let a plain truth go around naked — they have to dress it up a bit, or it just wouldn't be decent.

**Affinity**: Nature

**Birthrights:**

**Shapechanging**: Each pooka has an affinity for one type of animal (usually a mammal, but not always), and when completely alone the pooka may transform into that animal by spending a Glamour Trait and counting out 10 seconds. This animal shape is a perfectly normal specimen of its type (the character retains her intellect, and can speak to other fae normally, but may not speak to mortals unless the form can also approximate human speech), and the Storyteller should assign up to three Traits and Negative Traits to reflect the transformation. (A monkey pooka might gain *Nimble* and *Dexterous* but also *Cowardly* and *Delicate*.) The change must also be signaled with some hand gesture or body posture that the other players can easily decipher, which must be maintained as long as the shape is taken. Changing back requires only 10 seconds and privacy. (**Note**: Security cameras and the like count as someone "being around.")

This is a Wyrd Birthright — pooka cannot change while in the presence of the unenchanted, although a pooka already in animal form is unaffected by the arrival of mortals, who see her as a normal animal of her type.

**Confidant**: Pooka have an ability to befriend people that is almost beyond their control at times; their natural senses of humor and whimsical dispositions tend to get them past most people's emotional defenses. All pooka have a free level of *Subterfuge* and an *Ingratiating* Trait to reflect this innate talent for getting people to spill their guts.

**Frailties:**

**Lies**: Infamous liars one and all, pooka are incapable of telling the complete, straight truth — they must always mix in a lie of some kind. A Willpower Trait must be spent for each time a pooka wishes to say the straight, unadulterated truth. Pooka also receive a permanent *Untrustworthy* Negative

Trait that can never be bought off. This is a Wyrd Frailty, and a pooka need not always lie around the unenchanted, although these Kithain are often full of "blarney" in the mundane world, and are considered "colorful" speakers at best by those who know them.

## Redcaps (RED-kaps)

Savage fae who date back to the first mortal nightmares of things lurking in the night, redcaps are said to have been spawned from the same emotions as the sluagh. Where the underfolk became synonymous with lurking fear and intellectual terror, though, the redcaps became partnered with raw visceral horror and physical menace. Although by no means stupid, redcaps have never been ones for subtlety, and find the social intricacies of modern mortal and fae societies useless, preferring the more easily quantifiable standards of strength and skill at arms. Honor is not unknown to them, but mercy generally is, and even the best Seelie redcaps are rough knights who offend their lords at table as mightily as they serve them on the field. To their credit, redcaps give grudging respect to any who can play their games with them without getting squeamish, and they ask for no more quarter than they give. Their few Seelie make as steadfast friends as their Unseelie make bulldog enemies, and the Kithain who earns the friendship of a redcap has made a friend for life. So far, few outsiders have taken the kith up on either offer, which suits the clannish redcaps just fine.

Most often, redcaps find employment in rough, physical trades in their mortal seemings, such as bouncers, boxers, motorcycle gang members and professional bodyguards, making a name for themselves as much for their attitude as for their ability. They tend to be built stocky and powerful, with gray skin, bloodshot eyes and rubbery wrinkled faces. Rites of passage involving body piercing and tattooing are extremely common for wilders and grumps of this kith, and the current fashion for leather and metal suits their tastes perfectly. In battle redcaps fight quickly, savagely and dirty if necessary, using tactics and weapons that play to their image as fierce, inhuman monsters as much as possible. Wherever they go, redcaps give fae and humans alike a shock they seldom forget.

**Affinity**: Nature

**Birthrights:**

**Dark Appetite**: Redcaps can eat anything (and we do mean anything) they can get their mouths around; failing that, they break something into smaller pieces and eat it anyway. A Glamour Trait is required to eat a substance that no human could conceivably digest, however (i.e., toxic waste, tires, romance novels—Storyteller's decision on what is "conceivable"). This can be a Wyrd Birthright, depending on what the redcap is attempting to digest.

**Bully Browbeat**: Redcaps have such bad attitudes that even chimera are intimidated by their tough talk. All redcaps receive a free *Intimidating* Trait, and are two traits up on any Social Challenges involving sheer bad attitude.

**Frailties:**

**Bad Attitude**: No one likes a redcap; all redcaps must choose two of the following Negative Traits (or one twice) that can never be bought off: *Bestial, Callous, Ignorant, Impatient, Obnoxious, Tactless* or *Violent*. Childlings and wilders also cannot begin with Seelie Status (even with a *Title* Background), though Unseelie Status is unaffected in any seeming.

## Satyrs (SAY-ters)

Long openly scorned and secretly treasured by humanity, satyrs are the wild urge and the streak of inspired madness in Kithain society, the embodiment of mortals' lustiest dreams and the wisdom born of passion. Whether their passion is sex or Sartre, satyrs embrace it with all their heart, and they have both contempt and pity for those who live their lives without giving the same kind of emotion to something dear to them. Athletes without equal in the physical or the intellectual world, satyrs often seem an enigma to other kith, who can't reconcile their rampant lusts with their intellectual savvy. Never noted for their restraint, satyrs will cheerfully tell a redcap to swallow his own ugly face, then gallop away laughing. Life is nothing to these fae if not extreme, and as such satyrs find making lasting friends difficult, as few can endure their wild mood swings. Making a splash and finding some drinking companions, however, is easy for this kith, as they tend to exude a kind of rugged appeal. Satyrs claim this is due to their open-mindedness and freedom of expression, but most other Kithain think the *Gift of Pan* has a bit more to do with it. Wherever a satyr goes, the life of the party or the center of the debate is sure to follow.

Satyrs are often found in bands of their kith, called tragos, which form some of the hottest bands and gangs of party animals in the known world. When these boys and girls get their *Gift of Pan* going, the Banality goes down, the temperature goes up, and everybody gets a little bit crazy. Regardless of Court, love or hate, tragos stick together beyond most other bonds in a satyr's life, and any satyr who is about to fall to Banality is given a powerful send-off by his comrades. Satyrs can be found in any profession, though they much prefer the life of musicians, actors and itinerant professors.

Shameless performers on and off the stage, satyrs are straightforward folk, and their appearance tends to emphasize their… finer features. These Kithain treasure their hair, and both sexes often grow it long and luxurious; males rarely shave. What clothes satyrs wear are durable and easily removed. In their fae form, they have furry goat legs, cloven hoofs and horns growing from the tops of their foreheads. These horns grow longer and more intricate as the satyr ages, and are occasionally associated with sexual prowess among males.

**Affinity**: Fae

**Birthrights:**

**Gift of Pan**: Satyrs are capable of awakening the libidos or repressed desires of others through singing or playing. Satyrs receive a free level of *Performance* to reflect this affinity, and can engage a target (or targets, as satyrs often affect large crowds at concerts and the like) in a *Performance* Social Challenge which, if successful, forces the target(s) to act out a Negative Trait, Derangement or simply a repressed desire for the rest of the scene. The target's effective Banality is also lowered by one for the remainder of the scene. In the case of group challenges, the most banal person in the crowd must be defeated for the *Gift of Pan* to work, but if he is, everyone else in the area is affected too. Multiple satyrs may combine their efforts; each additional satyr adds one Trait to the bid for the *Gift of Pan* Challenge, and if it is successful, lowers the Banality level of the group an additional point (minimum of Banality 2). Combat or any other direct threat to the target(s) immediately cancels the *Gift of Pan*, unless the target's desire was somehow violent in nature. Kithain and Prodigals may also spend a Willpower Trait to retest the *Gift of Pan* Challenge; if successful, the Birthright may not be used on them for the remainder of the session.

**Physical Prowess**: All satyrs receive a permanent *Athletic* Trait, and in their goat-legged fae form can make an attempt at a Fair Escape by running away from combat. This is a Wyrd Birthright.

**Frailties:**

**Passion's Curse**: Satyrs are given to wild mood swings, especially when drunk, and often have trouble controlling themselves. Satyrs are two Traits down on any attempts to maintain self-control for any reason, and any supernatural powers that read, create or control emotions receive a free retest when used on satyrs. This penalty is doubled if the satyr is intoxicated. **Note:** Self-control applies to resisting the lure of a good party just as much as fighting the urge to flee from a hideous chimera.

## Selkies (SEL-kees)

Not all changeling politics are confined to the land. Indeed, the mysteries of the undersea races (merfolk, merrows, etc.) are barely known to the Kithain at large, much less understood, and the distrust of the aquatic fae for their landbound cousins leads to little communication between the two races. Legends on both sides paint the other as malicious, exotic and cruel, and as such the fae of Concordia have little to do with their watery cousins. Caught in the middle of this stony silence are the selkies, seal-folk who live for the constantly shifting shoreline and serve neither the Undersea nor the Oversea Courts. Once solely a phenomenon of the British Isles, like their clurichaun cousins, the selkies have since migrated to America, drawn by the vast beaches and plentiful seal kin they find there. They can now be found on both coasts, and while still relatively rare, many shore communities harbor one or two. They are contradictory creatures, shy and outspoken, playful and practical, and often stay away from other Kithain, not out of spite but simply because only their own kin seems to truly understand them.

Unlike pooka or even other shapechangers such as the werewolves, selkies are skinchangers; when they assume their human forms, they literally put their seal forms aside. A selkie's seal coat (be it in the form of a wetsuit, fur greatcoat, belt or something else) is the home of her fae soul and the source of her Glamour; without it she is unable to change skins or work cantrips. If it is destroyed, so too is her fae spirit, and she may never regain it. Selkies also do not come into existence as other changelings do — they must physically pass on their seal skins to another, usually younger, individual, who may then live the selkie's life. The new owner may transfer the Glamour to a new skin instinctively (from an old greatcoat to a new wetsuit, etc.), but once it's hers, she must find another to take it of his own free will to pass on the selkie legacy. This peculiarity alone is enough to make other Kithain view selkies with suspicion, and is one of the reasons this kith largely keeps to itself.

The other is their overpowering need to be near the sea; selkies cut off from the shore quickly fade away and their fae souls wither. No one quite understands the pull of the ocean like they do, and while most selkies are more than happy to show someone the glories of the sea, the other kith find the seal-folk's inability to leave it for an extended period of time frustrating. The passion these fae put in defending the seas and all their creatures is likewise conveniently overlooked by the others. For their part, selkies don't feel limited by their need for the sea — after all, they have the whole ocean to play in.

Selkies are frequently attractive and friendly, with healthy tans and weather-tested looks that many find irresistible. They have little trouble making friends, and as such typically have a wide variety of contacts wherever they live. They dress very casually but most refuse to let their seal coats, whatever they may appear to be, out of their sight for long. Obviously, any occupation which keeps them near the beach interests selkies; many find employment as fishermen and Coast Guard officers, or end up surfers and beachcombers. Grump selkies are even less common than grumps of other kith, as most of them pass on their skins to younger, less banal heirs when they feel Banality creeping up on them.

**Affinity**: Nature

**Birthrights:**

**Seal's Beauty**: All selkies are especially attractive to the appropriate gender, and when in a friendship or seduction contest with such parties receive *Seductive* and *Alluring* for free. These Traits can be bid as normal, and are lost and gained as any other Traits, *except* that they never apply to others who aren't attracted to their gender.

**Ocean's Grace**: All selkies automatically succeed at any non-combat or non-cantrip challenges or tests related to swimming in any form, and are two

Traits up on any challenges made while in the water. However, selkies are one Trait down on all Physical Challenges made on dry land.

**Seal Form**: A selkie, provided she is immersed in sea water and wearing her seal coat, may transform into a normal-seeming harbor seal (although abilities such as *Kenning* and *Heightened Senses* can see through this guise with a challenge). She gains *Nimble*, *Lithe*, *Dexterous* and *Athletic*, but also *Short-sighted*, *Bestial* x 2 (it's an animal, folks) and *Delicate*. To shift back, she must loosen a corner of her suit (undo a button, unzip a wetsuit) and surface. A selkie automatically knows where her coat is at any time, with no Glamour cost. The ability to change into a seal is a Wyrd Birthright, although all other effects involving the suit are not.

**Frailties:**

**Longing for the Ocean Shore**: Selkies are beach creatures; each day away from the shore, they gain one Banality Trait. If their Banality exceeds their Glamour, they forget their fae selves. These Banality Traits (even permanent ones gained from this separation) can be removed by the selkie spending one day per Trait in the ocean. However, they often must be "rescued" by others, who put them in their seal coats and drop them in the ocean. This risks Bedlam, but if it's not done....

**Seal Coat**: A selkie's faerie nature is contained in his seal coat, and if it is destroyed, the selkie's faerie nature is destroyed forever. Fortunately, only fire and cold iron have any effect on a coat, and cold iron does no chimerical damage whatsoever unless it injures the coat (actual damage is unaffected). A seal coat automatically wins all challenges not involving fire or cold iron (though this does not make it invincible armor, as it is simply sometimes more resistant than its wearer), and has as many Health Levels as its wearer does; damage to the coat should be recorded separately. A selkie cannot cast cantrips without his coat, though he need not be wearing it to do so. A selkie can automatically sense where his coat is if it is taken; no challenge is required to do so. Selkies can (and must) pass their Glamour through their coats, giving them to others as they see necessary or appropriate.

## Sidhe (SHEE)

For all the power and majesty of the Kithain, one can only imagine it would take beings of surpassing grace, resolve, imagination, courage and honor to rule them, let alone guide them and protect them. In the modern times, with Winter approaching, Glamour running thin and Banality consuming all who oppose it, such leaders would have to be nothing less than awesome to stand up to such threats and not lose their nerve.

The sidhe are such leaders.

Worshipped as gods and goddesses by some cultures, sidhe are always breathtakingly beautiful, and even in their mortal forms they stand out from the crowd. The sight of a sidhe in her full glory breaks hearts for a hundred yards and colors the local Dreaming with its beauty, and an angry sidhe knight makes redcaps turn tail with the intensity of her rage. Sidhe tend to have mortal lifestyles of influence and wealth — eccentric CEO, fashion model and jet-setter are all common. Whether this is an extension of their Birthrights or simply chance is a topic of debate, but sidhe seem to be successful in whatever field they choose. In mortal seeming, they tend to prefer stylish but not ostentatious clothing, and almost everything looks good on them. In fae mien, however, anything is possible: gowns of spring dew drops, armor formed of chilled flame and robes of diamond silk are some of the less impressive ideas. While an individual sidhe might give in to sadness, excess, arrogance or spite, by and large this kith is a dynamic and optimistic, if somewhat aloof, force in Kithain society. If there is any hope in fighting off the oncoming Winter, it lies in the hearts of these majestic fae.

**Affinity**: The sidhe have not been on Earth long enough to develop one.

**Birthrights:**

**Awe and Beauty:** All sidhe radiate the aura of born leaders and rulers; even the most beautiful or commanding mortals look wan and mundane when compared to the sidhe. To reflect this, all sidhe receive free *Gorgeous* and *Dignified* Social Traits and a level of the *Leadership* Ability. None of these can be permanently lost as the result of a challenge. This is a Wyrd Birthright.

**Noble Bearing:** No cantrip can ever directly make a sidhe look foolish, and any such attempt automatically fails (any Glamour or other Traits expended in the attempt is still lost, though). Mundane pranks or very indirect cantrips are unaffected by this Birthright, however.

**Frailties:**

**Banality's Curse**: Sidhe are acutely sensitive to the cold grip of Banality, and all Banality ratings are considered one higher for the purposes of the sidhe. This includes testing against Banality for cantrips. In addition, sidhe receive an extra Trait of Banality for each one earned, making them very vulnerable to the ravages of the mortal world. Sidhe also do not reincarnate as other faeries do. The uncertain fate of their souls is a source of constant fear and worry for the sidhe, which often makes these noble fae afraid to risk death.

## Sluagh (SLOO-ah)

Lurkers and loremasters, gatherers of secrets and shadows, the sluagh are said to have been given their shapes by mortal dreams of creatures in the darkness who heard every secret, saw every sin and punished the wicked when night fell. In older times many parents put unruly children back in line with threats to call the sluagh to discipline them, and even in the modern age the other Kithain look uneasily at the underfolk when they hear the word "fear." Called rumormongers and eccentric collectors at best, spies and assassins at worst, no other kith is as widely distrusted by its fellows, or considered quite as useful when it comes to dealing in a rival's dirty laundry. For their part, the sluagh say little, preferring instead to let centuries' worth of reputation they've gathered (fairly and otherwise) keep the foolish and idly curious out of their affairs.

Sluagh maintain ties with other denizens of the shadow community, most notably wraiths, who have been their allies for centuries. Gifted (or cursed) with the ability to see and speak to the spirits of the dead, sluagh often make bargains with wraiths, protecting the precious Fetters and Passions of their dead friends in exchange for having the wraiths spy on areas inaccessible even to them. Indeed, in their fae forms, sluagh are often mistaken for the dead; they appear impossibly thin and pale, with dark hair, piercing dark eyes and bodies that can make contortionists queasy. Younger sluagh often adopt full Goth dress, while their elders lean more toward Victorian fashions. Notoriously shy and agoraphobic, sluagh prefer quiet, solitary professions — museum personnel, librarians, scholarly hermits and freelance fiction or history writers are favorites. It is said that this kith is storing its lore in anticipation of some great change, or some calamity it sees as about to befall it, but if there is a dark secret or hidden motive at the heart of the sluagh, they are characteristically silent about it.

**Affinity**: Prop

**Birthrights:**

**Heightened Senses**: Sluagh have very keen senses, especially hearing and vision, and can act at no penalty in lightless or dimmed environments. Sluagh can automatically see past the Shroud and spy any wraiths in the area (unless a wraith is Skinriding — see **Oblivion** for details), and may even spend a Glamour Trait to speak to them, although the wraiths are under no compunction to respond or even hang around. However, these senses make sluagh even more sensitive than most creatures — any Trait penalties due to intense or excessive stimuli (bright lights, loud music) are doubled, and events that would ordinarily blind or deafen another character will do so for at least twice as long for a sluagh.

**Contortions**: The underfolk are very limber, and are able to bend and twist in the most disturbing ways. Each sluagh receives a free *Lithe* Trait, and is able to make a Simple or Static Test to escape bonds or straitjackets (cold iron negates this second advantage). However, having such delicate bones and joints also give sluagh a *Delicate* Negative Trait which they can never buy off. This is a Wyrd Birthright.

**Frailties:**

**Whispers**: Sluagh are completely incapable of speaking above a whisper, and automatically fail any cantrip or other test which requires them to do so. This poses an obvious problem for many Social Challenges — Traits such as *Expressive* or *Eloquent* are completely ineffective when the target cannot hear what is being said. As a rule, if any challenge requires a target to hear the sluagh's spoken words, the sluagh must whisper it, and the target's legitimate failure to hear it cancels the challenge immediately. *Whispers* is a Wyrd Frailty, although sluagh are soft-spoken at all times, and can never raise their voices above a light murmur regardless of who is present. When in the presence solely of changelings or enchanted beings, sluagh must always whisper.

Sluagh are agoraphobic and shy by nature as well — all have a permanent *Shy* Negative Trait which cannot be bought off, and are at a one-Trait penalty on all challenges in wide open spaces.

## Trolls (TROLS)

Rememberers of oaths long since lost to the world and defenders of places no other kith can recall, the trolls have not disappointed their creators' ambitions, even if modern mortals choose to ignore their faerie guardians. Trolls are the closest thing the Kithain have to a warrior class, but even so, it is rare to find a troll who abuses her strength and martial prowess; even Unseelie trolls abide by a code which prevents them from needlessly pushing around their "inferiors." It was trolls who acted as nobility during the Interregnum, it was trolls who organized the commoner war parties and peace councils during the Accordance War, and when things turn chaotic most commoners still look to trolls for leadership and support. For their part, trolls respect and look after their fellow commoners, often serving as the intermediary between them and the sidhe when one side has a complaint with the other. Stoic, strong, stern, sincere and silent — that is the image most of the other kith have about trolls, and it is one the trolls willingly put forth.

Trolls are easily the largest of the kith, with most of them standing over six feet in mortal form and eight or nine feet in their fae form. This can make some spaces uncomfortable for them, and trolls quickly gain Banality for denying their fae natures if forced into spaces too small for their fae shape (the back of a Volkswagen, a broom closet, Rhode Island). In fae form, trolls often have a bluish cast to their skin and a pair of small horns at the tops of their foreheads; Unseelie trolls sometimes have pointed teeth. In their mortal seemings, trolls tend to prefer occupations that uphold trust and the public good, especially if it allows them to work with their strength: police officer, forest ranger, farmer, athlete. Trolls' dress, like their living quarters, is Spartan and practical, but their weapons and armor are always kept highly polished and well-cared-for.

**Affinity**: Fae

**Birthrights:**

**Titan's Power:** All trolls are large and muscular; as such, they receive free *Brawny* and *Stalwart* traits, and wilders gain the advantage of an additional *Bruised* Health Level. Grump trolls receive an additional *Brawny* Trait and another *Bruised* Health Level; however, they lose one dexterity- or quickness-related Trait (beginning characters start with no more than two such Traits total), and cannot gain any more such Traits unless they somehow permanently lose a Trait of Banality as well. This is a Wyrd Birthright.

**Strength of Duty:** All trolls are loyal to a cause and extremely stubborn. This devotion manifests as an extra Willpower Trait per story that can only be counted or spent in direct support of an oath that the troll has sworn.

**Frailties:**

**Bond of Duty:** Trolls live for honor, and any breach of a troll's sworn word has an extremely detrimental effect on him. Any troll who violates a sworn oath immediately loses the benefits of *Titan's Power*, and loses Physical Traits at a rate of one per day until he runs out. These Traits cannot be regained, even with Willpower. If the troll has still not atoned for his breach of honor by the time his Physical Traits run out, he begins to lose Health Levels at a similar rate, and he will die the day he loses his last one. There is no known method for avoiding this fate, save to atone for the breach of honor and feel genuine remorse for the act.

# Step Two: Attributes

Attributes are everything a character naturally, intrinsically is. Are you strong? Are you brave? Are you persuasive? Questions such as these are answered by your character's listing of Attributes, the Traits that describe her basic, innate potential. Each Trait represents an aspect of your character's personality and allows her to perform deeds and actions specifically related to her strengths and weaknesses.

## Choosing Attributes

The first step in the process is to prioritize the different categories of Attributes (Physical, Social and Mental), placing them in order of importance to your character. Is she more concerned with the physical than with the social? Does her knack for quick thinking surpass her physical strength? You must figure out which category is most important to your character, which is second, and which is least important.

**Categories of Attributes:**

**Physical** Attributes describe the abilities of the body, such as power, quickness and endurance.

**Social** Attributes describe your character's appearance and charisma — her ability to influence others.

**Mental** Attributes represent your character's mental capacity and include such things as memory, perception, self-control and the ability to learn and think.

The concept, seeming, and kith of your character may suggest what your Attribute priorities should be — a redcap probably won't have Social as his Primary — but feel free to pick any way you please. For now, think in the broadest of perspectives — you can get more specific after you understand the big picture.

## Choosing Traits

After you've chosen the order of the three Attribute categories, you need to choose specific Traits from each category to flesh out your character. Think back to your favorite novel. Each of the characters in it is described with adjectives — "mysterious," "arrogant," "lithe" and so on, allowing you to draw a mental picture of what each character is like. For the purposes of **Mind's Eye Theatre**, Traits work the same way. They are the adjectives that delineate who your character is and what he can do. The only difference is that in **MET**, unlike a novel, Traits have other applications as well.

In your primary (strongest) Attribute category, you get to choose seven Traits. In your secondary category, you choose five. In your tertiary (weakest) category, you choose only three. Thus, you receive a total of 15 Attribute Traits. You can take the same Trait more than once, if you wish, reflecting greater aptitude in a specific area.

Traits have two primary purposes. The first and most important purpose is to enable you to describe your character concretely and thereby empower your roleplaying. The second is to enable you to interact with other characters in terms of the game system. The mechanics of **The Shining Host** revolve around the Trait system; almost every challenge is resolved using Traits in some fashion or other.

The premise of this system is that a character who is described by a specific Trait tends to be pretty good at things that involve that Trait, and is certainly better than someone who doesn't have the Trait at all. For example, someone who is *Brawny* is a better arm wrestler than someone who isn't. Likewise, a courier needs to be *Tireless* in order to deliver a document quickly and still be standing afterward, and a child who is *Persuasive* has a good chance of convincing his nurse that he isn't responsible for the broken mirror in the drawing room.

### Attributes (Bidding Traits)

Creative players can think of ways to use nearly any Trait in nearly any challenge. Though this is most praiseworthy, players can sometimes go too far. To avoid this, the general rule on bidding Traits is very strict: You can only bid Traits from the category that best suits the nature of the challenge (i.e., all Traits bid are from the same category — Physical, Mental or Social). Even then, however, not all Physical Traits (or Mental or Social) are appropriate to all Physical (or Mental or Social) challenges.

For example, beginners might think they can use all their Physical Traits in combat. This is incorrect. If your character is trying to kick someone, *Resilient* is not an appropriate Trait to bid as part of the attack. Likewise, if your character is trying to read an opponent's aura, *Creative* might not be an appropriate Trait to use in a bid.

For such an "inappropriate" Trait to be used, both parties in the challenge must agree to allow its usage. When an opponent bids a Trait that you feel is

68

extremely inappropriate, politely tell her that you're not going to allow its use. If she is insistent, reevaluate your grievance. If you still can't agree, appeal to any witnesses of the contest. Then, if there is still deadlock and no one is willing to compromise, seek out a Narrator to make a ruling. Appeals to a Narrator in these situations, however, should occur very, very rarely. Learn to handle confrontations on your own, quickly and politely.

To keep things simple, you *can* ignore the subtleties of Traits and, for example, use any Physical Trait in any Physical Challenge. This approach is particularly useful when you have a number of novice players. Eventually you will go beyond this boring convention and only allow players to use Traits appropriate to the situation at hand. This method is more complicated, but it can be a lot more fun. Try it out.

## Physical Traits

**Athletic**: You have conditioned your body to respond well in full-body movements, especially in competitive events.

Uses: Competitions, duels, running, acrobatics and grappling.

**Brawny**: Bulky muscular strength.

Uses: Punching, kicking or grappling in combat when your goal is to inflict damage. Power lifting. All feats of strength.

**Brutal**: You are capable of taking nearly any action in order to survive.

Uses: Fighting an obviously superior enemy.

**Dexterous**: General adroitness and skill involving the use of one's hands.

Uses: Weapon-oriented combat (*Melee*). Pickpocketing. Acrobatics. *Legerdemain* Arts.

**Enduring**: A persistent sturdiness against physical opposition.

Uses: When your survival is at stake, this is a good Trait to risk as a second, or successive, bid.

**Energetic**: A powerful force of spirit. A strong internal drive propels you and, in physical situations, you can draw on a deep reservoir of enthusiasm and zeal.

Uses: Combat. *Wayfare* Challenges.

**Ferocious**: Possession of brutal intensity and extreme physical determination.

Uses: Any time that you intend to do serious harm.

**Graceful**: Control and balance in the motion and use of the entire body.

Uses: Combat defense. Whenever you might lose your balance (stepping on a patch of ice, fighting on four-inch-thick rafters).

**Lithe**: Characterized by flexibility and suppleness.

Uses: Acrobatics, gymnastics, dodging, dancing and *Wayfare* Arts.

**Nimble**: Light and skillful; able to make agile movements.

Uses: Dodging, jumping, rolling, acrobatics. Hand-to-hand combat.

**Quick**: Speedy, with fast reaction time.

Uses: Defending against a surprise attack. Running, dodging, attacking. *Wayfare*.

**Resilient**: Characterized by strength of health; able to recover quickly from bodily harm.

Uses: Resisting adverse environments. Defending against damage in an attack.

**Robust**: Resistant to physical harm and damage.

Uses: Defending against damage in an attack. Endurance-related actions that could take place over a period of time.

**Rugged**: Hardy, rough and brutally healthy. Able to shrug off wounds and pain to continue a struggle.

Uses: When resisting damage, any challenge that you enter while injured. *Primal* Arts.

**Stalwart**: Physically strong and uncompromising against opposition.

Uses: Resisting damage, or when standing your ground against overwhelming odds or a superior foe.

**Steady**: More than simply physically dependable: controlled, unfaltering and balanced. You have firm mastery over your actions.

Uses: Weapon attacks. Fighting in exotic locations. Piloting ships over difficult waters.

**Tenacious**: Physically determined through force of will. You often prolong physical confrontations, even when it might not be wise to do so.

Uses: Second or subsequent Physical Challenge.

**Tireless**: You have a runner's stamina — you are less taxed by physical efforts than ordinary people.

Uses: Any endurance-related challenge, second or subsequent Physical Challenge with the same foe or foes. *Primal* Arts.

**Tough**: A harsh, aggressive attitude and a reluctance ever to submit.

Uses: Whenever you're wounded or winded.

**Vigorous**: A combination of energy, power, intensity and resistance to harm.

Uses: Combat and athletic challenges when you're on the defensive.

**Wiry**: Tight, streamlined, muscular strength.

Uses: Punching, kicking or grappling in combat. Acrobatic movements. Endurance lifting.

## Negative Physical Traits

**Clumsy**: Lacking physical coordination, balance and grace. You are prone to stumbling and dropping objects.

**Cowardly**: In threatening situations, saving your own neck is all that is important. You might even flee when you have the upper hand, just out of habit.

**Decrepit**: You move and act as if you are old and infirm. You recover from physical damage slowly, are unable to apply full muscular strength, and tire easily.

**Delicate**: Frail and weak in structure; you are easily damaged by physical force.

**Docile**: The opposite of the *Ferocious* and *Tenacious* Traits; you lack physical persistence and tend to submit rather than fight long battles.

**Flabby**: Your muscles are underdeveloped. You cannot apply your strength well against resistance.

**Lame**: You are disabled in one or more limbs. The handicap can be as obvious as a missing leg or as subtle as a dysfunctional arm.

**Lethargic**: Slow and drowsy. You suffer from a serious lack of energy or motivation.

**Puny**: You are weak. This could mean diminutive size, or just substandard strength.

**Sickly**: Weak and feeble. Your body responds to physical stress as if it were in the throes of a debilitating illness.

## Social Traits

**Alluring**: An attractive and appealing presence that inspires desire in others.

Uses: Seduction. Convincing others.

**Beguiling**: The skill of deception and illusion. You can twist the perceptions of others and lead them to believe what suits you.

Uses: Tricking others. Lying under duress. *Chicanery* Challenges.

**Charismatic**: The talent of inspiration and motivation, the sign of a strong leader.

Uses: In a situation involving leadership or the achievement of leadership.

**Charming**: Your speech and actions make you appear attractive and appealing to others.

Uses: Convincing. Persuading.

**Commanding**: Impressive delivery of orders and suggestions. This implies skill in the control and direction of others.

Uses: When you are seen as a leader. *Sovereign* Arts.

**Compassionate**: Deep feelings of care or pity for others.

Uses: Defending the weak or downtrodden. Defeating major obstacles while pursuing an altruistic end.

**Dignified**: Something about your posture and body carriage appears honorable and aesthetically pleasing. You carry yourself well.

Uses: Defending against Social Arts.

**Diplomatic**: Tactful, careful and thoughtful in speech and deed. Few are displeased with what you say or do.

Uses: Very important in intrigue. Leadership situations.

**Elegant**: Refined tastefulness. Even though you don't need coin to be elegant, you exude an air of wealth and class.

Uses: High society or Seelie celebrations. Might be important in some courts for advancement. *Sovereign* Arts (and defending against them).

**Eloquent**: The ability to speak in an interesting and convincing manner.

Uses: Convincing others. Swaying emotions. Public speaking.

**Empathetic**: Able to identify and understand the emotions and moods of people with whom you come in contact.

Uses: Gauging the feelings of others. Not useful in defense against Social Challenges (might actually make it easier to affect you).

**Expressive**: Able to articulate thoughts in interesting, significant, meaningful ways.

Uses: Producing art, acting, performing. Any social situation in which you want someone to understand your meaning.

**Friendly**: Able to fit in with everyone you meet. After a short conversation, most find it difficult to dislike you.

Uses: Convincing others.

**Genial**: Cordial, kindly, warm and pleasant. You are pleasing to be around.

Uses: Mingling at gatherings. Generally used in a second or later Social Challenge with someone.

**Gorgeous**: Beautiful or handsome. You were born with a face and body that is attractive to most people you meet.

Uses: Entrancing, posing. Nearly any sidhe challenge (against enchanted targets).

**Ingratiating**: Able to gain the favor of people who know you.

Uses: Dealing with nobles in a social situation. Defending against Social Challenges.

**Intimidating**: A frightening or awesome presence that causes others to feel timid. This Trait is particularly useful when attempting to cow opponents.

Uses: *Sovereign* Arts. Inspiring common fear. Ordering others.

**Magnetic**: People feel drawn to you; those around you are interested in your speech and actions.

Uses: Seduction. *Chicanery* Arts.

**Persuasive**: Able to propose believable, convincing and correct arguments and requests. Very useful when someone else is undecided on an issue.

Uses: Persuading or convincing others.

**Seductive**: Able to entice and tempt. You can use your good looks and your body to get what you want from others.

Uses: *Subterfuge*. Seduction.

**Witty**: Cleverly humorous. Jokes and jests come easily to you, and you are perceived as a funny person when you want to be.

Uses: At celebrations. Entertaining someone. Goading or insulting someone.

## Negative Social Traits

**Bestial**: You have started to resemble something wild. Maybe you have claw-like fingernails, heavy body hair or a feral glint in your eyes; however this attribute manifests, you definitely seem inhuman.

**Callous**: You are unfeeling, uncaring and insensitive to the suffering of others. Your heart is a frozen stone.

**Condescending**: You just can't help it; your contempt for others is impossible to hide.

**Dull**: Those to whom you speak usually find you boring and uninteresting. Conversing with you is a chore. You do not present yourself well to others.

**Naive**: You lack the air of worldliness, sophistication or maturity that most carry.

**Obnoxious**: You are annoying or unappealing in speech, action or appearance.

**Repugnant**: Your appearance disgusts everyone around you. Needless to say, you make a terrible first impression with strangers.

**Shy**: You are timid, bashful, reserved and socially hesitant.

**Tactless**: You are unable to do or say things that others find appropriate to the social situation.

**Untrustworthy**: You are rumored or perceived to be untrustworthy and unreliable (whether you are or not).

## Mental Traits

**Alert**: Mentally prepared for danger and able to react quickly when it occurs.

Uses: Preventing surprise attacks. Defending against Mental Arts.

**Attentive**: You pay attention to everyday occurrences around you. When something extraordinary happens, you are usually ready for it.

Uses: Preventing surprise attacks. Seeing through *Veiled Eyes* when you don't expect it. Preventing supernatural mind control (*Dominate*, *Sovereign* Arts, etc.)

**Calm**: Able to withstand an extraordinary level of disturbance without becoming agitated or upset. A wellspring of self-control.

Uses: Resisting frenzy or commands that provoke violence. Whenever a mental attack might upset you. Primarily for defense.

**Clever**: Quick-witted resourcefulness. You think well on your feet.

Uses: Using a Mental Art against another. General trickery.

**Creative**: Your ideas are original and imaginative. This implies an ability to produce unusual solutions to your difficulties. You can create artistic pieces. A requirement for any true artist.

Uses: Defending against another's plots. Creating anything. Being a changeling.

**Cunning**: Crafty and sly, possessing a great deal of ingenuity.

Uses: Tricking others. Setting up pranks.

**Dedicated**: You give yourself over totally to your beliefs. When one of your causes is at stake, you stop at nothing to succeed.

Uses: Useful in any Mental Challenge when your beliefs are at stake. Upholding an oath.

**Determined**: When it comes to mental endeavors, you are fully committed. Nothing can divert your intentions to succeed once you have made up your mind.

Uses: Facedowns. Useful in a normal Mental Challenge.

**Discerning**: Discriminating, able to pick out details, subtleties and idiosyncrasies. You have clarity of vision.

Uses: *Kenning*-related Challenges.

**Disciplined**: Your mind is structured and controlled. This rigidity gives you an edge in battles of will.

Uses: Riddling contests. Facedowns. Useful in Mental Art contests.

**Insightful**: The power of looking at a situation and gaining an understanding of it.

Uses: Investigation (but not defense against it). Seeing through *Veiled Eyes* when you expect it.

**Intuitive**: Knowledge and understanding somehow come to you without conscious reasoning, as if by instinct.

Uses: Taking a wild guess. Seeing through *Veiled Eyes*.

**Knowledgeable**: You know copious and detailed information about a wide variety of topics. This represents "book-learning."

Uses: *Gremayre* contests. Remembering information your character might know.

**Observant**: Depth of vision, the power to look at something and notice the important aspects of it.

Uses: Picking up on subtleties that others might overlook.

**Patient**: Tolerant, persevering and steadfast. You can wait out extended delays with composure.

Uses: Facedowns or other mental battles after another Trait has been bid.

**Rational**: You believe in logic, reason, sanity and sobriety. Your ability to reduce concepts to a mathematical level helps you analyze the world.

Uses: Defending against emotion-oriented mental attacks. Defending against the use of an Art with Banality. Not used as an initial bid.

**Reflective**: Meditative self-recollection and deep thought. The Trait of the serious thinker, *Reflective* enables you to consider all aspects of a conundrum.

Uses: Meditation. Remembering information. Defending against most Mental attacks.

**Shrewd**: Astute and artful, able to keep your wits about you and accomplish mental feats with efficiency and finesse.

Uses: Defending against a Mental Art. Outwitting a prank in progress.

**Vigilant**: Alertly watchful. You have the disposition of a guard dog; little escapes your attention.

Uses: Defending against investigation, *Sovereign* and *Chicanery*. Seeing through *Veiled Eyes*. More appropriate for mental defense than for attack.

**Wily**: Sly and full of guile. You can trick and deceive easily.

Uses: Tricking others. Lying under duress. Confusing mental situations.

**Wise**: An overall understanding of the workings of the world.

Uses: Giving advice. Defending against *Sovereign* Challenges.

## Negative Mental Traits

**Forgetful**: You have trouble remembering even important things.

**Gullible**: Easily deceived, duped or fooled.

**Ignorant**: Uneducated or misinformed, never seeming to know anything.

**Impatient**: Restless, anxious and generally intolerant of delays. You want everything to go your way — immediately.

**Oblivious**: Unaware and unmindful. You'd be lucky if you noticed a herd of cattle headed straight toward you.

**Predictable**: Because you lack originality or intelligence, even strangers can easily figure out what you intend to do next. Not a very good Trait for chess players.

**Shortsighted**: Lacking foresight. You rarely look beyond the superficial; details of perception are usually lost on you.

**Submissive**: You have no backbone. You relent and surrender at any cost rather than stand up for yourself.

**Violent**: An extreme lack of self-control. You fly into rages at the slightest provocation, and frenzy is always close to the surface. This is a Mental Trait because it represents mental instability.

**Witless**: Lacking the ability to process information quickly. Foolish and slow to act when threatened.

75

# Step Three: Advantages

Advantages delineate what and whom your character knows, and are divided into four categories: Backgrounds, Abilities, Arts and Realms.

## Choosing Abilities

Abilities are the skills, talents and knowledges of a character on the live-roleplaying stage. While most are incorporated into **The Shining Host**, not all translate well, and others have been subsumed into Attribute Traits so as to be more easily performed with challenges. An Ability allows a character to participate in, if not dominate, a type of challenge that she would otherwise be unable to take part in. Additionally, if a character is defeated in such a challenge, she may choose to temporarily expend one level of the appropriate Ability to call for a retest. While any Traits risked are still considered lost, it is possible to win the challenge through retests in this manner. Any Ability levels lost in this manner are returned at the beginning of the next session. If a character loses all her levels in an Ability, she may not use that Ability until those Traits have been recovered.

If a player wishes to demonstrate a character's high degree of mastery in a particular field, or familiarity with a wide variety of specialties, she may take an Ability multiple times. For example, taking the *Science* Ability more than once would be the hallmark of a bright and dedicated scientist, while several levels of *Linguistics* indicates mastery of a like number of languages.

The use of Abilities is often accompanied by a challenge of one sort or another. Some of these will be performed as a Static Challenge with a Storyteller who will not only assign the relative difficulty of a challenge (measured by a number of Traits), but will actually perform the test with you. As a rule, one or no Traits are risked for trivial things, two to four are at stake in novel, unusual or challenging projects, and five or more indicates a taxing and groundbreaking attempt in progress. More details on difficulty are included in each Ability's description. Note that some Abilities, such as *Subterfuge* and *Brawl*, can be used directly against another player and thus do not often require the involvement of a Storyteller.

**Brawl** — You are proficient at using your hands (paws, etc.) as weapons. You might be skilled in some form of martial art, or may have acquired your skill from numerous street and barroom fights.

**Computers** — We live in an Information Age where data pulses and flows through silicon circuitry and fiber optic lines. With this Ability, you have learned many of the secrets of the digital world and can use them to your advantage. You can infiltrate other systems, swap data, steal business and science secrets and access records. A Mental Challenge is required to accomplish these and other similar acts, with difficulty based on system security and accessibility, equipment, time and the rarity of information, as interpreted by a Storyteller. Failure can lead to investigation by mortal and supernatural agencies.

**Crafts** — This Ability imparts knowledge of master artisan techniques — woodworking, leatherwork, glassblowing, gem cutting, etc. One trade should be chosen each time this Ability is taken, although general craftsmen are not unheard of. You can make functional objects from various substances; the quality of these objects depends on how long you take to perform the task (Storyteller's discretion), the materials available and difficulty of the task in question.

**Drive** — A character who also has this Ability is an adept driver capable of tailing and avoiding tails, avoiding collisions and using her vehicle as a weapon. These actions often require a Physical or Mental Challenge. Factors influencing difficulty could include the type of vehicle, road conditions and the sort of stunts attempted.

**Enigmas** — You have a knack, if not a fascination, for the perplexing permutations of riddles and problems of both the physical and intellectual varieties. When posed with a conundrum of this sort, you may request a Mental Challenge to gain insight (but not the solution) into the problem. The Storyteller may require you to risk a variable number of Traits, depending on the relative difficulty, character familiarity with the problem and existing information on the enigma.

**Firearms** — Sometime during your existence, you have spent the time to familiarize yourself with a range of guns and similar projectile weapons. You not only understand how to operate them, but can also care for them, repair them and possibly make minor alterations. The most common use of this Ability is in combat, but a Storyteller may also allow a Mental Challenge to allow the character other functions, such as trick shots, hunting, etc.

**Gremayre** — You are conversant in the knowledge of myths, legends and rituals of the Kithain and all things fae — the lifeblood and history of all changelings. With sufficient knowledge of this Ability, you can create new oaths, or even a new Art. Along with the *Remembrance* Background, it is an essential Ability to deciphering fae things, and can be used with a Mental Challenge to understand or remember facts about other kith, the Dreaming and fae society, the difficulty of which is decided by the Storyteller based on familiarity with the subject of the question, obscurity of the lore, etc. You may also use this Ability to try to counter cantrips cast against you (see cantrip casting rules on page 153).

**Investigation** — You possess the learned skills of a diligent investigator. This sort of attention to detail is often found among private investigators, police officers, government agents and insurance claims personnel. In any case, you can often pick out or uncover details and clues that other individuals would overlook or ignore. You may request a Mental Challenge with a Storyteller to see if any clues have been overlooked, piece together clues or uncover information through formal investigation.

**Kenning** — *Kenning* is the Ability of faerie sight. It is the Ability to sense Glamour in whatever form it takes, be it a chimera, a changeling, a cantrip, whatever. Although often linked with sight, this Ability doesn't require it — it is an instinctive sense rather than a simple visual trick. With a successful use of this Ability, the user may identify a "sleeping" changeling through her mortal guise, sense a cantrip (and possibly who cast it), and otherwise determine if Glamour is in the area. For an area or item, this is typically a Simple Test and successful on a win or a tie; for a cantrip, chimera or freehold, it is a Static Mental Challenge with a Storyteller-assigned difficulty based on the strength of the Glamour and the pains with which it was hidden. Finally, to sense another changeling or a changeling "sleeping" in Banality requires a Mental Challenge. As a rule, any place or item marked with a green circle is chimerical, and can only be seen by Kithain or enchanted characters. Characters who are unenchanted must completely ignore all things marked with green circles (of course, they cannot be affected by them, either).

**Law** — Laws, whether civil or criminal, Seelie or Unseelie, are based on layer upon layer of confusing tradition, precedence and procedure. Your experiences with it, however, allow you to make the system work for you. In the world of humans, you can use the *Law* Ability to write up contracts, defend clients and know the rights of yourself and others.

In the world of the fae, it can be an invaluable guide to the traditions and practices of the sidhe and the Seelie Court — or a way to save your neck if you find yourself the subject of a Shadow Court trial. The difficulty of the Mental Challenges involved depend on factors like precedence, severity of the crime, legal complexity of the subject and the legal action desired.

**Leadership** — You have a gift for influencing or inspiring others. This is a function of confidence, bearing and a profound understanding of what motivates others. You may use this Ability to cause others to perform reasonable tasks for you. They must first be under your command or somehow be your subordinates. Examples include: a duchess to her court, a commander to his soldiers, a CEO to her employees, a gang leader to his followers, or a changeling to those under the effects of *Sovereign* cantrips such as *Protocol* or *Geas*. These requests cannot violate a subject's current Legacy, and the subject must be defeated in a Social Challenge. If the action endangers the characters who would follow you, they should be given a choice, but a challenge can assist in roleplaying this.

**Linguistics** — You have received tutelage in one or more languages other than your native tongue. This can be anything from ancient runes and hieroglyphics to common national languages or complex dialects. The language known must be specified when the *Linguistics* Ability is chosen and may not be changed; one new language is chosen each time the Ability is taken. This skill allows you and anyone who also knows the language to speak privately. Furthermore, you can translate data for yourself or others, though a Static Mental Challenge may be required depending upon the complexity of the text.

**Medicine** — This Ability represents an adeptness at treating the injuries, diseases and various ailments of living creatures. A living being under treatment may recover a single Health Level per night with time and a Mental Challenge. The difficulty is determined by the severity and nature of the damage, equipment at hand and any assistance or distraction. Note that changelings heal much faster in a freehold than normal, but otherwise are considered normal humans for purposes of healing. This Ability covers chimerical wounds as well. Other uses include forensic information, diagnosis and pharmaceutical knowledge.

## Whatever Should I Wear?

At first, the difference between a mortal seeming and a faerie mien may seem difficult to delineate in live-action play, but in reality, a few simple rules and props can deal with most problems. If a chronicle deals almost entirely with changelings and enchanted beings, players should feel free to dress to match their fae forms and forget armbands entirely, as they can simply describe their mortal selves to any mortals who wander into the action.

If a chronicle contains unenchanted mortals and Prodigals on a regular basis, all players with Kithain characters should wear a green armband on their left arms to indicate their changeling natures to the other players. A non-changeling who has been enchanted should wear a green button prominently on his costume to demonstrate his enchanted status. A changeling player in a mixed game may dress as either his mortal or faerie self, but should be ready to describe his other seeming to other players, perhaps even by pinning a description card to his costume and directing the right folks to read it. If the changeling dresses fae, he must tell unenchanted characters what his mortal seeming is like, and vice versa. In either case, the green armbands and pins tell enchanted and mundane alike which characters merit a little bit of extra description — people react very differently to a buff nine-foot-tall troll than to his puny mortal seeming!

Of course, there are a few special cases. If a character Forgets her fae nature, she should try to dress as her mortal self if at all possible, but still wear the armband (other changelings can still see her fae soul with a *Kenning* Challenge). Most importantly, if a character calls upon the Wyrd to make her fae self real for a time, she should try to be dressed and outfitted as her fae form. In that case, she can remove her armband for the duration of the call upon the Wyrd.

**Melee** — You are skilled at armed combat. You are proficient in the use of a variety of weapons, from broken bottles to swords. This skill may be the result of hard street lessons or more formal training, but is very handy indeed in the neo-feudal society of the Kithain, where chimerical duels by blade and other melee weapons are common.

**Occult** — There exists, on the fringe of mundane society, a wealth of arcane and alternative knowledge, most of which offers enlightening insight into the nature of our mysterious universe. This Ability allows you to tap that information and use it to your advantage. Examples of these uses include, but are not limited to: identifying the use and nature of visible magicks, rites and rituals, understanding basic fundamentals of the occult and having knowledge of cults, tomes and artifacts. Most uses of the *Occult* Ability require a Static Mental Challenge based on the obscurity of the knowledge in question, the amount of existing data and your degree of understanding.

**Performance** — You have the gift to make your own original creations and/or express these creations to your peers. The genius of your creativity or the power with which you convey it is determined by a Static Social Challenge, with a difficulty given by a Narrator. The difficulty is based on what you wish to achieve, your materials, the mood of your audience, etc. You should declare a particular field of artistic expertise each time you take this Ability: short stories, poetry, storytelling, playing an instrument, acting, singing, sculpting, dancing or any other form of artistic expression. This Ability may, of course, be taken more than once to indicate widespread artistic talent, virtuosity in a particular field or perhaps a bit of both. The creativity this Ability represents is vital to the sensitive, artistic Kithain — without art and mortals devoted to it, Glamour would become rare indeed. Use of this Ability is essential to Rapture and Reverie, although not necessarily for Ravaging. You may attempt to particularly impress or entrance others (like sensitive Toreador vampires) with a display of your art and a successful Social Challenge.

**Repair** — You possess a working understanding of what makes things tick. With time, tools and parts, you can fix or slightly alter most of the trappings of modern society. This knowledge also allows you to excel at sabotage, should you choose to do so. Using this Ability calls for a Static Mental Challenge, difficulty of which depends on factors like the item's complexity, tools and parts available, the extent of the damage and time spent on repairs. Note that this Ability can only fix and alter existing things; creation of new items is the domain of the *Crafts* Ability.

**Science** — You have a degree of factual and practical expertise in a single field of the hard sciences. This knowledge will allow you to identify properties of your field, perform experiments, fabricate items, obtain data or access information a player could not normally utilize. A Static Mental Challenge is necessary for all but the most trivial uses of this Ability. The difficulty depends on resources (equipment, data, etc.) available, complexity of the task and time. A field of study must be chosen when this Ability is taken. Examples are *Physics*, *Biology*, *Electronics* and *Chemistry*. Other fields are allowed at Narrator's discretion.

**Scrounge** — *Scrounge* allows characters to produce items through connections, wits and ingenuity. Many individuals who lack the wealth to purchase the things they desire or need develop this Ability instead. Materials acquired with *Scrounge* aren't always brand new or in perfect working order, and usually require some time to come by. However, this Ability sometimes works where finance or outright theft fails. A Static Mental or Social Challenge is necessary to use *Scrounge*. Some factors that influence the difficulty of the challenge include rarity and value of the item and local supply and demand.

**Security** — You have a degree of expertise and knowledge of the variety of ways people defend and protect things. Not only can you counter existing security, such as locks, alarms and guards, but you can also determine the best way to secure items and areas. Other uses include breaking and entering, infiltration, safe-cracking and hot-wiring. Almost all applications of the *Security* Ability require a Static Mental Challenge. Difficulty depends on the complexity and the thoroughness of the defenses, and the time and equipment the intruder has available.

**Streetwise** — With this Ability, you have a feel for the streets. You know its secrets and how to use its network of personalities. You can get information on current events on the street, deal with gangs and the homeless, and survive (if somewhat squalidly) without apparent income. Some uses of *Streetwise* require a Static Social Challenge influenced by such things as composition of the local street community, familiarity with the area and the current environment on the street.

**Subterfuge** — *Subterfuge* is an art of deception and intrigue that relies on a social backdrop to work. When participating in a social setting or conversation with a subject, you can attempt to draw information out of him with trickery and careful social probing. This includes finding out someone's name, nationality, Negative Traits or friends and enemies. The first requirement to doing this is getting the target to say something dealing with the desired knowledge, such as entering a conversation about foreign cultures to determine a subject's nationality. If you can succeed at this, you may pose your true question and initiate a Social Challenge. If you win, the subject must forfeit his information, hopefully by roleplaying his *faux pas*. To use this Ability again, you must once again lure your target into a conversation. Furthermore, *Subterfuge* may not reveal more than one Negative Trait per session, although it may be used to defend against others with *Subterfuge* as well.

**Survival** — You have the knowledge and the training to find food, water and shelter in a variety of wilderness settings. Each successful Static Mental or Physical Challenge allows you to provide the basic necessities for yourself or another living creature for one day. This Ability can be used to track or hunt in a wilderness setting as well. The difficulty depends on available resources, time of year, equipment used and type of wilderness (tundra versus forest, etc.).

Other possible Abilities: *Animal Ken, Archery, Bureaucracy, Finance, History, Instruction, Lore* (Kindred, Garou, Shadow Court, etc., each purchased separately), *Meditation, Riding*

# Arts and Realms

Arts and Realms are the areas of power faeries exercise over Glamour. They can be combined to create a multitude of magical effects, which are detailed in the Arts and Realms chapter on page 125.

## Glamour

Glamour describes the daydreaming spirit — the enchanted, whimsical soul. It is worldly delight sprung whole from the seeds of creative bounty. It is insight created by the appreciation of beauty and the expression of the imagination. The ability to live in your dreams, to let yourself perceive the real essence of things, comes from Glamour. All things have it, even humans, but only the fae can make it real.

Glamour is used in **The Shining Host** to exert direct control over the Dreaming, and is often used to fuel cantrips. Each seeming starts with a different amount of permanent Glamour Traits: childlings five, wilders four and grumps three, and more may be purchased with Negative Traits. Glamour appears to users of *Kenning* as multicolored light, and can be very easily detected by other changelings if the caster isn't careful. There are many ways in which Glamour may be used; but a few follow here.

Glamour may be spent to add an additional Bunk to a cantrip being cast; only one Bunk per cantrip may be added in this manner, and both Bunks must still be performed to cast the cantrip.

Glamour may be spent to create a token to enchant a mortal or Prodigal to perceive Glamour, chimera and changelings' faerie selves — one Trait of Glamour per day of enchantment, and the target must willingly accept the token or have it surreptitiously placed on her for the enchantment to work. Tokens can be anything from brownies to a tattoo to a bouquet, and should be represented with prop cards.

Glamour may be used to enchant a target forcibly, without creating a token, either by using a technique called the *Enchanted Stroke* (page 183) or by spending a Glamour Trait and defeating the target in a direct challenge of the changeling's permanent Glamour rating versus the target's permanent Banality rating. The target may not actively use her Banality to gain more Traits in this challenge. If he succeeds, the changeling can spend one Glamour Trait per day of enchantment he wishes to inflict on the subject. The enchantment produced is identical in every other respect to the less violent token method, although many Kithain find the target more traumatized by the transition than normal.

Glamour Traits are required while performing some cantrips; the specific costs are covered in Chapter 3.

Glamour Traits must be spent to use some Birthrights or innate abilities of certain kith; sluagh, for example, can speak to wraiths with the expenditure of a Glamour Trait.

Glamour may be gained from using dross, items that contain a measure of Glamour, but which possess no special power on their own. Any item that has intimately witnessed a great deal of creativity or history may be dross: moon rocks, Lincoln's pen, unreleased Hendrix tapes, etc. Sometimes particularly beautiful or interesting natural objects such as rocks or shells may contain Glamour as well. It is up to the Storyteller to determine how much Glamour a piece of dross has, but it usually does not exceed five Traits. A Kithain may choose to "use up" Glamour Traits from dross instead of spending her own Glamour. However, this is a one-shot deal — if a Kithain wants to use dross for its Glamour, it's all or nothing. She cannot use one Trait and leave the other two for later; she must use them all at once, or any unused excess is lost.

Once a Glamour Trait is spent, it can be recovered only in certain ways. One is the *Dreamers* Background, which is described on page 87. Another is actively experiencing a Reverie, Rapture, Ravaging or Rhapsody, which may yield a number of Glamour Traits as is described under the section on the three Epiphanies (page 189). Using dross is another — a Narrator can tell you how much Glamour can be gained from a piece of dross, which is consumed in some way in the process. Spending a restful night in a freehold or glen also gives the option of recovering either a Trait of Willpower or Glamour. Finally, some oaths may give temporary or even permanent Glamour Traits, although the cost of failure is equally high, and the casual swearing of oaths for this purpose is severely frowned upon by both Courts.

## Willpower

Within each of us is the ability to do incredible things. A determined individual can even fight off Death itself if she truly has the will to live. In **The Shining Host**, this ability to do the nigh-impossible is governed by a Trait known as Willpower. This Trait gives a character the extra strength necessary to succeed in the direst of circumstances, and is often required by many Advanced Arts as well. You start play with one to three Willpower Traits, depending on your character's seeming, although you can gain more by purchasing Negative Traits (see below).

Willpower can be used to replenish all traits lost in a session in any one category: Physical, Social or Mental.

Willpower allows a character to ignore the effects of any wounds, up to and including Incapacitated and chimerical wounds, for the entire duration of one challenge.

Willpower can be expended to ignore the effects of one Social or Mental Challenge; this includes Arts or the supernatural abilities of Prodigals requiring such challenges. This usage must be declared before the result of the challenge is determined.

Willpower can be spent to retain self-control or courage in the face of overwhelming temptation, rage or fear. This lasts until the source of the emotion is gone or 10 minutes have passed, whichever comes first.

A Willpower Trait can be spent to succeed automatically at a Simple or Static Challenge.

Once Willpower has been spent, it is gone for the remainder of the story. At that time, all the Willpower spent is regained. At the Storyteller's discretion, a character who is roleplaying her Legacy, Negative Traits or Derangements well may receive a Willpower Trait, and resting in a freehold restores a Trait of either Willpower or Glamour each night. If a particularly long time passes in the game between sessions, the Storyteller may rule Willpower is regained in the interim. Finally, some oaths may also give temporary or even permanent Willpower Traits, although the cost of failure is equally high, and the casual swearing of oaths for this purpose is severely frowned upon by both Courts.

## Banality

This Trait describes the extent to which the mortal world has infected your soul. If your Banality exceeds your Glamour at the end of a story (not a session), you are in danger of losing the memory of your faerie self and will gradually revert to your mortal seeming until some other Kithain can rescue you and remind you of what you are. This lapse in your fae life is known as the Forgetting. Those who gain 10 permanent Banality Traits or otherwise have their fae souls completely suppressed are said to be Undone, a fate far worse than death to a changeling. Banality itself is an aura of frigid disbelief, a denial of the inherent magic and wonder of life — it is anti-Glamour, and refuses to accept any traces of imagination in its clean, scrubbed-up version of reality (hence the Mists). You start with one to five Banality Traits, depending on your seeming, and may gain more during the game. It can be gained or used in the following ways:

Banality may be used to resist cantrips. By declaring you are using your Banality to resist a cantrip, you receive additional Traits on the challenge equal to the number of permanent Banality Traits that you have — one for a Banality of one, seven for a Banality of seven, etc. However, such a banal action immediately earns you a Trait of temporary Banality, regardless of the outcome of the challenge.

Banality is given if you deny your faerie self or a chimera your character carries, such as a troll failing to stoop when his mortal self passes through a doorway too small for him or, or swinging a chimerical sword through the wall of a real-world location. This usually earns the offender one Trait of temporary Banality per instance.

Banality can be arbitrarily assigned to you if a Narrator feels you are acting too banal, usually no more than a temporary Trait at a time. You may attempt to arbitrate with the Storyteller on this, but in the end her word is final.

Banality is gained for destroying treasures, using dross improperly or killing certain chimera — usually a temporary Trait or so per offense, depending on the power of the chimera, treasure or dross in question.

Banality is always assigned for killing another changeling's faerie form — one temporary Trait. If you actually kill another changeling's mortal form, you automatically earn at least two temporary Traits of Banality. If you do the deed with cold iron, you can expect a permanent Trait of Banality.

A permanent Banality Trait can be gained if your temporary Banality Traits ever exceed 10 in number. The 10 are exchanged for another permanent Trait, thus marking your slow decline into mundanity. You must approach a Narrator when this is the case. If you ever acquire 10 permanent Banality Traits, your fae has been Undone and permanently forgets her faerie self. No amount of Glamour can save her; you must wait until her next lifetime to reawaken her fae spirit. (In the meantime, creating another character works well.)

Banality inevitably creeps over your faerie soul, no matter how hard you resist. When you gain temporary Glamour Traits, such as from the *Dreamers* Background or an Epiphany, you may decline to accept the Trait in exchange for disposing of a temporary Banality Trait on a one-for-one Trait basis (this is the only time in the game such an exchange can be made). You may also ask at any time to suffer a Nightmare instead of taking a temporary Banality Trait, but you will then be subjected to whatever twisted aspect of the Dreaming the Storyteller feels is appropriate to the level of Banality being "dodged." Everything from a persistent cough to an ever-present chill breeze to terrible hallucinations can be visited on you at this time, with the effect lasting for as long a time as the Storyteller considers appropriate. A character may only be under the effect of one Nightmare at a time, however, which means you cannot take advantage of this rule in order to dodge every single assignment of Banality. Finally, some quests are said to be able to reduce a character's permanent Banality rating, but these seekings are truly epic in scope, and result in the gain of even more permanent Banality if failed.

## Backgrounds

These Traits determine certain things about your character and your character's past, such as what chimera you might possess, whether or not you are a noble, what powerful mortal friends and contacts you have, etc. They are quite special, and players should pick them with an eye toward fleshing out their character concepts, not mini-maxing to create the perfect super-characters. Furthermore, some Backgrounds may be lost as the result of a story (a mortal *Ally* dies, a *Treasure* is lost), but most can't be bought with experience points. A Background lost, then, is usually lost forever.

Once play begins, Backgrounds are gained as a result of actions, not points (a *Title* is conferred, a *Companion* is gained). A Storyteller should be consulted if a player feels she has earned the right to purchase and/or be granted a new Background.

### Chimera

This Background allows you to possess a chimerical object of some kind. While every changeling can imagine himself a basic chimerical costume for his fae mien at no cost, any practical or usable items (those which require item cards, which always includes workable weapons and armor) in addition to costuming require purchasing this Background. Chimerical items are always much more striking than their mundane counterparts, and anything from a simple longsword or diary to a full suit of sci-fi movie bounty hunter armor or a woven tapestry of dreams can be owned. However, an item's actual power and usefulness is determined by how many Traits of this Background you take.

1 — A basic chimera (a conversation piece)
2 — A minor chimera (a chimera with some benefits)
3 — A useful chimera (a chimera with some impressive benefits)
4 — A significant chimera (a powerful item)
5 — An incredible chimera (a legendary relic)

The Storyteller is still the final arbiter of what kind of items may be taken with this Background, and should generally be consulted about chimera of three or higher for approval, as they can have quite an impact on a chronicle. Note that living chimera are the province of the *Companion* Background, below. This Background may be taken more than once to reflect owning more than one item.

### Companion

This Background allows you to have living chimerical friends and companions, most likely the same ones who helped you through your Chrysalis. The Storyteller should be consulted as to the Traits and Abilities your *Companion* might have, although he need not tell you all of them at first, and the more powerful you make the *Companion* the more of an independent mind it will have. However your *Companion* may appear, his general aspect is indicated by the number of Traits you put into the Background:

1 — A basic companion (intelligence up to the level of a dog; no Arts)
2 — A minor companion (human intellect, some minor powers; no Arts)
3 — A useful companion (smarter than you; a level of an Art)
4 — A significant companion (quite bright; several levels of Arts)

5 — An incredible companion (a dragon, a genie; who knows how strong?)

This Background, like *Chimera*, may be taken more than once for additional *Companions*. In any case, *Companions* should be represented by cards or other props that are clearly marked and placed where they would be visible (to *Kenning*, anyway).

### Dreamers

This Background demonstrates a connection with certain mortals whom you regularly patronize in order to gain Glamour. These mortals can also perform a number of services (mostly artistic) for you, and are friendly (although they are not your servants or your true friends, and under no compunction to obey your orders). You may gain a number of Glamour Traits equal to the number of Traits you placed into this Background once per session — this takes at least 15 minutes per Trait, and possibly more depending on who and where the artists in question are in the context of your game location. You must, of course, remain out of character during this time. You should detail who these artists are, where they live, what artistic mediums they use, and how you came to be their friend, as it may become important in the chronicle at a future date. This Glamour-gaining is assumed to be benign Reverie; you may attempt to gain more Glamour or use this Background more often than once per session, but you risk accidentally (?) Ravaging and drying up your source at Narrator discretion.

### Remembrance

This Background is your unconscious memory of Arcadia, as well as your intuitive knowledge of the fae and of your previous incarnations. Any time you need to know something general about the fae (no questions about other characters), you may expend a level of *Remembrance* and make a Simple Test. On a win, you are struck with a realization, usually of what you needed to know, but not always. A Narrator must answer the question, although the presentation of it may be quite cryptic in nature. You may also use this Background to retest *Gremayre* Challenges, although doing so in this manner gives you no visions or any other special insight. All expended levels cannot be recovered until a good night's sleep has come.

### Holdings

You are the heir/owner of a faerie freehold of some type. The number of points put into it equals the rating of the freehold (not to exceed five) and how much Glamour can be gained from it daily (one Trait per Background level, per night). Furthermore, while within a freehold, Kithain do not age, and don't have to contest with Banality when performing their cantrips (although it can still be invoked as an active defense). Spending too much time in a freehold is a quick ticket to Bedlam, however. Putting one Trait into this Background indicates a tiny freehold, barely scraping by, while three would be a thriving local Kithain center, and five is something that recollects the legendary freeholds of times past. As whole chronicles can and have been built around freeholds, you and the Storyteller must work together to detail the freehold: its politics, its regulars, its powers, and its mundane and chimerical appearance. Keep in mind that the more powerful the holding, the less likely it is to be held by commoners or low nobles, although it would not be unheard of. This Background may be "pooled" by several characters to create a powerful freehold, although it is up to the players to then determine details of ownership, rulership and the like.

### Influence

A Kithain with Traits in the *Influence* Background has gained a certain degree of control in aspects of normal human society. While many Kithain avoid taking such an active role in human affairs, fearing the Banality of such high-pressure positions, other fae see it as a way to take the fight against Winter to the very heart of the enemy, and a means of keeping Dauntain and Autumn People away from Kithain centers. *Influence* can also be seen as access to contacts, minor allies or even kinain (humans with fae blood) in the field. Possible areas of influence are listed on page 91.

One level of one area of *Influence* may be chosen for each Trait put into this Background. Note that *Influence* does not give you knowledge of a particular area (Abilities do that), but at the least it gives you power over those who have such knowledge. Certain *Influences* are often considered too banal by most Kithain (*Finance, Industry*), and are notably ill-populated by the fae folk, while others (*Occult, High Society*) are relatively common. A character with *Influence* is usually given cards, one for each level of each *Influence*, to represent their ability to get things done in their field, or to be able to loan them to other people as "favors." Characters may expend *Influence* Traits to accomplish goals relating to a specific aspect of mortal society. The actual charts for *Influence* levels are at the end of this section.

### Mentor

This Background denotes a mentor who looks after and guides you in some fashion. Typically, he was assigned to guide you through the changes during and after your Chrysalis, and you two have stayed friends. The specifics are up to you, however.

Your mentor can provide many benefits: guiding you away from dangerous situations you might be getting into, speaking on your behalf to more powerful changelings, and of course providing you with lots of advice. You may occasionally be asked to perform favors for your mentor, but usually you get more from it than you have to do directly in return. The Storyteller or a Narrator will most likely play your mentor, so you must ask permission to take this Background; keep in mind that your mentor cannot perform noble favors for you, as that is the domain of the *Patron* Background.

Another player might also be allowed to act as a mentor, with the permission of the Storyteller. The Traits you spend roughly determine about how much your mentor knows and/or how often you can meet them (a mentor who knows little but is constantly around can of as much use as one who knows everything but who lives in the Deep Dreaming and can only be contacted once every lunar cycle):

1 — Mentor knows little of import.

2 — Mentor has noteworthy pieces of information.

3 — Mentor has significant secrets to share.

4 — Mentor has extraordinary knowledge to pass along.

5 — If your mentor doesn't know it, it ain't worth knowing.

This is an ideal Background for beginning players in many ways, as a mentor can help steer them away from situations more experienced players naturally avoid.

### Patron

This Background details a particular noble who has taken a liking to you, and who thus favors you over her other subjects; you and she are friends. She may render you favors in times of need, although services will sometimes be required of you in return, and the two of you must be careful that this favoritism is not too public in nature — jealous changelings of all types would soon descend *en masse* to correct the impropriety. Most likely, this *Patron* should be a Storyteller or Narrator character, although another player is possible, with her consent. Note that this Background does not imply the same relationship as the *Mentor* Background, although they may be combined to create a friendly noble mentor who's willing to use her influence on your behalf. The number of Traits expended equals the rank of the noble who is your patron — one for a knight or lady, two for a baron/baroness, three for a count/countess, four for a duke/duchess, five for a king/queen. (Talk to the Storyteller about that last one in particular.)

### Political Connections

This Background is not quite the same as *Title* or *Influence*, but rather a little of both — you are the appointed representative and spokesman for a freehold or mew of some kind, and as such are something of an ambassador. You can expect to be taken in and treated reasonably well by most nobles, and while you certainly do not have diplomatic immunity, you are most likely forgiven minor *faux pas* that would get others in trouble. However, as a member of the Parliament of Dreams, you must attend as many sessions of that body as you can, which may limit somewhat your options for adventuring. (It is normally assumed that your character spends some of his "down time" in-between sessions attending these meetings.) The laws, coalitions, and movements of Concordian politics are fairly well known to you and you have a voice, small as it may be, in how they are shaped. The Traits put in this Background represent how strong a freehold/mew you represent.

1 — Very small freehold/medium-size mew

2 — Small freehold/large mew

3 — Medium-size freehold/huge mew

4 — Large freehold

5 — How did you land this cushy job?

**Title**

This Background denotes your rank in changeling society. Not all Kithain have a title; in fact, few rise above the rank of squire, if they attain any title at all. *Title* bestows little in the way of actual power, but is an important source of social influence. You receive one Status Trait per level of *Title*, which can be used in place of a normal Trait in a Social Challenge and adds to your total Social Traits in the event of a tie or overbid.

Status Traits should be written in the category for regular Social Traits, with a "(T)" notation next to it. This is one of the few ways to gain Status in Kithain society, although being given honors by the king or duke is another such method. (If you wish to start play with Status but no title, you must take it with freebie points or Negative Traits, and a good story.) You need not have *Holdings* to be a noble; this is in fact more and more common as land (and freeholds) becomes rare on Earth. Sidhe characters are required to have at least one point in *Title*. The number of Traits you invest determines your title and the Status Trait that usually accompanies each particular station.

1 — Squire (*Loyal*)

2 — Knight/Lady (*Valiant/Noble*)

3 — Baron/Baroness (*Wise*)

4 — Count/Countess (*Trusted*)

5 — Duke/Duchess (*Exalted/Cherished*)

**Treasure**

This Background represents a chimera or a physical item you possess that is imbued with Glamour, and which can perform feats equal to the Arts and Realms it was invested with. This Background may be taken more than once to reflect ownership of more than one treasure. The number of levels of *Treasure* reflects how potent a device you possess:

1 — A minor treasure (a glowing rock)

2 — A useful treasure (a magic herring that cuts down trees)

3 — A treasure of significant power (a blade that cuts chimera as well)

4 — A very powerful treasure (a circlet of command over mortals)

5 — An incredibly powerful treasure (a horn that summons dragons)

You should work with the Storyteller to determine what your treasure does, how you can use it, and if it has any requirements for its use (spending Glamour, certain words or phrases, being covered in gold cloth, etc.) — very often the most potent treasures have strict requirements on their use, and it is very common for rulers to cast *Protocol* on potent items to prevent their misuse. However, in general, let your imagination run wild.

**Trod**

This Background represents your access to a trod that is open at least semi-regularly, and is relatively safe. You do not need the *Holdings* Background to take *Trod*, though combining the two is very appropriate. Trods are tied to the cycles of nature, and thus may not be used as "changeling subways" for player convenience all the time; the Storyteller will decide when and how they can be used, although player suggestions can be welcome. However, when a trod is usable, traveling to the trod's destination takes one-fourth normal time. (The Storyteller should be contacted when a trod is being used, usually to describe the journey itself and assign travel time.) The points put in it determine the regularity and destination of the trod(s).

1 — One local destination, accessible one-fourth of the time

2 — One local destination, accessible half the time, or 2-3 local destinations, accessible one-fourth the time, or one local destination open all the time

3 — 2-3 local destinations and one regional half the time; or 2-3 local, one regional, and one Near Dreaming, accessible one-fourth of the time; or 2-3 local, accessible all the time

4 — 4-5 local, two regional, one national (e.g., Concordia) and two Near Dreaming accessible half the time; or 4-5 local, two regional, one national, one Near Dreaming, one Far Dreaming, accessible one-fourth the time; or 2-3 local and one regional, all the time; or 2-3 local, one regional, and one Near Dreaming, half the time

5 — 5-6 local, three-four regional, two national, two Near Dreaming, one Deep Dreaming, half the time; or 4-5 local, 4-5 regional, four national, two Near Dreaming, two Far Dreaming, one Deep Dreaming, one-fourth the time; or 2-3 local, one regional and one Near Dreaming, all the time.

## Influence Charts

To use Influence actively, you should explain to the Narrator what sort of effect you wish to create with your Influence. The Narrator then decides the Trait cost, the time involved (both real and in-game) and any tests required to achieve the Influence effect. Influence Traits used this way are temporarily considered to have been expended and are not recovered until the next session. The effects of using Influence can be instantaneous and brief, or slow to manifest and permanent, depending on the nature of the manipulation and the degree of power the character wields.

The difficulty of a task is set by a Narrator, and equals the number of Influence Traits that must be expended to accomplish the task. A given chore's difficulty can be subject to sudden change, depending upon circumstance. The suggested guideline listed along with each area of Influence can change dramatically between chronicles or even between sessions. After all, you may not be the only Kithain attempting to Influence something.

Sometimes a Narrator will require a challenge of some sort to represent the uncertainty or added difficulty involved when exercising Influence. Some uses of Influence may not actually cost Influence to use, but rather require that the Kithain simply possess a certain level of the Influence in question.

Kithain can trade Influences with each other much like children swap toys. These trades may be permanent or temporary. In the case of permanent trades, the old owner erases the Trait from his sheet and turns over the appropriate Influence card (if your chronicle uses these) to the new owner. The new owner then records her newly acquired Influence Trait on her character sheet. Temporary trades of Influence occur when a Kithain is merely doing a favor or loaning her Influence to someone else. In this case, the owner does not erase the Trait, but instead makes a note that it is no longer in her possession. The holder of the Influence Trait may use it immediately or hold onto to it until she feels she needs it. However, the original owner of the Influence Trait may not regain the Trait until the current holder expends or voluntarily returns it.

## Time Limits

Obviously, an unwise Kithain can find his Influences tied up in the hands of others for a long time if he is not careful. For this reason, some chronicles dictate that the Trait reverts to its original owner after a certain time. A good rule of thumb for this is that one month is the maximum duration of any loan of Influence. If your chronicle's sessions are scheduled less frequently than once a month, the Narrator(s) should probably expand this window of opportunity. Any exchange of Influence Traits requires the presence and assistance of a Narrator.

Sometimes characters may wish to try to counteract the Influence of other characters. In such cases, it generally costs one Trait per Trait being countered. The Kithain willing to expend the most Influence Traits (assuming she has them to spend) achieves her goal; all Traits used in this sort of conflict are considered expended.

In practice, the use of Influence is never instantaneous and rarely expedient. While a character may be able to, say, condemn any building in the city, it will not be torn down that night. For sake of game flow, a Narrator may allow trivial uses of Influence to only take half an hour. Major manipulations, on the other hand, can become the center of ongoing plots requiring several sessions to bring to fruition.

The guidelines below by no means limit the number of Influence Traits that can be spent at one time or the degree of change a character may bring about. They are merely an advisory measure to help Narrators adjudicate the costs of certain actions.

Actions followed by an asterisk (*) below indicate that their effects can generally be accomplished without expending an Influence Trait.

### Bureaucracy

The organizational aspects of local, state or even federal government fall within the character's sphere of control. She can bend and twist the tangle of rules and regulations that seem necessary to run our society as she sees fit. The character may have contacts or allies among government clerks, supervisors, utility workers, road crews, surveyors and numerous other civil servants.

| Cost | Desired Effect |
|---|---|
| 1 | Trace utility bills* |
| 2 | Fake a birth certificate or driver's license; Disconnect a residence's utilities; Close a small road or park; Get public aid ($250) |
| 3 | Fake a death certificate, passport or green card; Close a public school for a single day; Turn a single utility on a block on or off; Shut down a minor business on a violation |
| 4 | Initiate a phone tap; Initiate a department-wide investigation; Fake land deeds |
| 5 | Start, stop or alter a city-wide program or policy; Shut down a big business on a violation; Rezone areas; Obliterate records of a person on a city and county level |
| 6 | Arrange a fixed audit of a person or business |

### Church

Not even churches are without politics and intrigue upon which an opportunistic person may capitalize. *Church* Influence usually only applies to mainstream faiths. Sometimes other practices fall under the *Occult* Influence. Contacts and allies affected by *Church* Influence include: ministers, bishops, priests, activists, evangelists, witch-hunters, nuns and various church attendees and assistants.

| Cost | Desired Effect |
|---|---|
| 1 | Identify most secular members of a given faith in the local area; Pass as a member of the clergy;* Peruse general church records (baptism, marriage, burial, etc.) |
| 2 | Identify higher church members; Track regular members; Suspend lay members |
| 3 | Open or close a single church; Find the average church-associated hunter; Dip into the collection plate ($250); Access to private information and archives of a church |
| 4 | Discredit or suspend high-level members; Manipulate regional branches |

| | |
|---|---|
| 5 | Organize major protests; Access ancient church lore and knowledge |
| 6 | Borrow or access church relics or sacred items |
| 7 | Use the resources of a diocese |

## Finance

The world teems with the trappings of affluence and stories of the rich and famous. Those with the *Finance* Influence speak the language of money and know where to find capital. They have a degree of access to banks, megacorporations and the truly wealthy citizens of the world. Such characters also have a wide variety of servants to draw on, such as CEOs, bankers, corporate yes-men, financiers, bank tellers, stock brokers and loan agents.

| Cost | Desired Effect |
|---|---|
| 1 | Earn money; Learn about major transactions and financial events; Raise capital ($1,000); Learn about general eco nomic trends;* Learn real motivations for many financial actions of others |
| 2 | Trace an unsecured small account; Raise capital to pur chase a small business (single, small store) |
| 3 | Purchase a large business (a few small branches or a single large store or service) |
| 4 | Manipulate local banking (delay deposits, some credit rating alterations); Ruin a small business |
| 5 | Control an aspect of city-wide banking (shut off ATMs, arrange a bank "holiday"); Ruin a large business; Purchase a major company |
| 6 | Spark an economic trend; Instigate widespread layoffs |

## Health

In our modern world, a myriad of organizations and resources exists to deal with every mortal ache and ill, at least in theory. The network of health agencies, hospitals, asylums and medical groups is subject to exploitation by someone with *Health* Influence. Nurses, doctors, specialists, lab workers, therapists, counselors and pharmacists are just a few of the workers within the health field.

| Cost | Desired Effect |
|---|---|
| 1 | Access a person's health records;* Fake vaccination records and the like; Use public functions of health centers at your leisure |
| 2 | Access to some medical research records; Have minor lab work done; Get a copy of coroner's report |
| 3 | Instigate minor quarantines; Corrupt results of tests or inspections; Alter medical records |

| 4 | Acquire a body; Completely rewrite medical records; Abuse grants for personal use ($250); Have minor medical research performed on a subject; Institute large-scale quarantines; Shut down businesses for "health code violations" |
| 5 | Have special research projects performed; Have people institutionalized or released |

### High Society

An clique of people exists, who, by virtue of birth, possessions, talent or quirks of fate, hold themselves above the great unwashed masses. *High Society* allows the character to direct and use the energies and actions of this exceptional mass of talents. Among the ranks of the elite, one can find dilettantes, the old rich, movie and rock stars, artists of all sorts, wannabes, fashion models and trend-setters.

| Cost | Desired Effect |
|---|---|
| 1 | Learn what is trendy;* Obtain "hard to get" tickets for shows; Learn about concerts, shows or plays well before they are made public* |
| 2 | Track most celebrities and luminaries; Be a local voice in the entertainment field; "Borrow" $1,000 as idle cash from rich friends |
| 3 | Crush promising careers; Hobnob well above your station* |
| 4 | Minor celebrity status |
| 5 | Get a brief appearance on a talk show that's not about to be canceled; Ruin a new club, gallery, festival or other high society gathering |

### Industry

The dark world of the Gothic-Punk milieu is built by pumping and grinding machinery and the toil of endless laborers. A character with the *Industry* Influence has her fingers in this pie. Industry is composed of union workers, foremen, engineers, contractors, construction workers and manual laborers.

| Cost | Desired Effect |
|---|---|
| 1 | Learn about industrial projects and movements* |
| 2 | Have minor projects performed; Dip into union funds or embezzle petty cash ($500); Arrange small accidents or sabotage |
| 3 | Organize minor strikes; Appropriate machinery for a short time |
| 4 | Close down a small plant; Revitalize a small plant |
| 5 | Manipulate large local industry |
| 6 | Cut off production of a single resource in a small region |

### Legal

There are those who quietly tip the scales, even in the hallowed halls of justice, and the courts, law schools, law firms and justice bureaus within them. Inhabiting these halls are lawyers, judges, bailiffs, clerks, district attorneys and ambulance chasers.

| Cost | Desired Effect |
|------|----------------|
| 1 | Get free representation for minor cases |
| 2 | Avoid bail for some charges; Have minor charges dropped |
| 3 | Manipulate legal procedures (minor wills and contracts, court dates) Access public or court funds ($250); Get representation in most court cases |
| 4 | Issue subpoenas; Tie up court cases; Have most legal charges dropped; Cancel or arrange parole |
| 5 | Close down all but the most serious investigations; Have deportation proceedings held against someone |

### Media

The media serves as the eyes and ears of the world. While few in this day and age doubt that the news is not corrupted, many would be surprised at who closes these eyes and covers these ears from time to time. The media entity is composed of station directions, editors, reporters, anchors, camera people, photographers and radio personalities.

| Cost | Desired Effect |
|------|----------------|
| 1 | Learn about breaking stories early;* Submit small articles (within reason) |
| 2 | Suppress (but not stop) small articles or reports; Get hold of investigative reporting information |
| 3 | Initiate news investigations and reports; Get project funding and waste it ($250); Access media production resources; Ground stories and projects |
| 4 | Broadcast fake stories (local only) |

### Occult

Most people are curious about the supernatural world and the various groups and beliefs that make up the occult subculture, but few consider it anything but a hoax, a diversion or a curiosity. This could not be farther from the truth. Occult Influence, more than any other, hits the Garou close to home and could very well bring humanity to its senses about just who and what shares this world with them. The occult community contains cult leaders, alternative religious groups, charlatans, would-be occultists and New Agers.

| Cost | Desired Effect |
|------|----------------|
| 1 | Contact and make use of common occult groups and their practices; Know some of the more visible occult figures* |

| | |
|---|---|
| 2 | Know and contact some of the more obscure occult figures;* Access resources for most rituals and rites |
| 3 | Know the general vicinity of certain supernatural entities (Kindred, Garou, mages, mummies, wraiths, etc.) and possibly contact them; Can access vital or very rare mate rial components; Milk impressionable wannabes for bucks ($250); Access occult tomes and writings; Research a Basic Ritual |
| 4 | Research an Intermediate Ritual |
| 5 | Access minor magic items; Unearth an Advanced Ritual |
| 6 | Research a new or unheard-of ritual or rite from tomes or mentors |

## Police

"To protect and serve" is a popular motto among the chosen enforcers of the law. But these days, everyone can have reason to doubt the law's ability to enact justice. Perhaps they should wonder whom the law defends, whom it serves, and why. The *Police* Influence encompasses the likes of beat cops, desk jockeys, prison guards, special divisions (such as SWAT and homicide), detectives and various clerical positions.

*Cost* *Desired Effect*

| | |
|---|---|
| 1 | Learn police procedures;* Hear police information and rumors; Avoid traffic tickets |
| 2 | Have license plates checked; Avoid minor violations (first conviction); Get "inside information" |
| 3 | Get copies of an investigation report; Have police hassle, detain or harass someone; Find bureau secrets |
| 4 | Access confiscated weapons or contraband; Have some serious charges dropped; Start an investigation; Get money, either from the evidence room or as an appropriation ($1,000) |
| 5 | Institute major investigations; Arrange setups; Instigate bureau investigations; Have officers fired |
| 6 | Paralyze departments for a time; Close down a major investigation |

## Politics

Nothing ever gets done for straightforward reasons any more. It's all who knows who and what favors can get paid off in the process. In other words, it's politics as usual, and there's a whole class of people who thrive in this world of favors and policy flacks. Some of these individuals include statesmen, pollsters, activists, party members, lobbyists, candidates and politicians themselves.

| Cost | Desired Effect |
| --- | --- |
| 1 | Minor lobbying; Identify real platforms of politicians and parties;* Be in the know* |
| 2 | Meet small-time politicians; Have a forewarning of pro cesses, laws and the like; Use a slush fund or fund raiser ($1,000) |
| 3 | Sway or alter political projects (local parks, renovations, small construction) |
| 4 | Enact minor legislation; Dash careers of minor politicians |
| 5 | Get your candidate in a minor office; Enact encompassing legislature |
| 6 | Block the passage of major bills; Suspend major laws temporarily; Use state bureaus or subcommittees |
| 7 | Usurp county-wide politics; Subvert statewide powers, at least to a moderate degree |
| 8 | Call out a local division of the National Guard; Declare a state of emergency in a region |

**Street**

Disenchanted, disenfranchised and ignored by their "betters," a whole collective of humanity has made its own culture and lifestyle to deal with the harsh lot life has dealt them. In the dark alleys and slums reside gang members, the homeless, street performers, petty criminals, prostitutes and the forgotten.

| Cost | Desired Effect |
| --- | --- |
| 1 | Has an ear open for the word on the street; Identify most gangs and know their turfs and habits |
| 2 | Live mostly without fear on the underside of society; Keep a contact or two in most aspects of street life; Access small-time contraband |
| 3 | Often gets insight on other areas of Influence; Arrange some services from street people or gangs; Get pistols or uncommon melee weapons |
| 4 | Mobilize groups of homeless; Panhandle or hold a "collection" ($250); Get hold of a shotgun, rifle or SMG; Respected among gangs, can have a word in almost all aspects of their operations |
| 5 | Control a single medium-sized gang; Arrange impressive protests by street people |

**Transportation**

The world is in constant motion, its prosperity relying heavily on the fact that people and productions fly, float or roll to and from every corner of the planet. Without the means to perform this monumental task, our "small" world would quickly become a daunting orb with large, isolated stretches. The forces that keep this circulation in motion include cab and bus drivers, pilots, air traffic controllers, travel firms, sea captains, conductors, border guards and untold others.

| Cost | Desired Effect |
|---|---|
| 1 | A wizard at what goes where, when and why; Can travel locally quickly and freely* |
| 2 | Can track an unwary target if he uses public transportation; Arrange passage safe (or at least concealed) from mundane threats (robbery, terrorism, etc.) |
| 3 | Seriously hamper an individual's ability to travel; Avoid most supernatural dangers when traveling (such as hunters and vampires) |
| 4 | Temporarily shut down one form of transportation (bus lines, ships, planes, trains, etc.); Route money your way ($500) |
| 5 | Reroute major modes of travel; Smuggle with impunity |
| 6 | Extend control to nearby areas |
| 7 | Isolate small or remote regions for a short period |

## Underworld

Even in the most cosmopolitan of ages, society has found certain needs and services too questionable to accept. On every age, some organized effort has stepped in to provide for this demand, regardless of the risks. Among this often ruthless and dangerous crowd are the likes of hitmen, Mafia, Yakuza, bookies, fencers and launderers.

| Cost | Desired Effect |
|---|---|
| 1 | Locate minor contraband (knives, small-time drugs, petty gambling, scalped tickets) |
| 2 | Obtain pistols, serious drugs, stolen cars; Hire muscle to rough someone up; Fence minor loot; Prove that crime pays (and score $1,000) |
| 3 | Obtain a rifle, shotgun or SMG; Arrange a minor "hit"; Know someone in "the Family" |
| 4 | White collar crime connections |
| 5 | Arrange gangland assassinations; Hire a demolition man or firebug; Supply local drug needs |

## University

In an age when the quest for learning and knowledge begins in schools, colleges and universities, information becomes currency. *University* Influence represents a certain degree of control and perhaps involvement in these institutions. In this sphere of Influence, one finds the teachers, professors, deans, students of all ages and levels, Greek orders and many young and impressionable minds.

| Cost | Desired Effect |
|------|----------------|
| 1 | Know layout and policy of local schools;* Access to low-level university resources; Get records up to the high school level |
| 2 | Know a contact or two with useful knowledge or skills; Minor access to facilities; Fake high school records; Obtain college records |
| 3 | Faculty favors; Cancel a class; Fix grades; Discredit a student |
| 4 | Organize student protests and rallies; Discredit faculty members; Acquire money through a grant ($1,000) |
| 5 | Falsify an undergraduate degree |
| 6 | Arrange major projects; Alter curriculum institution-wide; Free run of facilities |

# Step Four – Finishing Touches

### Negative Traits

At this point, you may increase your character's power by selecting counterbalancing flaws. By taking a Negative Trait, you can, for example, add a new Trait to your Attributes or take another Ability. Negative Traits are Attributes that have a negative effect upon your character. They can be used against you in a challenge (a contest staged between you and other characters). Each Negative Trait is equal to one positive Trait; for each Negative Trait you take, you receive a positive Trait of your choice. You can take no more than five Negative Traits unless you have the Narrator's permission. You can take whatever Negative Traits seem to fit your character; you need not take the full five, or any at all.

Each Negative Trait you take allows you to choose one of the following options:

Take one additional positive Trait in any category of Attribute: Physical, Social or Mental.

Take one extra Ability or Background

**Optional**: Your Narrator may allow you other options for modifying your character. Possible options are:

Three Negative Traits allow the purchase of one Basic Art.

Two Negative Traits allow the purchase of one level of a Realm.

### Health

Characters are considered to be at full health at the beginning of each story unless the Narrator states otherwise. Of course, characters can be hurt or even destroyed during a story, and changelings must keep track of both damage to their fae and human forms during the course of an evening's play.

There are three "levels" of Health beneath Healthy: "Bruised," "Wounded" and "Incapacitated," and changelings have identical levels for both mortal and fae miens. For more information on Health, see page 166.

# Spark of Life

Characters do not consist of Traits alone. Other aspects, such as motivations and secrets — while not necessarily important in terms of game mechanics — are vital to roleplaying. In many cases, the Narrator provides, or at least suggests, these "sparks of life" for you. Your character needs to be woven into the story, and these flourishes allow the Narrator to do just that.

## Other Aspects

**Background Story** — You need to create a background narrative for your character, describing her life before the Chrysalis: what she did, how she lived and what was unique about her. This background may describe what your character did for a living, how she saw herself and what others thought of her. It will probably influence who she is now — indeed, changelings must still cling to their former lives as protection from Bedlam.

**Secrets** — Each character has secrets of some sort, things that he doesn't want others to discover. One secret almost all changelings possess is a True Name, learned upon Saining, but this is hardly the only secret a changeling can have. The Narrator is likely to give you any number of secrets that you will need to protect over the course of the chronicle.

**Motivations** — Changelings are creatures of emotion. What is your purpose? What motivates you on a day-to-day basis? Is it hate, fear, lust, greed, jealousy or revenge? Describe your motivations in as much detail as possible; ask the Narrator for help if you can't think of anything.

**Appearance** — Find props and a costume that will help others understand or at least recognize your character at a glance. You may find it helpful not only to act like your character, but to look like him as well — especially if you're playing multiple roles in a single chronicle. Your character's appearance makes his Physical (and many Social) Traits apparent to other characters. You may want to get a "fantasy feel" for your costumes, to reflect your character's faerie nature. Good resources for these fashions are local renaissance faires and consignment stores — there you'll find flowing gowns, tunic-type shirts and anything else you feel will add flair to your character's wardrobe. Remember, however, the restriction on weapons still applies to all costumes, no matter what your *character* might be carrying.

**Equipment** — Your character likely begins the game with equipment of one sort or another. Ask a Narrator for more details on your personal possessions and assets. If you want to spend money on equipment right away, feel free. Changelings must also specify whether or not their equipment is mundane or chimerical, as this designation will determine whether it can interact with the mortal world. You may buy weapons, clothing, land, boats, horses — anything. Use an appropriate reference book for prices, or approximate.

Owning items with magical powers falls under the Background stage of character creation. (By the way, be sure to get your Narrator's approval if you wish to buy anything unusual or dangerous.)

**Quirks** — By giving your character quirks (interesting personal details), you add a great deal of depth and interest to her. Write a few sentences on the back of your character sheet about the strange and interesting things that define your character. Examples of quirks include a dark sense of humor, a gentleness toward children or a habit of mumbling when nervous.

## Merits and Flaws

Merits and Flaws are optional defining Traits that give you a way to make your character unique. A Merit is a descriptive Trait that applies to your character and gives him a slight advantage in some area, while a Flaw gives your Kithain a slight disadvantage. You may buy Merits only during character creation, unless you earn them during a story (and have Storyteller approval). To buy Merits during character creation, you may only spend Traits from Flaws (maximum of seven; you may take more Flaws than that, but they will not be counted), Backgrounds (maximum of five), Abilities (maximum of five) or Traits earned from Negative Traits (maximum of five); the maximum number of Merit Traits allowed is 22. Your character will not suffer if you do not have Merits and Flaws, but putting all your points into Merits and Flaws will surely handicap you in other areas.

You can also take Flaw Traits and use them to buy other Traits — Abilities and Backgrounds — at a one-for-one ratio.

Merits and Flaws may be restricted in some stories, or not available at all in others. Make certain that you get Storyteller approval before buying any Merits or Flaws, as some of the ones listed below may be disallowed in your game. Merits and Flaws are *optional* parts of a character, and **The Shining Host** can be played quite well without them.

Remember that you must have Storyteller approval on all Merits and Flaws you want for your character. Once gameplay starts, you may only purchase or buy off Merits and Flaws with Storyteller approval, and at double the Trait cost listed for them. You must also have given excellent proof of your worthiness to earn a new Merit or your dedication in buying off a particular Flaw in the story.

You are not allowed to take a Merit that doubles up an existing advantage of your character's, or that is identical to one of your character's Frailties, unless it is otherwise stated that you can do so.

## Aptitudes

These Merits and Flaws establish your changeling's special capacities and abilities, or modify the effects and powers of his other Traits.

**Ability Aptitude (1 Trait Merit):** You have a particular facility with one (not combat-related) Ability, and are considered to be two Traits up on all tests directly related to that Ability.

**Ambidextrous (1 Trait Merit):** You have a high degree of off-hand dexterity, and can perform tasks with the "wrong" hand with no Trait penalty.

**Animal Affinity (2 Trait Merit):** You possess some of the legendary fae affinity for animals, and with a successful Social Challenge you may calm down a frightened or enraged animal, or befriend a neutral one. By spending two Social Traits, you may gain a rudimentary ability to understand the intentions of a particular animal, and even communicate with it in a way it understands well.

**Busy Helper (5 Trait Merit):** This Merit is identical to the boggan Birthright: *Craftwork.*

**Chimerical Craftsman (5 Trait Merit):** This is identical to the nocker Birthright: *Forge Chimera.*

**Jack-of-All-Trades (5 Trait Merit):** You have a large pool of miscellaneous skills and knowledges obtained through your extensive travels, the jobs you've held, or just all-around know-how. You may automatically attempt any action even though you do not have the appropriate Ability, although you must risk an extra Trait to do so. However, if you lose this challenge, both Traits you bid are also gone. You can, of course, spend a Willpower Trait to avoid losing the Traits you just bid.

**Water Baby (5 Trait Merit):** This is identical to the selkie Birthright: *Ocean's Grace.*

**Inept (5 Trait Flaw):** You have never trained extensively in any skill or craft, and therefore can purchase no Abilities. You also cannot purchase new Abilities or Influences above one until this Flaw has been bought off.

**Endless #@%$#*$@ Frustration (5 Trait Flaw):** This is identical to the nocker Frailty: *Flaws,* except you may choose the Ability it affects — having a Flawed *Performance* Ability means that something is always wrong with any art you create, while the effects of Flawed *Repair* are generally dangerous for those around you. The Storyteller has the final say on what Abilities may be *Flawed,* and how it comes into play each time it is used. She is under no compunction to be merciful, either.

## Awareness

These Merits and Flaws involve perception (or the lack thereof).

**Acute Sense (1 Trait Merit):** You have an exceptionally keen sense (hearing, smell, taste, vision). You are automatically two Traits up on all challenges that involve that perception.

**Cat Senses (5 Trait Merit):** This is identical to the sluagh Birthright: *Heightened Senses*, except you may not speak to wraiths, and you do not suffer the sluagh difficulties of *Heightened Senses* (susceptibility to light, etc.).

**Natural Appreciation (5 Trait Merit):** This is identical to the ghille dhu Birthright: *Nature's Bounty*.

**Weak Sense (1 Trait Flaw):** You have a sense that's not quite up to snuff (hearing or vision, choose one). You are automatically two Traits down on perception tests related to that sense. Obviously, you may not have *Acute Sense* and *Weak Sense* on the same sense.

**Color Blindness (1 Trait Flaw):** You can only see in black and white. Color means nothing to you, although you are sensitive to color density, which you perceive as shades of gray. In the vibrant and magical world of the Kithain, this is considered a sad condition indeed. **Note:** Color blindness actually indicates an inability to distinguish between two colors, but we fudged a bit for the sake of playability. It's a *game*, after all.

**One Eye (2 Trait Flaw):** You have one eye — choose which, or determine the missing eye randomly during character creation. You have no peripheral vision on your blind side, and are two Traits down on any test requiring depth perception. This weakness extends to missile combat. To simulate this Flaw, you may choose to cover one eye while you're playing.

**Deaf (3 Trait Flaw):** You cannot hear at all. If you are not truly deaf, this Flaw can be difficult to roleplay and you should get your Narrator's approval before selecting it.

**Blind (6 Trait Flaw):** You automatically fail all tests involving vision. You cannot see — the world of color and light is lost to you. **Note:** This Flaw can be difficult to act out in a live-action setting, and must never be allowed to take precedence over safety.

## Changeling Ties

These Traits reflect your status among your fellow Kithain, and any capabilities and drawbacks that result from that.

**Boon (1-7 Trait Merit):** An elder fae owes you a favor because of something either you or your mentor once did for him. The extent of the boon owed to you depends on how many Traits you spend. One Trait would indicate a relatively minor boon, while seven Traits would indicate that the elder probably owes you his existence.

**Kith Affinity (2 Trait Merit):** You have a knack for interacting with members of another kith — perhaps it's the way you look, or maybe you have a reputation for helping them out when they're in need. Maybe you were a great aid to them in a past life (perhaps you were one in a past life!). Regardless, you are two Traits up on all Social Challenges on all friendly social interactions with this kith, or when sincerely attempting to gain their trust. However, if that kith has any enemies in the area, beware — you will be marked as a sympathizer.

**Enemy (1-5 Trait Flaw):** Sometime in your life, you offended an unknown being with the power to cause you grief. The power and influence of this enemy are determined by the Flaw's value. Someone about your equal would be one Trait, while a Methuselah vampire or a noble of the Shadow Court would be worth five. You and the Narrator should discuss the severity of your enemy's hatred, and whether or not you are aware that he is pursuing you. The Narrator awards the freebie points for this Flaw.

**Twisted Upbringing (1 Trait Flaw):** When you were led through your Chrysalis, the group that Sained you put all the wrong ideas into your head about changelings and changeling society. Now you have trouble shaking these notions. Perhaps your "benefactors" did it for some dark purpose, or maybe just for kicks, but all the bad info has been implanted in you just the same, and it's going to take a lot to get what they told you out of your head. You also resist others who try to tell you the "truth" of what's really going on, sticking to your beliefs until hard lessons teach you otherwise. The Storyteller will tell you when you have learned enough to buy off this Flaw.

**Kith Enmity (2 Trait Flaw):** For some reason, you just don't get along with another kith — it can be anything from the way you dress to the ideals you hold, but you have trouble interacting with other members of this kith, and no matter what you do, they seem to be naturally disposed to dislike you. You are two Traits down on all non-cantrip related Social Challenges with this kith, even intimidation attempts. You will also automatically be considered an enemy of any local motleys of this kith, regardless of your real intentions.

**Notoriety (3 Trait Flaw):** You have a bad reputation among your peers; perhaps you violated the Escheat once too often, or you belong to an unpopular motley. Maybe it isn't even your fault, but the reputation of your mentor. Regardless, you are two Traits down on anything that has to do with social dealings with other Kithain of your area.

## Mental

These Merits and Flaws deal with the mind — its strengths, weaknesses and special capacities.

**Common Sense (1 Trait Merit):** Your have a significant amount of practical, everyday wisdom. Whenever you are about to do something contrary to common sense, the Narrator should alert you to how your potential action might violate practicality. This is an ideal Merit if you are a novice player; it allows you to receive advice from the Narrator concerning what you can and cannot do, and (even more importantly) what you should and should not do.

**Celestial Attunement (1 Trait Merit):** You have an innate link to the passage of time and the movement of celestial bodies. You can estimate the time until sunrise or sunset within a minute or two, and can follow the phases of the moon in your head. Those with some training in astrology and this

Merit can even foretell certain astrological conjunctions without access to charts. You can accomplish any of these feats with only a minimum of concentration. This Merit is especially common among the faerie folk who are in tune with the cycle of nature. It can also help resist the effects of "faerie time" inflicted by the *Chronos* Art; all such difficulties to confuse a changeling with this Merit are down two Traits.

**Eidetic Memory (2 Trait Merit):** You can remember things you have seen and heard with perfect detail. You are up two Traits on any memory-related challenges, and can recall any sight or sound accurately, even from a passing glimpse or snatch of sound. The Narrator relates to you exactly what was seen or heard, and can be queried about what you do and do not know.

**Iron Will (3 Trait Merit):** When you are determined and your mind is set, nothing can divert you from your goals. You cannot be *Dominated*, and you receive a free retest on any other mental attacks or magic against you, whether you are aware of them or not. At the Storyteller's discretion, resisting especially strong magic may require a *Willpower* Trait.

**Amnesia (2 Trait Flaw):** You are unable to remember anything about your life prior to the Chrysalis. You past is a blank slate, and may come back to haunt you. You may, if you wish, take up to five other points of Flaws without specifying what they are. The Narrator can supply the details. Over the course of the chronicle, you and your character will slowly discover these hidden Flaws. *Amnesia* can be a dangerous Flaw; your Narrator is under no obligation to be merciful.

**Confused (2 Trait Flaw):** You are often confused, and the world seems to be a very twisted and distorted place to you. Sometimes you are simply unable to make sense of things. You need to roleplay this behavior to some extent at all times, but your confusion becomes especially strong whenever strong stimuli surround you (such as when a number of people talk all at once, or you enter a cavern with an overpowering stench). You may spend Willpower to override the effects of your confusion, but only for the duration of a scene.

**Absent-Minded (3 Trait Flaw):** Though you do not forget such things as knowledges and skills, you do forget things like names, titles and the last time you had a meal. In order to remember anything more than your own name or the location of your freehold, you need to spend a Willpower point.

## Mortal Society

These Merits and Flaws, along with your Influences, help to define your interactions with the mortal world.

**Mansion (2 Trait Merit):** You own a large mansion — a home with 25 or more rooms — as well as the surrounding estate. The servants, if you have any, are provided for you if you have this Merit, although they cannot be used as *Dreamers* unless you purchase the appropriate Background. While the mansion can be in as poor or as good repair as you wish, the more inhabited it appears to be, the more attention it will garner (from tax men and the like). Similarly, superstitious mortals go out of their way to avoid a "haunted" manor, although you may have to fight off the zoning board from time to time. There are also down sides to living in a decrepit building, not the least of which is personal safety.

**Nightclub (2 Trait Merit):** You own a nightclub of moderate size, perhaps one of the hottest nightspots in the city. It brings you in enough money to support a decent lifestyle ($1000 allowance a month, which may be augmented by taking *Influences*), and also provides provide an excellent place for a freehold (although that requires the necessary Background) or even just a general rendezvous. The name of the club, its style, its design and the description of its regular patrons are all up to you (within reason). Variations on this Merit could include a restaurant, theater, comedy club, sports arena or retail store, with the Storyteller's permission, of course.

**Persistent Parents (2 Trait Flaw):** This Flaw is the bane of many childlings. You may have run away to join faerie society, but your parents have refused to let the mystery of your disappearance lie. They actively use missing children programs to find you, and employ private investigators to help in the search. The Storyteller determines how close they are to finding you, but the trail is hot enough to make you uncomfortable, and any violent confrontation with one detective will only bring the rest of them closer to you. Implicit in this Flaw is the fact that for some reason you simply cannot tell your parents what you are or talk your parents out of searching for you (though you may try); perhaps they loyally serve a Prodigal master, or they are Autumn People.

**Ward (3 Trait Flaw):** You are devoted to the protection of a mortal. You may describe your ward, though the Narrator is the one who actually creates her. This character is often a friend or relative from your pre-Chrysalis days. Wards have a talent for getting caught up in the action of stories, and are frequent targets of a character's enemies.

**Hunted (4 Trait Flaw):** You have come to the attention of a Dauntain or similar individual who seeks your destruction. This hunter is beyond reason and has some form of power, influence or authority that puts you at a disadvantage. Because of you, your friends, family and associates are likewise endangered. Sooner or later, this Flaw results in a confrontation. The resolution should not be an easy one, and until such time as you and your pursuer have your showdown, you are in for a hellish time.

### Physical

These Merits and Flaws deal with your health and physical makeup, and the unusual physiology of the fae.

**Double-jointed (1 Trait Merit):** You are unusually supple. You receive one free retest per session on a challenge related to body flexibility. The

Storyteller determines if this Merit applies if there is any debate. Squeezing between bars is one example of a use for this Merit.

**Changeling's Eyes (1 Trait Flaw)**: Your eyes are a startling color, perhaps burning crimson or the color of the full moon. Whatever they are, they are clearly not normal, and visible even in your mortal seeming. This makes you easily tracked by those who know of your… distinction. You must describe your unusual eye color to everyone you meet.

**Huge Size (4 Trait Merit)**: You are abnormally large in size, possibly over seven feet tall and 400 pounds in weight. You therefore have one additional Health Level, to reflect the fact that you are able to withstand more punishment than most before you are incapacitated. When acting this part, players should dress appropriately with bulky clothes, unless they already have a stature that approximates this Merit. **Note**: A troll may purchase this Merit, as it affects her mortal seeming as opposed to her fae self.

**Short (1 Trait Flaw)**: You are well below the average height, and have trouble seeing over high objects and running quickly. You suffer a two-Trait penalty to all pursuit rolls, and you and the Narrator should make sure your height is taken into account in all situations.

**Disfigured (2 Trait Flaw)**: A hideous disfigurement makes you easy to notice as well as to remember. You cannot take any Social Traits that would compliment your appearance.

**Child (3 Trait Flaw)**: You are a child in body, if not in mind, and while you may be extremely precocious, you're still just a kid. You have the *Short* Flaw (above), and are subject to many parental controls and curfews. You might even be barred from things (like bars or clubs) due to your being "underage." You also may have some trouble being taken seriously by non-Kithain (two-Trait penalty to all relevant tests). Not all childlings need take this Flaw; those who don't are assumed for some reason to be considered more "adult" by others.

**Deformity (3 Trait Flaw)**: You have some kind of deformity — a misshapen limb, a hunchback, a club foot — which affects your interactions with others and may inconvenience you physically. You are one Trait down on all tests of a physical nature. Furthermore all challenges related to physical appearance are two Traits down.

**Lame (3 Trait Flaw)**: Your legs are injured or otherwise prevented from working effectively. You suffer a three trait penalty to all tests related to movement, and may require crutches or other aid to move around effectively.

**One Arm (3 Trait Flaw)**: You have only one arm — choose which, or determine the missing limb randomly at character creation. You are accustomed to using your remaining hand, so you suffer no off-hand penalty. However, you do suffer a two-Trait penalty to any test in which two hands would normally be needed to perform a task.

**Mute (4 Trait Flaw)**: Your vocal apparatus does not function, and you cannot speak at all. You can communicate through other means — typically writing or signing. Obviously, you may not take any Traits pertaining to vocal expression.

## Supernatural

These extremely rare Merits and Flaws give you different kinds of supernatural benefits or detriments. Because of the unbalancing potential of these particular Traits and the liberal way in which they deal with the "laws of reality," the Storyteller may not allow you just to choose from this category — ask before you pick one. Furthermore, you should not select such Traits unless they firmly fit your character concept and you can explain why your character possesses them. In general, it is not recommended that anyone have more than one or two Supernatural Merits or Flaws — they should be strictly controlled by the Storyteller.

**Fae Songs (1-5 Trait Merit)**: Through accident or training, you have learned some of the ancient songs of the fae, which allow you to weave special powers over your audience with a successful *Performance* Challenge. You have learned one song per Trait of this Merit, and each has a different supernatural effect — sleep, passion, lure a type of target (rodents, children) away, or happiness. These songs are covered by the Mists, meaning that any mundanes affected will be unable to remember the tune that so enchanted them except in dreamy snatches....

**Past Life (1-5 Trait Merit)**: Most fae only recall hazy memories from their past lives in dreams, but those with this Merit can remember much greater detail — perhaps even entire lifetimes. Sometimes, these visions even provide insight into a problem in a current lifetime; a character may call on this Merit a number of times equal to the Trait rating per story, although what exactly a character remembers is the province of the Storyteller. The information recalled may be cryptic, but is always useful in some way or another. Of course, you never know who might have shared a past life with you....

**Mass Appeal (1-5 Trait Merit)**: You have learned how to harness the Glamour of an appreciative audience to your own ends; for each Dreamer in the vicinity, or for every five mundane beings enjoying a performance of which you are a part, you are considered to have one extra Glamour Trait, up to the limit of the number of Traits of the Merit. These extra Glamour Traits may only be spent on enchantment or cantrips directly related to the performance, and fade away once the performance is over if they are unused. You must successfully employ a *Performance* Social Challenge to use this Merit.

**True Love (1 Trait Merit)**: You have discovered, but may have lost (at least temporarily) a true love. Nonetheless, the mere existence of this love provides you with transcendent joy. Whenever you are suffering, in danger or dejected, the thought of your true love is enough to give you the strength to persevere. In game terms, this love allows you two extra Traits in a challenge, but only when you are actively striving to protect or come closer to your true love. Also, the power of your love may be enough to protect you from other supernatural forces (Narrator's discretion). However, your true love may also be a hindrance and require aid (or even rescue) from time to time. Be forewarned: this is a most exacting Merit to play over the course of a chronicle.

**Danger Sense (2 Trait Merit):** You have a sixth sense that warns you of danger. When you are in a perilous situation that would potentially surprise you, you have five seconds in which to react instead of the normal three seconds.

**Shaman/Medium (2 Trait Merit):** You possess a natural affinity with spirits, either natural spirits such as animals or plants (*Shaman*) or the ghosts of the departed (*Medium*) — choose one. Though you cannot see spirits unless they reveal themselves, you may speak freely to any spirits of your affinity in the area, and you can even summon them to you with pleading and cajoling. Spirits never offer their powers or advice for free, however — they always want something in return. Sluagh who take *Medium* are two Traits up on all Social tests with wraiths they encounter.

**Poetic Heart (3 Trait Merit):** You possess a truly romantic, inspired soul, and are destined to be a great hero or artist. In any event, Glamour shields you from some of the worst effects of Banality; once per story, you may spend a Willpower Trait to avoid gaining Banality Traits from one test.

**Unbondable (3 Trait Merit):** You are immune to being Blood Bound. No matter how much blood you drink from vampires, you can never be Bound to one, although this is no protection from the Banality that comes with drinking vampire blood.

**Luck (4 Trait Merit):** You were born lucky — or else the Fates look after their own. Either way, you can repeat three failed tests per story. Only one repeat attempt may be made on any single test.

**Iron Resistance (4 Trait Merit):** Although cold iron is still a threat to your faerie soul, you suffer less from its proximity than other fae do. You can tolerate touching cold iron without the detrimental physical side effects that most fae suffer. Cold iron still inflicts aggravated wounds on you, however, and a fatal wound from the metal will still destroy your fae soul utterly.

**Seeming's Blessing (5 Trait Merit):** All of your Birthrights are effective in your mortal seeming, (even ones that are normally considered Wyrd Birthrights) and function in front of mortals. For example, trolls gain extra Physical Traits and Health Levels, sidhe gain extra appearance-related Traits, etc.

**Faerie Eternity (5 Trait Merit):** After your Chrysalis, you began to age strangely — you had received a touch of the immortality once inherent to all fae, and now you age at one-tenth the rate of a normal human. Should you fall permanently into Banality, or have your fae self destroyed, you will begin to age normally.

**Art Affinity (5 Trait Merit):** You possess a great degree of natural skill with one Art of changeling magic (your choice). You are automatically one Trait up on any tests with this Art, and it costs one fewer experience Traits than normal to learn new powers in that Art. This Merit may only be purchased once.

**Immortal Passion (5 Trait Merit/4 Trait Flaw):** You possess one of the legendary passions of the fae, and tend to feel this emotion with a depth unfathomable to most mortals. You must work with your Storyteller to determine what your passion is, and to what situations it might apply. Whether or not you are able to easily control this passion, however, dictates whether this is a Merit or a Flaw. If you take this trait as a Merit, you receive a free retest on any test directly pertaining to your passion (this does not include most combats, unless the object of your passion is defenseless or otherwise in dire need of your aid), and any attempts (magical or otherwise) to create emotions in you that would contradict your passion automatically fail. However, if you take this trait as a Flaw, your passion can also take control of you at inopportune moments, and you must either spend a Willpower Trait or make a Static Challenge of your current Willpower against six Traits to retain control of yourself.

**Note:** This does not mean that you must act unbalanced or melodramatic when it comes to expressing your passion; indeed, some of the most emotional moments in our lives are times of quiet strength and devotion. This Merit is also not cumulative with the effects of the *True Love* Merit, although they can be combined (most wonderfully) for roleplaying purposes, and taking this Flaw with *True Love* is one way to ensure an epic, though most likely tragic, romance. Some passions include: love, honor, compassion, righteous anger, freedom and a desire to learn. At the Storyteller's discretion, you may take darker passions (lust, greed, etc.), but they are generally only acceptable as Flaws.

**Regeneration (7 Trait Merit):** Your faerie spirit is exceptionally strong, and even your mortal frame recovers quickly from damage. You heal one Health Level of chimerical damage every five minutes, and one level of actual damage every hour.

**The Bard's Tongue (1 Trait Flaw):** You speak the truth, and with uncanny accuracy. This is not a talent for prophecy, but rather a facility for blurting out unpleasant truths at inappropriate times. Once per session, the Storyteller may approach you with an unpleasant truth you must spit out, and you may only swallow the urge by spending a *Willpower* Trait. Pooka with this Flaw are destined for frustration.

**Geas (1-5 Trait Flaw):** You begin play under a *geas* of some kind — most likely a Ban, but possibly a long-term quest. The number of Traits in the Flaw indicates the difficulty of the Ban to follow — a Ban against eating with red-haired people is worth one Trait, while a Ban against sleeping in the same bed more than once would be worth five. You must work with the Storyteller to define the specifics of your Ban and the consequences of failure to uphold it.

**Slipped Seeming (1-5 Trait Flaw):** Your fae self bleeds over into your mortal seeming; the degree of the slipped seeming depends on the number of Traits of a Flaw you take. One Trait might mean pointed ears for a sidhe, while five would mean goat legs for a satyr. These slips, however, do not confer any of the usual Birthrights associated with them — a satyr with goat legs cannot make a Fair Escape, for example. The Mists do not protect *Slipped Seeming*.

**Surreal Quality (2 Trait Flaw):** You exude an aura of otherworldly mystery to those around you; unfortunately, this means mortals often become fascinated with you in an unhealthy way. They might attempt to strike up conversations at bad times, or try to get close to you in ways that you might find unfavorable. Even worse, mortals of a criminal persuasion will often target you for their illicit actions, as you seem particularly appealing to them.

**Winged (2 Trait Flaw/4 Trait Merit):** You have beautiful wings, be they feathered bird's wings or batwings or a brilliant butterfly's tapestry. They are chimerical, but you must accommodate them nonetheless, which can make for some bizarre scenes as you try to explain why you've cut slits in the backs of all of your coats. If your wings are restrained improperly, you are down on Trait on all Physical Challenges. If you take *Winged* as a Flaw, you cannot fly, but are one Trait up on all uses of *Wind Runner*. If it is a Merit, you may indeed fly for short periods of time (no more than a scene or two at a stretch), although you may not use this ability in the presence of the unenchanted.

**Echoes (2-5 Trait Flaw):** You are affected by mortal beliefs, like many of the fae of old, and exhibit many behaviors that faerie hunters and superstitious mortals will recognize. The Trait value of this Flaw describes how many superstitions you are affected by. Two Traits would indicate something like milk curdling in your presence, three might mean that mortals who say your name backward are invulnerable to your Arts, and five might mean that you take damage from walking on holy ground. This Flaw is cumulative, so taking five Traits of it means you suffer lesser effects as well. These can have some beneficial effects for you (for example, picking four leaf clovers might bring you luck), but generally it's more trouble than it's worth. You must work with the Storyteller to determine what superstitions affect you, and how often you come in contact with them.

**Cleared Mists (3 Trait Flaw):** Although they are the result of Banality, the Mists help hide the magics of changelings from the eyes of mortals. Unfortunately, for some reason the Mists do not shield your Glamour, and any use of cantrips or other fae powers you use will be fully remembered by any mortals who observe you. This makes you easily noticed and tracked by Dauntain.

**Bound Essence (5 Trait Flaw):** This is identical to the selkie Frailty: *Seal Coat*, except that you may have your fae self bound into any kind of item you desire (with Storyteller approval): jewelry, a weapon, even an old book.

**Bad Moon (5 Trait Flaw):** The moon is the traditional home of both the Seelie and Unseelie Courts, and for some fae it still has a powerful effect on their attitudes; it can even cause a temporary form of madness which wilders sardonically call "lunacy." Whenever the rays of the moon strike your unprotected skin, you immediately adopt your Unseelie Legacy, or if already Unseelie, become violently antisocial in your ways. For most Kithain, the change lasts for the span of a full day. For unknown reasons, sidhe suffer the effects of the change for an entire week.

Obviously, you must cover yourself well when traveling at night, although you may stand under the moon if you are within the radius of another light source (such as a streetlight); the other light is considered to "drown out" the moonlight and render it unable to trigger this Flaw. The Storyteller should be called if there is any debate as to whether or not a character's bare skin has indeed been exposed to moonlight.

**Greedy Glamour (5 Trait Flaw):** Glamour always asks a lot of you, and your cantrips seldom come easily. You must perform an additional Bunk, for which you receive no bonus Bunk Traits, whenever you cast a cantrip, and you may never cast a cantrip without using a Bunk. You may still spend Glamour to do an additional Bunk while casting.

**Banality's Curse (5 Trait Flaw):** You are extremely susceptible to Banality, much like the sidhe, and suffer from the Frailty of the same name. You are assigned extra Banality Traits each time you gain Banality, and the level of Banality in an item or area is always considered one higher than normal for your purposes.

**Chimerical Magnet (5 Trait Flaw):** You tend to attract chimera, and as a result you gain the attention of rampaging monsters more easily than do others. While this can sometimes be a help to you, more often than not it means trouble, as nervosa and harmless pixies alike target you for their attentions. Worse, you might as well have "dragon magnet" tattooed on your forehead in some territories.

**Oathbound Health (5 Trait Flaw):** This Flaw is identical to the troll Frailty: *Bond of Duty*.

**Dark Fate (5 Trait Flaw):** You are doomed to experience a horrible demise or, worse, suffer eternal agony. No matter what you do, someday you will be out of the picture. In the end, all your efforts, your struggles and your dreams will come to naught. Your fate is certain and there is nothing you can do about it. Even more ghastly, you have partial knowledge of this, for you occasionally have visions of your fate — and such phantasms are most disturbing. The malaise these visions inspire in you can only be overcome through the use of Willpower, and returns after each vision. At some point in the chronicle, you will indeed face your fate, but when and how is completely up to the Storyteller. Though you can't do anything about your inevitable doom, you can still attempt to reach some goal before it occurs, or at least try to make sure that your friends are not destroyed as well.

## Personality

These Merits and Flaws deal with the personality of your character, and describe ideals, motivations or pathologies. Some Personality Flaws can be temporarily ignored by spending Willpower Traits, and are noted as such. If you possess such a Flaw and do not roleplay it when the Narrator thinks you should, then she may inform you that you have spent a Willpower Trait for the effort. Flaws cannot be conveniently ignored.

**Code of Honor (1 Trait Merit)**: You have a personal code of ethics to which you strictly adhere. You can automatically resist most temptations that would bring you in conflict with your code. When battling supernatural methods of persuasion (*Dominate*, mind magic, etc.) that would make you violate your code, you gain one automatic Trait for the challenge. You must construct your own personal code of honor in as much detail as you can, outlining the general rules of conduct by which you abide. As always, double-check what you create with a Storyteller.

**Higher Purpose (1 Trait Merit)**: Everyone has "reason to live," but you have a special commitment to a single ideal. Your chosen goal drives and directs you in everything. You do not concern yourself with petty matters, because your higher purpose is everything. Though you may sometimes be herded along by this aim and find yourself forced to behave in ways contrary to the needs of personal survival, having this sort of motivation can also grant you great inner strength. You have two extra Traits on any challenge having to do with your higher purpose. You need to decide what your higher purpose is before you start playing; make sure you talk it over with the Storyteller first. (You cannot take both this Merit and the Flaw: *Driving Goal*.)

**One Bad Dude (5 Trait Merit)**: This is identical to the redcap Birthright: *Bully Browbeat*.

**Loyal Heart (5 Trait Merit)**: This Merit is identical to the troll Birthright: *Strength of Duty*.

**Compulsion (1 Trait Flaw)**: You have a compulsion of some sort, which can cause you a number of different problems. Your compulsion may be for cleanliness, bragging, stealing, gambling, exaggeration or just talking too much. A compulsion can be temporarily avoided for one scene at the cost of a Willpower Trait, but it is in effect at all other times.

**Cyclical Court Change (1-3 Trait Flaw)**: In times past many fae were Seelie in spring and summer and Unseelie in autumn and winter, and you are still bound by the cycles of the natural world in your choice in Courts. Although you may have some control over your actual Court, you are forced to adopt one particular Court a certain number of times per year based on some regular natural cycle — the tides, the lunar calendar, etc. The number of Traits this Flaw is worth depends on how regular the change is and for how long each switch lasts (involuntarily changing to your Seelie/Unseelie Legacy for one day every month is worth one, while being forced to stay one Court for an entire season is worth three).

**Intolerance (1 Trait Flaw):** You have an unreasoning dislike of a certain thing, It may be an animal, a class of person, a color, a situation or just abut anything at all. Some dislikes may be too trivial to be reflected here — an aversion to rare comic books, for instance. The Narrator is the final arbiter on what you can pick to dislike.

**Nightmares (1 Trait Flaw):** You experience horrendous dreams every time you sleep, and memories of them haunt you during your waking hours. Sometimes the nightmares are so bad they cause you to be down one Trait on all of your actions for the next day (Narrator's discretion). Some of the nightmares may be so intense that you mistake them for reality. A crafty Narrator will be quick to take advantage of this, and in the dream-centered world of the Kithain, this can be a horrible Flaw indeed.

**Overconfident (1 Trait Flaw):** This is identical to the eshu Frailty: *Recklessness*, except the possessor of this Flaw does not receive Negative Traits for it.

**Shy (1 Trait Flaw):** You are distinctly ill at ease in social situations, and have trouble relating with large groups of people. You are one Trait down with all social dealings, and another Trait down when you are the center of attention for a large group of people (over 10).

**Soft-Hearted (1 Trait Flaw):** You cannot stand to watch others suffer — not necessarily because you care about what happens to them, but simply because you dislike the intensity of emotion it causes in you. If you are the direct cause of suffering and you witness it, you experience bouts of nausea and nights of sleepless grief. You avoid situations where you might have to witness others' pain and will do anything you can to protect people from it. Whenever you must witness suffering, you are one Trait down on all challenges for the next hour.

**Low Self-Image (2 Trait Flaw):** You lack self-confidence and don't believe in yourself. You are two Traits down in situations where you don't expect to succeed (at Narrator's discretion, though the penalty might be limited to one Trait if you help the Narrator by pointing out times when this Flaw *might* affect you). At the Narrator's option, you may be required to use a *Willpower* Trait to do things that require self-confidence in situations when others would not be obliged to do so.

**Vengeance (2 Trait Flaw):** You have a score to settle. You are obsessed with wreaking vengeance on an individual (or perhaps an entire group), and make revenge your first priority in all situations. The need for vengeance can only be overcome by spending a Willpower Trait, and even then it only subsides for a single scene.

**Wyld Mind (2 Trait Flaw):** You possess the chaotic sensibility of the true fae, and have trouble keeping your mind on one subject for too long. You suffer a one-Trait penalty on any successive tests in an extended confrontation (not including combat, but including actions such as a facedown) as a result of your inability to keep your mind focused.

**Curiosity (2 Trait Flaw):** You cannot resist mysteries or puzzles of any kind, and when confronted with a situation where you might be tempted to investigate ("What harm could it possibly do to follow the Shadow Court assassin home?"), you must make a Static Mental Challenge against a number of Traits determined by the Storyteller. You may avoid the temptation for a while with a Willpower Trait, but if another mystery appears....

**Driving Goal (3 Trait Flaw):** You have a personal goal, which sometimes compels and directs you in startling ways. The goal is almost limitless in scope, and you can never truly achieve it. "Overcome Banality" or "Destroy all Dauntain" are acceptable goals, while "Become a titled noble" is not — after all, you might pull the latter off. Because you must work toward your goal throughout the chronicle (though you can avoid it for short periods by spending Willpower), your fixation can get you into trouble and supersede other actions that you might prefer to take. Choose your goal carefully, as it is the focus of everything your character does.

**Hatred (3 Trait Flaw):** You have an unreasoning hatred of a certain thing. This hate is total and largely uncontrollable. You may hate a color, animal ("ARRRGHHH! IT'S A LEMUR! I *HATE* LEMURS!"), class of person or situation — anything. You constantly pursue opportunities to harm the hated object or to gain power from it. The Narrator may, of course, rule a particular hatred too trivial for game purposes.

**Lifesaver (3 Trait Flaw):** You cannot bring yourself to take the life of another, and even chimerical combat makes you uncomfortable. You have a two-Trait penalty on any tests which result in the death of another (chimerical or otherwise), and if you ever kill another person's mortal form, you will suffer a long period of agonizing self-doubt. You may be able to slay creatures entirely of evil (such as feral chimera or crazed vampires), but be very careful at how you define "evil"....

**Phobia (3 or 5 Trait Flaw):** You have an overpowering and irrational fear of something. You instinctively and illogically retreat from and avoid the object of your fear. Common objects of phobias include certain animals, insects, crowds, open spaces, confined spaces and heights. You must make a Simple Test whenever you encounter the object of your fear. The consequences of failure depend on the severity of the Flaw. If you have taken a three-Trait phobia, you must retreat from the object upon failure. If the fear is worth five Traits, you will not approach the object with fewer than three successes. If you fail, you will flee in terror. The Storyteller has final say over which phobias she allows in a chronicle.

# Experience

Humans — and changelings — are creatures of experience By doing, we learn how to improve what we've done. Thus, characters can take Experience points (awarded for superior roleplaying, expert leadership or even simple survival) and convert them into improved statistics. Only one Ability, Trait, Art or Realm should be gained per session.

## Using Experience

After experience has been awarded, it may be spent to purchase new Abilities, Traits, Arts and Realms, improving upon the character and giving the player a sense of satisfaction as he watches his character grow. The following lists the cost of improving the various aspects of a character.

- New Attribute Trait — One experience point per Trait.
- New Ability — One experience point per Ability Trait.
- New Art — Three experience points for Basic Arts, six for Intermediate Arts, and nine for Advanced Arts.
- New Realm — Two experience per Realm.
- New Glamour — Three experience per Trait.
- New Willpower — Three experience per Trait.
- New Banality — Two experience per Trait. Go on, take it. You know you want it. (It'll get you sooner or later anyway.)
- Buy off Negative Trait — Two experience per Trait.
- New Background — One experience point per Background Trait, with Narrator approval.
- New Merit/Flaw — Double the cost of the Merit or Flaw, with Narrator approval. This should not happen instantaneously. It is recommended that Narrators find a way to integrate the addition of a Merit or removal of a Flaw into a character's ongoing plotline.

# Handing Out Experience

Experience in The Shining Host is represented by giving each character one to three experience points at the end of each session. The number of points awarded is based on how well the character performed during the course of the story and how active the player was in the game. The Narrator will decide how many points each player receives upon completion of the game. All players receive one point — this is standard. Exceptional roleplayers, those who played a particularly memorable part, should receive two. Three points should be awarded to those characters who portrayed acts of incredible insight and courage, making the game more memorable for the Narrator and other players. On a normal night, each player will receive one experience point.

If you are a Narrator, you should be consistent and fair awarding of experience. Do it in the open, and be prepared to explain your rationale for your decisions in accordance with the rules. If the players disagree, hear them out and make sure you know the whole story, then award experience to those who have earned it.

Be careful, as awarding too many experience points can make the characters in the game too powerful too quickly. Awarding too few disheartens the players and seriously damages their feeling of achievement.

Awarding experience points, therefore, requires a delicate balance between satisfying the players and maintaining the balance of the game. If you follow the guidelines below, you probably won't get into too much trouble, but feel free to experiment.

• **Automatic** — Each character receives one experience point per game. This represents the acquisition of common everyday knowledge.

• **Roleplaying** — Narrators should encourage roleplaying. The best way to do this is by rewarding it tangibly with experience.

• **Leadership** — You should award one point to those few players who played a starring parts in the story. Someone who got involved, and by her efforts propelled the plot, deserves a third point. It should be noted that if more than one of the players were integral in the progression of the story, then each of the players who showed such leadership should be awarded this point.

# Example of Character Creation

Bored with the politics of the undead and the endless slaughter of the werecreatures, Cindy has decided to join the local group for a game of **The Shining Host**, and is enchanted by the idea of beings who exist on the power of creativity. Having never created a changeling character before, Cindy hunkers down with the rulebook and puts on an inspirational CD, as her Storyteller, Lucas, sits by, ready to give her a hand if she needs it and answer any questions she has. The process of character creation begins.

## Step One: Concept

Cindy thinks about this stage for a while. She wants to play a character with a childlike sense of wonder, but who hides her fascination behind a tough facade. Although her character's a child of the streets, Cindy doesn't want the cynicism of that life to have gotten to her yet. Thinking it to be the best balance of these aspects, she decides her character will be a wilder, or teenage fae. When the other characters first see her, they'll see a young creature of the night, who likes to rebel against both mortal and faerie society, but when someone really gets to know her, they'll find she has an aptitude for art history and a deep love of the Dreaming. While she's definitely not evil, she has no great love of rules either, so Cindy decides her character will be Unseelie, a fae of change and chaos.

The pooka kith, a natural one for tricks and paradoxes, also seems to stand out in her mind, and she decides her character will be a pooka who can change into a lynx, as she sees something catlike in her character. Since a lynx isn't normally an animal a pooka can be, she asks Lucas if it's OK, and after thinking it over, he agrees, seeing some potential for good-natured havoc in it.

Cindy still has to pick her Legacies, her fae personality, and eventually settles on *Cerenaic* for her Unseelie Legacy and *Troubadour* for her Seelie Legacy. As her Unseelie side is usually dominant, her character normally lives life to the sensory fullest and throws cares to the wind, but those who coax out her Seelie side find a sensitive soul dedicated to romance and art. Cindy decides her character will be a runaway, but she wants to put a bit of a twist on that common theme to make her character stand out more. After some consideration, she determines her character didn't run away from home to get away from her parents, but to find them, since they mysteriously disappeared one day shortly after her Chrysalis, her awakening to her fae nature. Lucas, smelling a good future plot hook, takes note of this as well.

Cindy wants her character's name to be exotic and fae-sounding, as she always loves characters with mysterious names in novels. Following several minutes of doodling and sounding things out, she decides the name "Cybelle" contains the right balance of mystery, beauty and plain old pooka wit for her. With a better grasp of her character's concept, she moves on to fleshing it out.

## Step Two: Attributes

Cindy is now ready to pick Cybelle's Traits, and starts by setting priorities. Right away, the Social category leaps out at her — Cindy sees Cybelle as a beautiful, captivating person, and it even goes well with the pooka kith's natural talent for talking to just about anyone (not to mention talking themselves into a great deal of trouble). She selects Social as her primary category (with seven Traits). Figuring Cybelle to be a pretty naturally intelligent person, Cindy decides to make Mental Traits her secondary category (with five Traits), leaving Physical to tertiary (with three Traits), as Cybelle has been battered around a bit by life on the streets. Cindy looks at the lists of Traits — there are many that she thinks would apply, but she knows she'll have to take the essential ones first and worry about the others later. She starts with Social Traits, and winds up selecting *Alluring, Beguiling, Eloquent, Expressive, Magnetic, Seductive,* and *Witty.* For Mental Traits, she picks *Clever, Creative, Intuitive, Intuitive* and *Knowledgeable* (which reflects her art history study, and departs wildly from the street urchin stereotype). Finally, for her three Physical Traits, she chooses *Energetic, Lithe* and *Nimble;* she wishes she could pick more, but those will have to do for now, and she's still far from done.

## Step Three: Advantages

Cindy now gets to pick her five Abilities. After studying the list, she decides to take a wide range and not specialize in any one Ability, to reflect her character's diverse interests. *Performance* is Cindy's first choice, and she decides Cybelle is secretly something of a poet, since that Ability requires her to choose a type of art she pursues. Of course, Cybelle wouldn't be where she is today without some *Streetwise,* so Cindy takes that. A level of *Gremayre* goes down as well, since Cybelle has learned a thing or two about the fae during her time on the road. Ditto for the *Kenning* Ability, as Cybelle wants to be able to detect Glamour wherever she goes. With her final Ability, Cindy chooses *Melee,* since Cybelle has learned quite well how to wield a knife in her time on the street.

Next comes Backgrounds. Cindy decides to take a level of *Remembrance,* since her interest in art is fueled by dreamy memories of another time and place, and she puts a level into the *Street* Influence, to reflect her contacts in the local community. Having a sudden vision of a beautiful mask of comedy she can use to magically alter her appearance, she puts the last three levels into *Treasure,* giving herself an item fused with Glamour. She talks to Lucas about it, decides it will be a physical treasure, not a chimerical one, and eventually gets it approved. Cindy jots down what it does on the back of her character sheet, and Lucas signs it, to show other players it's authentic. She makes a mental note to buy and decorate a mask for a prop, and moves to the next phase.

Arts and Realms take a long time for Cindy to choose, since they all sound so appropriate for Cybelle, and she's fascinated by the concept of changeling

magic. Eventually, however, she figures out what her character will have, and chooses the Basic levels of *Chicanery* (*Fuddle*, *Veiled Eyes*) and the first Basic level of *Wayfare* (*Hopscotch*) for her three levels of Arts, reflecting Cybelle's tricky, elusive nature. Since she had taken both Basic powers of *Chicanery*, Cindy could have chosen instead to take the first Intermediate *Chicanery* power for her third level of Arts, but she decided that *Hopscotch* was going to be a bit more useful, as Cybelle might find herself in a situation where she needs to get away in a hurry, and Cindy moves to picking Realms to accompany her Arts. As she deals with a large number of mortals in her time on the streets, she takes three levels of the *Actor* Realm (*True Friend*, *Personal Contact*, *Familiar Face*), letting her use her cantrips on a wide range of mundane people. It's always good to be able to cast cantrips on yourself, Cindy reasons, and she takes a level of the *Fae* Realm (*Hearty Commoner*); since she has no title, this will do just fine. After tinkering a bit, Cindy has Cybelle choose to take one level of the *Prop* Realm (*Ornate Garb*), explaining it by saying Cybelle has a private taste for enchanted fashions. This step is now complete, and Cindy is nearly finished creating her little pooka.

## Step Four: Finishing Touches

Cindy copies down her beginning Glamour, Willpower and Banality Traits—since she's a wilder, she starts with four Glamour, two Willpower and three Banality Traits. She also fills in temporary Willpower and Glamour equal to her starting Traits, as all characters begin play with full Glamour and Willpower. She looks up her pooka Birthrights, and writes down her ability to shapechange into a lynx, noting that it costs one Glamour Trait to do so. She also receives an *Ingratiating* Social Trait and a level of the *Subterfuge* Ability from her second Birthright, and adds these to their respective areas. Cindy looks at her Frailty and smiles; she's going to enjoy the wordplay involved in her pooka inability to tell the truth. (Lucas, on the other hand, merely groans.) She also gains an *Untrustworthy* Negative Trait from that Frailty, and records this next to her other Social Traits, marking it with an "(N)" to show it is a Negative Trait.

Cindy reads the Musing and Ravaging Thresholds, and after contemplating them a while, asks Lucas if he would mind Cybelle taking a Musing Threshold, even though she's Unseelie. She explains that Cybelle hates Ravaging, and in fact loves to promote the spread of art around her; on these grounds, she'd like to take the *Inspire Creativity* Musing Threshold. Lucas questions her for a while, making sure she really wants this for her character (since this would be a departure from the rules), and, satisfied with her concept, approves it at last. Cindy happily jots her new Musing Threshold down.

Finally, there is the question of whether or not Cindy wants to give Cybelle any Flaws or Negative Traits in order to purchase Merits or more Traits for her character. She decides to add another *Untrustworthy* Negative

Trait, as Cybelle often seems unreliable to those around her, and takes the *Impatient* Negative Mental Trait as well, reflecting Cybelle's overly restless spirit. She takes the *Surreal Quality* Flaw, which is worth two Traits, to reflect how Cybelle's enchanting aura on those around her can get her into trouble. She knows that those Traits, along with her pooka nature, are going to make her life interesting, but she feels they reflect her character well. Plus, with these four extra points, Cindy can now buy some extra Traits or Merits and improve Cybelle a bit. She decides to improve her physical potential, purchasing the *Dexterous* and *Tough* Traits, giving her a total of five Physical Traits. With her remaining two extra Traits, she takes the *Danger Sense* Merit, reflecting Cybelle's knack for coming out of tricky situations alive. She looks the list over, sees nothing else she wants to take, and goes to the last stage.

## Step Five: Spark of Life

Cindy has finished what will go on her character sheet, and must now revisit her concept and settle some of the more intangible facts of Cybelle's life, and how she'll portray her character. How does Cybelle dress? How does she walk? Does she speak with an accent, a habitual cough, a sultry laugh? Does she pace when she's angry, or have a habit of rolling her eyes when she's lying? There are many layers of subtleties that can be added to a character when they're played, and Cindy now has to think about just how she'll convey her character to the other players in an entertaining and memorable way. She also has to give more thought to Cybelle's past and personality — she has a decent start on twisting the usual runaway stereotype, and a good cluster of motivations and goals to begin play with, but some more detail couldn't hurt. Who were her childhood friends? What was she like in school? Does she miss anyone from her mundane life? Cindy spends a while thinking about these things, until Lucas coughs loudly and she remembers she has to finish sometime, that a character is really only complete when she's been played. She'll think up the rest later, and practice her character's Traits when she plays. She passes her character over to Lucas, who makes sure everything adds up before approving her character. She's certainly already shown enough of a character and a history! Cybelle is now ready to play in the next session.

122

Abilities

Performance  Subterfuge  Melee
Streetwise
Gremayre
Dextrous
Kenning

Backgrounds
Remembrance
Street Influence
Treasure x3
(Mask)

Merits/Flaws
Danger Sense (2)
Surreal Quality (2)

Birthrights/Frailties
• Turn into lynx – One Glamour
• Ingratiating & Subterfuge Traits
• Cannot resist lying w/out a
  Willpower Trait
• Wyrd Frailty

Nimble
Lithe
Energetic
Dextrous
Tough

Clever
Intuitive x2
Creative
Knowledgeable

Impatient

Alluring    Expressive
Beguiling   Ingratiating
Eloquent    Witty
Seductive   Magnetic
Untrustworthy x2

Fuddle
Veiled Eyes
Hopscotch

●●● ○○○○○○○
□□□□□□□□□□

●● ○○○○○○○○
□□□□□□□□□□

●●● ○○○○○○○
□□□□□□□□□□

Realms

Actor x3
Fae
Prop

THE SHINING HOST

Player: Cindy
Character: Cybelle
Chronicle: Jeweled Birds
Seeming: Wilder
Legacies: Cerenaic/ Troubadour
Kith: Pooka (lynx)
Motley:
Court: Unseelie
House: Commoner
Ravaging / Musing Threshold:
    Inspire Creativity
Experience:

# Chapter Three:
## Changeling Magic

Cantrips are the powers of faerie magic, the combined efforts of a changeling to use the Dreaming to affect the world around her, enchanted or otherwise. Cantrip casting is broken into several different parts, all of which are essential to creating a particular effect.

# Arts

Arts are the distillation of raw Glamour to create magical effects for a changeling. The range of Arts represents the spectrum of ways of using Glamour to achieve certain ends, but all Arts draw upon the same pool of imaginative energy. In the old times, faeries could do nearly anything imaginable at the slightest whim, drawing on the boundless Glamour that existed before the Sundering. Modern Arts are but the faded legacies of that magical time. Arts themselves are still quite powerful, however, and thus require Realms to act as magical "funnels" through which to channel their magic in order to create any kind of constructive product. Many Kithain, particularly those involved in the fine arts, look upon an Art as a muse, the raw notion of what change or improvement needs to be made through the power of Glamour. As such, an Art is potent but still formless, and needs discipline and direction (e.g., a Realm) to be put to any measurable use. Simply having an idea doesn't guarantee anything to come of it, after all, as countless failed Dreamers can attest.

# Realms

If the Art is the muse of a changeling, the Realm is the medium through which she chooses to work. Just as an artist must choose some method of expressing herself to communicate her ideas — writing, singing, photography, sculpture or whatever — the Kithain must use a Realm to specify what the power of her Art is to affect. Doing so makes the cantrip a little more demanding, but also allows a versatile changeling with a wide range of Realms to achieve many different uses of one Art.

**For example:** The outcast sorcerer Lord Dywer has the Art of *Hopscotch* (Basic *Wayfare*). That's not too impressive on its own, but with his wide range of Realms he can achieve many different effects: with *Actor* or *Fae*, he can bestow the power to make great leaps on someone; with *Prop*, he can fire an object into the air; with *Nature*, he can give an animal jumping power, or jump higher than a thunderstorm himself; with *Scene*, he can combine another Realm to allow a whole group to spring like kangaroos on steroids; and with *Time*, he can set the cantrip to go off just when he needs it.

Thus, command of a wide range of Realms makes even the lowliest Arts formidable in the hands of wily Kithain, just as a wide range of media makes a human artist more versatile in displaying her talents. However, the power that Arts and Realms grant comes with a quirky price to be paid.

# Bunks

Bunks are the often downright silly requirements that Glamour forces changelings to perform in order to use their cantrips. Before even the smallest cantrip can produce a result, a Kithain must carry out whatever inner price her Glamour demands. This is known as a Bunk. The form the Bunk takes can be anything from quoting Keats to doing an Elvis impersonation to launching a triple backflip, but it's always interesting. Fortunately, most Kithain quickly learn the general sort of demands their Glamour makes on them, and can prepare accordingly.

A Kithain character should have a number of Bunks equal to her permanent Glamour rating written on her character sheet. In addition, the Storyteller should assign to each Bunk the number of Traits it is worth when successfully completed, and if necessary the time required to complete the Bunk. Quick, easily performed actions might be worth one Trait; longer, more complicated Bunks might be worth three or four. Truly difficult or specific Bunks might be worth five. In no case should one Bunk be worth more than five Traits. These extra Traits are called Bunk Traits, and they serve multiple purposes. They add to the number of Traits a changeling is considered to have in a cantrip-related challenge, and some Arts also use them to determine such things as the damage and duration of a cantrip.

Usually all this work should be done before play begins. Preparing thus gives Narrators time answer any questions players might have about their capabilities, as well as helping to ensure the Storyteller knows what his band of wacky fae might be up to. There should also be some way for each player to pick a Bunk randomly (numbering them works best) from her list, as this sort of luck of the draw is essential to the casting process. Players may use the same Bunks over multiple sessions if they like, but must make sure that said Bunks are re-randomized every time. Also, Kithain who use the same Bunks time and again risk gathering Banality for being so repetitive, and allow enemies take advantage of their predictable patterns. As long as the Storyteller is consulted about the legality, power and time requirement of each new Bunk, players are encouraged to make their Bunks as creative and distinctive as possible. Just keep in mind as well that all live-action rules, especially those pertaining to running, touching and performing dangerous acts still apply (more strictly than normal, actually) to Bunks.

There are no prefabricated Bunks listed in this book. You should make up your own Bunks and give them whatever names you choose. The idea is to come up with tasks that are simultaneously cogent and fun. Your Storyteller is the final authority on all Bunk Trait ratings, so don't argue too strenuously over whether something is two Traits or three. Just have fun with it — after all, that's what Bunks are all about.

# Duh

White Wolf is not responsible in any way, shape or form for hospital bills for players who decide things like actually performing a three-story fall or smoking 10 packs of cigarettes would make neat Bunks for their characters. If natural selection hasn't weeded out such folk already, the Storyteller should. Given practice, though, the time spent making up and exchanging Bunks before a session can become quite wild in and of itself!

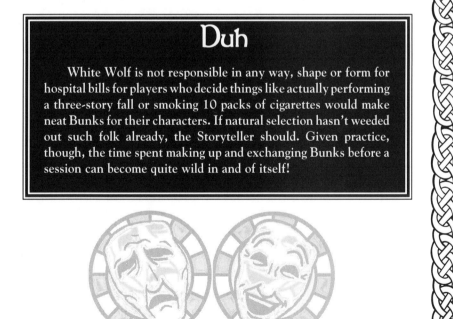

# Chicanery

This is the Art of trickery and mental deceit. It is favored by many commoner Kithain for its usefulness in dealing with mortals. *Chicanery* was one of the first Arts to be rediscovered after the Shattering. Kithain known to possess *Chicanery* are watched closely, especially by the nobility. A few nobles have become infamous for their judicious uses of this Art, although it is generally thought to be a commoner's Art and therefore "vulgar."

**Type of Challenge**: Social

**Art Note**: Many uses of *Chicanery* on unenchanted mortals are protected by the Mists. Once the cantrip ends, the mortal often forgets that anything out of the ordinary occurred. As a rule of thumb, the higher the Banality of a target, the less he remembers about this Art.

**Basic**

**Fuddle**: With this Art, you can trick the perceptions of another. This Art cannot create something from nothing, but can alter existing phenomena. Police sirens can be made to sound like barking dogs, or one person can be made to look like another, but a person cannot be conjured out of thin air, or barking dogs from silence. Furthermore, a target cannot experience anything beyond his capability; a blind person could not be made to see the ocean, but could be *Fuddled* into smelling the salt air. This Art can never be directly harmful to another, although those affected may be injured accidentally due to their confused perceptions, and if any directly life-threatening situations arise, *Fuddle* is immediately negated. Otherwise, it disappears after the passage of 10 minutes per Bunk Trait gained. The Realms required for this Art determine who is to be *Fuddled*; for example, *Fuddling* a gang of angry vampires requires *Actor* 5 (*Dire Enemy*) and *Scene* 2 (for the group). Note also that *Fuddle* cannot change a target's perception of itself.

**Type**: Chimerical

**Veiled Eyes**: With this Art, you may hide people, places or things from the eyes of others; this is not so much a sudden supernatural vanishing as it is a function of having others "filter out" the existence of the *Veiled* object. The effect lasts for as long as the target remains relatively unobtrusive (no combat, no picking up/manipulating objects, etc.), and must be recast every time the power is broken. This enchantment may be renewed on inanimate targets as often as the changeling spends Glamour (once per day, usually), but may not be renewed on living targets without a new cantrip. Characters should cross their arms to indicate that they are *Veiled*; Storytellers should be notified of *Veiled* areas.

Sluagh *Heightened Senses* and other, similar powers may be used to detect invisible objects and people as normal. Making multiple targets invisible requires the *Scene* Realm; if the caster drops the power or is discovered at any point, the cantrip is broken for the entire group. Otherwise, if one member of the group makes himself visible, the rest of the group is fine so long as they abide by the unobtrusiveness rule.

**Type**: Chimerical

**Intermediate**

**Tip of the Tongue**: *Tip of the Tongue* allows you to remove or steal specific memories and thoughts from the mind of another. The memory affected can be as minor as the color of someone's watch to the fact that the target is a supernatural being. This is also very useful in covering one's tracks and reinforcing the Mists. Note that *Tip of the Tongue* cannot add memories in any way. One 15-minute period of memory may be affected per Bunk Trait gained in casting *Tip of the Tongue*, and the effects last for one day, at which point the target may make a Static Mental Challenge against the Glamour of the caster to figure out what was done to him. Only the Realm of the target to be affected is needed for this Art.

**Type**: Chimerical

**Switcheroo**: A more refined version of *Fuddle*, this devious Art allows you to make a target believe he is something else, which can be just about whatever you tell him to be. A target could be told he was a two-headed alien, a sperm whale or a bowl of petunias, and will do his best to act the part (singing, jumping, barking, swimming or even simply standing still), so long as it doesn't directly endanger him, at which point the cantrip instantly fails. This Art costs one Glamour Trait per 10 minutes the subject is to be affected, to a maximum of the number of Bunk Traits gained in casting. For the duration of the effect, the target should adopt gestures and mannerisms as consistent with his "new shape" as possible, as he truly believes he is that thing. Kithain and other supernatural beings may cancel this Art with the expenditure of a Willpower Trait. Only the Realm of the target to be affected is needed, although you must be able to somehow tell the target what you wish him to be for the cantrip to work (talking, telepathy and even writing are acceptable). If you wish him to change roles at any time, you must communicate your wish to him.

**Type**: Chimerical

**Advanced**

**Captive Heart**: This powerful Art allows you nearly complete control over a subject's heart and mind; he becomes pliant to your commands, and you may stir his emotions at will through the power of your Glamour. This power costs two Social Traits and two Glamour Traits to use, in addition to the Bunk for the casting. However, if it works, the target gains the Negative Trait: *Submissive* x2 for the remainder of the session, and may not attack or even be rude to you as long as the *Captive Heart* is effective. You may also create a specific emotion or passion in him at any time at the cost of one Glamour Trait per five minutes of passionate experience. (Truly alien or bizarre passions allow the subject a Simple Test to resist, but success will not break the *Captive Heart* enchantment itself.) If you create a passion tied to a particular event or thing (a hatred of mailmen, or distrust of bodies of water), and the target already possesses something like that (he hated mailmen already, or nearly drowned as a child), the time of effectiveness is doubled, simply out of habit. Attacking or being obviously crude and disrespectful to the target immediately cancels *Captive Heart*, and the cantrip may not be attempted again on the same target for the rest of the session. Willpower Traits may be spent to resist *Captive Heart*, but each Trait spent allows only for a retest on the outcome of the challenge, not complete immunity. Even if he loses the original challenge, the target may attempt to resist every hour with a similar expenditure of Willpower Traits.

**Type**: Chimerical

## Chronos

This Art is the ability to control time itself. Its application is responsible for stories like "Rip Van Winkle," wherein time flows differently for mortals trapped in the lands of the fae. *Chronos* is a difficult Art to learn, much less master, and must be taught by a mentor of some kind, as even the brightest changeling can't just pick it up on his own. However, those who are patient enough learn secrets that are potent even by the standards of the fae.

**Type of Challenge**: Mental

**Art Note**: This is a rare Art for non-sidhe to have, and as a general rule, any non-sidhe using it is one Trait down, although certain commoners display a facility that offsets this penalty. Due to the potential complications inherent in the Art, a Storyteller should be present for most uses of *Chronos* and may even disallow this Art if it becomes too problematic.

**Basic**

**Wyrd**: This Art distorts the target's perception of time, confusing him and making him see things after the fact or a split second before they occur. Such confusion should be played as a dizzy stagger and a far-off look in the eyes of the target. In game terms, this effect translates into a one-Trait penalty on all challenges for five minutes per Bunk Trait gained in casting. Note that certain sidhe are immune to this Art, as are very rare commoners.

**Type**: Chimerical

**Backward Glance**: This Art allows you to look into the past. It is automatically successful if you wish to recall something from your own memory (if your memory has been altered, you remember only the alteration), although the usage still costs one Glamour Trait. You may also use this power to read the pasts of other people and places with a successful cantrip, and thus ask them for exact details of what occurred at such a time and place. Doing so is often considered somewhat rude, of course, and any character being "read" in this way will automatically sense it. The Realms used with this Art cover either what the Art is to be used on, or what the subject of the memory is. This power covers one incident and one incident alone per use, and is also useless on anything of the Mists or that has been touched by them. In no case can *Backward Glance* access a memory more than a year old. If players have problems with what can be "remembered" this way, a Storyteller should be consulted as to what "really" happened.

**Type**: Chimerical

**Intermediate**

**Dream Time**: This bizarre Art allows you to manipulate the passing of time, speeding it up or slowing it down as you wish (though no use of this cantrip can stave off the onset of Banality). *Dream Time* requires the expenditure of Mental Traits on the caster's part, so that for every two Mental Traits expended you can accelerate time or slow it down by one "degree," according to your wishes. For an object or place, a degree equals 10 years of time added or subtracted, while for a plant, animal or sentient a degree is a year added on or taken off. This cantrip cannot be cast on a target more than once per scene/hour, and the number of Mental Traits you spend cannot exceed more than twice the number of Bunk Traits gained in the cantrip casting. Premature aging caused to animals or sentients by this Art can be undone by a special casting of this Art, which has the same cost as the cantrip which inflicted the aging plus a Willpower Trait.

**Type**: Wyrd

**Advanced**

**Reversal of Fortune**: Any use of this Art must be approved and overseen by the Storyteller, as this is the power to "undo" a recent event, and it is entirely within the Storyteller's power to disallow use or even possession of this Art in a chronicle. *Reversal of Fortune* requires a permanent expenditure of one Glamour and one Willpower Trait, plus one permanent Mental Trait for each minute of peacetime or round of combat that you wish to "take back," up to a maximum of your current Bunk Traits. You must use the *Scene* Realm when casting this cantrip, and anyone outside of the range of the manipulation must stop play until the new outcome of the scenario has been determined, at which point they are told the new, true version of what "actually happened." Players cannot walk in on this cantrip while it is in effect. Instead, they must wait for the reality affected by the cantrip to "catch up" to the real world.

**Type**: Wyrd

## Dream Craft

This Art allows a Kithain to explore the Dreaming itself, in particular the Near and Far Dreaming. The Deep Dreaming is also a possibility, but only the insane or foolish go out so far, and none who do so have ever returned. This Art allows for control over and understanding of the Dreaming. While the sidhe are particularly strong at it, many commoners, particularly eshu, show a facility for it as well.

**Type of Challenge**: Mental

**Basic**

**Walk the Silver Path**: The Silver Path travels through all trods, enabling Kithain to travel from location to location within the Dreaming in (relative) safety. Leaving the path is a good way to get oneself eaten by giant chimera or trapped in a Nightmare Realm. Therefore, when traveling the Dreaming, it is a good idea to know where one is going and what might be there, not to mention staying on the Silver Path itself. This Art is designed for that exact purpose.

With the expenditure of one Mental Trait, the character becomes able to stay on the Silver Path regardless of circumstances (although this becomes a challenge if someone attempts to conceal the true Silver Path). Plus, with an expenditure of one Mental Trait per question, a Kithain may ask a Narrator about who/what is at the other end of the trod she is using, provided the appropriate Realms are used in the casting of the cantrip. (In other words, if you want to see if the sidhe nobles are really waiting for you, the *Fae* Realm of *Lofty Noble* must be invoked, etc.) The questions asked must be entirely visual in nature and may be resisted with a Mental Challenge, but must be answered truthfully if successful. Note that invisibility of any kind defeats this power except if someone is attempting to cloak the Silver Path itself.

**Type**: Chimerical

**Intermediate**

**Homestead**: This Art allows you to create stable pockets in the chaotic areas of the Dreaming, "anchoring" certain people or things against the constant shifts in the reality of the landscape. Each use of this requires the caster to expend a Glamour Trait, then one Mental Trait for each item or person to be affected. More Glamour may be required to protect truly grand or powerful things at a Narrator's discretion. Each thing so protected gains an additional "Healthy" Health Level, usable only in the Dreaming, and allows for a Static Mental Challenge to avoid penalties due to sudden shifts in the

132

local paradigm. Note that if this Health Level is lost, it cannot be regained without another casting of *Homestead*.

**Type**: Chimerical

**Advanced**

**Dream Weaving**: This Art is similar to the *Legerdemain* Art, *Phantom Shadows*, but it is more versatile. On the other hand, *Dream Weaving's* creations are confined entirely and absolutely to the Dreaming, and any encounter with mortal Banality destroys them very quickly. These creations also may not be made real by a changeling's calling upon the Wyrd — such an action instantly destroys the chimera. However, this is the Art of pure chimerical creation, and can allow a Kithain to achieve truly legendary feats. To use *Dream Weaving* requires the expenditure of two permanent Glamour Traits and one permanent Willpower Trait (more in the case of very grand creations). At that point, whatever the caster desires, be it castle, creature or chimerical item, comes into being, fully sentient and ready for existence. (The Storyteller controls the new item or being, and gives it whatever Traits and powers he and the player agree are appropriate, although the Storyteller is under no compunction to tell the character exactly what her creation is capable of.) The new creation will be friendly and grateful to its creator, and loyal if well-treated, but not necessarily a zombielike minion.

**Type**: Chimerical

## Legerdemain

Demonstrations of this Art are the basis for many mortal imitators and their sleight-of-hand and petty illusions, although the magic of Glamour allows changelings to transcend such simple tricks and affect physical reality. All sorts of effects, from perfect illusions to objects that move with no apparent source of propulsion, are possible through this Art.

**Type of Challenge**: Physical

**Art Note**: Many instances of *Legerdemain*, particularly the low-level abilities, involve an invisible force; this force can be resisted and retested by all strength-related powers such as vampiric *Potence* or Garou Gifts; however, any such considerations must be made when the cantrip challenge is undertaken.

**Basic**

**Gimmix**: This Art allows you to move things telekinetically; whatever is affected feels an invisible hand grasp it and move it about. Note that you cannot directly damage someone with a telekinetic "punch," though pushing someone off of a building might ruin his day. This Art can be used on things you cannot see, but requires you to gesture the type of action you wish the *Gimmix* to perform — lifting, pulling, etc. — in addition to whatever Bunk you have been given. *Gimmix* costs one Physical Trait per use. Note that fine manipulation such as typing or tying shoes is impossible with *Gimmix*, although actions such as flipping a switch or pushing a button are possible.

**Type**: Wyrd

**Mooch**: With this Art, you can relocate objects from one place to another, usually from someone else's pocket to your own. The object in question must be in sight or have been seen during the last minute; if neither of these are true, you cannot *Mooch* something, even if you're absolutely certain the item is still there. Living (and undead) things cannot be *Mooched* in any case, nor can the target be more than about the size of a fist or weigh more than about two pounds. Changelings who overuse *Mooch* cantrips often begin having trouble hanging onto their own possessions.

**Type**: Wyrd or Chimerical (depends on item)

**Intermediate**

**Effigy**: With this Art, you can create things from pure Glamour, copies of objects or people that you are touching or looking at. These copies are chimerical and exact in every visible, tangible way, although they do not have the original's capabilities — an *Effigy* doctor cannot diagnose or treat the sick, and the *Effigy* of a computer cannot run programs. For each "special effect" that you wish an *Effigy* to simulate, you must spend a Trait appropriate to the activity (a Social Trait for the doctor to speak, a Mental Trait for a computer to seemingly "boot up" or display static), and all challenges attempted by an *Effigy* are in fact done by you at a two-Trait penalty. *Effigy* costs two Glamour Traits, plus any costs incurred with "maintaining" the *Effigy* itself, and ceases to exist when in direct contact with Banality or whenever you cease to concentrate upon it. Note also that an *Effigy* cannot inflict anything other than chimerical damage, and ceases to exist if it attempts to do otherwise, even if made real by calling upon the Wyrd.

A Kithain using this power is at a one-Trait penalty on any challenges while using *Effigy*, and cannot engage in any stressful activity (such as combat) while doing so.

**Type**: Wyrd or Chimerical

**Ensnare**: With this Art, you can animate the features of an area so that they trap or hold a person; even if convenient features (tree limbs, cables, etc.) are not available, a successful use of this Art makes the target believe there are. This costs one Glamour Trait to enact, and the victim of *Ensnare* must make a Static Physical Challenge to break free, with a difficulty equal to the Kithain's current Physical Traits at the time the cantrip is cast (Traits from Bunks count). Additionally, you may spend Physical Traits during the casting of the cantrip, and each Trait so spent adds one to the difficulty of the Static Challenge. If the difficulty exceeds the target's Physical Traits, she is unable to break free until the *Ensnare* fades. Vampires with *Vigor* and *Puissance* may continue to contest *Ensnare* every two minutes, but receive no other benefit from their Discipline.

This power often allows for Fair Escape, and the *Ensnare* fades as soon as the caster leaves the area, the Static Challenge is won, or when 10 minutes have passed.

**Type**: Wyrd

**Advanced**

**Phantom Shadows**: This Art allows you to create illusions that mimic reality. The true nature of an illusion created thus is very difficult to discern, unless one is mystically aware or has faerie sight. The illusions in question, however, are very specific. For example, a soldier created with *Actor* would have a rudimentary uniform, but without use of the *Prop* Realm, he wouldn't have a gun. However, unlike an *Effigy*, those chimera created by *Phantom Shadows* are imbued with sentience and will seek to carry out your wishes on their own, without your needing to spend additional Traits or maintain concentration.

Any number of Realms may be woven into the illusion to make it more exact. *Phantom Shadows* itself costs a Willpower and Glamour Trait to enact, and a minimum of a Glamour Trait per day to maintain. If denied its "sustenance," a *Shadow* may even strike out on its own, seeking Glamour any way it can. Such chimera can be a nightmare to the changeling who made them, as he will also be held responsible for them. Unlike *Effigy*, these illusions can chimerically injure all creatures, even unenchanted mortals who believe in them. If made real by calling upon the Wyrd, they inflict real damage. *Heightened Senses* and the like may attempt to penetrate an illusion with a Mental Challenge, but each Realm beyond the first used in creating it puts such snoopers at a one-Trait penalty in any challenges to reveal its true nature.

**Note**: You cannot use *Phantom Shadows* to disguise yourself or anything else.

**Type**: Chimerical (any *Shadows* made real by calling upon the Wyrd cost a Mental Trait per five minutes to maintain).

**Rattle**: Much like *Gimmix*, but stronger and more controlled, the Art of *Rattle* allows you to slam and toss your opponents directly, or to put on displays of telekinesis that are nothing short of stunning. To use *Rattle*, you must spend a variable number of Physical Traits. Each Trait spent allows you to manipulate or throw 100 pounds' worth of material, or for a single target to be thrown 10 feet. Using this power for damage inflicts one Health Level and allows you to position your target wherever you want within the range dictated by your Trait expenditure. At this level of control, fine manipulation such as typing is also possible, though you must concentrate on nothing else, and can only perform the cantrip for a number of actions/minutes equal to the number of Bunk Traits gained in the casting. Most uses of *Rattle* are clearly supernatural, and are often protected only by the Mists (but beware, for one never knows when Dauntain are watching).

**Type**: Wyrd

## Naming

This is the Art of True Names and runes, the Art that allows power over letters and the inherent potential of an individual or thing. While all changelings undergo a Saining to determine their True Names, this Art goes deeper, ferreting out their powers and weaknesses simply through arrangements of words and letters.

**Type of Challenge**: Mental

**Art Note**: This Art, like *Chronos*, is extremely rare and usually known only to high-ranking members of the nobility. It is not normally available for beginning characters, and anyone seeking to take this Art should consult the Storyteller first. In no case can a character begin with more than Basic *Naming*. Any character who wishes to get far in this Art had better also have dedicated some Abilities to learning the rune languages themselves, as this Art is useless unless one knows the right runes to use. The Storyteller may disallow this Art if it threatens game balance.

**Basic**

**Rune**: With this Art, you can unleash the mystical power inherent in the words and symbols known as runes. In addition to your Bunk, you must know the appropriate rune to use this Art, and have inscribed or displayed it in some fashion related to the item or person you intend it to affect. If you do so successfully, the Traits gained from the Bunk used in the casting may be added to one challenge or test appropriate to the rune used; after that use the power of the rune is lost. (Although runes may be re-used with additional castings, they cannot be cumulative.)

**Example of play**: Baroness Rhiannon, a proficient user of the *Naming* Art, wishes to enchant a sword with a rune to let it burst into flame for a friend heading off to battle. Hurriedly sewing the rune into a ribbon, she ties the ribbon around the hilt of the blade and performs a cantrip casting that gives her four Bunk Traits. That means when her friend uses the power of the rune, the sword will flare briefly into flame, putting her friend four Traits up on one challenge while wielding the blade. After that, the rune must be re-inscribed to be used again.

**Type**: Chimerical (Wyrd for especially flashy rune effects)

**Intermediate**

**Runic Circle**: With this Art, you can create a circle or enchant a ward that can be used to protect its bearer against supernatural forces. You must take the time to inscribe the necessary runes (at least 10 minutes, real time) in the circle as well to insure that the magical protection is complete and thorough. Once this is done, you may spend a variable number of Mental Traits on the cantrip. For every two Traits spent making a ward, you receive a free retest on supernatural challenges of any kind, and attempted physical attacks on the bearer of the ward are that number of Traits down. If you created a circle, then supernatural entities must make a Static Mental

Challenge against a difficulty determined by the number of Traits expended to cross into or use their powers on anyone within the circle.

Note that retests are always used up, won or not, and that once a challenge has been successfully performed against a circle or ward, the winner of that challenge is immune to that ward or circle for the remainder of the story. Also, if a caster wishes to make the ward or circle permanent, she must permanently expend the Mental Traits involved, and a Willpower Trait must be spent each time the ward or circle is activated.

**Type**: Wyrd

**Advanced**

**Saining**: By this Art, you may discover the True Name of a subject, which in turn often gives you power or control over the item or person thus known. This Art is often used on newly awakened kithain, but can be used for other, shadier purposes. A True Name typically has from two to 20 letters (the exact number should always be determined by the Storyteller, preferably randomly) and for each Bunk Trait you gain, you learn an additional letter of the target's True Name. This process is often rather lengthy and can be resisted by the subject, even if unconsciously, for a True Name is extremely powerful in the right (or wrong) hands, and thus this cantrip is almost always a challenge.

A True Name cannot be used until all of it is known, and you can never be certain as to how many letters remain. In addition, you cannot "guess" at what letter(s) might be missing, even if you're certain only one remains; the remaining letters must be discovered by this Art to be of any use. Supernatural beings are always aware of use of this Art on them, even if they fail to defend themselves against it, and are usually not amused.

**Type**: Chimerical

**Reweaving**: By switching the runes in a subject's True Name, you may fundamentally and permanently alter aspects of the subject itself. One Trait of permanent Willpower must be expended for each use of this Art, and the target's True Name must have been gained through use of the *Saining* Art, above. If you are successful, such changes may be made as: switching Natures or Legacies, exchanging Mental Traits for Social Traits and vice versa, Seelie to Unseelie, buildings to bulldogs, Autumn People to aardvarks, and more. Any alterations done, however, must be switches, not deletions, and anything lost must be replaced in some fashion. One such change may be made per Bunk Trait gained in casting.

**Note**: The Storyteller is perfectly within her right to deny a use of this Art, increase its cost for truly radical changes, or even forbid this level of *Naming* altogether. In no case should this Art be used without a Storyteller present, and any such attempts are automatically void. A target may retest this Art at the cost of a permanent Willpower Trait per retest.

**Type**: Wyrd

**Prerequisite Art**: *Saining.*

137

## Primal

This Art allows understanding of the fundamental connection between the changeling soul and the forces of the earth and nature. Those who specialize in this Art are often nature lovers or those who feel a strong call to nature, such as trolls, selkies and ghille dhu. No *Primal* cantrip can create or otherwise have any effect on cold iron, although alloys such as steel are affected normally.

**Type of Challenge**: Physical

**Basic**

**Willow-Whisper**: This Art allows you to speak with anything you have the Realms to describe. If the cantrip is successful, you may whisper questions and conversation to your target for as long as you want, although you are required to expend a Mental Trait to work with subjects of roughly human-level sentience. Also note that many inanimate objects have little in the way of perception and memory, fascinating as they may be to talk to, and often have truly bizarre viewpoints.

This Art cannot be used to force an unwilling subject to talk, although it is most useful for communicating with people otherwise unable to talk, and sleeping targets can easily be coaxed into a conversation with a successful casting.

**Type**: Chimerical

**Eldritch Prime**: The user of this Art can make one of the following natural elements appear: fire, water, earth, wind or wood. The cantrip causes the element to appear in its most natural form possible: water showers down or bubbles from the ground, wood sprouts or an object "grows" bark, etc. The element can appear in an unnatural setting (an indoor rainstorm, or an inferno from a cigarette lighter) but cannot appear in an unnatural or manufactured form (no party ice or finished marble floors). A basic use of this Art costs one Physical Trait in addition to the requirements of the cantrip casting. If used to injure another, this Art costs two Physical Traits per Health Level of damage to be inflicted, up to a maximum number of levels equal to the Bunk Traits gained. If used to create a protective shield, this Art costs one Physical Trait per Health Level the barrier has, up to a maximum of the Bunk Traits gained in casting. The shield is considered to have Physical Traits equal to its caster's for the purpose of challenges.

Note that once the element is created, the cantrip must be recast if the caster wishes to control it — a summoned fire is out of control unless you cast a second cantrip with as many Bunk Traits as the first. If you are simply creating natural elements, the *Nature* Realm is all that's required for this Art. If you use it to affect another individual, however, you must use both *Nature* and another appropriate Realm.

**Example of play**: Sam the boggan is being chased by an angry Garou. Looking for a way to distract the werewolf, Sam uses *Eldritch Prime* to create a blazing fire — he could not have one simply spring up from the linoleum of his kitchen, but fortunately he left his oven door open while cooking, and the roast had started to smolder a bit. With a successful casting, Sam gets his burst of flame, the werewolf ignites and runs off, and the plucky boggan begins thinking about how to get the smell of burnt fur out of his kitchen.

**Type**: Wyrd

**Intermediate**

**Heather Balm**: This is the Art of healing, and is most useful to those who walk the way of the warrior. This Art works on both real and chimerical wounds, as well as aggravated injuries. Wounds healed by this magic heal permanently, leave no scars or marks, and cost the subject no permanent Traits. All that is needed to heal chimerical wounds is a successful casting, and as a result the subject heals a number of Health Levels equal to the Traits gained by the Bunk. For actual wounds, an expenditure of one Glamour Trait per Health Level healed is required (up to a maximum of Traits gained from the Bunk). Aggravated wounds are treated like regular physical wounds, except two Glamour Traits are required instead of one. Regeneration of limbs and the like is possible at the Storyteller's discretion, but such a feat would likely require the expenditure of a permanent Glamour Trait, as well as a day of rest in a glen or freehold. This cantrip may be cast any number of times on a subject, but must be cast separately for each subject affected. Bonus Health Levels from magics like *Oakenshield* cannot be healed. Items may be repaired with this cantrip as well; the Storyteller must determine how much Glamour must be spent before an item can be considered repaired.

**Type**: Chimerical (Wyrd if the damage to be healed is aggravated)

**Oakenshield**: This Art allows you to fortify a subject with the mystical power of your Glamour. The Health Levels the target gains are considered to be extra "Bruised" Health Levels, and apply to both chimerical and actual wounds. By casting the cantrip and expending a number of stamina-related Physical Traits up to the number gained by the Bunk, you may bestow additional "Bruised" Health Levels upon the target. These levels last until they are lost through damage, Banality erodes them, or a month passes (game time). You cannot cast this cantrip on a target again until any levels gained previously in this manner are lost. Any others attempting to do so will find the efforts result in similar failure (but not until it's too late).

**Type**: Chimerical

**Prerequisite Art**: *Heather Balm*

**Advanced**

**Holly Strike**: This Art allows you to inflict damage upon a person or thing. The wounds done by this are actual damage, in the form of vicious cuts and bruises, and use of this Art on another changeling save a Dauntain is a clear violation of the Escheat.

139

With a successful casting and the expenditure of two strength or damage-related Physical Traits (*Ferocious, Muscular, Brutal*, etc.), you inflict a Health Level of actual damage upon your target. The subject may resist by spending a Willpower Trait and entering Physical Challenge; no powers other than stamina-related ones may be used, but no retests are allowed, either. Note that each casting allows for only one level of damage; you cannot pile on the Physical Traits and completely devastate someone in a single blow, though repeated castings may have the same effect. The source of this Art is always obvious, and the method of defense (Willpower) is instinctive; you must mention it to your target when you use it if she is unaware. If you use *Holly Strike* on an object, the Storyteller determines how many Health Levels of damage the object can absorb before it breaks.

**Type**: Wyrd

**Elder-Form**: This mighty Art allows you to alter your own shape or that of another, provided you have the appropriate Realms to do so. While in your new form, you gain all the advantages and drawbacks of that shape, and should consult the Storyteller about changes to appropriate Traits (rocks gain a lot of Physical Traits, but say bye-bye to almost any Mental or Social Challenges). Sentience, if not speech, is always retained, and you retain at least a basic perception of the outside world, though your perceptions are limited by the form itself. Turning into a fantastic form such as a dragon or vampire does not confer any special powers on you — a dragon shape might have wings and claws, and a vampire shape might be pale and fanged, but the dragon could not breathe fire, and the vampire wouldn't get Blood Points or Disciplines.

However, the change is real for all other purposes, and cannot be seen through with powers such as *Heightened Senses*. Using this Art on yourself requires merely a successful casting and the expenditure of a Willpower Trait; particularly difficult or bizarre forms may also require a Static Physical Challenge (Bunk Traits count). When you use *Elder-Form* on someone else, it is a direct Physical Challenge, and the subject may be forced into the desired form for one hour per point of Willpower you spend. The subject may spend Willpower every hour to retest and revert to his original state. Under no circumstances does the transformation last for more than a single night or day.

Also, any contact whatsoever with an unenchanted being immediately forces a test of the transformed changeling's Glamour versus the interloper's Banality — you may work a Bunk to add to your rating, but that is all. If you fail, you immediately revert to your original form. Due to the radical character changes often involved in such transformations, you must consult the Storyteller when using this Art, and you must adopt props, dress and/or gestures that clearly indicate your altered state to the other players. Casting this Art on another requires two Realms — one for the subject and one for what you wish the subject to become. Casting it for yourself it requires only the Realm of whatever it is you wish to become.

**Type**: Wyrd
**Prerequisite Art**: *Holly Strike*

## Pyretics

This Art allows for control over fire, which has fascinated and inspired mortals for centuries. Both chimerical and actual flames can be created through use of this magic, although neither sort are quite what they seem at first.

**Type of Challenge**: Physical
**Basic**

**Will-o'-the-Wisp**: With this Art, you can create a glowing ball of chimerical flame, and with the expenditure of a Physical Trait you can command it to seek out or illuminate a particular person or object. In game terms, for the next half-hour you may ask people out of character if they have seen the person or thing you are looking for and where it was heading; they must answer truthfully. If the person is using a power to conceal himself, such as *Obfuscate* or *Veiled Eyes*, you must still somehow penetrate the veil in order to locate him. That effect holds firm, although the *Will-o'-the-Wisp* leads you to your target's general vicinity regardless of what spells she has on her, and players must still tell you if they saw the target even if their character couldn't. If used to illuminate an area, the *Will-o'-the-Wisp* gives off light equal to a full set of candles. Note that the flame created by this cantrip can never injure anyone, although people illuminated by this cantrip make easy long-range targets. Any such attacks are two Traits up.

**Type**: Chimerical
**Intermediate**

**Prometheus' Fist**: With this Art, you can create chimerical or normal fire that completely engulfs the target of your cantrip. For chimerical flame, a Glamour Trait must be spent to start the flame, in addition to a Physical Trait for each turn you wish to maintain the blaze. To create actual flame, you must spend a Willpower Trait to initiate the flames, followed by a Glamour Trait per turn. In either case, the flames inflict one Health Level of damage per turn a subject is engulfed, although the target may attempt to put out the flames with a successful Physical Challenge; if this works, the cantrip immediately ends. If you use this cantrip on yourself or on a melee weapon such as a sword, you inflict an extra Health Level of damage for close combat challenges, and the victim or anyone else near you must win or tie a Simple Test to avoid catching fire for each turn or challenge she is exposed to you. Note that chimerical flames cannot harm you, whether released or not, but actual flames can once they are released from direct control.

**Type**: Wyrd or Chimerical
**Advanced**

**Star Body**: With this potent Art, you may transform your target into living flame, while allowing it to keep all of its intrinsic powers and abilities: a cat is still a cat, a sword is still a sword, a person can still think, speak and move freely, etc. and so on. The flames are magical, and cannot harm you; they also do not ignite materials unless the transformed creature or the owner of the transformed object wills it to be so. Two extra actual Health Levels of damage are done in combat by the extreme heat of the flames, although a Simple Test must be won for each of these additional levels of damage, and; as with *Prometheus' Fist*, above, the target must win or tie a Simple Test to avoid catching on fire herself. This Art costs the caster a Willpower Trait and one Glamour Trait per turn it is in effect, and cannot exceed a number of turns equal to the Traits gained from the Bunk.

**Type**: Wyrd

## Soothsay

The Art of divination, Fate and prophecy, *Soothsay* is used by many changelings to help them understand Glamour, the Dreaming and themselves. Some type of oracle — Tarot cards, Ouija board — is useful, but is in no way required. Any cantrip performed with such a divination aid in addition to the Bunk required is considered to be one Trait up. Although *Soothsay* is thought to be a commoner's Art, many nobles privately find it very useful for court intrigue, and at least one court seer inevitably has a high level of ability in this Art. A particularly ardent user of this Art sometimes catches glimpses of the Dreaming itself… or of the rather nasty fate which awaits one of her companions.

**Type of Challenge**: Mental

**Art Note**: Because of its clairvoyant and precognitive powers, *Soothsay* can place great demands on Storytellers, and its power over Fate can potentially unbalance some situations. It is recommended that Storytellers keep tabs on all omens and predictions to avoid confusion later on, or perhaps assign a Narrator, called the Oracle, to keep track of uses of this Art (this is an especially good idea in large chronicles). A sense of the balance of Fate must also be maintained for this Art to avoid becoming overly powerful; Fate rewards the faithful and the dedicated, but never lets one person get away with murder indefinitely.

**Basic**

**Omen**: This Art allows you to get a glimpse of your place in the tapestry of Dan, and can be a helpful guide to finding the resolve to face a difficult decision. Once the cantrip has been cast, a perception-related Mental Trait (*Discerning, Observant*, etc.) must be spent while you spend 30 seconds simply watching the setting around you. You may speak or walk at a normal pace, but any action more involved than that immediately negates this cantrip. This power may be granted to others by use of the appropriate Realms, although you must still pay the Mental Trait. A sign of some kind representing the character's current position in the world and a possible near future will appear. What exactly the sign is and how cryptic it may be are up to the Storyteller, but the affected character feels refreshed and reassured of her place in the tapestry of Fate, and instantly regains one Willpower Trait. A target may only benefit from this effect once per day/session. At the Storyteller's discretion, a character who blatantly ignores Fate's advice (i.e., one who walks into a burning building after watching his likeness burn to ash) may not receive the benefit of this Art, which is instead replaced by a feeling of dread and uneasiness.

**Type**: Chimerical

**Fair is Foul and Foul is Fair**: This Art allows you to bestow minor doses of good or bad luck on a target. A target will not suddenly die or win the lottery, but some elements in her life which might have fallen either way will now tip in the direction you wish. After making a successful cantrip casting, you may choose to bestow a bonus or penalty of Traits equal to the number of Traits gained in the casting on one Trait category of the target for the duration of one challenge. You may choose the category (Mental, Social, Physical) and challenge to be affected, and this bonus or penalty applies to all retests or overbids of this challenge as well. At the Storyteller's discretion, this Art can have less direct results, although in this case you cannot control what will occur, merely identify which situation the cantrip alters. Multiple castings of this Art are not cumulative, although those who continually use it to inflict bad luck on others often find their cantrips rebounding back on them.

**Example of play**: Devon the sluagh wishes good fortune to befall his friend Lord Magbane in a coming duel. He casts *Foul is Fair* on him, and performs a four-Trait Bunk. Now, during one challenge in the duel, Devon may give Lord Magbane four extra Physical Traits for the purposes of ties and overbids, most likely giving him enough Traits to carry the challenge. If Magbane won but his foe retested the challenge, those extra Traits would still apply.

**Type**: Chimerical

**Intermediate**

**Tattletale**: This Art allows you to scry on distant places or things, and you may make challenges with such perception-related Abilities as *Kenning* once contact has been established. Use of this Art requires only that the cantrip casting be successful, although those hidden by supernatural power must be defeated in another direct challenge to be detected. Five minutes of uninterrupted, out of game meditation must be performed in addition to the usual Bunk, and one Mental Trait must be spent for each sense beyond sight that the user wishes to invoke. Targets cannot detect a use of *Tattletale* unless they have some kind of supernatural power which specifically allows them to detect such things as astral presences and distant observers, and have such

143

powers already activated at the time the Art is used. There is no limiting range for *Tattletale*, although mystic wards such as those created with *Weaver Ward* and the like automatically stop it. The time limit for uses of *Tattletale* is one minute per Bunk Trait gained. Due to the divinatory power granted by this Art, a Storyteller's help should be required when *Tattletale* is used.

**Type**: Chimerical

**Advanced**

**Augury**: The Art of prophecy and prediction, this mysterious power allows you to look into the future in a limited fashion. You must spend 10 minutes in out of game meditation to activate this Art, in addition to the demands of the casting Bunk, and spend a Willpower Trait. Once this is done, you may ask one question related to the Realms you invoked in the casting per Bunk Trait gained. Obviously, a Storyteller is required to answer your questions. You have no control over how far in the future the cantrip looks, though typically the farther out you go the hazier the visions are. While most of the time you will receive visions of events that will happen later this session, there's no guarantee that will be the case, and in any event the future is always a very fluid thing.

Those who overuse this power, especially for trivial concerns, tend to begin receiving visions of their own unpleasant ends and other similarly disturbing sights instead of their desired prophecies. As *Augury* can be a complicated and frustrating Art for a Storyteller to deal with, it may be modified or even disallowed if it places too many demands on the Storyteller.

**Type**: Chimerical

**Prerequisite Art**: *Tattletale*

**Dance of Destiny**: A particular favorite of eshu, who view this power as a dance with Lady Fate herself, this Art makes you destiny's darling… for a time. Accidents which should cripple come short of harm, enemies find it difficult to land even the slightest shot, and fortune just seems to throw things your way. Once under the effect of the *Dance of Destiny*, you automatically win all ties in contests, regardless of who has more Traits. Plus, you gain the advantage of a Fair Escape once per combat you enter, as Fate covers her tracks. You may also ignore the first wound delivered to you in combat unless it is given by cold iron, and you may not be Surprised by your foes. This Art lasts for one hour.

At the Storyteller's discretion, if you invoke this power in a non-combat situation you may find yourself temporarily receiving free favors or Influence Traits as Fate makes things break your way. The duration and limits of this type of effect are up to the Storyteller, but should be in line with the daring, dramatic nature of the Art, and not simply used for a quick power grab. Similarly, if you use this Art on a regular basis in combat simply to butcher and humiliate foes, you'll eventually find Fate favoring the new "underdog" against you! However, for her attention, Fate requires you prove your willingness to throw stability to the wind; each time this power is invoked, in addition to the casting Bunk, you must permanently give up something of value to you, be it a treasure, chimera, Influence Trait or other important possession. If the item is deemed insufficient or to have been deceitfully offered (in her guise as the Storyteller), the Art may simply not function, or it might even turn against you.

**Type**: Chimerical, as this Art is always is careful to manifest in ways which appear coincidental.

## Sovereign

The Art of command and leadership, *Sovereign* has traditionally been wielded only by rulers (i.e., sidhe), although this has changed in recent years. *Sovereign* allows court functions to be held even in the chaotic and unruly modern world, and gives nobles the power to command duties that still need to be done, even if no one will shoulder them voluntarily. Many wilders, particularly Unseelie commoners, consider this Art "fascist traditionalism," and despise those who use it openly.

**Type of Challenge**: Social

**Art Note**: This Art is traditionally known only by the sidhe nobility, although in recent years some commoners, particularly commoner nobles, have gained access to its secrets. Although its usage is somewhat unpopular in the democratic modern age where everyone has a multitude of rights, even the most rebellious commoner acknowledges that this Art is sometimes needed to keep order and get things done. *Sovereign* has absolutely no effect on someone with a higher *Title* Background rating than yourself, no matter how strong a cantrip you cast.

**Basic**

**Protocol**: This Art allows you to enforce the rules of changeling court protocol on the target, and is generally used by nobles as part of court preparations to prevent Unseelie outbursts and hyperactive childlings from disrupting the proceedings. A subject may resist by spending a Willpower Trait. This cantrip lasts until sunup or sundown, or whenever the caster or reigning noble cancels it. The Storyteller has final say over what is suitable "protocol" for a situation, and is encouraged to come up with different types of court settings, each with its own rules and traditions. Use of this Art on multiple targets requires both the Realms of the targets and the *Scene* Realm.

**Type**: Chimerical

**Dictum**: This is the power of command. While not as powerful as a *Geas*, *Dictum* allows you to issue a direct request and it expect it to be carried out, provided it takes no more than half an hour to perform and does not place the subject in direct danger. (A request to guard someone or something is usually acceptable.) A Willpower Trait may be spent to counter the request, but this must be declared during the casting of the cantrip to be effective. However, as a *Dictum* must be carefully worded and formally stated in some fashion to the target, most changelings are aware when one is about to be directed at them, though Prodigals and mortals may not be. Telepathy or other nonverbal communication of the request is permissible as long as the target can clearly understand you; language is a barrier to *Dictum*. Furthermore, unless they are shielded by the Mists, most beings will remember this cantrip's use on them, which has made this Art an increasingly sore spot with wilders and commoners as of late.

**Type**: Chimerical

**Prerequisite Art**: *Protocol*

**Intermediate**

**Grandeur**: This Art is proof as to why noble changelings, particularly sidhe, were once regarded as gods and goddesses by the rest of the world. By performing a Bunk and expending one appearance-related Social Trait (*Gorgeous*, *Dignified*, etc.), you become imbued with unearthly grace and radiance. So awe-inspiring are you that any who wish to harm or even directly speak ill of you must first overcome you in a Social Challenge (you receive the benefits of your Bunk Traits in regards to all such challenges). Failure means the subject must mutely humble herself before you. The effects of *Grandeur* last for one hour, and should be indicated by holding your arms down and away from your sides (like *Majesty* in **The Masquerade**). Anyone who still wishes to contest you, even after losing the first necessary Social Challenge to do so, must spend a Willpower Trait for each retest, and automatically loses on all ties, regardless of who has more Traits.

**Type**: Wyrd

**Weaver Ward**: This Art allows you to place a lock or seal on an object, door or entrance, preventing it from being used or entered. The area is quite literally unable to be picked up, touched, passed through or used by anyone except those who you designate when you create the *Ward*. Optionally, you may create some kind of password, bit of poetry or other "security measure" that deactivates the *Ward* temporarily. (**Note**: Only those who actually use the correct security measure will be able to use/open the Ward; others can't come along for the ride without also pronouncing the proper phrases.) *Weaver Ward* requires a Willpower Trait in addition to the cantrip, but lasts until the next new moon, another cantrip cancels it, or Banality erodes it. A Storyteller should be notified when this Art is used, and an envelope or sign describing the nature of the magic at work should be placed on/near the object.

This Art is directly opposed by the *Wayfare* Art of *Portal Passage*, and a successful casting of that cantrip will negate this Art. However, the user of *Portal Passage* must spend a Willpower Trait in addition to the other costs of the Art, and if the caster of the *Ward* is actually present, he may contest an intrusion with a Social Challenge — the winner's cantrip holds, although all Traits bid are still spent.

**Type**: Wyrd

**Advanced**

**Geasa**: *Geasa* are patterns of Glamour that direct, guide and control behavior. Unlike the *Chicanery* Art of *Captive Heart*, *Geasa* doesn't control the target's mind. It does, however, give him a mission and the drive to perform it. Some *Geasa* are created through an oath, some simply by raw magical force, but all have fundamentally the same basic effects. A *Geas* itself is a quest of some kind that the target must perform to the letter; if not, he suffers from some kind of curse, usually named at the time of the casting and always related to the size and scope of the task. Failure to deliver doughnuts to the duke's wife might earn you embarrassing b.o. for a week, but failing to hunt down and slay the Unseelie raider who slaughtered the freehold's childlings with cold iron might mean your own death as well. The other type of *Geas* is a *Ban*; where a *Geas* is a quest, a *Ban* is just that — a prohibition against doing something, or else the subject suffers a curse of some kind. Exiles are often placed under a *Ban* to never return. Placing a *Geas* requires a successful cantrip and the expenditure of a Glamour and Willpower Trait; an oath of some kind is atmospheric, but not necessary. The subject may only resist fulfilling the *Geas* (without being cursed) by attempting to fall into Banality, hoping the *Geas* becomes null (if you have a *Geas* to kill someone who's already dead, for example, it becomes nullified), or by spending a permanent Willpower for each retest of the *Geas* Challenge.

Obviously, this Art is weighted in the caster's favor, but it is also used most sparingly by the few nobles who have it, for fear of risking a commoner revolt. A Narrator at least should be present when this Art is cast, and should record the exact wording of *Geas* or *Ban* to avoid any semantic arguments in the future.

**Type**: Chimerical

## Wayfare

The Art of traveling and movement, *Wayfare* was created by bards, warriors, heralds and messengers. Those who possess it and advertise the fact are carefully watched, as this Art allows for passage into restricted places; however, many modern changelings find its mobility and utility a very handy combination. As an added benefit, the Mists cover the more blatant uses of this Art handily. While *Wayfare* is costly (almost all of its effects are Wyrd effects), it is often the only solution to a problem facing a changeling. In many cases, this Art also provides the generally nonviolent Kithain the means to get a variety of Fair Escapes when confronted by hunters or bloodthirsty Prodigals.

**Type of Challenge**: Physical

**Art Note**: Many uses of *Wayfare* involve radical changes in the location of a player or group of players; these changes should be done in a "timeout" fashion, where the game pauses while the players take up their new positions. During the this timeout, no actions may be taken by any involved party unless a Storyteller specifically permits it (such as snapping off a shot at a flying changeling before he gets away).

**Basic**

**Hopscotch**: This Art allows you to make fantastic leaps and bounds. By using this power you can jump up to the top of a building and down again safely, provided of course you pay the necessary cost of the cantrip. A Fair Escape may be called due to a use of this Art, depending on the nature of the jump and the attacker trying to prevent the getaway. A person wielding a hatchet won't be able to strike a bounding faerie, but one with a shotgun might. ("Pull!") Once you perform the Bunk, a variable number of Physical Traits may be spent to enact the magic of the cantrip; each Trait allows for a jump one story straight up or 10 feet across — it also covers jumping back/getting down safely. The action should be paused while the jumping is done, but the jump takes place at the conclusion of the turn's sequence of actions. If you use the Art on another, you must still be the one to spend the necessary Traits.

**Type**: Wyrd

**Quicksilver**: This cantrip allows you to move as fast a flicker of light, but only for an instant. After performing a successful Bunk, you may spend Glamour Traits to gain additional actions this turn at a rate of one per additional action, up to a maximum of the number of Bunk Traits you received in casting the cantrip. No other tests or challenges are required. So if you received a three-Trait Bunk, you may not spend four Glamour for four extra actions, only three. These extra actions take place at the same time normal extra actions take place (e.g. *Rage*, *Celerity*, etc.), and opponents without extra actions may only bid defensive Traits (*Tough*, *Stalwart*, etc.), cannot injure the changeling as a result of the challenge, and are at a Trait penalty equal to the number of actions that have been unanswered so far this turn.

**Type**: Wyrd

**Prerequisite Art**: *Hopscotch*

**Intermediate**

**Portal Passage**: With this rather cartoony Art, you can open a portal in order to pass through a barrier. The portal will either conform to the barrier (at its smallest) or will be as large as a normal door (at its largest). This Art requires a Physical Trait in addition to the cantrip to enact, although a challenge is necessary if banal witnesses are nearby; failing the challenge means the cantrip is null. (Use the most banal observer for the purposes of the challenge.) More Physical Traits may be spent to hold open the door for 10 seconds per extra Trait, although no more Traits may be spent this way than Bunk Traits were gained in casting. This Art is directly opposed to *Weaver Ward* (above), and magical wards made by Prodigals may also block it — consult the Storyteller for a ruling if such is the case.

**Type**: Wyrd

**Wind Runner**: You can use this Art to make yourself or others fly. This can be momentary levitation or an all-out flight. Note that the Mists, thankfully, protect the mortal world from such visuals, and observers will quickly forget such a blatant demonstration of Glamour. ("No, officer, I certainly did not see a man with butterfly wings flying over the Wilsons' backyard!") This Art cannot be used to hurl objects or people telekinetically, nor can it be used to levitate them against their will; that is the province of the *Legerdemain* Art. *Wayfare* requires the expenditure of a Willpower Trait, plus a number of Physical Traits for every target affected, plus a number of Glamour Traits equal to the number of minutes you wish the targets to stay aloft (you get a free minute, but after that you're on your own). This time must be divided for each target involved, i.e., if you have eight minutes and four targets, you can give each person two minutes, or give one person six minutes and the others 30 seconds each, etc. You are included in this time division, although only you (and a Narrator) know how much flight time everyone has left. Once in the air, the targets have complete control over their own flight, for however long it lasts. This Art is a wonderfully flashy way to make a Fair Escape, but be warned that this is a tough cantrip to keep going for extended periods of time, and can be truly nasty to try to re-cast when falling….

**Type**: Wyrd

**Advanced**

**Flicker Flash**: This Art allows you to blink out of existence in one place and reappear in another. Both the subject and the destination should be known to you, or you should possess at least a part or image of them. If you do not, then you must make a Simple Test after the cantrip is cast. Failure means you take a Health Level of actual damage from the stress of the journey, and win or lose you still must count out fifteen seconds on the ground of disorientation during which you may only defend yourself. In addition to the regular cantrip, this Art requires a Glamour Trait and takes five real minutes to complete; this process may be made instantaneous (and thus a Fair Escape) with three Glamour Traits. During the time of transport you must not be interrupted, or the cantrip fails. In addition, you must make a Static Physical Challenge if the destination is particularly far off, well hidden or well guarded. Failure means you arrive in an embarrassing or inconvenient place. Difficulty is the Storyteller's discretion. With her permission you may transport multiple targets at once, but each additional Realm or target costs another Glamour Trait.

**Type**: Wyrd

# Realms

## Actor

This Realm has to do with people, characters of all kinds. Normal mortals, enchanted mortals, Autumn People, mages, psychics, Dreamers, werewolves, vampires, fomori and wraiths are all covered by the *Actor* Realm, even if in animal or otherwise not quite human form. However, other changelings (including Nunnehi), Dauntain and chimera are not covered by the *Actor* Realm, even if in their mortal seemings or if the Wyrd has been called upon.

**Note**: Realms must be purchased with experience in the order in which they are listed below. You can't start with *Dire Enemy*; you have to work your way up through *True Friend* and so on.

**True Friend** — A well-known confidant, a buddy.

**Personal Contact** — You must have had a long conversation with this person, and you must know his name.

**Familiar Face** — You need know nothing about this person, but you must recognize her face.

**Complete Stranger** — You must know absolutely nothing about a person, although she cannot be hostile toward you.

**Dire Enemy** — You must be opposed to someone, hate him, or otherwise be in competition or conflict. Note that a friend with whom you are engaged in a genuine conflict falls under this Realm as well.

## Nature

This Realm comprises the awesome forces, elements, denizens and raw power of Nature.

**Raw Material** — Unliving, organic materials: wood, rope, paper, etc. If it's inorganic or still alive, it doesn't fit this Realm.

**Verdant Forest** — Living, organic plant material (not animals).

**Feral Animal** — Living, nonsentient animals. Self-aware and intelligent animals, or such creatures as werewolves or vampires who have assumed animal forms, are not covered by this Realm; they are covered by the *Actor* Realm. (You might not know this until it's too late, though.)

**Natural Phenomena** — Natural phenomena: weather, volcanic eruptions, geothermal reactions, etc.

**Base Element** — Governs natural elements in pure form (Einsteinium is right out), or the traditional four: fire, air, water and earth.

## Fae

This is the Realm of the fae, and includes all things of the Dreaming: the kith, the Nunnehi, chimera, cantrips, freeholds, treasures, faerie seemings, etc.

**Hearty Commoner** — Commoner changelings only. Note that you may not know if another changeling has a title until after the cantrip fails.

**Lofty Noble** — Noble changeling. Any sidhe or commoner with the *Title* Background is fair game.

**Manifold Chimera** — Chimera and chimerical items of all kinds.

**Elusive Gallain** — All fae beings not covered above: Nunnehi, inanimae and anything else unexplainable but still related to the Dreaming.

**Dweomer of Glamour** — Anything composed of Glamour: cantrips, treasures, freeholds, glens, dross, etc.

## Prop

This Realm allows you to affect the tools of humanity. In distinguishing a *Prop* from a *Nature* object, you must be aware that anything touched or worked by the hands of humanity (or the fae) becomes a *Prop*. For example, if a man found a branch while walking through the woods and used it as a walking stick, it would not become a *Prop* until he shaved off a few inches to make it more comfortable or carved his name into it. Until then, it would still be covered by the *Nature* Realm.

**Ornate Garb** — Objects commonly worn: jewelry, clothing, even tattoos.

**Crafted Tool** — An item having no moving parts. Weapons like clubs, staves, and swords apply; guns or even morningstars do not.

**Mechanical Device** — An item that has moving parts, but does not require fuel (or electricity).

**Complex Machine** — An item containing with movable and sometimes electronic components, but which is relatively easily explained and understood. Toaster ovens, cars, printing presses, and many nocker machines — when explained to other nockers — fall into this category.

**Arcane Artifact** — Any item not covered above, usually with complex components.

## Scene

This Realm determines the area of a casting. It allows cantrips to have an "area-effect" quality, when combined with other Realms to affect the targets within that area. For example, a changeling would need *Actor* as well if she wanted to use *Scene* 4 to affect a playground full of kids.

**Closet** — Up to 10 square feet.

**Bathroom** — Up to 20 square feet.

**Guest Room** — Up to 50 square feet.

**Ground Floor** — Up to 100 square feet.

**House** — Up to 500 square feet.

## Time

This Realm allows you to put a "delay" on a cantrip; you can then leave the area, confident that your cantrip will take effect at a later time. This Realm may be combined with any cantrip in order to delay its activation, although high Banality erodes the effectiveness of cantrips that ware delayed too long. The downside of this Realm is that for each level of the Realm you use, you're considered to be one Trait down for the purposes of the challenge related to the cantrip. If *Time* is used in combat, the number of turns delay you pick corresponds to the number of challenges that must pass before the cantrip takes effect. You need not use the full amount of time delay possible for a level of the Realm, but once you cast, the delay cannot be changed without canceling the cantrip somehow.

**That Instant** — Up to one turn/five second delay.

**Just A Moment** — Up to three turns/30 second delay.

**One Mighty Minute** — Up to 10 turns/one minute

**Nice Siesta** — Up to one scene/hour (whichever comes first).

**What Was I Saying?** — Up to one week.

# Cantrip Casting Made (Relatively) Simple

The following steps are the order that all cantrip casting must follow. Though they may seem complicated, once practiced they (Bunks aside) go as fast as any other challenge in live-action. Also, while the Golden Rule remains in effect, it is recommended that players and Storytellers be familiar with this system before any changes are made to it, as excessive tinkering can easily throw the balance of changeling magic out of whack.

## 1) Art

The first thing you have to do is decide what Art you'll be using in casting the cantrip. There can never be more than one Art involved in a cantrip, and the Art must be defined as either chimerical or Wyrd (specified in the Art description). Chimerical cantrips affect either only enchanted beings (Kithain, enchanted mortals or Prodigals, chimera) or appear coincidental to the mundane world, and thus do not directly violate the laws of reality. Wyrd cantrips affect both realities in a direct and obvious way, and are only protected by the Mists. A Wyrd cantrip automatically costs an extra point of Glamour.

## 2) Realm

You must decide how it is you'll perform your fae magic, or what you'll use it on, by picking a Realm. Typically your choice of Realm describes what you will affect with your Art, although you can get quite creative with your interpretation so long as the Art doesn't specify otherwise (and the Storyteller permits). For example, a changeling who wishes to use the *Hopscotch* Art on a mortal but who doesn't have the *Actor* Realm might try using the first level of *Prop* to catapult the mortal's clothing (and hope the mortal doesn't die from the resulting wedgie). Not all Realms are necessarily compatible with all Arts, however, and the Storyteller's judgment is final in deciding what combinations do and don't work.

At this point, you must also declare it if you are using the Realms of *Scene* (to affect a group or area) or *Time* (to delay the time the cantrip will take effect) in addition to whatever other Realms the cantrip requires. If your kith has an Affinity with the Realm you wish to use, you are one Trait up on any tests related to the cantrip.

**Note:** To affect a group of animals or sentients, such as another band of changelings, you must combine the right level of *Scene* with the appropriate level of *Fae*.

### 3) Bunk

Randomly select a Bunk and perform whatever action(s) it requires. Numbering the Bunks on back of your character sheet and having someone else call out a random number works best, although any random system can work. At this time a Glamour Trait may also be expended to allow you to select randomly one additional Bunk. Both of these Bunks must be performed for the cantrip to be successful, but doing so can greatly increase the changeling's chances of success, as both Bunk Trait totals are added together. Keeping track of the number of Bunk Traits gained is quite important to some Arts, as Bunk Traits are always added to the number of Traits a changeling has for the purposes of the challenge itself, and can determine such things as damage and duration of a cantrip. Failure to perform the Bunk(s) immediately cancels the cantrip.

Once the Bunk is complete, the player may immediately move on to the rest of the cantrip casting phases. If the Bunk requires a player to perform an action which their character is currently capable of but which the player cannot or will not do, he may opt to sit out for an amount of time recorded on the character sheet by the Storyteller as being equivalent to the time that performing the Bunk would have taken. During this time, the player must count aloud (this can be waived if the Bunk takes several minutes or more), and he may still be interrupted as normal, which may in turn negate the cantrip. He must also describe what his character is doing to any other characters in the area who would notice, and he is still capable of interaction with those in the game to the extent the Bunk itself might allow.

**Note:** A player may, due to the demands of preference or circumstance, choose to pass on performing a Bunk by spending a Glamour Trait. This action must, however, be declared before the player would have been assigned a Bunk for a cantrip; you can't wait to see if you've gotten a lousy or complicated Bunk and then decide you'll skip it. Any cantrips that use Arts which require Bunk Traits to operate cannot be performed without a Bunk, although cantrips which merely add Bunk Traits to a caster's bid or determine the duration of the magic can allow for this substitution; the caster simply is considered to have zero Bunk Traits for those purposes. Sometimes, however, a changeling needs a quick cantrip so badly he is willing to accept this reduction in power.

## 4) Realm Check

You reveal to the target (or to the Storyteller, if the target is an animal, place, or thing) what Realm you used to cast the cantrip. If the Realm you chose is inapplicable, for whatever reason, your cantrip immediately fails. For example, if you used the Realm of *Hearty Commoner*, and found out your target had been knighted, your cantrip is immediately rendered void. If there is a irresolvable dispute over the accuracy of the Realm, a Storyteller or Narrator should be consulted — their judgment is final in all cases. **Note**: All Traits spent and actions taken up to this point are still considered spent and/or performed, even if the cantrip fails.

## 5) Banality

The target may now choose whether or not to use its Banality in its defense, or the Kithain asks the Banality of an item or area from a Storyteller or Narrator. Everything has a permanent Banality rating ranging from zero to 10, with 10 being the highest; each permanent Banality Trait allows the target to go up one Trait on any cantrip-related tests or remove one Simple Test retest for the cantrip in question, though choosing to use Banality in this way immediately earns the user a Trait of temporary Banality. If the target is an item or area, its permanent Banality either sets the difficulty of any Static Challenges against the item/location or removes one Simple Test retest per Trait; it may not "actively" use Banality to resist, and does not gain additional Traits or Banality. If you are performing a cantrip in the presence of Banal witnesses, but not directly on those witnesses, the difficulty of any Static Challenges is still automatically at least the rating of the observer with the highest Banality rating.

## 6) Tests

Perform any tests or challenges required by the Art, following any rules or guidelines about retesting as specified in the Art description. Each Art notes the type of challenge — Physical, Mental or Social — that it requires. The rule of thumb to use when testing is:

• Against an object or place, it is either a Simple Test or a Static Challenge with the Storyteller.

• Against an animal or another mortal, fae or Prodigal, it is always a regular challenge against that character unless otherwise specified. Unlike a regular test, however, your target doesn't have to bid a Trait from the same category as you do.

If you are attempting to cast on a group of characters by using the *Scene* Realm, treat it as a regular group challenge, with all the retest and Trait rules of a cantrip in effect. So when casting against another player, unless the Art says otherwise, assume it's a normal rock-paper-scissors challenge of the appropriate category.

## Average Banality Ratings

Since players will inevitably seek out Prodigals, mortals, and other amusing playthings not strictly of the enchanted stripe, the following chart is a general indication of the Banality levels of such creatures to use when casting cantrips. If at all possible, however, a target's individual personality and outlook should be weighed when assigning Banality, as this chart is just a quick and dirty reference. Prodigals and other characters who possess the Merit: *Faerie Affinity* should subtract at least two from the ratings given for their Banality (to a minimum of 1, of course).

| Target | Banality Rating |
| --- | --- |
| Children | 3 to 5 |
| Natural spirits | 4 |
| Wraith | 4 |
| Drunks | 5 |
| Lunatics | 5 |
| Tradition mages | 5 to 7 |
| Malkavian and Ravnos vampires | 6 |
| Normal humans | 6 to 7 |
| Werewolves | 7 |
| Wyrm creaturs | 7 |
| Mummies | 8 |
| Other vampires | 8 to 9 |
| Autumn People | 8 to 10 |
| Technocracy mages | 9 to 10 |

## 7) Retests

Assume no retests are possible unless otherwise stated — Simple Tests are often an exception to this, and sidhe of House Eiluned may use the Boon of their house to retest any cantrip they cast (but not which is cast on them). Additionally, a fae with the *Gremayre* Ability and the same Realms as the caster used may spend levels of this Ability to retest a cantrip cast on her on a one-for-one basis, although she cannot retest her own cantrips this way. Note that a target may not necessarily realize a cantrip has been cast on him, even if he wins a challenge, unless some evidence is provided or it is somehow brought to his attention. Of course, a pooka screaming out an obscene limerick as the prelude to a violent *Holly Strike* cantrip might just tip someone off that something's not quite right, and Prodigals (or worse yet, Dauntain) are often adept at noticing faerie magic.

## 8a) Sucess – Now Pony Up

If your cantrip succeeded and the Art requires any Trait expenditures, you must pay them at this time. The effects of the cantrip should of course be explained to the target(s), as well as to all in the area who would notice the effects and/or might soon also be affected by them. All Bunk Traits gained are immediately lost. Standard cantrip casting costs, in addition to whatever might be required in the Art description, are as follows:

• A Wyrd cantrip costs one Glamour Trait. If a changeling has called upon the Wyrd to make his fae self physical reality, all cantrips are automatically considered Wyrd.

• Chimerical cantrips cast on enchanted beings or inanimate things cost no Glamour.

• Any cantrip cast on a Banal target costs one Glamour Trait. (This is not cumulative with the cost of a Wyrd cantrip above.) Banal targets are unenchanted mortals or Prodigals, "sleeping" fae, and anyone without a Glamour rating. Note that having Banal witnesses doesn't count for this requirement.

• Choosing to perform a cantrip without a Bunk costs a Glamour Trait.

• A Glamour Trait may be spent to put a changeling one Trait up on a cantrip Challenge; up to five Glamour Traits may be spent this way on a single cantrip. This is cumulative with Bunk Traits.

• A Glamour Trait can be spent to gain one additional Bunk for a cantrip.

• Use of the *Scene* or *Time* Realms purely as a modifier — to increase area or delay the cantrip's effects — costs an additional Glamour Trait.

## 8b) Failure – Ouch!

If the cantrip failed, and the target actively used Banality to resist the cantrip (to get Traits up on the challenge, etc.), the Kithain who lost gains an additional Trait of Banality. Also, she loses any Bunk Traits she gained from the cantrip at this time.

# Examples of play

## Contested Challenge

Random, a pooka in a jam, wants to cast a cantrip using the Advanced *Wayfare* Art, *Flicker Flash*, to teleport himself away from Marie, an eshu he's accidentally annoyed. He knows he's not nobility, so therefore he can use his Fae Realm of *Hearty Commoner* to affect himself. Jim, Random's player, notes that he has no Affinity for the Realm in question; if he did, he'd be one Trait up on any challenges already. He's picked his Art and his Realm to use, so he moves on to the next stage: the Bunk. He could skip this step by spending a Glamour Trait, but Jim feels he's going to need the Traits when it comes to a challenge — Marie out-muscles him by quite a bit, and *Wayfare* Arts call for a Physical Challenge. So he bites the chimerical bullet and decides to do a Bunk, praying for a quick, easy one.

Random has a Glamour of five, which means he should have five Bunks written on his sheet. Jim asks Marie's player, Sarah, to pick a number between one and five to randomly determine his Bunk. She picks number three; that corresponds to *Whistle Tunelessly*, a four-Trait bunk (and an easy one!). This means that for the Physical Challenge required by the *Wayfare* Art, Random will be four Traits "up" — considered to have four more Physical Traits than he actually does if the challenge comes to a tie or an overbid. Random could spend Glamour and get another Bunk, but he's already looking at a four-Trait Glamour expenditure to instantly teleport himself (a requirement of this *Wayfare* power), and he might not have the time to do two Bunks anyway; *Whistle Tunelessly* will have to do. Random whistles a few bars of his favorite song as Marie closes in, and thus completes his Bunk just in time. (Jim can skip the Realm check phase in this case, since he knows the Realm is correct because he's using it on himself alone; it's awfully unlikely that he was knighted and didn't notice!) Furthermore, since the cantrip doesn't directly affect her, Marie can't elect to use her Banality to resist Random's cantrip. She'll just have to hope her knife hand is quicker than his magic. The two are now ready to challenge.

Marie declares she'll attack Random as her action: "I'll *Ferociously* stab your pink pooka butt!" Random doesn't have to declare a specific Physical Trait for his bid, since he's casting a cantrip. The two do rock-paper-scissors, and both play rock, producing a tie. The two then compare Traits. Marie has seven Physical Traits, and Random has only four, but wait — he gets to add the four Bunk Traits from *Whistle Tunelessly*, bringing him up to eight Physical Traits. Random wins, and Marie cannot retest, so the lucky pooka vanishes an instant before the chimerical dagger would have found his Adam's apple. As he moves to his new location, Jim notes that he has lost the Bunk Traits from the cantrip, bringing him back down to four Physical Traits again.

## Static Challenge

Count Brendan Beaumain, sidhe hacker extraordinaire, is doing a bit of legwork to try to rescue his love, Kelli, from a nasty gang of redcaps . Climbing up onto the roof of a building overlooking their hideout, he decides to use his *Wayfare* Art of *Hopscotch* to jump off the building and sail gracefully over the walls into the compound. He has prepared the *Hopscotch* Art, the Fae Realm of *Lofty Noble* (for himself), and since he wants the better chance of success Bunk Traits give him (and has a lot of time on his hands), he gets the Storyteller to pick a number to select his Bunk. The Bunk turns out to be *Gluttony*, which requires the count to smoke an entire pack of cigarettes at once, and is a four-Trait Bunk. The count carries cigarettes for just such an occasion, but his player, Pete, doesn't smoke (and even if he did, that would probably be a little much for him). He instead looks at the time the Bunk requires him to sit out if he doesn't want to perform it in actuality — one minute. Pete sits out of play, counting out loud, for a minute, during which time the count is considered to be puffing away. If anyone approached, Pete would have to tell her what she saw the count doing, and she could interact with him if she liked. Fortunately for the intrepid sidhe, nobody knows he's up here, so his Bunk is uninterrupted.

At the end of allotted time, Pete stands up and resumes playing (and hacking and coughing) the count normally. Pete asks the Storyteller the Banality level of the area, since no one is actively opposing him, and is told it is a six. That means the Static Physical Challenge from the *Wayfare* Art will be against a difficulty of six Traits. The count is a little wimpy, with only three Physical Traits normally, but the four Bunk Traits he got from the *Gluttony* Bunk bring him up to seven — just enough to have a chance at this challenge! He shoots rock-paper-scissors against the Storyteller and wins. The count, coughing as quietly as he can, soars off the roof, ready to give those dirty rotten redcaps quite a scare.

# Chapter Four:
## Systems and Rules

# Time

Time in **Mind's Eye Theatre** works as it does in real life, moving forward relentlessly. During gameplay, pretty much everything is played out in real time, and players are expected to stay in character unless a rules question necessitates a stop in the action.

During the course of a story, it is assumed that a player is *always* "in character." There is a reason for this: Dropping out of character ruins the atmosphere for everyone involved, and players should do so only under certain circumstances. If a player wishes to talk through challenges or needs to take a break, he should inform a Narrator and should not interact with any of the other players while out of character. By schmoozing with an in-character player, you're taking her out of the game as well — and robbing others of the chance to interact with her character.

The only other reason for dropping out of character during gameplay occurs when a Narrator calls for a "hold." This may be necessary to resolve a dispute or to change the scene if the story requires it. When "Hold!" is called, all players within hearing distance must stop whatever they are doing until the Narrator calls out the word "Resume." Holds should be kept to a minimum, since they interrupt the flow of the story, but matters of safety, honesty and fairness are *always* good reasons for a hold.

# Challenges

During the course of most stories, there inevitably comes a time when two or more players will come into a conflict that cannot be resolved through roleplaying alone. This system allows for conflicts to be resolved simply and quickly, whether they're firefights or tests of will. This faceoff is called a challenge. In most cases, a Narrator does not need to be present when a challenge is played.

## Using Traits

Before you can begin to learn how challenges work, you must first understand what defines a character's abilities. You create a character by choosing a number of adjectives that describe and define that person as an individual. These adjectives are called Traits, and are fully described in Chapter 2 of **The Shining Host**. These Traits are used to declare a challenge against another character or against a static force represented by a Narrator.

## Initial Bid

A challenge begins when a player "bids" one of her Traits against an opponent. At the same time, she declares what the conditions of the challenge are, e.g. firing a gun or attacking with a rapier. The defender then decides how to respond — either by relenting immediately (and accepting the conditions of the challenge) or by bidding one of his own Traits.

During bidding, players should only employ Traits that seem sensible within the context of the situation. In other words, when bidding Traits, a player should use Traits from the same category as her opponent does, whether Physical, Social or Mental. Experienced players may offer each other more creative leeway, but only by mutual and prior agreement.

If the defender relents, she automatically loses the challenge (for example, if she were being attacked, she would suffer a wound). If she matches the challenger's bid, the two immediately go to a test (described below). The Traits bid are put at risk, as the loser of the test not only loses the challenge, but the Trait she bid as well.

## Testing

Once both parties involved in a challenge have bid a Trait, they immediately go to a test. The test itself is not what you may think — the outcome is random, but no cards or dice are used. The two players face off against one another by playing Rock-Paper-Scissors (see below). It may sound a little silly, but it works. If you lose the test, you lose the Trait you bid for the duration of the story (this usually means the rest of the evening). Essentially, you've lost some of your self-confidence in your own capabilities. You can no longer use that Trait effectively, at least not until you regain confidence in your Traits.

A test works like the moment in poker when the cards are turned over and the winner is declared. There are two possible outcomes of a test: either one player is the victor, or the result is a tie.

If one player wins, then the loser accepts the conditions of the challenge (taking a blow, losing a staredown, etc.) and gameplay resumes. In the case of a tie, the players reveal the number of Traits they possess in the category which they have bid (Physical, Social or Mental). The player with the lesser number of Traits loses the test and thus loses the challenge. Note that the number of Traits you've lost in previous challenges (or for any other reason, such as a Flaw) count toward this total.

You may lie about the number of Traits you possess, but only by declaring fewer Traits than you actually have — you may never say that you have more Traits than you actually do. This allows you to keep the actual number of Traits you possess a secret, although doing so may be risky.

The challenger is always the first to declare his number of Traits. If both players declare the same number of Traits, the challenge is considered a draw and both characters lose the Trait(s) they bid.

**Example of Play**: Marie the eshu has caught up with that pesky pooka Random, and is about to put some hurting on him. She gets within combat range, and makes her initial bid ("Time to start singing soprano from a *Ferocious* kick, bunny boy!"). In response, Random tries simply to evade her attack and get away, so he bids *Nimble* ("I'm far too *Nimble* for you to catch!"). They test, and both shoot Scissors — a tie. They must now declare the number of Traits they have to resolve the tie. Marie has nothing to hide, so she declares all seven of her Physical Traits. Random, on the other hand, only has four. He now suffers a wound, as well as losing the *Nimble* Trait he bid, and Marie can choose to continue to attack him if she wishes. To say that Random is not loving life at this point is a serious understatement.

Incidentally, certain advanced powers allow some characters to use gestures other than Rock, Paper and Scissors. Before players can use these gestures in a test, they must explain what they are and how they are used.

## Rock-Paper-Scissors

If you don't happen to know (or remember) what we mean by Rock-Paper-Scissors, here's the concept: you and another person face off and, on the count of three, show one of three hand gestures. "Rock" is a basic fist. "Paper" is a flat hand. "Scissors" is represented by sticking out two fingers. You then compare the two gestures to determine the winner. Rock crushes Scissors. Scissors cuts Paper. Paper covers Rock. Identical signs indicate a tie.

## Adjudication

If you have question or argument about the rules or the conditions of a challenge, you need to find a Narrator to make a judgment. Try to remain in character while looking for a Narrator. Any interruption in the progress of the story should be avoided, so work problems out with other players if it is at all possible. If you don't know the exact correct application of a certain rule, try to wing it rather than interrupt the flow of the story. Cooperation is the key to telling a good story.

### Complications

There are a number of ways in which a challenge can be complicated. The above rules are enough to resolve most disputes, but the following rules help to add a few bells and whistles.

## Negative Traits

Many characters have Negative Traits; Traits that an opponent can use against a character. After you have each bid a Trait during the initial bid of any challenge, you can call out a Negative Trait that you believe your opponent possesses. If he does indeed possess the Negative Trait, your opponent is forced to bid an additional Trait, although you must still risk your one Trait as usual. If he does not possess that Negative Trait, you must risk an additional Trait. You may integrate as many Negative Traits as you wish one by one during the initial bid phase of a challenge, as long as you can pay the price if you're wrong.

If your opponent does not have additional Traits to bid, then your Trait is not at risk during the challenge. Additionally, if you guess more than one Negative Trait that your opponent cannot match, you gain that many additional Traits in the case of a tie or an overbid. The same works in reverse, favoring your opponent if you do not have additional Traits remaining to match incorrect Negative Trait guesses.

**Example of Play**: Sir Killian, pooka knight, is trying to impress Raphael, a Toreador vampire, into coming along with him to investigate a strange disturbance. Killian starts with his initial bid ("I'm very *Persuasive* about my recruiting efforts."), but Raphael, in no hurry to run off with a bunch of fae, responds with his bid ("I'm too *Dignified* to be seen running around town with a bunch of kids."). Sir Killian then suggests that Raphael is *Callous* ("I know you're *Callous*, but you've got a personal stake in this."). However, Raphael does not possess this Trait ("I'm not *Callous*; I just don't want to go!"). Now Sir Killian has to risk an extra Trait, such as *Beguiling*, if he wants to continue the challenge.

It can be risky to bid Negative Traits. If you're sure you'll be successful, though, the use of these Traits can be a great way to raise the stakes for your opponent, perhaps to the point where he relents rather than risk additional Traits. Just make sure your sources are good before you try....

164

## Overbidding

Overbidding is the system by which experienced characters (who often have considerably more Traits than younger opponents) may prevail in a challenge, even if they lose the initial test. An experienced grump with 18 Social Traits should be able to crush a fledge with five. This system is designed to make that possible.

### Using Overbids

Once the players have made the test, the loser has the option of calling for an "overbid." In order to do so, you must also risk a new Trait; the original one has already been lost. At this point, the two players reveal the number of Traits they possess, starting with the player who called for an overbid. If you have at least double your opponent's number of Traits in the appropriate category, you may attempt another test. As with a tie, you may state a number of Traits less than the actual number you have and keep your true power secret. This can be dangerous, though, unless you are completely confident in your estimation of your opponent's abilities.

**Example of Play**: Lord Vandermere, an Unseelie sidhe magician, is being annoyed by a childling named Remi, who persists in trying to prank him when he has wizardly business that needs attending. Vandermere tries to scare her away with a Social Test ("I am far too *Intimidating* for you to do this to me."), while she persists in playing with him ("I'm too *Witty* to ignore, you big dork!"). They test, and Remi wins, but Vandermere, confident he has enough Social Traits to crush this pest, calls for an overbid. He imperiously announces that he has 14 Social Traits, and Remi admits that she only has five. Vandermere risks another Trait ("I am now using a *Commanding* tone of voice to get you to leave me alone!"), and they do another test. This time Vandermere wins. Remi must scurry away to pester someone else while Vandermere goes and advances his evil machinations. Vandermere loses the first Trait he bid, as does Remi, but thanks to the overbid he has now won the test itself.

A challenger who fails on a normal Social or Mental Challenge must wait at least five minutes before attempting the failed challenge on the same target again (and not after spending the next four and a half minutes arguing the rules call with a Narrator, either). This does not include tests that are failed but later redeemed through overbids.

## Static Challenges

Sometimes you may have to undergo a challenge against a Narrator rather than against another player, such as when you are trying to pick a lock or break a code. Under such circumstances, the Narrator chooses a difficulty appropriate to the task you are attempting and you bid the appropriate Trait, then immediately perform a test against the Narrator. The test proceeds exactly as it would if you were testing against another character. Of course, you may overbid in a Static Challenge, but beware, because the Narrator can overbid as well.

Sometimes Narrators may leave notes on objects, such as books and doors. These notes indicate the type of challenge that must be won for something to occur (such as understanding a book, opening a door or identifying an artifact). With experience, you may learn how difficult it is to open a locked door. However, difficulty ratings can be as different as lock types.

## Simple Tests

Simple Tests are used to determine if you can succeed at something when there is no real opposition. Often used when determining the extent of a Discipline's effect, most Simple Tests do not require you to risk or bid Traits, although some may.

When a Simple Test is called, players use the Rock-Paper-Scissors test against the Narrator. In most cases, the player succeeds on a win or a tie, although at Narrator discretion, it may be necessary for the player to win.

# Health

A character in **The Shining Host** has four Health Levels that represent the degree of injury the character has suffered: Healthy, Bruised, Wounded, and Incapacitated. If a Healthy character loses a combat challenge, she becomes Bruised. If she loses two, she becomes Wounded, and so on. Note that a character has four levels of Health each for both the mundane and enchanted world — these wounds must be counted separately. If a character is injured chimerically as well as actually, he takes the highest level of damage for consideration of wound penalties. Chimerical and "real" damage should not be combined in any way, shape or form.

**Example of Play**: Lord Thomas Magbane, sidhe warrior of House Gwydion, has had a rough day on the field. He's been shot by a group of mortals and attacked by a raging dragon chimera. In game terms, he has taken a Bruised Health Level of actual damage (from the gunshot), and has been Wounded chimerically (from the dragon's claws). When considering wound penalties, he ignores the Bruised actual level and suffers only the effects of being chimerically Wounded, because he is more injured chimerically. This does not mean the Bruised level of actual damage has gone away; it simply means that he's feeling more pain from the dragon's claws. If the situation had been reversed and Thomas had been Wounded by the gunshots and Bruised by the claws, he would ignore the chimerical pain in favor of the actual one — the difference in the two examples being that unenchanted mortals wouldn't be able to see his chimerical wounds (and thus believe him an excellent mime — brrr), whereas the gunshot is pretty obvious to anyone, enchanted or otherwise.

• **Bruised** — When a character is Bruised, she is only slightly injured, having perhaps suffered a few scrapes and bruises, but little more. In order to enter a new challenge, a Bruised character must risk an additional Trait. Thus, in order to have even a chance in a challenge, a Bruised character must bid at least two Traits.

• **Wounded** — When a character is Wounded, she is badly hurt. She might be bleeding freely from open wounds, or may even have broken bones. A Wounded character must bid two Traits to have a chance in a challenge. In addition, she will always lose when she ties during a test, even if she has more Traits than her opponent. If she has fewer Traits, her opponent gets a free additional test.

• **Incapacitated** — When a character is Incapacitated, he is immobilized completely out of play for at least 10 minutes. After 10 minutes has passed, the character is still immobile and may not enter into challenges until he has healed at least one Health Level. He is at the mercy of other characters, is only capable of whispering and is barely aware of his surroundings while in this state. A character who takes another wound in this state dies, chimerically or otherwise.

## Healing

Although changelings possess some Arts which allow them to withstand and recover from damage with greater ease than mortals, they are still very delicate creatures, particularly when compared to such Prodigal combat machines as vampires or werewolves. The balance between faerie and mortal halves results in a creation of a being that is both finely balanced and yet vulnerable in two worlds.

• **Chimerical Damage**

Chimerical damage represents damage caused to a changeling's faerie self, and is not detectable to unenchanted beings. A changeling may be in great pain from a chimerical sword wound, but normal mortals will be unable to treat or even see anything other than someone doing an excellent rendition of a person in pain. A changeling "killed" by chimerical damage does not truly die, but merely falls unconscious and forgets her faerie nature for a time; the number of Banality Traits she possesses determines how long she remains comatose, and what of the Dreaming she remembers upon waking. Chimera and chimerical weapons inflict chimerical damage, unless otherwise noted, as do certain Arts.

Chimerical damage may also be aggravated. Aggravated damage is a deep wound on the fae self that cannot be healed in quite the same way as normal chimerical damage. While aggravated wounds are often quite dramatic-looking, and changelings can be so badly chimerically wounded as to be missing eyes or even limbs, chimerical wounds are not simply blood and guts injuries. Instead, they represent damage to the hold the Kithain has on his faerie self. Suffering too many aggravated wounds drives a changeling to forget his fae nature temporarily or (in rare and horrible cases) permanently. Still, the ability to let loose "without consequences" remains an important reason most changelings only battle each other chimerically.

• **Actual Damage**

Actual damage is the type of damage caused by most every normal, non-chimerical or enchanted source: guns, bombs, knives, fists, feet, swords, clubs, etc. — all the tools and toys of the modern world that are not chimerical. Fire, vampire fangs, werewolf claws and even certain sorts of treasures cause aggravated damage in real life.

## Recovering

A changeling can recover Health Levels at a rate of one actual wound per day of full bed rest and good sleep. Chimerical wounds can also be recovered in this way, or a changeling can choose to spend a temporary Glamour Trait to heal a Health Level's worth of chimerical damage. Glamour cannot be applied to actual damage.

Aggravated wounds, either actual or chimerical, cannot be healed with a day of rest and/or Glamour Traits; they require three days of bed rest per Health Level and a Willpower Trait each to heal fully, at least without magical attention.

Health Levels, normal or chimerical, are completely refreshed if the wounded changeling spends a night of undisturbed rest in a freehold. They awaken completely healed, although they do not receive the usual benefit of Glamour or Willpower from sleeping in a freehold. Aggravated wounds of either type heal at a rate of one level per night of sleep in a freehold, but no additional charge is needed. Only one changeling may benefit from a freehold's healing powers per night, and they must be kept near the balefire that powers the freehold to do so.

Health Levels lost to cold iron in any form are always considered aggravated actual damage; each such wound level suffered also garners the changeling a temporary Trait of Banality.

# The Mob Scene

During the course of many stories, you are inevitably going to be drawn into a challenge in which several people are involved. Multiparty challenges can be confusing, but if you follow these simple guidelines, you shouldn't have much difficulty in resolving them. These rules are most useful in combat challenges, but they can be used with nearly any sort of group challenge.

The first thing you need to do is to decide who is challenging whom. This is usually obvious, but when it's not, you need a quick way to work things out. Simply have everyone involved in the challenge count to three at the same time. On three, each player points at the individual he is challenging.

The first challenge that must be resolved involves the person who has the most people pointing at him. Determine which category of Traits is most appropriate — Physical, Social or Mental — for the challenge. Each player pointing at the defender bids one appropriate Trait, and the group chooses a leader. The attacking group cannot exceed five people — physics demands that there is a limit to the number of individuals who can attack a single person at one time.

The defender then bids as many Traits as there are people opposing him. If he does not have enough Traits to do so, he automatically loses the challenge. If he does have enough Traits, he performs a test against the chosen leader of the attackers. The rest of the challenge continues as normal, although only the group leader can compare and overbid Traits.

If the defender wins the test, he remains unharmed, but he can choose to affect only one member of the attacking group — usually by inflicting one wound (as during combat). Additionally, the attackers lose all Traits they bid. If the attackers win, they may inflict one wound, and the defender loses all the Traits he risked.

After the first challenge is concluded, go on to the next one. Continue the process until each character who has declared an action has been the target of a challenge or has donated Traits.

### Order of Challenges

Some players wonder exactly how to respond when challenged. Typically, if someone initiates a Physical Challenge, the defender can only respond with Physical Traits. He cannot respond by using a cantrip or another ability until after the first challenge has been completed. Some cantrips, which specify this contingency in their descriptions, are the exceptions to this rule. Social and Mental Challenges work the same way.

## Combat

The basic challenge system used in **The Shining Host** has already been presented. This section contains a few basic modifications to the combat system and elaboration on it.

Combat is the usual intent behind Physical Challenges. Essentially, combat involves two characters in physical conflict. The players agree what the outcome of the challenge will be, each player bids an appropriate Trait, and a test is resolved, determining the victor. The following rules allow for variances to those basic rules, such as situations using surprise or weapons.

The agreed outcome of a Physical Challenge usually involves the loser being injured. This is not, however, the only result possible. For instance, you could say that you want to wrest a weapon from your opponent's hands or that you're trying to trip him. In short, the result of a challenge can be nearly anything the two parties agree upon, from slapping someone's face to dramatically throwing someone through a window. The results of a combat

169

challenge may also be different for both participants. (For example, a rampaging redcap may wish to attack the satyr who offended her, while the satyr may just want to escape pronto).

## Surprise

If a player does not respond within three seconds of the declaration of a Physical Challenge, the character is considered to have been surprised — he is not fully prepared for what's coming. Sometimes a player is busy with another activity, doesn't hear a challenge or is playing a character who just isn't prepared for the attack (i.e., the character is led into an ambush). It is considered highly improper to sneak around whispering challenges to try to get an element of surprise.

Surprise simply means that the outcome of the first challenge in a fight can only harm the surprised defender, not the challenger. For instance, if a player did not respond in time to an attack, but still won the challenge, the challenger would not be injured. Furthermore, if the challenger loses the test, she may call for a second challenge by risking another Trait, since she was operating from the benefit of surprise. With the second challenge, play continues, and winners and losers of a challenge are determined as normal. Overbidding is permitted for both challenger and challenged in surprise situations.

Surprise is only in effect for the first challenge of a conflict; all further challenges are resolved normally, as explained below.

## Weapons

**No real weapons are ever allowed in Mind's Eye Theatre games.**

Even nonfunctional props are forbidden if they can be mistaken for weapons. This system does not use props of any kind, nor are players required (or allowed) to strike one another. Weapons are purely an abstraction in this game. Weapon cards, which display the facts and statistics of a particular weapon, can be used instead. The damage a weapon inflicts is limited only by mutual agreement, although it is generally assumed that an injury incurred from a blow reduces the target by a Health Level.

While some weapons have special abilities, most weapons give their wielders extra Traits, although sometimes a Negative Trait disadvantage offsets this advantage. Each weapon has one to three extra Traits; you can use these in any challenge in which you employ the weapon, but you cannot use them in place of your Traits when placing your initial bid. Instead, they add to your total when comparing Traits during a tie or an overbid (for instance).

Opponents may use a weapon's disadvantages, or weaknesses inherent in the weapon, in precisely the same way they do Negative Traits. The weapon's Negative Traits can only be used against its wielder and only when appropriate to the situation. For instance, if you're firing a longbow and your opponent wants to apply the weapon's Negative Trait *Clumsy* against you, you can ignore that Negative Trait if you've taken the time to set up your shot beforehand.

If your opponent names your weapon's Negative Trait and it is appropriate to the situation, you suffer a one-Trait penalty (i.e., you are required to risk an additional Trait). If your opponent calls out a Negative Trait that doesn't apply to the situation, your opponent suffers a one-Trait penalty in the challenge.

Along with your character card, you carry cards listing the statistics for your weapons. Weapon cards specify the capacities of each weapon and allow other players to see that you actually possess a weapon — when you have a weapon card in your hand, you are considered to be holding the weapon.

Each weapon also has a concealability rating. If you cannot conceal a weapon, you must display that card at all times — you cannot, for example, pull a two-handed sword out from under your trenchcoat. Optionally, you can pin weapon cards to your shirt, indicating that, for instance, you have an unconcealable weapon slung over your shoulder.

Note that some weapons have special abilities, such as causing extra Health Levels of damage or affecting more than one target.

### Bidding Traits with Weapons

During a normal hand-to-hand fight, you bid your Physical Traits against your opponent's Physical Traits. However, if you're using *Archery*, you can use Mental Traits instead. If your opponent is also using a bow or other ranged weapon (crossbow, spear, Roman pilum), he too bids Mental Traits. If your opponent is not using a distance weapon and is merely trying to dodge, the attacker uses Mental Traits to attack, while the defender uses Physical Traits to dodge. This is one of the few instances when Traits from different Attributes are used against one another.

**Note**: Obviously, we can't go into every single variety of sword, dagger, shotgun and shortbow extant in the Gothic-Punk world. The weapons listed below are generalized examples, designed with ease of play (and not necessarily historical accuracy, per se) in mind. Kithain often use both modern and archaic weapons as they go from the enchanted to the mundane world, which means that a well-armed knight might well carry both a longsword and a gun. Please keep this in mind before getting upset over the fact that you're not going to find Trait listings for every implement of destruction ever designed in this game.

### Weapon Examples

• **Knife/Dagger** — This easily concealed weapon is very common.
Bonus Traits: 2
Negative Traits: *Short*
Concealability: Sleeve

• **Club** — This can be anything from a chair leg to a tree limb.

Bonus Traits: 2

Negative Traits: *Clumsy*

Concealability: Short cloak

• **Pistol** — The classic handgun, from flintlock to Saturday Night Special.

Bonus Traits: 2

Negative Traits: *Loud*

Concealability: Pocket

• **Broken Bottle** — A good example of a weapon made from scratch.

Bonus Traits: 1

Negative Traits: *Fragile*

Concealability: Sleeve

• **Shotgun** — A powerful weapon that fires a spray of pellets.

Bonus Traits: 3

Negative Traits: *Loud*

Concealability: Trenchcoat

**Special Ability**: A shotgun may affect up to three targets if they are standing immediately next to each other and are at least 20 feet from the person firing the shotgun. This is resolved with a single challenge against the group. The Traits risked are against the entire group. Up to three separate tests are performed (one for each target). In this fashion, it is possible for an attacker to simultaneously wound up to three targets with one challenge. If any of the three defenders wins, the attacker loses the Trait; however, it is still good to be used in the challenge against the other targets of the test. Also, a shotgun can do two levels of damage to a target standing within five feet.

• **Short sword** — This blade is usually 18 to 24 inches long and used for stabbing.

Bonus Traits: 2

Negative Traits: *Short*

Concealability: Short cloak

• **Longsword** — This single-edged blade is nearly impossible to conceal.

Bonus Traits: 3

Negative Traits: *Heavy*

Concealability: Full-length cloak

• Submachine Gun — This weapon is very powerful, but difficult to conceal.

Bonus Traits: 3

Negative Traits: *Loud*

Concealability: Jacket

**Special Ability**: The submachine gun may affect up to five targets if they're standing immediately next to each other and are further than 10 feet from the person firing the gun. This is resolved with a single challenge against a group (as described in the section for shotguns).

• **Greatsword** — This blade is impossible to conceal, and requires two hands to use.

Bonus Traits: 5

Negative Traits: *Heavy, Slow, Clumsy*

Concealability: (sound of hysterical laughter)

• **Rifle** — Favored by hunters and snipers.

Bonus Traits: 3

Negative Traits: *Loud*

Concealability: Not in this lifetime.

• **Longbow** — This weapon has tremendous range and shocking power, but is so tall that it cannot be used indoors.

Bonus Traits: 6

Negative Traits: *Fragile, Clumsy, Heavy*

Concealability: None whatsoever

**Special Ability**: Chain armor does not protect against longbow attacks, and it only takes one shot from a longbow to render a shield useless. (In real life, often the arrow would punch through the shield and the arm behind it as well.)

Trebuchets, ballistae, catapults, mangonels and other siege engines lie outside the scope of this game.

## Protection

### Armor

Armor is the second-best defense against weapon-based attacks (the best, of course, is being somewhere far away from the combat). **Mind's Eye Theatre** uses a simple armor system to determine the effects of armor in combat. There are four types of armor in **Mind's Eye Theatre**: leather, chain, modern and plate.

Leather armor consists of hardened leather stitched together. A character wearing leather armor does not gain any Negative Traits by doing so, and the armor absorbs the first health level the character takes in combat during a session. After the first health level has been absorbed, the armor is useless.

Chain armor is made from hundreds of tiny rings of steel interwoven to form a "fabric" of metal. While chain mail absorbs the first two Health Levels of damage for its wearer, it comes with the Negative Trait: *Heavy*. Chain armor is also permeable to arrow fire, which goes through this defense as if it were nonexistent. Modern armor usually consists of either plastic body armor or Kevlar vests. In either case, modern armor can absorb two Health Levels of damage before being rendered useless. However, modern armor is unknown in the Dreaming, and thus is useless for stopping chimerical damage.

Plate mail is, as one might expect, the stereotypical solid steel armor one sees in movies and on the cover of fantasy novels. This sort of armor is fantastically heavy, and gains the Negative Traits: *Heavy* and *Clumsy*. Plate armor sops up the first three Health Levels of damage.

**Shields**

A shield is nothing more than an edged board, usually round or targe-shaped, worn on the arm to block opponents' blows. Shields are often reinforced to stand up to multiple blows, and some have metal bosses in the middle for bashing purposes. (Treat shields as having a single bonus Trait and the Negative Trait: *Clumsy* for attack purposes.) Shields are considered to be indestructible, except in the special cases noted above.

For purposes of **Mind's Eye Theatre**, there are two classifications of shield: small and large. Using a shield precludes using a bow or two-handed melee weapon. Also, shields are impossible to conceal.

A small shield has the Negative Trait: *Heavy*. Whenever anyone attacks the bearer of the shield successfully, the attacker must then succeed or tie on a Simple Test, or the shield absorbs the damage. A large shield has the Negative Traits: *Heavy* and *Clumsy*. Whenever anyone attacks the bearer of the shield successfully, the attacker must then succeed on a Simple Test, or the shield absorbs the damage.

## Etiquette of Arms and Armor

While one might wish to be as well-armed and armored as possible at all times, there are certain problems with tromping around in plate mail and wielding pointy objects all of the time. For one thing, it gets heavy and uncomfortable. For another, it is extremely rude to wear armor indoors, unless one is a guard or man-at-arms who specifically needs to wear armor to fulfill his duties. Toting weapons around, sheathed or otherwise, is also considered insulting, and may well get you in more trouble than having your mace at hand could possibly be worth.

### Ranged Combat

Many weapons allow you to stand at a distance from a target and engage him in combat. In such situations, you still go over to the target (after shouting "Bang!" or "Twang!") and engage in a challenge. Ranged combat, incidentally, is one of the few instances in which Traits of a similar type are not bid against one another; in ranged combat the attacker uses Mental Traits while the defender uses Physical (unless, of course, he is returning fire, in which case both characters bid Mental Traits).

If you have surprised your opponent, even if you lose the first test, you have the option of calling for a second test. Once you call the second challenge, play continues as normal. Your target is considered surprised for the first attack, and if he has no ranged weapon with which to return fire, he is considered "surprised" for as long as you can attack him without facing resistance (that is, if he wins on a challenge, you don't take damage).

If your target is aware of you before you make your initial ranged attack and has a ranged weapon of his own, he is not considered surprised for your first attack. He may shoot back right away, and your challenges are resolved as stated below. After your first arrow or bullet is fired (the first challenge is resolved), your target may attempt to return fire, assuming he is armed. The loser of a firefight challenge loses a Health Level.

If the defender is unarmed, he may declare his victory condition as escape, providing he is not cornered. If the defender wins the challenge, the attacker remains unharmed, but his target, the defender, has escaped from view and must be searched out if the attacker decides to press the attack. In instances such as this, a new challenge cannot be made for at least five minutes.

## Cover

Fighting with hand-to-hand weapons — clubs, knives or swords — requires that combatants be within reach of each other. Fighting with ranged weapons allows combatants to stand apart; participants can therefore "dive for cover." When you resolve each ranged combat challenge, you can present one Trait of cover to add to your total number of Traits. These cover Traits can't be used for bidding, but they do add to your total when comparing Traits. You can find cover behind nearby obstacles as long so they are within your reach (don't actually dive for them). A Narrator might be required to tell you what cover is around, but if combatants know the area, they can agree upon what cover is available without slowing the action. In some instances, there may be no cover, leaving a combatant in the open with only his own defensive Traits.

If cover is extensive — a brick wall, perhaps — it may be worth more than one Trait for one challenger. The number of Traits available for cover is left for challengers to agree upon, or for a Narrator to decree. Hiding behind a car, for example, might be worth two cover Traits, while hiding behind some sheetrock might only count as one. If one combatant goes completely under cover — so that he cannot be seen at all and is thoroughly protected — he is considered impossible to hit. The attacker must change his position to get a clear shot.

# Glamour Systems

## Calling Upon the Wyrd

This special action allows a changeling to bring her faerie self and any chimera or chimerical companions she possesses into the real world for a time. To call upon the Wyrd, a changeling must spend a Glamour Trait and Willpower Trait, and do nothing but concentrate for a full 10 seconds — this process can be made instantaneous with the expenditure of two additional Glamour Traits. At the end of this time, the changeling appears to the real world exactly as she does to the enchanted world — a troll now stands nine feet tall with blue skin, a pooka bears her animal features, a satyr has goat legs and horns, etc. All chimera worn or carried, and all chimerical companions owned also become real, and can inflict real damage on anything, even unenchanted mortals. A chimerical sword now does real damage, and can actually kill a foe instead of merely damaging him chimerically; a chimerical dragon can consume family pets with reckless abandon, and will deal real damage with its fiery breath.

While using this power, the changeling may still see and interact with both the real and enchanted world normally. In addition, Wyrd Birthrights such as a troll's *Titan's Power* or a sidhe's *Awe and Beauty*, which are normally ineffective around the unenchanted, grant the changeling full benefits; Wyrd Frailties also apply to their full extent.

However, the downside of calling upon the Wyrd is that all cantrips cast are considered Wyrd cantrips automatically, and the changeling takes real damage from all chimera and chimerical weaponry. The effects are real, regardless of whether a changeling's opponent has also called upon the Wyrd. As a result, a Kithain who has called upon the Wyrd cannot suffer regular chimerical defeat, only actual death.

The transformation is canceled after one hour or if the character is rendered unconscious, at which point the fae soul retreats back into the Dreaming for a while and the mortal seeming reappears. For roleplaying purposes, when a character uses this power she drops her green bandanna (if such was used) and makes any other chimerical prop or creature cards she is carrying noticeable to the rest of the group. Furthermore, if she is not already attired and outfitted as her character's faerie self, the fae should immediately describe her guise to everyone in the area, and to everyone who sees her for as long as the call upon the Wyrd lasts. Note that any unenchanted beings who view the changeling's fae form automatically come under the effects of the Mists once they have left the changeling's immediate vicinity.

# Creating Chimera

The creation of chimera can be as easy as waking from a nightmare or as difficult as threading a needle with bungee cord. Below are extremely simplified rules for creating chimera; if you want to get more detailed, see the chimera creation rules in Changeling: The Dreaming.

Note: These are the rules for creating chimera for everyone except nockers and DreamCrafters, who get off easy. Chimera creation for non-nockers can be difficult, time-consuming and expensive.

To create a chimera requires an investment of Glamour, typically two Glamour Traits per level of chimera desired. However, there's more to the process than that.

1 — Design the chimera you want. Is it a *Companion?* A *Treasure?* What does it look like? Does it have any distinguishing features? How about special powers?

2 — Show the design to your Storyteller. Work with him to make sure it works within the context of the game. (For something silly off the cuff, a Narrator will do just fine.) Your Storyteller should also assign a creation time, which, depending upon the type of chimera, can be anywhere from a few seconds to months. So a flower, for example, would take only a few moments, but a magical sword might take three or four sessions to complete.

3 — With the design approved, you must spend a number of Glamour Traits equal to twice the chimera's level. These Traits are considered to be spent instantaneously.

4 — At the end of the creation time assigned by your Storyteller, your chimera is available for play. Make sure to remind your Storyteller of what you agreed upon, especially if the creation time is more than a single session.

5 — Spend a Willpower Trait to make the chimera "permanent." If you do not spend a Trait, the chimera will vanish into smoke at the end of the session. If the chimera is particularly intricate or intelligent, the Storyteller has the option of forcing a Simple Test to see if your design fails at the last minute. This isn't easy to do, you know....

While you are creating one chimera, you are not permitted to work on another. The process of making your imagination real is time-consuming and difficult, and not something you can give only part of your attention to.

Storytellers, of course, should feel free to create random chimera (particularly nightmare nervosa) from the dreams of characters whenever they feel like it. These monsters are one-half the normal to create, but they do drain the character who spawns them of Glamour. Nervosa are considered to be instantly ready for action, and most will follow around their creators looking for affection, attention or vengeance.

# The End of Enchantment

The chart below should be consulted whenever a changeling or enchanted being is "killed" by chimerical damage, or whenever an unenchanted mortal (or supernatural) witnesses a chimerical effect or creature. This chart is also used to determine what happens to an enchanted mortal or Prodigal who is subsequently returned to the mundane world after visiting the Dreaming, and how much he remembers. Note that the memories of previous sojourns return if a character is enchanted again.

At the Storyteller's discretion, the duration of a character's coma may be modified if he is given a powerful dose of Glamour, is somehow magically healed, or otherwise has his faerie self "jolted" back online by an infusion of creativity. Of course a more classic method, such as the kiss of true love, is also acceptable, but such things are hard to come by these days.

| Banality | Duration of Coma | Memory |
|---|---|---|
| 0 | One minute | **Total Recall:** Everything is remembered with perfect clarity. |
| 1 | One hour | **Startling Clarity:** The entirety of the encounter is remembered as if it were yesterday. |
| 2 | Six hours | **Hazy Memory:** Everything is remembered, although some details might be hazy. |
| 3 | 12 hours | **Disoriented:** The individual is slightly confused and possibly shaken, but is able to recall most of his experiences, though many details are vague. |
| 4 | One day | **Uncertainty:** The person has a vague memory of what occurred, but is plagued by doubts as to the validity of the experience. |
| 5 | Three days | **Haze:** A hazy recollection of the experience is possible, but the individual doubts her own memories. She dismisses the experience as a momentary delusion unless she is shown physical proof. |
| 6 | One week | **Flashbacks:** The person may have occasional vivid flashbacks of his experiences, but they otherwise seem like a distant dream. |
| 7 | Two weeks | **Dreamlike Quality:** The individual recalls only vague, dreamlike images, and doubts the experience ever occurred. |
| 8 | One month | **Distant Dream:** Something must provoke the memory, and even then the experiences are hazy. |
| 9 | Two months | **Complete Denial:** The character has only completely denies the experience ever occurred. |
| 10 | One year | **Complete Blank:** The person remembers absolutely nothing of his experiences with the fae. Bummer. |

### The Dolorous Blow

Similar to both calling upon the Wyrd and the Enchanted Stroke (below), this technique is an especially nasty use of chimera, but it sometimes the only way for a changeling to defend himself. By spending two Willpower Traits, a changeling may make a single chimerical weapon (and nothing else) become real to an unenchanted being for the duration of one challenge *and one challenge only*. The weapon will inflict actual damage, and can kill enchanted and unenchanted alike. To mundane observers, the weapon seems to spring from nowhere, and the Mists will cover any uses of this technique in time.

If the challenge fails, the changeling must still spend the Willpower Trait. Furthermore, killing still incurs the usual Banality penalty for the fae wielding the weapon. At the Storyteller's discretion, changelings with multiple actions due to Arts such as *Quicksilver* may retain their weapon for the duration of all their attacks that turn, but regardless the blade becomes chimerical again after the last additional action is taken.

The Dolorous Blow is a secret known to few modern fae, and to employ it the changeling must have at least three levels of the *Gremayre* Ability, though at Storyteller discretion this requirement can be altered or waived for the sake of drama (a troll protecting her charge, an impassioned sidhe dueling, etc.). Still, those few Kithain aware of the secret employ it to great effectiveness; many mundanes and Prodigals have discovered too late the true potential of the chimerical rapier of a seemingly "unarmed" faerie opponent....

# The Mists

The Mists is the name changelings have for the mystic barrier that separates the fae world from the mundane. The Mists cloud the minds of mortals so that they do not remember their encounters with Glamour and things faerie. There are both good and bad sides to this; a changeling at a block party who uses *Wayfare* to fly to the top of his roof won't have to explain this talent to his neighbors later. On the down side, he wouldn't be able to show the wonders of the Dreaming to a group of children and have them remember what they'd seen for very long, unless he somehow enchanted the children more permanently or brought them into a freehold. Similarly, while the Mists keep hunters from discovering the power of Glamour, this mystical shroud does cloud a Kithain's own memory when she is injured or killed chimerically. Thus, the Mists make it even more difficult for a changeling to maintain her dual existence. A side effect of Banality, the Mists exemplify the force of human rationality.

## Bedlam

Many childlings and wilders wonder why, once they've discovered their fae natures, they can't simply disavow the mortal world entirely and exist purely in the world of the Dreaming. After all, abandoning the "real" world would seem to be the perfect way to counteract the power of Banality. Such logic often leads a young changeling to scorn and disparage her mortal shell, instead of realizing the protection it offers. For, as all grumps know, even as the Banality of the mortal world threatens to squelch the fae soul, so too does too much Glamour threaten to sweep one's mind away. Like it or not, changelings are creatures born of two worlds, and abandoning one entirely invites doom from the other. Changelings who spend too much time around the Banality of the mortal world eventually Forget, or are even permanently Undone; Kithain who embrace the Dreaming without minding enough of their mortal ties invite a soul-twisting madness known as Bedlam.

Bedlam progresses in three distinct stages, called thresholds, and its advance is under the strict control of the Storyteller. In some cases it takes years for a changeling to move from one threshold to another, but sometimes a Kithain can rocket through them in a matter of days, or even hours. There are warning signs, however. The following are not strict requirements for entering Bedlam, but if a character exhibits three or more of these symptoms, he might be a candidate for Bedlam.

### First Threshold

The first threshold is mainly perception-based; a character begins having trouble distinguishing between mundane and chimerical things, and sees chimera which aren't really there. First-threshold faults should be annoying but bearable. Some examples of first-threshold Bedlam include: shifts in the color spectrum, hearing disembodied whispers of madness or prophecy, inexplicable feelings of fear, the distortion of shadows into monstrous shapes or bright lights that flash in and out of existence without warning. A Storyteller might choose to add more such flaws onto a character, or simply drop him to the next threshold.

## When To Go Nuts

As one mad changeling can ruin an entire chronicle, the Storyteller is encouraged to inflict Bedlam only when she feels it is appropriate (regardless of what the signs say), but if a balance between the real and fantastic worlds is to be encouraged, Bedlam must be a threat with teeth.

**Second Threshold**

Bedlam's second threshold gets much more serious, as chimerical reality seems to become mundane reality to the unfortunate changeling. A player whose character is so affected should be pulled aside and have her reality explained to her; she no longer heeds any but the most obvious dangers of the mundane world, and is completely oblivious to any other goings on in regular reality. The character simply ceases to interact with anyone or anything not in her little corner of reality. Furthermore, she may suffer additional afflictions. Some examples are:

• Don Quixote Syndrome, when the character believes everything to be from an ancient or mythical time;

• Delusions of Grandeur, in which the character believes she is superior to everyone around her, regardless of her actual power and station;

• Social Darwinism, under which the character sees everyone as predator or prey, and her own lot to be that of a predator of great skill and guile;

• The Walls Have Ears, in which the changeling believes absolutely everything to be alive and sentient.

Since the next threshold of Bedlam is nearly impossible to cure, Storytellers should give characters at this stage a chance to heal, and should make sure this madness fits the character's personal story. Of course, if the player of the mad character is having fun, and the character is reveling in his insanity by staying up all night to party with the local horned chimerical teddy bears, the Storyteller can go ahead and drop the character to the final threshold.

## Warning Signs Checklist

The following are warning signs that a changeling might be falling into Bedlam. Although none of these are a sure sign of impending madness, the more of these signs a character regularly exhibits, the more likely he is to have Bedlam looming on the horizon.

You spend more nights in freeholds than in the mortal world (If you spend all your time in a freehold, madness is almost assured).

•You have more than one faerie treasure.

•You interact with more than three chimera on a regular basis.

•You are a constant Ravager.

•You have no mortal friends.

•You are almost exclusively nocturnal.

•You drink alcohol, use drugs or have sex to excess.

•You spend more than half your waking time creating art of some kind.

•You have no mortal family.

•You have no mortal possessions.

•You are in a state of unrequited love.

### Third Threshold

At this point, the character is almost completely swallowed by his madness. What's worse, third-threshold Bedlam is highly contagious, and those who associate too often with such a character may develop first-threshold symptoms themselves; only the devoted or the foolhardy try to treat such changelings. Often, the only recourse is to destroy the poor unfortunates, albeit with great remorse.

While they retain all the previous traits of their madness, characters in third- threshold Bedlam gain even more inhuman and insidious quirks, which include such taints as: a berserker response, when the character attacks all around her with whatever is at hand; an autistic complex, when the character withdraws completely inward, not recognizing the outside world at all; feral cunning, wherein the character reverts to a cunning, predatory animal seeking only to stalk and kill; or perversity, as the character descends into the depths of her soul and performs unspeakable acts. What's even more terrible is the fact that many changelings this far gone birth nightmare nervosa chimera, which attempt to protect the character and keep others from "harming" her. If left untreated, the character eventually disappears from reality one night while Dreaming, and the player must make a new character. (the Storyteller might require this step earlier if the Bedlamite has grown too disruptive to the game). Perhaps worst of all, though, are the spells of lucidity a character in this stage goes through, during which time he seems perfectly normal and unaware of his plight.

## Treating Bedlam

First-threshold Bedlam is easily curable and recoverable if the changeling realizes what's going on and takes the appropriate steps. Ironically, a short time spent in the mundane world, away from court and cantrips, usually cures first-threshold Bedlam, acting as a splash of cold water on the overexuberant fae soul. However, most Glamour-bent changelings are unwilling to accept such a, well, *banal* solution so quickly, and stubbornly hold onto their fae selves, even if they realize what is happening. Denial almost always quickly leads to a more rapid deterioration.

The second threshold is a bit more different, and requires a bit of magical healing (with the Primal Art) along with the same Banality therapy as the first threshold. By the time a changeling reaches the second threshold, her madness has progressed to her fae soul, and both mortal mind and fae spirit must be healed for the character to completely recover.

Third-threshold Bedlam is nearly impossible to cure; the only known method is to drink from the Cup of Dreams, an ancient and powerful faerie treasure said to have been lost long ago to the Dreaming. Some also whisper that dragons know the secret of curing third-threshold Bedlam, but there are precious few wyrms friendly enough to approach in this manner, and even fewer Kithain with the courage to try. No Banality cure or *Primal* healing has ever worked on souls in this state, and any mortal psychiatrists who treat these unfortunates are astounded at their resistance to medication and normal therapeutic techniques.

## The Enchanted Stroke

A favorite of many cinematically inclined wilders, this flashy technique duplicates the effects of enchantment in every way, with a special twist. The changeling must spend a Glamour and a Mental Trait and make a *Melee* Challenge to attack an unenchanted target with a chimerical weapon (not even physical treasures count). If the challenge is successful, the target becomes enchanted for one day, willingly or not. The newly enchanted target suffers no damage from this first stroke, but is likely to be quite taken aback at the new world he's been thrust into! If the challenge fails, the Glamour and Mental Traits are still spent. As this technique requires a bit of knowledge about chimera and enchantment, a Kithain may only attempt it if he has at least one level of the *Gremayre* Ability. The Enchanted Stroke is one of the few ways available to enchant a mundane against his will, and many Seelie avoid it if at all possible,. As such, the Storyteller may increase the cost or even disallow the tactic entirely if it is abused by the players — enchantment is nothing to be taken lightly. However, even the Seelie admit that the stroke can be such a stylish way of enchanting someone, especially a bitter mundane foe....

# Enchantment

At times, a changeling may want to bring others into her fantastic world, a process known as enchantment. A Kithain's motives for this can vary from desiring to show a friend the true nature of one's fae life to terrorizing hapless mortals, but once the target has been enchanted, he has become a part of the fae world whether he likes it or not.

The system for enchantment (creating tokens, duration of enchantment, etc.) is covered under the Glamour section; this section explains exactly what enchantment is, how long it lasts, and what happens afterward. For the purposes of ease and clarity (although they can be enchanted only at the Storyteller's discretion), consider Prodigals included as well whenever the text refers to unenchanted mortals.

Once a changeling has managed to enchant a mortal, that individual is brought fully into the Dreaming. She can perceive and interact with chimera and chimerical items, and see changelings' faerie aspects. Furthermore, all Wyrd Birthrights and Frailties are effective/in effect around an enchanted mortal, and chimera can even damage or chimerically "kill" her. The mortal gains the normal number of chimerical Health Levels to resist such damage, however, and may even create voile, or chimerical clothing, for herself. However, if an enchanted mortal is chimerically "slain," the enchantment immediately fades as she falls unconscious and the Mists take over (see the Mists chart for how long she remains unconscious).

Enchanted mortals cannot cast cantrips; their Glamour is borrowed, and they have none of their own. In addition, enchanted mortals may not actively use their Banality to fight cantrips — they have no choice but to believe now! The only exception to those rules are kinain, or faerie kinfolk, who can sometimes learn a few Arts and Realms from a changeling mentor, and who know enough about Banality to use it in their own defense if need be.

Enchantment lasts for a base time of one day per Glamour Trait invested in the token created to enchant the mundane, or the number of Glamour Traits spent after the challenge to forcibly enchant a mortal. However, if the mortal is kept in a freehold, the time limit on the enchantment is suspended for as long as she is kept there; such is the origin of "Rip Van Winkle" legends of mortals who seem to have passed a summer afternoon in a faerie glen and return to find decades missing. Unfortunately, Bedlam is even more of a threat to mortals than to the fae, so changelings are careful not to let their retainers remain enchanted and in a freehold for too long at a stretch. Unless carefully guided through the experience by a Kithain, most humans will think of enchantment as some kind of hallucinogenic effect or strange drug. Even creative and imaginative folk have no idea what really lies in the chimerical world, and the "truth" of the matter can be quite a shock.

**Note**: Enchanted Prodigals can be exceptions to the rules, and the duration and effectiveness of the enchantment is dependent upon the amount of Banality a given Prodigal possesses (see the normal Banality ratings chart for examples) and whatever other factors the Storyteller deems appropriate. Once the duration of the enchantment has passed, the mortal goes unconscious and unresponsive for a time equal to the duration dictated by her Banality. A supernatural creature can resist falling into this comatose state by spending a Willpower Trait, although this tactic is not effective if he's been chimerically "killed," and in any case his memory of the fae realm still deteriorates as his Banality level dictates. At the Storyteller's discretion, some powerful intervention, supernatural or otherwise, might be able to wake the comatose character, but this is extremely rare.

When re-enchanted, characters who have forgotten previous encounters with the fae, including changelings who have temporarily fallen to the Forgetting, immediately regain all memories of their previous fae experiences. Otherwise, a character who is repeatedly enchanted is treated exactly as a normal target enchantment, down to the effects of the Mists and the duration of the enchantment.

# Oaths

While changelings can be as capricious as the Glamour which flows through them, there are occasions where a person or situation demands some kind of great commitment from a Kithain, and the fae can be frightfully serious about such business. From this state of affairs the practice of swearing of oaths arose, wherein two parties enter into a verbal contract concerning one issue or another through the swearing of specific and demanding terms to the other party. The power of Glamour itself enforces the tenets of an oath even if a changeling's honor doesn't, and those who break their word of honor find themselves suffering dire consequences. Even Unseelie abide by their oaths if possible, although they are much more selective than Seelie in their oathtaking, and try to avoid swearing any oaths that don't directly serve their own interests.

Oaths can last for a variable amount of time. and grant varying rewards or punishments to those who swear by them, but oaths are one thing even the trickiest pooka or most savage redcap takes seriously. Particularly foul or repeated oathbreakers are chimerically marked, and henceforth shunned and reviled by all Kithain society.

Some of the most common oaths and their wordings are included here, but this list and even the wordings of these oaths are by no means final, as there exist as many oaths and variations on oaths as can possibly be dreamed. Oaths are intended to add to the pageantry and mythic quality of **The Shining Host**. Players who try to tweak their characters into war machines by selecting oaths solely for their benefits should be brought strongly in line, lest the balance and mystique of the oath system be lost for everyone. Similarly, the players should never be forced into having their characters swear oaths they themselves do not fully understand. After all, an oath taken under duress is not binding, and being manipulated by a mysterious, omnipotent "Storyteller" certainly counts as duress.

### The Oath of Clasped Hands

*Blood for blood, bone for bone, life for life, until only we stride the earth. My life is in your hands, my blood is in your veins. Hold me well and I will lend you my strength, break your bond and may we both perish. Friendship I swear to you, an oath of clasped hands and shared hearts.*

This oath is one of true friendship, a bond as strong as that one might feel for a lover, and is never sworn lightly. It is the cornerstone of any oathcircle and many motleys and households. Those who swear it gain a permanent Willpower Trait, but lose two if it is ever broken. Swearing to a group gives one Willpower Trait total, not one per member. (Glamour knows when you try to cheat on this provision!)

### The Oath of Fealty

*I swear fealty to you, lady/lord. Your command is my desire, and your request my desire. May my service always please, and may my sight grow dark if it does not. As the tides to the moon, my will to yours, my liege.*

This oath is commonly sworn at Sainings, knightings and investitures. Swearing this oath costs the speaker one temporary Willpower Trait, but all attempts to mentally control or dominate the speaker from now on are at a two-Trait penalty. Breaking this oath costs two permanent Willpower Traits, and especially heinous betrayals may strike the betrayer blind for a year and a day.

### The Oath of Escheat

*I take you as my vassal. You are of my house, even as the very stones. I pledge to hold you, guard you, and to keep you. I pledge to honor your service as it deserves, and to reward loyalty in kind. As the moon to the seas below, my will to yours, I pledge the Escheat to you.*

With this oath, a noble formally accepts another fae as her vassal. This oath is commonly spoken in conjunction with the Oath of Fealty, but not always. When the oath's words are spoken, the speaker loses a temporary Glamour Trait, and a chimerical gold coin, stamped with her likeness, appears in her hand. The oath is not actually binding until the oathmaker offers, and the proposed vassal accepts, this token. Failure to abide by the terms of this oath indicates a fall from true fae honor, and gives the oathbreaker a permanent Banality Trait. However, any fae bound by (and holding to) the terms of this oath, even if only to one vassal, regains a temporary Willpower Trait at the end of every week.

### The Oath of the Accepted Burden

*Lay down your burden, that I might take it up. The road is long, and I swear I shall bear it for you, until all roads end. I shall [name the actual task here], else may the road cease to lay beneath my feet.*

Superficially similar to a *geas*, this oath is a promise to perform a certain deed. The nature of the deed itself is irrelevant, and can be anything from a kiss to retrieving the still-beating heart of a foe. This oath is always made to another, and is made to verify that a task he desires will be performed. When these words are spoken, a temporary Willpower Trait is regained by both the oathmaker and the one to whom the promise is made. Casual oathtakers beware, though — if the oath is not kept, each loses two temporary Willpower Traits.

### The Oath of Adoption

*As the sea to the river, as the tree to the seed, as the mountain to the stone, so do I now recognize you to me. From this day forward, you are of my blood, of my family, and of my hold. I swear to offer you my wisdom, my love and my regard, for you will carry my name and my memory when I am no more. Should I abandon you, I abandon myself. It fills my heart to call you son/daughter.*

*Response*: *As the river to the sea, as the seed to the tree, as the stone to the mountain, so do I now recognize myself in you. From this day forward, I am of your blood, your family, and your hold. I swear to offer my respect, my devotion and my love, for you offer me a home where I have none. Should I abandon you, I consign myself to loneliness. It fills my heart to call you mother/father.*

This oath, once known only to the trolls, is gaining popularity as many changelings, especially runaway childlings and wilders, seek a sense of family in the enchanted world, and grumps look to the young to carry on their heritage. This oath ranks next to the Oath of the Truehearts and the Oath of Clasped Hands as the deepest personal bond a changeling can have for another, for the two oathmakers are truly considered parent and child from the swearing of the oath onward. There are no special benefits or penalties derived from swearing this oath, outside of those qualities one normally receives from a family, which makes this oath possibly greater than any other oath imaginable. Those who break this oath are considered among the most vile beings in the world, and they are scorned and shunned without mercy or relent.

### The Oath of Guardianship

*As the sun guards the earth by day, as the stars by night, so shall I serve thee. This is my duty — I shall not abandon [object of oath] till [duration of oath], else may the stars close their eyes and sleep.*

This is a fearful oath, and those who fail to uphold it are cursed never to spend two nights in the same bed until a century has passed. The Oath of Guardianship binds the oathmaker to protect a single object, place, or individual from any and all harm, to the point of ultimate self-sacrifice. Those who swear this oath gain an extra temporary Willpower Trait, which can only be spent while defending the subject of the oath, but there is no other cost to make the Oath of Guardianship other than that extracted by its keeping.

### The Oath of Truehearts

*I give a gift of myself to thee. Take it freely; freely it is offered, and forever thou hast me in thy keeping. I swear love unto you and pledge you my troth. May those who watch over love watch over this oath and those who keep it, and may we never find fault in their eyes.*

This oath needs no explanation. It is spoken in unison by the two (or more) lovers it binds, and it takes a Trait of temporary Glamour from each to craft a chimerical songbird visible only to the lovers. The instant the oath is broken, the bird ceases to sing, perching silently on the shoulder of the oathbreaker, and becomes visible to all as the sign of betrayal. In addition, both betrayer and betrayed gain a permanent Banality Trait as a result of this cowardly action. On the other hand, an Epiphany resulting from Rapture the lovers share bestow an additional Glamour Trait. The songbird cannot be affected by any known means of tampering.

### The Oath of the Long Road

*I swear that I shall [nature of quest undertaken], or lose my honor, that I shall [nature of quest] or lay down my sword, that I shall [nature of quest] or Dream no more. You and the sky my witnesses, so mote it be.*

The Oath of the Long Road is the most potent of the oaths known to most fae, and it is usually sanctified by some small but significant personal sacrifice on the part of the oathmaker and any witnesses present. It is always spoken in front of one, or preferably three, witnesses. The oathmaker receives a free permanent Willpower and Glamour Trait, but the consequences of failure are most dire. Simple failure of the quest causes the loss of three Willpower and Glamour Traits, one of each permanently. Abandoning the quest altogether strips the oathbreaker of all temporary Willpower and Glamour Traits and a permanent Willpower Trait, and gives the oathbreaker two permanent Banality Traits.

### The Oath of Crossed Blades

*Where two stand, there will be one. I swear enmity unto thee until the setting of the last sun. May my heart cease to beat and my hand lose its strength should ever I show favor to thee, as the bones of the earth are my witness.*

This oath is generally only sworn by trolls and sidhe, as the other fae consider announcing such black feelings counterproductive to their intentions. This oath remains a way to lay everything out on the table in the sometimes confusing world of fae politics. In addition, there is just something inherently stylish to swearing eternal hatred, and obviously (though not always) this oath can be sworn by two fae in conjunction. Those who do swear the Oath of Crossed Blades trade a temporary Willpower Trait for a temporary Glamour Trait, and are one Trait up on all challenges to oppose their hated foe directly. (Of course, if the oath is sworn together, this advantage is somewhat nullified.) Should the oath be broken, a permanent Willpower Trait is lost and a pair of matching scars, akin to those left by a rapier's point, appear on the face of the oathbreaker, which cannot be healed by any kind of Glamour.

### The Oath of the Undoing

*An eye for an eye, a tooth for a tooth. No slight shall go unnoticed, no wound unavenged. I shall hunt my undying enemy, [name of enemy], to the four corners of the Earth, and I shall not rest until either I or my enemy is fully Undone. I shall do everything in my power to reduce my enemy to nothing and to less than nothing, with a keen cold iron blade.*

Though superficially similar to the Oath of Crossed Blades, this foul and forbidden oath is much more serious than that, for while the Oath of Crossed Blades calls merely for bitter rivalry, this oath demands the final death of another fae. The oath is, in fact, one of the easiest ways Banality seduces fae into becoming Dauntain, the hated hunters of all things faerie, and many a tragic tale is told of those who swore this oath in the heat of passion and became trapped in lives of apathy and misery, regretting their swearing to the end but too honor-bound to turn from the path they had chosen. Fortunately, this oath is not widely known, though it sometimes seems to come — unlearned and unbidden — to the lips of many enraged wilders.

A changeling attempting to swear this oath must immediately enter a Static Challenge of his Glamour against his Banality; success means he feels the dread consequences of this oath and may break it off if he wishes. Failure, or a willful ignorance of the warning signs, means the changeling completes the oath, and immediately gains a permanent Trait of Banality as a result. If the oath is broken, a permanent Willpower Trait is lost; if it is fulfilled, another permanent Banality Trait is gained. This is indeed a terrible oath, and most likely not one a player will ever utter, unless he deliberately chooses the dark fate of the Dauntain for his character.

# Epiphany

Every changeling needs Glamour to live, at least if he wishes to keep his fae soul from withering. From learned eshu to ravenous redcaps, all Kithain spend their lives seeking out Glamour in all its forms, teasing or taking it out as they choose. Moments when a changeling gains a true appreciation of a particular kind of creativity, and thus gains Glamour from it, are called Epiphanies. Such revelations come in several distinct varieties, from benign Reverie to vicious Ravaging to transcendent Rapture. Not only are these moments addictive in and of themselves, but the surge of Glamour that accompanies them often leads a Kithain to a lifetime of seeking out and patronizing various artists, waiting for that moment of transcendent creation. Kithain need mortals the dreams they make — changelings are composed of that very essence. Not every mortal has this capability, though, to produce Glamour in this fashion, and perhaps one in every thousand humans has enough of it to be called a Dreamer.

## Reverie

Most changelings regain their Glamour through the process of inspiring mortal artists to greater and greater masterpieces, and then enjoying the Glamour this process slowly creates; "farming" Glamour in this fashion is known as Reverie. Though it may take time, Reverie harms neither the changeling or the artist, and ensures that the artist retains her creativity indefinitely. While gaining Glamour through the *Dreamers* Background is usually considered to be Reverie, and thus safe for both parties, it is possible to gain additional Glamour Traits by acting as a mortal's muse, but the process is a bit more lengthy.

**System**: The changeling must approach the Storyteller and announce that he is considering acting as a particular artist's muse. If the Storyteller deems the patronage appropriate, the player must win a Social Challenge

## Musing Thresholds

**Inspire Creativity:** You love to inspire the imaginations of all those around you, especially those who might someday become great artists. Uniting such brilliant and creative minds is a demanding task that you find just too much fun to pass up.

**Create Hope:** Nobody can live without hope, and you go above and beyond the call of duty to keep everyone's spirits up.

**Create Love:** Ah, *l'amour!* Fae are romantic, but you're contagious! A firm believer that love can make everything work out in the end, you strive to keep good couples together, keep singles searching for that one true love, and be there to heal the heartbroken.

**Create Calm:** Peace is the garden from which happiness springs, and while you realize that conflict is part of life, you prefer to prevent particularly ugly situations by keeping tempers down. You act as a constant balance for those around you.

**Foster Trust:** Nobody can walk this world alone, and you go out of your way to encourage everyone to keep everyone working together. Helping friends old and new realize the strength of their bonds of affection is your mission and your joy.

**Helping Those in Need:** Some people are lost or need guidance to get them back on their feet. You exist to fill that need, and will gladly give of yourself to help give another something to believe in. Dependence and sloth are foes to be conquered, not masters to bow to.

**Foster Dreams:** This variety of musing involves inspiring people to dream of things they want to achieve, from getting children to think of themselves as astronauts and presidents to helping an adult finally write her Great American Novel. As long as the subjects believe in their dreams and strive to make them come true, the musing is a success.

against *and* roleplay out befriending the artist. If that combination of actions is successful, the player must announce the time period over which he wishes to patronize the mortal (ideally, this is an extended process), and the number of Glamour Traits he would like to gain from the procedure.

Basing the difficulty on those considerations, the Storyteller issues a Static Mental Challenge. If the changeling is successful, he gains as many temporary Glamour Traits as there were levels of difficulty (not to exceed his permanent total). A failure in either challenge means that the artist is put off and/or blocked by the Kithain's attentions, and can't provide Glamour.

Note that while this procedure would seem to take a long time (and should), it can be the most lucrative Epiphany of all. Furthermore, once a relationship is established, there is no limit as to how long a changeling may continue to gain Glamour from that artist (on a fairly regular schedule, no less).

## Musing Thresholds

Certain Seelie fae demonstrate a facility for specific types of inspiration, and their attempts to create Reverie in these situations are often especially fruitful. A character may never have more than one Threshold, but those who begin play without one may gain one with practice, and those who start with a threshold can change it as their character demands. A Kithain need not be Seelie to have a Musing Threshold (nor Unseelie to have a Ravaging threshold), but things tend to fall along those Court lines. (Clever change-lings will note that the Musing and Ravaging thresholds directly oppose each other; by no coincidence, those who indulge in opposite thresholds often find themselves at each other's throats. This is one of the subtler ways in which parties of the two Courts still war, although it is also one of the ones with the longest-running affects on the mortal world.)

**Note**: If there is any doubt on whether a Musing or Ravaging Threshold applies, the Storyteller has the final say. Like Reverie, Musing Thresholds can develop into long-term relationships, providing an especially lucrative source of Glamour for a patient and gentle changeling.

**System**: Any time the changeling engages in a Reverie in accordance with her Musing Threshold, she gains one extra Glamour Trait if the challenge is successful, or (at Narrator discretion) two Glamour Traits if the scene is played out well and for the full beautiful effect.

## Rapture

Perhaps rarest of all forms of changeling inspiration, Rapture is that wonderful state in which the changeling gives herself Glamour through the creativity of her own thoughts. Such a feat requires a Zenlike calm and between a changeling's fae and human halves, but the reward — moments of pure and total ecstasy as the direct link to the Dreaming makes whole the changeling's fragmented soul and infuses it with Glamour — is incalculable. Most changelings, like most mortals, are incapable of transcending mere patronage to reach the direct link between art and artist, but it is a goal to which many Kithain rightly aspire.

**System**: Even more so than Reverie, there is no set "system" for playing out Rapture, as it must be the ultimate culmination of a long and dedicated process of artistic discovery, but if one needs rules, here they are: When the Storyteller feels that a changeling has spent enough long, trying, soul-searching hours working on improving and changing her art (a long, long, *long* process), she may allow the character to make a Static Challenge using the Trait category associated with her preferred art form, with a difficulty based on how much Glamour is to be gained and the complexity of the art to gain it from. If successful, the changeling experiences Rapture and gains the amount of Glamour specified in the Static Challenge; if not, the changeling must once again re-work her art and begin the process anew. The Storyteller is encouraged to grant bonuses to players who actually choose a medium and try to create what their character is working on (at least in their heads), and who constantly improve and detail the piece. Yes, that's difficult, but Rapture is a glimpse at the perfect synthesis of the fae soul and the mortal mind — that doesn't come easily. Some changelings spend lifetimes trying but failing to reconcile the two.

## Ravaging

It is a tragically simple matter to rip Glamour from a mortal or work of art, and although the resulting Epiphany is tainted by the psychic anguish of the victim, it is quick and in its own way, perfectly satisfying. However, individual mortals don't have an infinite supply of Glamour and must take time to replenish their pools; too much Ravaging can dry up the well once and for all.

Changelings who Ravage run the risk of gaining Banality while doing so, for Ravaging actually involves making use of one's own Banality. Most Seelie consider this practice abhorrent. On the other hand, Unseelie fae tend to think there'll always be more Dreamers, so what's the worry? Some particularly energetic Unseelie tend to have raised Ravaging to such an art form they develop "Ravaging Thresholds" (explained below), but even the most upright Seelie sometimes resorts to Ravaging if he needs "quick Glamour" from someone he knows (or has a lust for a certain mortal's dreams). Victims of a Ravaging feel no physical pain, "merely" the weight of Banality growing on them, and they are often terrified and exhausted by the entire experience.

**System**: A Ravager must know her victim fairly well before she can attempt to rip away his dreams, a result typically gained through roleplaying. Once a player feels she has learned enough about a target to Ravage him, she must go to the Storyteller, who will question her to see if she knows the other character well enough to perform a Ravaging. If the Storyteller believes the character does, the player must first make physical contact with the target (a Physical Challenge if the target resists). She then makes a Static Challenge against the number of Glamour Traits she wishes to gain by Ravaging, using her own permanent Banality rating as her bid. If she succeeds, she gain the Glamour; if she fail, she gains a permanent Trait of Banality (there are a lot of risks involved). **Note**: Retesting the Ravaging Challenge is possible for either party only with the expenditure of one Willpower Trait per retest.

**Ravaging Thresholds**: Certain Unseelie, particularly those of the Shadow Court, develop one particular method of Ravaging to such a fine degree they are able to gain extra Glamour Traits each time they perform this particular type of Ravaging upon a target. As with the Musing Thresholds, a character may never have more than one of these thresholds, although those who begin play without one may gain one due to roleplaying, and those who start with one can switch along with a shift in their dark pleasures. Unlike Musing Thresholds, Ravaging Thresholds often are as short-lived with a particular target as the regular means of Ravaging.

**System**: Any time the changeling Ravages in accordance with his Threshold, he gains one extra Glamour Trait if the challenge is successful. Narrators can award an extra Glamour Trait if the Ravaging is roleplayed particularly well.

## Ravaging Thresholds

**Exhaust Creativity:** You are jealous of mortal inspiration, and Ravage those with more talent than you. Ultimately you corrupt or destroy your victims' work in the process, and leave the artist burned out and bitter in your wake. Few objects of value, artistic or otherwise, survive your attentions for very long.

**Destroy Hope:** You take pleasure in snuffing out your victims' belief in anything good, and will gladly supply the shove that sends them over the precipice into despair.

**Destroy Love:** Exactly what it sounds like. No relationship is safe from you and your devious ways, and the more attached a couple is, the more determined you become to break them.

**Create Anger:** You delight in your own composure, and love making others mad until they can't take it. You enjoy leading a target to violence and self-destruction, then simply walking away as they suffer the consequences. (You are, however, a very bad friend to have around when, say, Brujah vampires or Garou caerns of any type are nearby.)

**Break Trust:** You've had your trust broken, and now others are going to pay for what happened to you. Those targeted by your cold and methodical Ravaging ultimately withdraw from the world, trusting no one and becoming easy prey for terrible things coming in the Endless Winter....

**Exploit Dependence:** You're proud of your self-sufficiency, and so you delight in slowly destroying those who depend on you, feeding their "addiction" to your presence and then painfully, breaking it off before they're ready.

**Destroy Illusions:** You're jaded, and the sight of anyone who is still innocent annoys and disgusts you. This type of Ravaging is easiest to enact by childlings, who get "good kids" to perform all kinds of wickedness while dodging any of the blame. Santa Claus and the Easter Bunny are also noticeably absent from the fantasy lives of children for blocks around where you live.

## Rhapsody

Once thought to be known only to the members of the forbidden Unseelie House Leanhaun (who must use it in order to survive), this sinister and twisted form of Epiphany has slowly crept into Kithain society in the modern age. Expressly forbidden by all faerie laws, Rhapsody is the process of infusing a mortal's soul with Glamour directly from the Dreaming without passing it through an intermediary such as art or changeling inspiration. Such a raw dose of power makes the mortal devote his whole heart and soul to his artwork, and the potent infusion of Glamour drives the victims of Rhapsody to create masterpieces of craftsmanship and beauty. The mortal whose life is so touched burns with enhanced creativity, like a flare in the middle of a dark night. Unfortunately, like a flare, the mortal's brilliance sputters to nothing far too quickly. Even if death doesn't follow the passing of the Glamour from Rhapsody, a permanent loss of creativity (not to mention lengthy bouts depression and rage) does.

In the meantime, the fae indulging in the Rhapsody drink in the supremely potent dreams of the mortal, often becoming the lovers of the mortals they are touching in this manner so as to be close to the source. Some Rhapsodizers even become vaguely concerned with the mortal's welfare, if for no other reason than the longer they can maintain such a link the longer they can revel in the Glamour. Even the best-intentioned user of Rhapsody knows what inevitably comes of his touch, though, and there is no escape from the price that must be paid.

**System**: As with Ravaging, a Rhapsodizer must know her target well in order to have any effect on them; however, she doesn't necessarily need to be in physical contact to Rhapsodize, merely close enough to enjoy, experience and absorb her target's artwork. (This doesn't stop many users of Rhapsody from getting physically close anyway, though.) She must also put Glamour Traits into the target at least once a week while the target is in the throes of the creative process. At the end of each week, the artist makes a Static Challenge related to his artwork; if he fails, the Glamour Traits added that week are effectively lost, and the mortal gains a permanent Banality Trait. If he succeeds, the Traits are added to the total number of Glamour Traits spent in that fashion. When the mortal completes the work, he makes a Static Challenge for his art; the number of Traits at risk is added to the Glamour Trait total. If the is successful, all the Glamour Traits invested in the composition are distributed to the user of Rhapsody, along with a number of additional Traits equal to those risked in the final Static Challenge. Unseelie receive two Traits of Glamour for every one they earn at this stage — sometimes it's good to be bad. The mortal, on the other hand, gains a permanent Banality Trait for every two regular Glamour Traits the Rhapsodizer gains.

**Note**: Storytellers must always keep careful track of how the Rhapsodized mortal is faring, alert any particularly watchful changelings or other art sensitive types in the area to the presence of a seemingly unnaturally powerful Dreamer. Narrators should *always* make sure they inflict the eventual punishment on any victim of Rhapsody at some point, or the tragedy of Rhapsody is lost. The effects can be fast or slow, depending on the individual mortal and how much the Rhapsodizer pushes him, but eventually the bill has to come due. Otherwise, there's no reason for everyone not to Rhapsodize, and game balance goes out the window.

There is no known way to cure or prevent damage to a mortal caused by Rhapsody; if the mortal survives his abuse at changeling hands (and remember, artists in the throes over overwhelming bursts of creativity have been known to ignore such necessities as food, sleep and medical attention), the abuser might very well earn a powerfully angry and bitterly disillusioned enemy.

# Fair Escape

Fair Escape is a simple rule that allows players to escape from potentially deadly situations without actually vaulting over tables or charging headlong out of a room, possibly causing harm to themselves or others. This rule also allows players to avoid combat without going through cumbersome challenges to see if they can "get away."

When you use this rule, you can call "Fair Escape" anytime you see another player approaching with whom you do not wish to interact. Once you call "Fair Escape," you may leave the area without being pursued. There are several guidelines which must be followed when using this rule, however:

• You may not use the Fair Escape rule if the person approaching is nearby (within conversational distance). In such cases, you must initiate a challenge in order to flee. Use common sense in places where there is a great deal of noise and conversational distance is reduced to a minimum (e.g., a crowded nightclub).

• Situations which involve an ambush (all exits are blocked or the target is surrounded) can negate the use of Fair Escape. Again, use common sense.

• A character with *Veiled Eyes* may employ Fair Escape at any time before a challenge has been initiated, unless someone with some form of *Heightened Senses* counters him.

These guidelines are intended to quicken play, not to obstruct it. Always try to use common sense when employing Fair Escape.

# Chapter Five: Storytelling

This chapter is for Storytellers and, to a lesser extent, Narrators. Storytelling **The Shining Host** is very different from Storytelling **Changeling: The Dreaming**, or even any other **Mind's Eye Theatre** game. **The Shining Host** involves running a game displaced in time and possibly space as well, meaning that not only the players, but the world of the game will demand constant attention. Both the enchanted and the mortal societies of your game need to be developed, and costuming and setting the scene can take creativity, effort and time. Running a live roleplaying game, especially this one, is not for the lazy. With proper preparation, however, **The Shining Host** allows you to tell epic stories of high dark fantasy, mythic conflict, courtly intrigue and anything else you can imagine. In the end, your effort is what creates something thrilling.

## Chronicles

If characters are the lifeblood of **Mind's Eye Theatre**, then the chronicle is the body those characters sustain. Although **The Shining Host** can be used and enjoyed as a series of loosely connected stories, such games often lack a sense of continuity and offer little opportunity for character development. Furthermore, most characters grow around long-term goals (power, prestige, status, revenge, knowledge — to name just a few); one story is rarely enough to resolve anything satisfactorily. In a chronicle — an ongoing series of stories — characters not only reside in a familiar environment, but also one that evolves as they interact with it. Developing and maintaining a chronicle is a satisfying task, but it requires continuous effort and dedication on the part of both you and your Narrators.

# Setting the Stage

The first element to consider in chronicle construction is the atmosphere you desire. The two aspects of atmosphere are mood and theme. Each is a fundamental ingredient in the alchemy of a chronicle.

## Mood

Mood is the underlying emotional sentiment of a chronicle. It sustains and flows through everything you do, unobtrusive yet omnipresent. While the mood of a chronicle is intangible, your choice of mood can be one of the most important ones you make as regards plot, character and theme. After all, if you're going for a mood of court elegance, a hack-n-slash plot (and a brigade of drooling redcaps to match) won't make much sense.

## Theme

Themes are central ideas of a chronicle, ones that help define the shape of the action. They can be as visceral as the struggle for freedom or as intellectual as the age-old questions of good and evil. Themes can emerge as seemingly inconsequential encounters or as the major focus of a chronicle. Avoid overemphasizing theme, however. Overemphasis makes related events expected and predictable rather than haunting and prophetic.

## Setting

The setting is the stage upon which the drama of a chronicle is played. Setting is composed of environment and locale. Environment describes the overall scheme of the world. The environment of **The Shining Host** involves the many levels of the enchanted existence: conflicts between and within kith and Courts, noble feuds, the struggles of the youth to stay young, the search for true Glamour, the menace of Dauntain, forbidden knowledge, ancient vendettas and much, much more. A myriad of potential alternatives are available. It's your reality — do with it what you will.

Locale, or the physical place where you choose to set your chronicle, is the next step toward chronicle creation. Obviously, your setting must have some basis in the real world as well as the enchanted, and therefore it is often easiest to take a setting you have some knowledge of, if possible. Setting your game at Stonehenge when you've never even cracked a travel guide to England simply makes no sense. Creating a detailed setting takes a great deal of imagination, but the more work spent in developing a locale, the richer the chronicle will be for your efforts.

## Creating the Setting

Most chronicles are focused around a single setting or a town, even if the characters might travel widely from it as time goes on. This place is the locus of your chronicle. You need to present your setting in a realistic and consistent manner so that players believe in it. The setting must live and breathe for players and, until it does, there's no real way for characters to connect to the chronicle. The setting is where your stories take place, and the more interesting and exotic it seems, the more your stories come to life. With each story you run, define the setting a little more, but don't give away everything at once. If you make the setting interesting enough, the players will want to explore it on their own, and they might even start contributing details. As long as players' additions don't conflict with what you intended, let them. Allowing player contributions is often a good way of determining what the players like to see in a chronicle.

As the chronicle progresses, add details of geography, custom and plot. Build the setting bit by bit at whatever pace you choose — it's better to have a small, well-developed starting point than a huge, ambiguous location. The mortal half of the setting is fairly easy to establish. Learn the history of a place first and what types of mortals would be there. However, remember that your setting is fictional, and that you can do anything you want with it. Feel free to change a few details here and there to suit the mood of your game. On the other hand, don't spring massive changes on your players out of the blue ("Oh, yeah, didn't I tell you guys there was a massive Gothic cathedral where the mall used to be?"), or the players will feel as if they've been bullied.

Only after you have finished with the mortal aspects of your setting should you want to consider the enchanted half of the equation. The history and atmosphere of your locale should help, determining what types of changelings would live there, and of what kith, Courts, houses and seemings they might be. Still, you still need to be the one to decide where the local freeholds are, what other sites of mystic power might be nearby (Garou caerns, mage chantries, wraith haunts, etc.), and where the local Dauntain and other Autumn People reside. You should also decide how the local chimerical landscape differs from the mortal world — if you want a magic forest to stand where the subdevelopment the characters live in is located, you should make this clear to the players before gameplay starts.

Last but not least, you should make sure the design of the setting meshes well with the motif of your overall chronicle. If the chronicle is going to be about corruption, the setting ought to be corrupt as well, both in its mortal and Kithain aspects.

# Casting the Parts

Once you know *what* is in your setting, it's time to think about who is in it. You should be concerned with both mortals and Kithain; neither side is terribly effective without the other. It's generally best to start at the top — who rules. Who are the local nobles? Their advisors? Whom does the nobles' lord serve? Are the commoners happy or rebellious? Who are the local Autumn People? Who are the Dreamers? You should think about whether Dauntain or other enemies of the local changelings have infiltrated the enchanted society. On the mortal side, consider which mortals are most likely to fight against the Kithain. If there is another supernatural presence in your setting, you will want to detail that as well. The local vampire, werewolf, wraith and mage populations, and their relations to the changelings, are all important things to have mapped out in advance.

## Intrigue

Intrigue is a vital ingredient of your chronicle. For people to play out intrigue, they need to be drawn into it — there has to be a tangible reward for all the scheming. Power is often an effective lure, but if power is a reward it needs to be immediate and real, visible and obtainable. Most importantly, it needs to be given out often enough to inspire characters to pursue it, but not so often that opportunities are passed on because they're too plentiful, or that the power level of the game rises to unmanageable levels.

## Ambition

Many characters eventually want to assume positions of power in the setting. In some games, this is just another aspect of the self-generating plots players contrive on their own. In other games, you may plan the characters' search for power from the beginning. In either case, you need to learn what long-term goals your players want to accomplish in the chronicle. You can then tailor an occasional session to the attainment of these goals, but don't give the players everything they want. Some characters may covet powerful positions from local nobles, or to advance the agendas of outsider motleys. Others may seek to return to Arcadia, or to uncover knowledge of the Dreaming.

On the other hand, more than a few players don't know or admit what they want in the long-term, or may not desire power. Don't worry, these folks will set their sights on something in time, especially if guided by their Legacies or other players. Practice stringing players along. Keep a carrot dangling before them. After all, you've got the whole world to play with as a Storyteller; you can certainly offer something to keep your Kithain coming back for more.

## The Price of Power

In most chronicles, it's likely that one or more characters might be in a position of power. If this is the case, the players need to know exactly what their responsibilities and advantages are. In general, any players in the role of nobles, mew representatives, motley leaders or, most rarely, Siochain, should be experienced enough to assist you as a Narrator. As powerful characters can have tremendous impact on lesser characters and the story as a whole, players should know and weigh the ramifications of their actions. Only experience in play develops this sort of insight, but it is vital that players with characters in positions of power understand both their responsibilities and their limits. Powerful characters, if abused, can discourage players with weaker characters. This drives off new players, and eventually the power-gamers may find themselves with no one to lord it over except one another. Nobles have as many responsibilities to their vassals as they have privileges, and it's important they recognize what their obligations are as well as their perks.

## Chronicle Dynamics

The key to a successful chronicle is a constant and uninterrupted flow of action. This doesn't mean there should be a gunfight every time someone goes to the corner store, but it should mean that something is always going on in one sense or another. In the real world, events never stop occurring, and everyone, in one way or another, gets dragged into life's chaos. Your chronicle should have the same ebb and flow to it. All characters should be drawn into the events around them. Every character should be doing something. Those in conflict may bide their time and pause to marshal their forces, but the tension never recedes. After all, if you give your players too much time to rest, relax and think, they may think about the fact that they're just playing a game. Too much time for reflection can shatter the most carefully crafted illusionary worlds.

# Trouble in all Shapes and Sizes

There are dozens of things in a story that can go wrong. This is particularly true of a chronicle. With the added level of complexity that comes with a chronicle, problems with continuity, advancement, numerous players, constant change and background plots are inevitable. A few of the more common chronicle problems, and how to deal with them, are detailed below:

• **Problem Players** — This problem is probably one of the most delicate and potentially disastrous you can face. For one reason or another, one or more players are disrupting the story and ruining everyone's good time. This can be the result of many things: cheating, excessive rule quotation ("rules lawyering"), personal vendettas or improper behavior. Once you detect a problem, your first action should be to approach the players privately and explain what they are doing and why you don't like it. At that point, most people attempt to change their ways, and that's that. Unfortunately, some players are prone to backsliding or just don't take the problem seriously. The next step to consider is some sort of penalty. Temporary suspension from the chronicle is usually effective. If players continue to make trouble, you may have to perform the distasteful task of barring them entirely from your chronicle. Do not be afraid to remove characters that unbalance your game. If the character's player is worthwhile, he'll understand the need for the sake of all of the other players. If not, you're better off without him.

• **Favoritism** — There is often a tendency to give your friends special treatment. Be vigilant in watching for this habit in all those who run and play the game, including yourself. If the problem does arise, try to remember that **Mind's Eye Theatre** is just a form of entertainment; no one can reasonably hold you responsible for a character's loss. If the problem continues, try to isolate problem individuals from encounters where favoritism might occur. As a final option, remove the offender from any position in which she can dispense favors to others.

• **Grudge** — In this situation an individual is treated unfairly for some reason that is not related to her character's nature or actions. Such is often the case with players who are not fond of each other in the real world. Handle it in a manner similar to favoritism problems.

• **Stagnation** — Even the most imaginative Storyteller occasionally runs out of ideas. Perhaps you're running the game too often to give yourself time to create new and original stories. If this is the case, consider spacing sessions further apart to provide yourself more planning time. Another solution is to take on more Storytellers or Narrators to give the chronicle a greater creative base to draw on. A plot coordination council of some sort is almost essential to running large-scale chronicles.

• **Logistics** — Problems with supplies and locations are bound to arise. If this is the case, be sure to communicate with everybody involved in the game. Players are often able to help procure a setting, props, incidental supplies and all manner of other vital materials.

• **Getting the News Out** — Sometimes you just don't have enough people to play the type of chronicle you've planned. This is more often a case of poor advertising than a genuine lack of bodies. Consider posting notices on electronic bulletin boards or on your local university network, in game and hobby stores, at conventions, at gaming organizations, with theatre or drama groups, on college campuses and anywhere else you think imaginative people with a taste for the original might be found.

• **Staying Focused** — At times your story may drift away from its original plot, or players may become lost. They may become too wrapped up in their own subplots or may be unable to unravel a puzzle that's vital to moving the plot along. When this happens, you need something to bring the story back on course. Having a few extra props available can be helpful when the story goes off on a tangent. Many of the prop ideas already suggested can be used to reorient players. For example, an intercepted letter with the Duke's seal on it, containing an important message (that just happens to be a vital plot point) can renew characters' interest in their original goal.

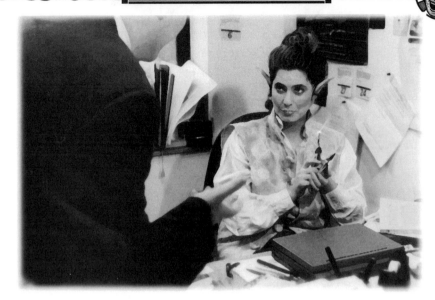

## Maintenance and Record-Keeping

It's a simple fact that the longer a chronicle runs, the more complex it becomes. The increased size of some chronicles only amplifies this fact. Developing a method for and the habit of keeping records is essential. The easiest part of the chronicle to keep records on is characters' statistics. Make a master copy of each character. Someone is bound to lose his character sheet and may need a replacement. Without a good memory or a master copy, this can pose a problem, especially with advanced characters. Storyteller records of characters also discourage unscrupulous players from altering their characters in the field. Furthermore, you can make use of character information when designing new stories. It's also a good idea to update your master copies after each story, given the inevitable changes arising from experience, rewards and penalties. A journal of events from each session proves equally invaluable, helping you understand changes the chronicle undergoes. You can then apply these changes to new stories.

Ideally, you, the Narrators and players should all file some sort of informal report after each story. Records from everyone can keep you appraised of all events and let you in on players' individual intentions. To encourage players to provide this information accurately, consider making reports mandatory or award experience only after you receive them. Make it clear that these reports are confidential and will not be used to "screw players over."

Finally, you should keep an ongoing private record of all the oaths, *geasa* and other bonds that the players enter into, including all the parties who swore to the oath and the exact wording of the oath itself. Not only can this provide you with a reminder of what your players may not be able to do (or be forced to do) by their oaths, but it also can be used to settle any future disagreements over what an oath requires of another. Remember that Glamour supports all oaths a changeling willingly swears to (or is magically bound by), and enforces the spirit of an oath, not necessarily the letter. (This is often an excellent device for you to prevent power-gamers from trying to control other characters with tricky oaths.) Nothing is worse, though, than setting up a challenging scenario only to find a group of characters is unable to participate due to an oath they've sworn, and players will quickly resent it if they think you're taking advantage of their oaths to force them to undertake certain actions. Keeping a clear record of oaths for those who have sworn them is the best way to head off this problem.

## Advancement and Balance

The greatest reward for some players is the sheer joy of playing. However, many players prefer to see their characters improve in status and power. The needs of both types of gamers need must be satisfied to keep your chronicle well-populated. Players who enjoy the story for its own sake are easy to please. In fact, they often please themselves by pursuing the goals their characters desire, which are often interpreted by the players themselves. Pleasing accomplishment seekers is a little more difficult, however. Allow characters chances to improve their station in the chronicle, if doing so is within the scope of your storyline. When characters reach tangible goals, their players are happy. However, to keep players happy without their characters achieving impossible degrees of power, be prepared to take characters down a peg or two, or allow other characters to do so for you. Besides creating revenge motives, such attacks fire players' desire to achieve more. Experience Traits, which players spend to improve their characters, are one form of reward, but there are others that are just as satisfying. Gaining the favor and support of other changelings can be more rewarding than any Art.

Furthermore, there are numerous positions of power that experience can't buy, but ambition and tenacity can. Even in well-planned chronicles, players may reach a point where they are bored and discontented with their place in the story, for no fault of yours. A player in this position actually has a couple of options. Starting a new character (and only playing the old one from time to time) helps players see if they still have what it takes to see a character grow and survive. As a Storyteller, make sure the player doesn't use this option to accumulate power for both his characters. Bringing in an old character's "relative" and allowing interaction between the siblings can mean trouble as they "work together." The easiest way to discourage this is to deny any direct ties between old and new characters. Another option to is to take the "advanced" character as a Narrator or Storyteller character. The character's experience with your chronicle and game as a whole can be used as a resource by lesser characters (i.e., other characters seek help from the experienced character), and the older character can be the basis for future stories.

Allowing the previous player to play the role of the mentor can be a great deal of fun in itself, as long as chronicle balance is maintained.

# Setting

Storytelling is more than simply voice and action. The effects that create your playing environment also make your story come to life. When you're running a story, you don't want your players to imagine they're playing in a world where enchanted beings walk in a world of wonder and beauty. You want them to feel they're actually there. Setting the stage for a convincing Gothic-Punk world is a challenge, unless you happen to have a real castle or forested glen nearby to use. With creativity, however, creating this sort of setting becomes surprisingly easy. It requires some effort and imagination, but with a minimum of difficulty you can have taverns, castles, fairy rings and mystical freeholds created in no time. To help you get started, we've provided some hints and ideas. Ultimately, though, creating an environment is limited only by your imagination. Take the advice we provide and run with it.

## Setting and Environment

More than any other element, the setting of a story has impact on that story's feel. Your setting should therefore be taken into careful consideration when deciding on your story's mood (which is discussed later). The fictional location you choose must fit the needs of your game as well as creating the atmosphere you have in mind.

### Finding Locations

The first practical step in planning a game is finding a good place to play. Where you play the game is influenced by the specific needs of your story. Factors like the number of players involved, theme, mood and nature of the plot all have an influence on the type of location you should choose. The scale of the game is your first consideration. Make certain you have enough room for all the players to move about. Multiple rooms or areas are helpful. The best layout usually involves a central meeting room that all the players can congregate in and multiple smaller sites for secret meetings. Choose a site that will work well logistically, and then worry about decorations later. Possibilities include college campuses, dorm lounges, museums, night clubs, coffee houses, conventions, parks, shopping malls, office buildings and warehouses. Obviously, extreme care must be taken when using these sites. You must ensure that all of the players are courteous and unobtrusive when playing in a public place. No one not involved in your game should ever be disturbed in any way by a game, and players need to understand that the session is over if anyone finds out about the game and is disturbed by what you're doing. If your players arrive in costume, sometimes you will draw attention, so always be polite and careful when "mundanes" come up and ask what's going on. Under no circumstances should you try to draw Glamour from innocent bystanders — feel free to explain at length what you're doing, but don't make mundanes a part of the game unless they specifically ask to play.

Some sites are more conducive to a certain types of stories than others. You may find a particular location is your favorite, but even then, you should keep your mind open to change. A change of locale, even if for only one scene, can help revive a dying chronicle. Most locations (or "sets") can be decorated to convey a specific mood. You must seek out sites that cater to the style of your game and nature of its plot. For best results, the setting should have a basis in reality. In other words, if it's a high energy social atmosphere you seek, stage your story in a nightclub (and find a place with good music, ambiance and a lot of room for people to move around.) If you're looking for a calm and intellectual setting, perhaps an art museum or library (and thus a real one) would be best. For politics and power plays, try a noble's hall. When choosing a location, look for an area that establishes the mood and atmosphere you're after. Because the enchanted world takes precedence to changeling eyes, try to find places you can decorate and describe that would be magical and fantastic, but don't overlook the mortal world either. Ideally, the players should have one location solely in the enchanted realm (a local freehold or glen, perhaps), and several others where both mortals and changelings might be found, so they can interact with other types of characters if they like.

## Changing Scenes

Sometimes it's necessary to use one area for different settings within the same story. Actual set changes should be performed quickly and efficiently. Lengthy set changes leave players bored. When your scene is changed, give it a last once-over, making sure everything is in place. A scene change should be just that. When the players enter the room again, they should have the distinct feeling that they're entering a new place. Your new decorations don't even need to be overly complicated. A quick shift of the couch or table, switching or removing a throw rug, draping a love seat and moving or removing chairs all help to change the feel of a room without necessitating major alterations. Changing the lighting and music can also make a big difference in a set's feel. Have the players help out to keep them involved, if it wouldn't ruin any surprises that you have in mind — you might just discover another artistic eye in your midst!

## Ambiance and Mood

**The Shining Host** offers you a chance to create a world from another time, in a mystical world, and challenges your creativity to do so. Establishing the right feel for a scene is governed by setting and environment. However, ambiance and mood are established and maintained by effects that are imposed upon the environment. Room decorations, recorded music and careful lighting are often the final touches for creating a scene.

• **Decorations** — Most modern rooms look, well, modern, and many are downright mundane. Playing **The Shining Host** in an accountant's office can be difficult, to say the least, because of the stifling sterility such a place is likely to exude. Some people are lucky and find a room they can decorate with all kinds of fantastic touches, but most games will be located in a modern meeting hall of some kind. Don't despair, though; all it takes is a few simple touches to spark players' imaginations. Try to cover up mundane features with cloth or something else suitable, and decorate the place with features the players will find interesting and intriguing. Wall hangings, either decorated or just plain cloth, are usually the first place to start if you're looking to create a local noble's hall, and **Changeling** has many crests, symbols and coats of arms that can be used to spice up such decorations. For an Unseelie dive, add some posters for local underground groups and keep the area poorly lit (but not so dark as to be a safety hazard). If you can't make a setting look 100 percent like what you want it to, aim for guiding the imagination of the players in that direction, and trust their good will to do the rest.

• **Music** — Music can be an integral part of establishing the mood of a story. It lends a hand in creating drama and, when appropriate, tension. When planning your story be certain to select music that complements your intended mood. Also make sure you have a variety of music on hand in case the mood changes.

There are two types of music that you should have on site: in-game and out. In-game music is what the characters actually hear in a scene, whether it's played by sprites or a mortal band brought into a freehold for an evening. It should be heavily mood-oriented and atmosphere-intensive, and while you may enjoy putting certain songs on for their value in terms of humor or out-of-character references, avoid doing so if the joke will break the game's mood. What kind of music suits a scene depends on what you want, but try to avoid having a lot of prominent lyrics (they're distracting) or having the volume at a level where it intrudes on the playability of the game. You may also be lucky enough to have a player or two who's willing to perform in-game. Take advantage of this (assuming your player won't be embarrassing himself by opening his mouth or taking out his guitar) and let his performance become part of the game. This is especially appropriate to the nature of **The Shining Host**, and can even be a good way to introduce players to a group or have some non-player friends stop by (as long as they know what they're walking into). Of course, if any music happens to be central to the plot, feel free to do whatever you like with it, but make sure the players know that as well.

You can also use music as background out-of-game music to enhance particular scenes. This is especially useful for combat scenes or settings in the Far or Deep Dreaming, away from the mortal world. If you use out-of-game music, feel free to use whatever creates the mood you are seeking. However, you still must take care not to let the music get obtrusive. If your players have to shout over thundering lyrics, your game will rapidly dissolve into chaos.

Celtic music is especially suited to many scenes in **The Shining Host**, and its recent popularity makes it easy to find good, authentic Celtic CDs — performers such as Loreena McKennitt, Clannad and Ashley McIsaac are a good start, but there are dozens more. Many folk groups provide excellent atmosphere as well, from Grey Eye Glances to Silly Wizard.

• **Audio Effects**: Above and beyond music, certain sounds and effects can enhance an evening. Horror and sound effect CDs, found in any music store, are a good place to start. A good FX CD can provide a variety of sound effects to simulate many different events, like screams, clashes of arms, clanging portcullises and so on. Proper timing of these sounds is critical. If you're able to pre-mix a tape of effects, you can play those sounds at appropriate moments in the story. Preparation is the key. Have your effects cued up ahead of time so that, with the mere touch of a button, hideous screams or church bells can be heard by all. Preparation makes for infinitely more drama than delaying the entire game while you search for the right sound.

• **Lighting Effects** — The Gothic-Punk world has a lot of dim lights and dark corners, and while real fire is absolutely out of the question for most sites, you can add a lot of atmosphere to a freehold by recreating the light of the freehold's balefire. You'll also want a lot of unusual lights for the enchanted world, to show the difference that Glamour makes. Remember, a few well-placed shadows can hide a great many anachronisms that might otherwise distract your players from the game.

When setting up your lights, follow these simple guidelines. Avoid high wattages and white light. Multicolored light bulbs have the broadest effect. By arranging multicolored light bulbs in different parts of the room, you can create shadowy areas and still have well-lit "white light" areas where the colors intersect. If you have track lighting, recessed multicolored bulbs work very well. If you can't get multicolored bulbs, cloth draped over lights works just as well (but avoid putting cloth in direct contact with hot bulbs). The key is contrast from low wattage bulbs. Keeping enough low-wattage lights to contrast with one another results in plenty of light to see by and plenty of shadows to hide in. Play around with different combinations to determine what works best for your mood and scene. While candles may be very atmospheric, they should be used extremely sparingly. Remember, burning down your site generally has a detrimental effect on a chronicle.

## Props

After you've got a story, players, a place to play and even selected an appropriate soundtrack to accompany the game, something else is still needed to bring the story to life. This is the point at which props come in. Props for a story don't need to be grandiose or expensive. Most props can be found in your own home or your grandparents' attic, or simply constructed. In **Mind's**

**Eye Theatre**, props should be kept relatively simple and should not attract more attention than the story itself. Only a few touches are needed to help a player's imagination fill in the blanks. Since **The Shining Host** is a storytelling game, imagination is of the utmost importance. This is not to say that you should be sparing with props; merely that your chronicle will survive without them. If you have the available materials, go wild. Just make sure that the props are not the focus of the story. The spotlight should always remain on the characters, not on what surrounds them.

## General Props

General props are items that can help you further a story by giving players something that they can physically examine. The Storyteller should be wary of how often physical props are used and what impact they have on the story. If physical props are allowed to dominate a story, players may begin to rely on them rather than interacting with one another. Be sure to inform players when props will be used in a story. Otherwise, characters are likely to disregard an important clue, considering it just another feature of the place you're playing in.

Many items can be used as general props to help enhance your story. Scrolls, jewelry, documents and pieces of artwork are a few examples. These props can be used to give game information, or they can merely grant insight into the character of the person possessing the prop. Sometimes an item has to be represented by an item card, as in the case of weapons. Also, a card may be discreetly attached to an item, giving more information to a player who inspects that particular prop. Creative and effective usage of general props can make a story more interesting for everyone, particularly if props are used to represent important items with plot (as well as character) significance. The important thing is to stay focused and avoid overloading yourself with gadgets and gewgaws. If you come up with an idea for a prop, but are unable to implement it, don't panic — your story can stand on its own without every last widget. After all, people, not things, make a story.

## Personal Props

Personal props, like costumes, can be used by players to help distinguish them as their characters. In a Gothic-Punk game, such props are very important to help with mood. This form of assistance can be particularly useful for Narrators, especially when they must often change from character to character. Cloaks, tunics, scarves, hats, canes and jewelry are only a few of the accessories that can give a character a distinctive look. You may want to provide certain items to players to aid them in this manner, especially if players are uncertain of the identities of the characters they are playing. For example, providing matching tunics for the freehold's guards, or a particular T-shirt for an Unseelie motley, will help to identify players as members of that group.

Many people feel intimidated about making "fantasy" clothing for their characters, but, again, providing the right feel is fairly easy. Sweatpants, tights or an ankle-length skirt, boots or sandals of any sort, and a simple "T-tunic" is the standard garb of most medieval gaming, and is easy to assemble. You can often buy "poet shirts" (shirts with puffy sleeves and ruffles) instead of making your own tunic. Of course, a changeling can look like just about anything, and eshu in Egyptian garb, pooka in multicolored trenchcoats, or nockers dressed in piepans and tinfoil are all possible. Costume shops sell simple inexpensive cloaks, as do vintage clothing stores. More complex clothing will come with time, as skilled sewers amongst your gamers and Narrators become involved, but the tunic/poet shirt, sweatpants/tights/skirt, and boots/sandals combination always works just fine.

For other personal props, items such as costume jewelry work best; real jewels can be far too valuable to lend out for a game. Should all else fail, second-hand stores can be great places to pick up a few last-minute props at an affordable price. All manner of clothing, including hats, canes and costume jewelry, can be acquired at such emporiums. In many stories, not much is needed by way of personal props. Sometimes, only a cane or piece of jewelry can make a character. The most important thing to remember is to have fun with props, avoiding dangerous ones.

# Combat

When people think of fantasy movies, they often think of glorious battle scenes and exciting tournaments. Such antics can be a part of your chronicle, but you must never allow players to try and act out large-scale combat too realistically. Follow the combat rules for Mind's Eye Theatre strictly, never allow players to touch, and always think about safety.

That being said, there are ways to make mass combat fun without the actual swinging of swords. After all, half of combat is planning, positioning and scouting. As a Storyteller, try to develop certain combat scenes ahead of time. Sculpt the setting as well as you would any other scene, and let the players work with the setting, organizing their forces, developing tactics and strategies. If the players blindly rush into things, then you and your Narrators (and perhaps other players) can take advantage of this, and recreate some of the disorientation of a surprise attack by positioning yourselves to come out of hiding from many directions without comprising safety. Small combats, one on one or two on two, are relatively easy, but make sure that any large-scale conflict has several Narrators around to guide it and keep it flowing quickly.

### No-Nos

Weapons should never be used as props. In addition, props must be understood to be someone's property, not some character's property. If your players start taking home the props that belong to their characters, perhaps it's time to reconsider using props at all. If you chose to go this route, cards (like those used to represent weapons) are the best way to go.

# Creating Stories

Story creation can be as simple or as detailed as you want. The more effort you put into preparing a story, the smoother the plot runs when it's finally executed. There is no small amount of satisfaction to be gained from writing a successful and well-appreciated story — but that's easier said than done. Finding the right combination of stimuli to ignite creative thought can be difficult. For some of us, creativity comes naturally. For others, it's more difficult to bring creative aspects of one's personality to the fore. However, this is exactly what you must do in order to create a good story.

Inspiration can come from any source. Magazines, movies, books, theatre, television, friends, family — you get the picture. The challenge is to take what you see and change it into something all your own. Inspiration can be, quite literally, any stimulus that ignites the process of creative thought. Hence, inspiration is very often as dependent on what's without as on what's within. What sends one person's mind racing may bore someone else. You must find the things that inspire you (if you don't already know what they are) and associate with them in order to ignite your creative fires.

## Plot

A story's plot is its progression of events. Plot not only involves the machinations of the powers that be, but the machinations of the characters as they pursue their own goals in the story. Plots are essential to the successful advancement of the story, as plot is really nothing more than a term for the series of events making up the story. A story can have any number of plots (see "Story Style," below, for more details on this). These plots should all be wound together with skill and care before the actual game begins, however, so you at least know how things are supposed to turn out. The trick is to have all the pieces of a plot already written in the characters' briefings so they can read about their own respective parts of the overall plot at the game's beginning — and then piece things together once gameplay starts. Together, the characters' backgrounds compose the main plot, and by pursuing their own parts of the plot, the characters advance the plot as a whole. During a story, it's often helpful to keep a schedule of events. This device is basically a pre-planned sequence of events (usually initiated by outside forces) that are going to occur regardless of the characters' actions. Typically, characters played by

Narrators keep the schedule on track. It is also helpful to integrate occasional Narrator characters into the story to assist the progression of the plot (or plots). These tactics should be used sparingly; otherwise players may grow dependent upon interaction with Narrators instead of with each other. However, occasional Narrator intervention can add a new level of unpredictability and excitement to a story.

# Elements of a Story

The elements of a story are best defined by its components or stages. It is often helpful to think of plot elements in terms of tense (past, present and future). In terms of story structure, these elements are addressed in the opening, climax and resolution of your chronicle. At the beginning of the story, characters reflect on events of their past that have brought them to the story. The story's climax is where the story's plot (or plots) are exposed and dealt with by some or all of the characters. Finally, there's the resolution, where the story comes to a close and you can set up story hooks for future tales.

## Opening

The opening can be any point at which you choose to begin your story. It can be a gradual, gentle start or a shocking plunge into the world of the Kithain. The latter works best if the characters start out as normal humans; the former is better for extended chronicles with older changelings. At the beginning of a story, each character should have a written synopsis of recent events that "everyone" would be aware of. This provides a basis for your plots, as well as laying down some common ground for characters to discuss. With such common knowledge, you're also helping to set the tone and theme of your game. The synopses of common knowledge and recent personal events should be brief explanations of the situation at hand. They should be precise and intriguing. These synopses should be the first media through which players get a feel for the story's mood. The synopses should also hint at the story's main theme. You may even wish to foreshadow the plot, but that depends on your personal style.

## Climax

When the main plot is on the verge of conclusion, the story is considered at its climax. This usually happens when characters have discovered all they need to know to solve whatever problem faces them and are on the verge of resolving the story. The tension is usually at its highest point at this time. If the opening was staged carefully, and the players are cooperative and imaginative, the climax can be reached with little additional effort on the part of Narrators. However, even the best of plans can be mislaid, or perhaps the Storyteller and Narrators prefer to take a more active role in the progression of your story's plot. Either way, there are times when a Narrator's intervention is warranted. The climax should be the high point of the story, something the players should always anticipate and work toward. However, this element should never be rushed. It's a matter of timing. Extended chronicles shouldn't have everything wrapped up in a single climax. After all, you need to have something for the changelings to do next week. Often, a story's climax takes the form of a combat, but this doesn't always have to be the case. Decisive votes, debates, unveilings, trials by fire and so on can all bear the dramatic weight of serving as a story's climax.

### Resolution

The story's resolution is where all (or most) of the pieces come together. The resolution should be used as a means of winding the excitement down while cultivating an interest in future stories. Players should always end a story feeling as though they have accomplished something. They do not have to uncover the big picture; merely knowing they've found another piece of the puzzle is often enough. In **Mind's Eye Theatre**, players often enjoy gathering for a group wrap-up session after a game. Unlike players of tabletop games, players of **The Shining Host** rarely see all of the action that takes place — they get wrapped up in their own plots, not the group's. During wrap-up sessions, many players look forward to learning more about "the big picture." At the wrap-up, players share their version of the story and, in so doing, give other players an opportunity to see more of the game they just took part in. Plus, it's a great chance for everyone to tell stories about their characters — and show off their accomplishments, which can be great fun as well.

### Off-Line Gaming

The game doesn't have to end when everyone puts down their character sheets. In-character e-mails, informal discussions at coffeehouses and the like can all serve both as roleplaying exercises and as ways to advance plots. As long as players keep some perspective on this sort of thing (Phone calls at 3 AM to discuss minor plot points generally signal a need for time out), off-line gaming can be a great way to shade in the gray areas of your game.

## Story Considerations

There are several factors that must be taken into consideration before you can begin scripting a story. The scale, number of players and general character types are all important elements that must be kept in mind. Rampaging chimerical teddy bears and vicious Unseelie raiders don't fit well into political chronicles; pacifist philosophers don't last long in hack-n-slash games. Tailor your plots to what you have to work with in terms of group, character and setting.

### Scale

Scale is the number of people you have playing. Games can range in size from handfuls to hundreds, and you need to ensure that no matter how many changelings are out there, there's something for everyone potentially to do.

Oftentimes, players set their own plots in motion based on roleplaying and character interaction, but there needs to be a metaplot, a grand scheme that gives everyone a starting point. Not everyone is capable of making his own fun, and as such you need to prepare a story that, at minimum, has something for everyone.

## Scope

The scope of your story is a very important consideration. Whether the story involves a massive plot to destroy the greatest of Dauntain or find a childling's lost toy is a matter of scope. Scope boils down to what's won or lost. Scope can be limited by the number of players in the game. You shouldn't always have stories with huge scope; players grow bored with "saving the world" every week. On the other hand, you should not keep the players from getting involved in potentially earth-shattering stories. Balance is the key. Metaplots should have bigger scopes than local plots. Obviously, the more characters involved in a plot, the higher the stakes should be. Don't forget your mortals when creating plots, either. The actions of the mundanes have a huge effect on the Kithain, in terms of audiences, influence and even emotion. On a more pragmatic note, it's no fun to sit around as a member of mortal society, waiting patiently to Ravaged. Make sure your humans have something worthwhile to do, too.

## Cast

Another factor to take into consideration is the type of characters players portray. The best way to determine this is to ask them. A story usually works best if players are enacting characters they are comfortable with, although it can occasionally be interesting to cast players in roles different from what they're used to playing. This variation in casting should only be done if you think it would be enjoyable for all the players. An important consideration is whether you are giving players premade characters, with complete backgrounds, Attributes and Arts, or if players are allowed to make their own characters. Sometimes the guidelines lie somewhere in-between. Obviously, the easiest of these options is to use pre- made characters. This allows you to customize your story to the characters, tying them to one another to make for a more intriguing plot. The problem with this is that players are sometimes disappointed with the characters they get. This can detract from everyone's enjoyment.

# Story Style

Style is the method you use in constructing your story. It describes how the subplots tie in with the main plot and how characters interact with the environment you have chosen. Style is the thread from which your story is woven. Without style, a story has no cohesive form and might well become boring for players. You need to develop and hone your style so as to be able to craft a finely tuned story, with many layers and intricacies for players to explore.

## Main Plot

The main, or metaplot is the root of a story, and any other lesser plots from the main plot. The main plot is what brings characters together, unifying their attention. The main plot of a story should be all- encompassing, in that all characters should be affected by it in at least a minor fashion. The main plot should illuminate every other aspect of the story. Not every character needs to be touched by your metaplot directly, but each character should be aware of the main plot at least on some peripheral level.

## Subplots

In most novels and movies, subplots are just filler material. Subplots are essential to **Mind's Eye Theatre**, however. These secondary stories keep characters busy and carry them from moment to moment. They are the stories that are woven around the characters. A story gives players ample opportunities to explore subplots, and due to the unique nature of this sort of game, subplots can be taken as far as the players want to take them. Each character should be involved in as many subplots as possible. A subplot can be any personal goal a character is trying to accomplish. Subplots should be crafted so as to intermingle with one another, so that characters become embroiled in a web of intrigue as one subplot leads them to another. The more layers of intrigue in a story, the more players enjoy untangling them. Indeed, if your setting is intricate enough, you may find players developing subplots of their own, adding to the confusion. This wild metastasis of plot should be encouraged, because it helps the story grow and gives it a life of its own. A subplot can sometimes be almost as large in scope as the main plot, the difference being that in a subplot, it is not necessary for everyone to be involved for it to come to fruition. However, you should take care that the subplot does not override the main plot; the word is prefixed with "sub-" for a reason.

## Character Relations

Character interaction is a part of every story and every chronicle. Intricate character interaction is essential to a story. That is not to say that all characters will get along harmoniously — character strife is usually much more interesting than One Big Happy Enchanted Family. However, making sure that characters relate to one another requires a bit of planning on your part. Making sure that players create backgrounds for their characters helps, as it gives you more material to work with to create common ground for Kithain characters to share. Spreading rumors that provide incentive for discussion, trade, and cooperation is another good way to go, as is the inclusion of a nasty villain who will force characters at least to discuss working together.

## Multiple Goals

Each of us possesses a multitude of goals and ambitions. Many of them conflict, and we have to choose between them. For instance, you might want to go to the movies on the same day you want to visit a friend. Multiple goals complicate matters, and while in real life that can be bothersome, in this game it only adds to the excitement. The more complicated you can make things, the better. Complications such as multiple goals give characters depth and keep players busy. A player with several goals is usually occupied throughout the course of a story and is rarely bored. Indeed, if players with multiple goals achieve even one of those goals, they probably leave the story with a sense of accomplishment.

# Narration and Storytelling

Now that you have written a story, you need to make it work in a live game. Narrating a story is an art akin to juggling; you have to keep up with all story threads, play judge and make sure that none of the players get bored — you'll have quite a few eggs in the air at all times. Storytelling requires a lot of work and planning and usually leaves you exhausted. There is a positive side to it, however. As Storyteller, you have a ringside seat to the story and can watch it unfold in its entirety. Because your control of the story is loose (tight control denies player freedom), you may be surprised by how the story twists and changes in the hands of your players. If you do your job well, you will be rewarded with the players' thanks and a great game as well. Of course, with the great rewards of storytelling comes a great deal of responsibility. You have to initiate and guide the story and present it in an entertaining manner. You, above all people involved, can most easily destroy the story. Even a very good story can be ruined if it's not presented well. If a few required player handouts are missing, or if players have no idea where the game is taking place, you have failed.

It is very important that you prepare every aspect of that story as far ahead of time as possible. If you try to prepare an entire game at the last minute, you'll be stressed out by the time the game begins. The game will suffer heavily from your exhaustion. Veteran Storytellers should take note that running a live game is very different from running old-style roleplaying games. You can no longer sit down an hour before play commences and dream up a quick plot. If you try to do this, your story will have lots of holes. If you change your setting in mid-story, you need to represent the change in some way so players realize where they are without having to ask. Prepare everything in advance or suffer the folly of sloth. The main rule to remember when preparing your story is "show, don't tell." You have to present your story so players can make their own impressions of the environment without your impressions being forced on them. Live games work because players can take the lead based on information they discover themselves. If you have not fleshed out your story enough — if you have to tell players what's going on over and over again — you might as well be playing a tabletop roleplaying game, because everything that's special about **Mind's Eye Theatre** will be missing. Fortunately for you, players usually cooperate in every way to help you maintain the illusion, but it's up to you to direct their attention from the game-like aspects of roleplaying.

## How to Host a Game

Running an entire chronicle can be exhausting unless you pace yourself. Expect to spend a minimum of an hour per player writing the story and setting everything up. Expect to actually play a story bi-monthly or even monthly. Trying to run a weekly game is very taxing and may result in the eventual death of your chronicle (not to mention your own nervous breakdown). Don't make your games frequent and tedious, but rare and spectacular.

## Storyteller Focus

As a Storyteller, your focus should always be on keeping the game running as smoothly as possible. To ensure that the game doesn't get out of hand, make sure you have enough Narrators. They'll serve to answer players' questions and resolve the majority of inter-player disputes, as your arbitration should only be required in the most extreme circumstances. More importantly, though, your Narrators will be an integral part of game action. As the arbiters of any large-scale conflict, noble courts, and a guide to how Banality might rear up at any moment to menace the Kithain, Narrators will be in constant interaction with players in all levels of your game. This requires a great deal of commitment from your Narrators, as they'll constantly be on the go, interacting with only a few characters at a time.

On the up side, your Narrators will have a good idea of who is working with who, and can keep you informed. They also can spread information and rumors through the many Narrator characters they animate. Rather than having to cook up a convoluted plot to let characters know that a grump sluagh is becoming a Dauntain, you can have a Narrator character whisper it quickly into a player's ear. Of course, that informant could be lying — which could lead to all new plots and paranoia. At the same time, if the action slows or people are getting frustrated, having your Narrators constantly on the floor enables you to pinpoint trouble spots quickly. Concentrate on where players stand in terms of resolving the plot or solving the mystery you have given them. If they are struggling, drop a few hints and spread a few rumors, then watch your changelings scramble to discover new information. If the players are too close to solving the mystery, throw in a red herring or create a new scene on the fly. Improvisation is a potent art, and Storytellers who learn to use it are well-rewarded.

If you are playing in public, you must serve as a buffer between the authorities of the real world and the potential mayhem players can create. Discretion is the better part of valor. Educate players on responsible playing and do not hesitate to hand out rewards or punishments as the need arises. Preparation is essential to running a successful story. The greater the preparation, the less you have to worry about maintaining focus. A well-prepared game frees you to enjoy your creation and interact with players, while a poorly prepared game leaves you scrambling to maintain control. When you maintain focus on story elements, the surroundings and your players, you need not fear the results of any game session.

## Pre-Game Tasks

There are several things you need to do to set up and run a game of The Shining Host.

1 — Make sure you know the size and scope of your game before anything else; it's the only way to make sure there's enough staff and plot for everyone.

2 — Get all of your props and costumes lined up well in advance. These usually require the most legwork and take the most time to round up, so you don't want to be chasing after them last minute.

3 — Choose a good core staff and delegate. You can't do everything yourself; don't even try. Find people you trust and turn them loose.

4 — Make sure everyone is working on the same page. A lot of work can be wasted by duplication or misunderstandings. Have everyone aware of what everyone else is doing.

5 — Keep a paper trail. Note when tasks are accomplished and where everything is. Keep track of who did well and who didn't. It'll make next time easier.

6 — Define everyone's role. Power squabbles and unfinished tasks are both unproductive.

7 — Set deadlines and keep to them for all tasks related to the game.

8 — Get your essential paperwork done. This includes arranging sites, briefing sheets, and plot creation. If you save this sort of work-intensive thing for the last minute, if there's a screwup your whole game may be left high and dry.

9 — Pace yourself. If you burn out creating the game, you'll have no fun running it.

10 — Relax. It's a game, not brain surgery. If one week's game doesn't go well, you can always learn from your mistakes and do better next time.

## Character Creation

It is your role as Storyteller (aided by Narrators) to guide players through the character generation process. It is generally best to have character creation go on off-line, well before your actual game action starts. This enables you to gauge accurately the power level and mood of your game. In addition, having access to character histories will enable you to create plotlines that force characters to interact. Knowing characters' backgrounds also allows you to bring in faces, places and items from a Kithain's past; always useful if the action starts to flag. After your players arrive for the game session, you need to introduce them to the basic premise of the game. Your main goal should be to make contributing to the story as easy as possible for players. If your players are beginners, show them the basics, but let them discover the intricacies of the game on their own. Hopefully everyone playing will have at least a basic idea of the rules, but be prepared to field questions and help out beginners. Start by laying out any briefing sheets you want to use on a table and invite players to look them over. You can pass out character sheets at the same time. Give the players time to look everything over and ask questions. If players can refer to the briefings and their character cards while they listen to your explanations, they'll understand how things work a lot better.

It's also likely that you have certain roles in the story that you need filled. Your story probably has requirements, in terms of characters and setting, that must be understood by all concerned. Even if you don't have specific requirements, you probably have a general idea of the types of characters you need. The best way to deal with this is to request certain players to fill those roles beforehand; usually the extra "oomph" that a precreated character is likely to have (not to mention its obviously central role in upcoming plots) will be enough to make up for the disappointment a player might feel over not being able to create her own character. If you're running an extended chronicle, odds are that most of your players will simply show up and start playing once you declare things "on line." This makes your job a lot easier — who wants to do briefings at the beginning of each session — but be careful to catch new players who might get lost in the shuffle. Bringing them into line with what the rest of the game is already doing will make everyone happier than if new players are forced into swimming upstream against established plots and characters.

## Introducing Your Story

When players begin to arrive, you need to give them information. You need to tell them what's happened since the last story (if anything) and should provide goals and motivations for the upcoming evening. Prepare as much information as you can in written form for players to read as they arrive. Here are some handouts that you can create to facilitate your story's introduction.

• **Character Cards** — You need to have enough of these for all your players. It's wise to have spare cards on hand, since players, who have their own characters, may forget their cards. In addition, you'll need pencils for everyone who's forgotten their own.

• **Timetable** — (For Narrators only) This sheet contains a chronological list of all events that take place. Timetable sheets are useful for planning complex stories, and help your Narrators coordinate where they have to be when. Events listed might be, "10:00 PM: Herald of the Duke arrives and announces Highsummer festivities will begin in half an hour." Make sure each Narrators has her own copy and go through the events on the handout during your Narrator briefing.

• **Background Briefing** — This is a one-pager that you can create to provide a short background for the important characters of your chronicle. You should include any important events that have occurred, rumors that are circulating throughout the setting and important things that have happened in previous games. A new player should be able to pick up this handout and immediately have an idea of what is going on. (Lost players tend to be bored players, and bored players don't come back.) The handout can mention things like what setting the chronicle takes place in and the name of the local movers and shakers. Make several copies of this document and give one to each player, or leave several out in the open for players to take.

• **Character Briefing** — Depending upon how thorough your character creation process is, you may need to let individual players know special tidbits that their characters know. It's best to have these written down; even the most talented roleplayers have to resort to their notes every now and then.

## Guiding Players

As your players begin to work out the story, it's possible that they may be unsure of themselves. New players in particular need some sort of guidance to help them learn the rules and get used to acting out their characters' actions. Step into a minor character in your story and engage a new player in a minor challenge to get her used to the rules. The challenge system works well in play, but most people do not immediately understand it until after they've actually defended themselves in a challenge, and gotten to try out the system in a non-life-or-death situation. Try to let new players win your challenge, as it builds their confidence, and confidence is sorely needed when newcomers play in the same game as more experienced players. Sometimes players also need help with their goals. A story that leans heavily toward investigation may frustrate players who miss one or two vital clues.

Eventually, some players may come over to you asking for help. Unless the players have a rules question, or you have to clarify some point that a character should know by virtue of his history or background, you might not want to give information away too easily at first. If a player receives immediate assistance from a Storyteller or Narrator, he may become dependent on outside help. Instead of giving direct answers to player questions, encourage players to figure things out for themselves. Later, if a player really does need help, have another Narrator, in the guise of a minor character, assist the player. If another Narrator is not available, you can approach the player and offer aid through your own character (although having another Narrator do it involves a touch of finesse). Pull your assistance off cleanly and the player will never know you have responded to his plea.

You also need to invent things to do for players who seem bored with the game. These players have usually either accomplished or hopelessly failed to achieve their goals, or can't find the motivation to pursue a difficult goal. Your best options are to get a bored player involved in another plot, or to make up a customized plot on the spot that centers on the bored player's character. If your character mentions a lead to a powerful treasure that others are looking for, the player may spend time following that lead. Alternatively, giving the bored player a clue that someone else has missed allows you to kill two birds with one stone, as other players will need to talk to this character — giving him all sorts of new chances for character interaction. It's a good idea to have a library of new plots on hand that you can drop into your chronicle as needed. Remember to be vigilant for bored players during your first few games; first-time players might not come back if they're bored all evening long. If you don't keep the players busy with plots, their characters may start swinging at each other just for something to do. At this point, the game quickly degenerates into a free-for-all. You'll probably find that players stay busy as your chronicle progresses because they spend more time dabbling in the plots of other players.

## Interacting with Players

Your key to interacting with players is the type of minor character known as an extra. An extra can be a pre-generated character already woven into the story, or a character created on the spur of the moment to fix a problem. You rarely need to create a character card for your extra; a basic concept is usually enough. (If the player characters really want to kill or otherwise interact with the extra so that Traits are called for, improvise as the plot demands.) Each character you introduce needs to have an easily identifiable mark so players can recognize which minor character you are playing. A wearable prop, such as a hat, coat, scarf, bandanna or amulet is usually enough. A distinctive speech pattern, like an accent, is at least as useful. Remember that the mark needs to be something that you can put on and take off quickly, since you may end up having to switch between several minor characters over the course of an evening's play. Your extra(s) should be enjoyable to play. During the middle of a story, you may find that you and the Narrators have little to do. You then have a chance to play your bit parts just for fun. Go a little wild. Try to provide some comic relief if you feel the game is getting too heavy, and most of all, enjoy yourself. If you're not having fun, even if the players are, something's wrong.

## Player Questions

Aside from having a way to deal with players within the context of the story, you need to handle players' questions outside the story. During the first half hour of a game, it's a good idea to keep a Narrator "out of game" to answer any questions players might have. When players step out of character to ask questions, you don't want them in the main playing area. Set the "outside"

Narrator up in another room. The most important thing to remember when interacting with players is to never remind them they are playing a game; addressing a Narrator as a Narrator does just that. You may occasionally need to impart information that a character can not offer. You have to provide such information as discreetly as possible without distracting players from their characters. If you want to be stylish about offering game information to players, you can prepare notes for Narrators to hand to players who discover things. You can also put notes in closed envelopes where clues might be found. You can write requirements on the outside an envelope, requirements that must be met before the player may look at the clue within. One thing you want to avoid when dealing with players is letting them overuse Narrators. Players may try to use Narrators as messengers, to summon other characters, or to try new and interesting abuses of Arts. If a player asks for such favors too often, Narrators can simply refuse their help. Tied to running plots and arbitrating conflicts, Narrators are simply in too short a supply to allow them to become hostages to individual characters or roles.

# Working with Narrators

As a Storyteller, you can't do everything yourself. It's not possible. No matter how good a Storyteller you are, you're going to need the help of Narrators (unless, perhaps, you have only five or six players). If you try to run the whole story, you will quickly become overwhelmed. It's best to delegate tasks and let your Narrators make judgment calls. Ideally, you, as Storyteller, should not have to deal with players very much (unless you establish yourself as a Narrator as well as Storyteller). You should wander around and observe to make sure the story is proceeding well. Players should learn to go to Narrators with their questions. A player should refer to you only if a Narrator has no idea how to handle a question.

To ensure that Narrators understand what's going to happen in the story, you should meet with them early in the evening. If no one but you knows what's going on, your Narrators aren't much use, and could even prove a hindrance if they direct events in the wrong fashion. You should assign tasks to Narrators at this time. For example, you can ask a Narrator to provide a clue to a character, but let the Narrator work out how and when that clue is delivered. Narrators need to keep you informed of their rulings and of story events. Avoid reversing a decision that a Narrator has made. Doing so makes Narrators seem indecisive and leads players to doubt them. If you want to run a large game, you are going to need assistants, and you have to learn to communicate with them effectively.

## The Teeming Hordes

For **The Shining Host**, you will need a large cast of willing Narrators. If you underpopulate your Narrative staff, you shortchange your players by creating long lines when multiple characters need Narrator assistance. Furthermore, a shortage of staff can make complicated scenes stagnate as Narrators try to run too much at once. Do whatever it takes to make sure that you have enough Narrators, or your story will fall apart under its own weight.

## Pacing the Story

More often than not, a story does not run according to schedule. It either drags late into the night or players work too quickly and become bored with their accomplishments. It's during times like these that you need to reach into your bag of tricks and adjust the pace of the story. Dealing with stories that are running too long is, thankfully, relatively simple. It's easy to push on the accelerator. You can start by doling out clues and information through character contacts and the introduction of new props. One of the simplest tools you can have in your repertoire is a number of characters to throw into the adventure. Simply introduce a character who has the tools to help solve the problem, but for a price.

Prolonging play time is a little more tricky than reducing it. Stretching out the action means prolonging the story, but if the story is complete, you have to make up new events in the spot. However, instead of creating an entirely new plot, you might be able to extend the "finished" story by going on past its logical conclusion. Extending stories works very well if you have a group of Narrators who are flexible, creative and who like to work "on the run." If you foresee the story ending early, there are ways of prolonging it by distracting players. Essentially, you can introduce subplots in order to pull characters off the beaten path. If you have a chance, work out one or two subplots for every story. Try not to overuse any particular devices for prolonging a story, or people will get bored, but an ever-new batch of red herrings can prove amusing.

The best way to slow players down is to present them with something new as a distraction. Bring in a Big Evil Nasty Thing (B.E.N.T.), or have the local Dauntain threaten, and you can be certain that the linear plot will be set aside in the face of the incipient threat. Just make sure the players don't feel that you'll sick a horde of rampaging foes on them every time they decide to take their time doing something, and you'll be fine. One of the more unusual tricks to use while improvising is to create a set of events with no obvious explanation. Then listen to the explanations your players propose and choose one to be the case, or base your explanation on the theory you like best. (Just don't let it show that you didn't have the foggiest idea what you were going to do with this twist when you introduced it.) While this tactic may seem cheesy, some absolutely amazing stories can be developed this way.

# Rescue 911

In **Mind's Eye Theatre**, the Storyteller and Narrators have only limited control over what occurs in the story. While you can often predict human behavior to know where a story might lead, things never work out as planned. Players have a tendency to ignore old goals, creating new plotlines without a second thought for your hours of preparation and cunningly laid plans. While such situations can be disconcerting, it's not always a bad thing for your players to improvise. Unforeseen plot turns are, in fact, what **Mind's Eye Theatre** is all about. The trick is to use what the players give you, instead of fighting with them. If players generate new plots, you can continue them in the next story, providing you with new material upon which to build. If you let players run with what they come up with, your story may go in entirely unexpected — but rewarding — directions.

While the story may go off on a tangent, headed toward no foreseeable conclusion, you can usually apply finesse to work things out. The hardest part is knowing when to say no, and recognizing when to stop destructive subplots in their tracks. The rule of thumb is, if a new direction adds depth to the story, entertains people and doesn't get in the way, let it run its course. As with all things, though, people can go too far in improvisation. The following are some signs indicating that events might be getting out of control:

• Characters begin attacking everything that moves for no obvious reason. (This is probably the best sign.)

• There is excessive character "death" during a game.

• A key antagonist is killed, disabled, captured or otherwise prevented from becoming a key figure in the story without good reason.

• Players begin acting on out-of-character knowledge (also known as "ninja sense," "metagaming" or "cheating").

• Important items or clues are destroyed, discarded or stolen with little or no cause.

• The essential center of the game (i.e., the struggle against Banality) is being casually discarded.

Try to avoid halting the story altogether, or telling players "No." Work within the story to put things right. Once a player puts a plan that would have a detrimental effect on the game into motion, rather than coming down like a ton of bricks, you can encourage other characters to work against the offending story. Doing so creates more plotlines and alleviating the suspicion that you are "out to get" any particular player.

Just try to avoid having players work against each so much that they carry such antipathy out of character. Only when things look bleak, and you have tried in vain to fix story problems, should you introduce a *deus ex machina* ending. Essentially a plot hammer, the D.E.M. should be reserved for those moments when the chronicle needs to be manhandled back into some semblance of playability. A *deus ex machina* can take many forms: An invading dragon that unites all of the squabbling characters, a visit from the High King, and so on. However, there are limitations on this sort of approach. Use a plot hammer too often, and players will feel hopeless, and that they're being controlled too tightly. Use it too seldom, and characters can run amuck. Good uses of the plot hammer include having problem characters fall into Bedlam, introducing a powerful outsider who'll force characters to cease pointless internal squabbling, bringing in an overwhelming threat that dictates that everyone work together to stop it, or, as a last resort, stopping the game until you've had time to regroup and your players have had a chance to calm down. Also, the downtime will allow you to introduce plot elements via e-mail or conversations with players that will serve to prevent recurrences of trouble situations.

## Laying Down the Law

It's your responsibility to ensure that players are not a hazard to others, including people who are not involved in the game. It is mandatory that the normal rules of social interaction be strictly adhered to. Most players will probably work with you in this regard. However, from time to time, there are those who prove disruptive to other players and the environment where the game is being played. Many times this disruption occurs by accident. However, there may be instances when players get out of hand on purpose. If such a situation presents itself, it's not considered bad taste to remove the offender from your game. It is, after all, your game and your creation. The integrity of your game should be preserved for the enjoyment of other players. The integrity of the game should also be upheld in the minds of those who do not play or understand **Mind's Eye Theatre**.

## Resolving Arguments

As Storyteller (and to a lesser degree as a Narrator), you have final word in any dispute that may arise between players. It is your responsibility to maintain peace between players to ensure the smooth flow of the story and its enjoyment by all. Players should be given the opportunity to speak their minds on a situation in which they disagree, but things should never be allowed to devolve into shouting or other such unpleasantness. It's a game, after all. While it is suggested that you listen to a player's grievances, remember that your decision is final and must be adhered to by all concerned. Once you make a call, that's that — the discussion is over. Be firm, or players will always be after you to change decisions you've made. Be consistent in the way you resolve rules conflicts, or people will think you're not being fair. It's best to combine an understanding ear and a firm hand. Keep your wits about you and your players will respect you for it. If a player's problems prove a disruption to the story, they may have to be put on hold and dealt with after the night's session. And remember, no single individual is bigger than the game. If someone becomes a distraction to the other players, you are perfectly within your rights to suspend or even to banish that player from the game.

### Breaking the Rules

The rules are yours to use and abuse as you see fit. Your concept of the way **The Shining Host** should be played may change constantly. Bend or break the rules to your liking. The rules serve the story; the story does not serve the rules. If you come upon a situation that isn't covered by the rules, don't panic — improvise. Improvising rules involves nothing more than applying common sense to a situation. Don't be afraid of going against the grain in such cases. Just do what makes the most sense for your story and your characters, and things will work out fine. After all, if it comes down to a question of rules versus story, story should win every time.

# Story Ideas

If you've never run a **Shining Host** story before, your first story ideas can be hard to develop. The traditional sword and sorcery plots from fantasy games don't quite capture the bifurcated worldview of changelings, but the sort of plots one might use in a **Masquerade** game simply aren't light enough for **The Shining Host**.

Luckily, we're here to help you out. Here is a quick list of story ideas and suggestions to spark your imagination. Come up with a story idea, choose a site to locate it, and then study the history of the land to decide how it might be changed by the events of your chronicle. Smaller chronicles need to be tightly focused, whereas larger ones need complex plots that allow players to interact with each other without the aid of a Narrator at every elbow. Plots can even be run with all the players as mortals, just learning of the Kithain element of reality! Here are a few suggestions to start you thinking:

• A long-lost changeling returns from the Deep Dreaming claiming to be the first of a new noble house, and displaying new standards and powers. Is he lying? What would the appearance of a new house mean?

• The characters visit a whole town run by Kithain (known as a "thorpe").

• The game recreates a traveling circus, moving its Glamour day by day from place to place.

• Unseelie revolutionaries fight to overthrow a cruel Seelie leader. Characters on both sides become embroiled in the conflict.

• A powerful treasure, perhaps the sword of the High King, is stolen. Now, everyone wants the sword — but no one knows who has it, or where.

• A prominent mortal is murdered, and evidence points to a Kithain assassin. Who killed him? Why did they kill him? Can the characters root out the killer before the investigation drops a weight of killing Banality on the area?

• While the cat's away — the local noble has gone off on a trip for some reason, leaving a group of happy-go-lucky, mischievous wilders in charge — the mice will play. What havoc will occur, and what happens if the noble comes back unexpectedly?

• A powerful Unseelie sorcerer seeks to harness Banality and the undying power of vampire blood to transform himself into a truly immortal being. The characters not only must stop him, but keep the Kindred from learning of the Dreaming's secrets.

• A knight of the Red Blade, one of the noblest orders in Concordia, has been murdered with cold iron, and the rest of the order is looking for answers.

• An ancient dragon comes searching for someone, but attacks all who cannot prove their nobility to it by answering three questions. Can the characters drive the dragon off, and should they even attempt to do so?

• A Prodigal falls in love with one of the noble characters. Is the love true? Will the noble risk his title and station for his love? Can a Kithain ever truly love a Prodigal (or even a normal mortal)?

• Can the area survive the effects of hosting the pooka prank festival?

# Index

# INDEX

# THE SHINING HOST

Experience: _____

Ravaging / Musing Threshold: _____

House: _____
Court: _____
Motley: _____
Kith: _____
Legacies: _____
Seeming: _____
Chronicle: _____
Character: _____
Player: _____

Realms

☐ ☐ ☐ ☐ ☐ ☐ ☐ ☐ ☐ ☐
O O O O O O O O O O

Banality

☐ ☐ ☐ ☐ ☐ ☐ ☐ ☐ ☐ ☐
O O O O O O O O O O

Willpower

☐ ☐ ☐ ☐ ☐ ☐ ☐ ☐ ☐ ☐
O O O O O O O O O O

Glamour

_____
_____
_____

Arts

## Abilities

_____
_____
_____
_____

## Backgrounds

_____
_____
_____

## Merits/Flaws

_____
_____

## Birthrights/Frailties

_____
_____
_____

## Physical Traits

_____
_____
_____

## Social Traits

_____
_____
_____

## Mental Traits

_____
_____
_____